WORTH
DYING
FOR

Also by N. Gemini Sasson:

The Crown in the Heather (The Bruce Trilogy: Book I)

*Isabeau, A Novel of Queen Isabella
and Sir Roger Mortimer*

WORTH
DYING
FOR

The Bruce Trilogy:
Book II

N. GEMINI SASSON

cader idris
press

For Eric –

Forever . . .
and ever . . .
and a couple of days after that.

Prologue

Edward II – Bannockburn, 1314

THE CRASH OF WEAPONS roars like constant thunder. Before me, my army—dropping to the earth like swatted flies. I have deafened to the screams. Gone blind to the sheen of blood. Dulled to the stench of death.

So many fallen. God's soul, *so* many. My nephew, Gilbert de Clare, among them. But how can that be? What unspeakable acts have those heartless heathens committed on him? Yesterday, he rode away on my command. Out of brash loyalty. And did not come back.

Hereford said that Robert the Bruce, that base traitor who dares call himself 'King of Scots', butchered him in a single blow. Hereford lies. He saw wrongly. Gilbert fought valiantly—to the last tooth and nail. He was my playfellow as an infant. Closer to me than my own brothers. Never my judge. Always at my side when I called. Often there when I did not. Gilbert with his wry quips and his lust for drink and merriment.

Aymer de Valence, Earl of Pembroke, grabs at my mount's reins. "We must leave. Now. To Stirling. Sire? Sire? Are you listening?"

I blink at him. Hot tears scorch my eyes. My sire always told me I failed at everything. That is why he fought so hard to keep from dying: so I could not have what was his and make ruin of it. I must prove him wrong!

"No," I say, "we stay. See this to the end."

His dark brows hood his eyes in foreboding shadow and I realize it is already the end.

"The day is lost," Pembroke says in harsh, cutting honesty, "but Stirling still belongs to the English. We must go there, now. Stay here a moment too long, fall into their hands and it well may be your death they'll be celebrating today."

Death? I should embrace it, for what have I left to live for? Piers is long gone. Gilbert, too. And now this . . .

Centuries from now, will they uncover the massed bones of my soldiers buried in this foreign earth? Or perhaps a shattered skull hidden among the stones and sand of one of these shifting stream banks after a cataclysmic storm?

One hand pressed to my chest, I feel for the lump beneath my coat of mail. It is there still: the lion pendant Piers always wore with such devotion.

I look back toward where the Bannock Burn carves at the earth. Last night while the planks and beams from the village were being scavenged and dragged over the boggy ground to be laid across the burn as bridgework, we found that its banks were steep, its waters swifter and deeper than one might have guessed merely by its width. Now those banks are slickened by an oozing of mud and blood and crowded with a squirming mass of bodies, grappling over one another, begging for mercy, desperate to live even in their abysmal agony.

A chill washes over my face. I feel the sweat beading on my upper lip, stiffen to the fever in my heart, see the white, blazing orb in the sky and yet I am wet-cold to the bone.

Again, Pembroke yanks on my mount's reins as he begins to lead me through the bedlam toward the Pelstream. My private guard surrounds us in a thick wall of armored knights and horses. But our own infantry presses in on them, blocking our route in a panicked jumble.

My guards to the front order them away and follow their threats with a slash of blades. Those that will not yield are cut down or trampled underfoot. From the corner of my eye, I see another and another swarm of Scots rushing down from the high ground. Their mouths open in a yip of battle cries, but the din is all a buzz in my empty, ringing head. The new mash of fighters melts into a blur as crazed and complete as a swarm of locusts devouring a field of grain.

My standard bearer. Where is my standard bearer? My soldiers will not know where I have gone to.

I clamp my knees to my horse's ribs and pull back on the reins as Pembroke fights to drag us forward. Some of the guard is already slipping down the banks of the Pelstream, their horses deftly avoiding the gored and leaking bodies that litter the slopes.

Young Hugh Despenser comes up on my left and the champion d'Argentan shoves his way through the web of death to be at my other side.

"I will see you to safety, my lord," d'Argentan declares.

"There will be no safety for us at Stirling!" I cry, as I loose my sword from its scabbard.

"I assure you there is less here." Pembroke pulls me onward as we slide down the bank and splash across the reddened stream.

A headless corpse entangles itself between my horse's legs, jostling me. My wrist is snapped backward by the jarring and my sword slips from my fingers, landing hilt first in the stream. A nebulous cloud of scarlet seeps into the murky water from the dead man's neck and floats over my weapon, lost to me. Pembroke guides my animal forward reassuringly. An arrow flicks out of nowhere and smacks against my breastplate. The jolt awakens me to reality. A wild Scottish arrow. Come from somewhere this side of the Roman road, by the little white church with the thatched roof. More shafts hiss through the air. A knight ten paces before me flies backward from his saddle with a white fledged arrow sticking from between his eyes.

My hand goes to my throat as I feel my heart there, choking out my air. "No, no! You're taking us too close! They'll kill us all."

"It's the only way," Pembroke insists. "Would you rather fight a handful of Scots or drown in the river?"

The land between where the Pelstream and Bannock Burn conjoin and the broad Firth of Forth lies is riddled with pockets of marsh and peat bogs, impassable in many places for our heavy warhorses. There is no way to Stirling but by the Roman road. Bruce knew that and used it to this end. And I, in my haste and spite, have been lured straight into the snare. Now it tightens and strangles my army. The rope closes around me, burning, cutting off my air.

Stirling looms ahead. Gray and imposing, like an eagle guarding its crag. We ride over the rough, choppy ground, strands of my broken columns of soldiers, racing in the same direction. One of my faint-hearted archers, who had been scattered in the first charge of Scottish cavalry, runs alone on the narrowing stretch of ground between the river and the road, his bow long lost in his frantic flight. He stumbles, spills the useless clutch of arrows from the bag on his back, and scampers to his feet. Two strides later a Scottish longsword hews into his spine.

I jerk my torso in the direction of the Scottish horseman—hobelars they call them, lightly armed fighters on swift mounts who can move through the mountains like wildcats. He is not alone. Twenty or more hobelars are swiftly riding down our heavier horses. My guard is yet in the hundreds. But the hobelars seem to know who they are heading for. They lash at their mounts with the flat of their swords and bypass my knights to the rear. Several times some of my knights veer off, trying to block them, taking down a hobelar, but the rest come on and all I can do is ride like the fires of hell on toward Stirling Castle. It could not have been more than a mile away by then, but it may as well have been a hundred.

Fear claws at my soul, shrieking for me to give up, to let fate grasp its own conclusion, written as plain as a mason's mark hammered in stone. For the moment, life exists only in flight. My head tells me to hurl myself down and yield, yet some primitive instinct pushes me impossibly on.

1

Robert the Bruce – Balquhidder, 1306

I DRAGGED MY FEET to the mouth of the cave, my bones grinding with weariness. The sun's rays, growing stronger, fell upon my face. I closed my eyes, inhaled the damp morning air, and thought of Elizabeth.

The last I had looked into her eyes, bright and green as summer grass slicked with dew, no words had passed between us. What would I have said, had I time to say anything at all? That we would be together again soon? I did not know. That she would be safe? That neither.

That I loved her? Achingly so.

For her, I had sacrificed everything. Turned my back on my fellow Scotsmen to scrape the ground at Longshanks' feet. With no more pride than some starving cur, groveling for fetid scraps. I thought I could have her *and* Scotland's crown—all without so much as a drop of blood shed. And so I took her as my wife and did Longshanks' bidding. What reason did he have then to give me more?

How I had hated every day of it. Hated him for his cruelty and deceit. Hated myself for my weakness, for yielding to him. But I had *believed* some good would come of it. What good? Not this, certainly. My army crushed at Methven by Pembroke's forces like grist beneath the millstone. My womenfolk wandering through the wilderness. So many more dead at Dalry.

Bloody and broken, we had made it as far as a glen pocked with rocky overhangs and small caves, somewhere near Balquhidder. We laid the worst of our wounded in the largest cave, stinking of mold and sheep droppings and crawling with insects, high up on the hillside. In a few days, God permitting, we would be on our way again. Yet every step would be clouded with the dread that John of Lorne's Highlanders might attack again. Ah, how could we drive out the English when we could not stop fighting our own?

Stubborn! Stupid! Fool!

"The sun out today, my lord?"

I turned at the sound of the voice, so feeble I might not have heard it, had I not been so close to its source. Behind me, near the cave's opening, a man sat propped crookedly against the wall. He was perhaps in his mid twenties, but the toll of battle had added a decade or more. A faint webbing of veins traced purple across his milk-pale skin. Curly, dark red hair lay in matted clumps on the top and right side of his head. But on the left . . . the hair was gone. An oozing mass of dried blood and mangled flesh marked the place where, only a day ago, his ear had been. The right eye was swollen shut, too, the lid a lumpy, mottled patch of blue and green.

"Aye," I said. "Bright and bold."

"Good." He half-smiled. "My Muriel will like that. She's an ill-tempered beast when it's gloomy." A shiver gripped him hard, made his teeth clack. When it had passed, he patted his lap and the ground. Finding nothing, he drew his hand to his chest to cradle the other arm against the chill. His right arm was nothing but a stump—a bloody, grotesque stump—the hand hewn clean off by a Highlander's axe. Someone had wrapped it in rags, but already they were soaked red.

I unclasped my cloak, flecked brown with battle-blood, and draped it across his legs. "Is Muriel your wife?"

"Daughter. My wife, she died last year." A tear squeezed from his good eye, blue as the winter sky, and streaked its way down his dirty cheek, leaving a jagged white trail. "My son, too. He was only three months old."

"I'm sorry to hear it. Children should never die so young. Nor wives." A wave of grief crashed inside my chest. My first wife, Isabella of Mar, had died in childbirth at not yet eighteen. Too young, too beautiful, and too much a part of me. Lately, every time I had looked at my daughter, who now tottered on the precipice of womanhood, it had sent a knife of sorrow through my heart because I saw so much of her mother in her: the sweeping, dark lashes that contrasted sharply with her corn-gold hair, the peculiar way she thrust her chin forward when determined to have her way, the dimples that creased her cheeks when she smiled. The pain of memories does not so much as fade, as it hides and waits in unexpected places. Even in the innocent face of a child. But Marjorie was not a child anymore.

A yellow dung-fly circled my head sluggishly, its annoyance yanking me back into the present. I swatted it away. "Tell me your name."

He laughed—a dry, raspy cackle, which quickly deteriorated into a hacking cough. Another violent shiver rattled his body, so that his words came out in broken bits. "N-never had a . . . k-king ask my name before. It's Col–Colin. "

"What happened to them, Colin?" I squatted down to hear him better. He had little strength left, even for words, but he told me his story, perhaps because he thought it was the last thing he would ever do.

"I was in the hills with Muriel. May. The hawthorn was in bloom—clouds and clouds of it. How my lass loved to watch the lambs play king of the cairn. She laughed until her belly ached." The vaguest of smiles curved his mouth, but soon the corners trembled and slipped downward. "And then, I saw the smoke above the hills. I knew, *knew* it was my home burning. I snatched her up and ran like the devil. But he was . . . they were already there. I was . . ." Colin paused, his disfigured face contorting even more with the agony of the memory. Several breaths passed before he whispered, "Too late."

No need to ask who 'they' was. It had been happening as long as anyone could remember—the English marching imperiously north every year when the days lengthened, plundering and murdering, striking terror wherever they went like the Hounds of Hell unleashed. Ever since Longshanks had cozened our nobles into signing the Ragman's Roll at Norham.

"Must have been twenty of the damned Englishmen," Colin said, little wheezes now leaking out in between strained breaths. "Maybe more, I don't know. There was so much smoke. Merciful Father, it was everywhere. The thatch was burning. Flames bursting from the door. When the roof fell in . . . I thought they were dead." His trembling stopped as he winced at a pain and drew his maimed arm tighter to his chest. Gulping, he struggled to pull in another ragged breath, before continuing. "Then . . . I heard my son cry. He was alive! But they'd heard him, too, and they went to the haystack where the sound had come from. One of them plunged his sword into it. Then another threw a torch on it. My wife jumped up and ran, holding the boy, but it was for naught. They were all around her. Everywhere, everywhere. They . . . they ripped my son from her arms and flung him to the ground. He stopped crying. Stopped moving." A long silence followed as he steeled himself to go on. "I knew if I went down there, I would die, too, and so would Muriel. So I hid. Like a coward, I hid in the hawthorns, my hand over Muriel's mouth so they wouldn't hear her whimpering. One after another, they raped my wife. Raped her, until she was bloody from her hips to her heels. I thought they would let her go, but . . . oh, sweet Jesus, they—" He tilted his head back, his mouth hanging open as he let out a sob. When he spoke again, his words were hollow with loss. "They c-cut her throat. Left her there to bleed like a butchered pig."

I laid a hand on his shoulder in comfort. Even through the cloth of his shirt, crusted with the dried blood from his missing ear, his flesh was ice cold. "Where's your daughter now?"

"In Aberdeen, with my sister. Her husband died at Methven. She has six children to raise on her own. Seven now." He swallowed hard, my cloak wadded in a shaking hand against his stomach. "Whoring bastards. I'll slice their bollocks off and shove them down their gullets, then strangle them with their own entrails." Bruised lips twisting in a sneer, he gazed down at his useless stump.

When they've killed your family and burnt your home to the ground, what is there left to do but dream of revenge?

If only a short while ago, I had wondered if the struggle was worth such sacrifices, I wondered no longer. Enough of suffering, enough of fear. No more.

A moan drifted from the back of the cave. Dawn stretched its pale light upon the clotted mass of battered bodies. Shapes came into focus, although it was a wretched, ugly site to behold. The stink of blood, urine and infection hung thick in the air. It might have turned my stomach, had I not been so accustomed to it. Somewhere, a body stirred. The scrape of a weapon over stone. Muffled weeping. The hushed whisper of desperate prayers. Another ghostly moan. Longer, more distressed.

I ventured further inside the cave. With dozens crammed tight in such a small space, there was barely room to walk between. I went slowly, carefully, I thought. My foot struck a stone. I stumbled, threw my hand against the wall to stop my fall and quickly righted myself. A sticky veil clung to the whiskers of my beard. I pulled back, my eyes focusing as I scraped at my stubbled chin. Before me, a cobweb glinted with morning dew like pearls strung on silver threads.

Last night, I had watched the wee spider dangling from the cave's ceiling, trying in vain to weave her web. Finally, a chance draft had wafted her to the wall, where she anchored her thread. Aye, the spider was still there, her intricate task complete. Resting now. Her creation still mostly intact, despite my clumsiness. Already a fly had become entangled in it, its meager movements tugging in vain at the fibers. The spider scurried forth, then froze, waiting for the fly to exhaust itself.

Beyond the web, a spindly, narrow-shouldered figure stood motionless. With an overturned kettle hat—doubtless taken from a fallen Englishman at Methven—tucked beneath his arm, Gil de la Haye gazed solemnly at James Douglas lying on the floor, as if studying him. Then he crouched down and balanced the helmet on his knees. With a thin hand, he brushed James' cheek. Next, he took a cloth from inside the helmet and twisted it. Brown water streamed into the helmet. As tenderly as if he were caring for a sick child, he dabbed James' forehead and temples. A fierce warrior in his own right, Gil was sometimes physician to us. He knew how to treat wounds, set bones, and what herbs to use to soothe an aching head or settle a disagreeable stomach. And when we were desperate for a prayer, it was Gil who repeated long verses of Latin, imploring God to guide our blades through English hearts and our shields and armor to ward off their arrows.

I picked my way through the tangle of bodies and discarded weapons. As I squatted down beside Gil, I said lowly, "Fever?"

"No, not so far, thanks be to God." Gil handed me the helmet, water sloshing onto the ground. He bent nearer to James, whose right arm lay across his chest. Between wrist and elbow, the arm was bent at an odd angle, the broken point of the bone jutting against the inside of his flesh. Gil rubbed a hand across his hawkish nose and sighed. "The sooner I set it, the better, I suppose. But he'll be in more pain then. He won't sleep. Best to let him rest for now."

We all needed our rest—only, I could not sleep with so many troubled thoughts crowding my mind. Last night after the battle, I had not slept at all and the night before that Elizabeth had thrashed beside me.

Yesterday, there was something she had wanted to tell me. A small thing, she said, that could wait. How long before I would see her again, before she could tell me? Would I ever know? Pray to God my brother Nigel could get her and the rest to Orkney: my daughter Marjorie and sisters, Christina and Mary. There, they could wait out the winter and join us in Ulster come spring, where Elizabeth's father was the earl. If he would have us. A distant hope, but what other sort was there now?

"Take care of him, Gil." I set the helmet down and rose on stiff knees. A faint breeze stirred the hair on the nape of my neck. At the opening of the cave, a tall shadow blocked the light from outside.

"Cursed spider," my brother Edward growled. In one arm, he clutched a small bundle of logs. Scowling, he waved his free hand in the air and, with a flick, smacked his palm against the wall, crushing the tiny creature. Then, too loudly: "Ah, dear brother, there you are!"

A collective grumble of protest rolled through the cramped space. Without grace or care, Edward made his way to me, kicking a wounded soldier in the shin. The man pulled his fist back, aiming for Edward's kneecap. But Edward was too quick. He snatched a log as thick around as his forearm from the bundle and swung it downward. Finger bones cracked. The man howled, then swore, "Virgin-fucking bastard!"

"I am no bastard,"—Edward's lips flickered in a wry smile, the log held out before him menacingly—"but I do favor virgins. Now get out of my way, you steaming puddle of dog vomit, before I piss on your wounds."

The man dragged himself backward, his teeth gritted as his wound scraped over rocks. Blood streamed from his leg, leaving a bright trail that darkened as it seeped into the dirt. Gil leered long at Edward, as he went to the man to tend to his freshly opened wound.

I took a step and banged my head on the low ceiling. Biting back a curse, I went to my brother.

"How many are we now, Edward?" My fingers probed the lump on my skull.

Shrugging, he heaved the logs upon the fading coals of the fire. A cloud of ashes burst upward. Soon, everyone was awake, those closest coughing, and those that were not . . . well, it was doubtful they were even still alive. "A guess? Eighty less than yesterday, give or take twenty. Sorry to be so vague, but I haven't had time to take a formal count. While you've been staring at the wall and lamenting your poor luck, I've been getting things done. Gathering firewood, for one. Sending men to fetch water and find food. Assigning the more alert ones to stand guard. Do you know that last night I tripped over a corpse in here? Boyd said his name was . . . och, I don't bloody know. Maybe he didn't say. Does it matter at this point? Anyway, we were all too tired until this morning to drag him outside and pile stones over him. The maggots were already at work on him. That's where I just came from. Burying a dead man whose festering wounds stank like rotted meat. A man I never knew. Soon, the buzzards will be circling. That's certain to alert the English to us." Sniffing, he looked around. "Dear God, it reeks of death in here still. Have you checked them all?"

He nudged at a nearby lump with the toe of his boot. The body rolled away, groaning.

"Hah, not that one then." Hands propped upon his hips, he swung around to face me. "Well, Robert, what next? We can't move on with this many ailing. And if we stay long we're sure to be found and slaughtered in our sleep. Doomed either way, it seems."

"We stay. For a few days, at least." I brushed past him, as weary of body as I was of his crassness.

"And eat *what*, exactly?" he said, his voice nearly lost against a cascade of coughing from behind him. "My gut's so empty I can feel my spine against the back of my navel."

Ignoring him, I stumbled out into the daylight. As I passed Colin, I saw that his eye was open, unfocused. His body an empty husk. Thank God he had not suffered long. I plucked up my cloak and slung it over a shoulder.

As I stepped outside, I squinted against the glare of sunlight. The chill was lifting. There would not be many warm days left in the year.

We needed to push on, find someplace safer. Those not gravely wounded and in the few caves tucked into the hillside were scattered on the slope below, some huddled behind boulders, as if they could hide. In truth, we were no better than lame deer, hoping the wolves did not stumble upon our scent. One keen pair of eyes from any vantage point within miles and we were fallen prey.

Close by, a sheep trail wended along the ridge before plunging downhill. I followed it, not so much because I had any purpose in mind, but because it was easier to let my feet carry me toward some unknown, than to stay and face the misery I had caused.

Far above, the first buzzard floated, held aloft by a gentle, but steady wind. Great wings etched a dark crescent against a gray sky. The grass around me stirred into a rising rustle. The buzzard dipped a wing and glided eastward, where clouds were gathering to blot out the sun.

Soon, I found myself in a thicket of brambles, canopied by a mosaic of ash and oak. Thorns caught on my sleeve and pricked my arm. I dropped to my knees amidst the tall grass and sank down. Wadding my cloak, I laid my head on it and pushed my fingers up over my face to trace the long scar that bordered my hairline: a reminder of Methven.

Before Methven, we had numbered in the thousands. Before Lorne's ambush as Dalry yesterday, over five hundred. And yet, was it only yesterday that I held my wife in my arms and spoke to her of what I dreaded most?

"Elizabeth, whatever you think, I'll not risk losing you. I swear it to both you and Our Lord. But I'm not ready to fight again. Not after Methven. Not yet. It's too soon. We've lost too many men and have neither the weapons nor the strength to defend ourselves."

"But you will fight," she said. "You'll have to. You . . . we . . . we can't keep running forever."

She drew back, gazed at me softly as her lips parted, then quickly buried her head against my chest again.

"What, my love? Something else?" I said.

"'Tis a small thing," she murmured. "It can wait."

"You'll tell me tonight then?"

"Aye, tonight," she whispered. "When we have more time."

That time had not come. Maybe, it never would.

2

James Douglas – Balquhidder, 1306

A SLAT OF YELLOW light pried between my eyelids. Hunched forms surrounded me. Voices wove together in a muffled buzz.

I tried to look around, but a dull throbbing mass of pain in my right shoulder seized me. A murky fog filled my head. Closing my eyes again, I succumbed to the unfeeling comfort, the nothingness. My body became heavier . . . slipping away, sucked down into some endless chasm of blackness.

Calloused fingertips clamped against either side of my jaw, snatching me back to awareness.

"Hold now. Tight," a voice said.

My eyes flew open.

Robert Boyd gripped my bare shoulders, while Edward Bruce held my head. Someone had removed my shirt and chain mail. My chest and arms were bare. I shivered at the cold. A tattered blanket lay across my lap. As I reached for it, pain jolted through my arm—the lower half bent at an odd angle. Dead might have been better than this.

Gil de la Haye positioned himself to set the bone.

"Pain me on your life!" I growled.

"James," Gil murmured with a patronizing smile, "I was mending bones long before your father and mother made you."

Boyd jammed the hilt of his knife between my teeth. "Quiet now, lad, and let Gil do his work. If you don't, y'may be able to thrash your sword with the other arm, but you'll have a damnable time stringing a bow."

Face fixed in concentration, Gil yanked and twisted. Bone ground against bone. White, hot pain shot up my arm, into my chest and opposite shoulder. I gnashed at the hilt. Edward clamped tighter. Not daring to watch, I pitched backward against Boyd. Finally, Gil stood back and scratched at his frosted head.

Peering over my shoulder, Boyd grunted. "No, doesn't look right. You need to turn it a bit more."

I prayed to be struck unconscious at that moment.

Gil nodded in agreement. With one slender hand, he clamped onto my right arm just below the elbow and with the other he pinched my wrist. I closed my eyes, expecting another excruciating flood of pain. I heard a little pop and he let go.

"Impressive, Gil," Boyd exclaimed with genuine wonder.

Edward slipped his hands from my head and pounded Gil on the shoulder. "Well done. Now if there are any of us not reeling too hard from all the blows, I need to find someone to relieve the sentries. Lorne may have left more of ours dead than his, but he won't swallow the humiliation of not having taken Robert alive."

The king's brother strode off and Gil, oddly skilled in plucking haft splinters and arrow shafts out of flesh, went to work elsewhere. Boyd took the knife from between my teeth and stood grinning above me.

"It will plump up like a piglet by sundown. A pleasure seeing you down for once," he gloated. "I was starting to think you were one of those fairy folk that live forever, like the Irish have."

"Maybe I am." I attempted a grin, but from his stiff reaction it must have looked more like a sneer. I think I had bruised my lip in the fall, as well. "That pleases you . . . that I was knocked from my horse?"

The numbness in my arm was beginning to wear off. My whole right side throbbed with every pulse.

"Every scar tells a tale, young Douglas. Some day you'll be an old man like me. No one will ever ask you what it was like to fight alongside Robert the Bruce, King of Scots. They won't believe you ever did with that pretty face of yours."

I didn't bother to mention the scars his wife had given him or the fact that he wasn't as old as he said. One day he was twenty-five, the next he was fifty. It was a habit of Boyd's to bend the truth. He gimped toward the mouth of the cave.

I called out, "Boyd?"

"Aye?"

"Thank you."

He shrugged. "For calling you 'pretty'? Tell anyone I said that—and I'll gut you like a fish." Sunlight curling around his bearish form, he turned and went outside.

FOR ONCE, BOYD HAD not exaggerated. From just above my elbow down to each fingertip, my arm swelled so much that I had to tear the lower part of my sleeve lengthwise for relief. While we loitered in the damp cave beyond Balquhidder, the first frost gripped the land. Gil, with his nimble fingers and keen eyes, mended the injured in a crude and sometimes unconventional manner. He made me drink a potion of juniper berries. Bitter, but it numbed my pains. Piece by piece, we ripped at the hems of our cloaks and shirts for bandages. I suffered the least. Beside me lay a man younger than me named Torquil. During that first week after Dalry, he bled so heavily that he was as wan as his silver-fair Viking hair. He had a wound in his chest, just below his right shoulder. One of Lorne's men had plunged a spear between his ribs. With his bare hands, he had pulled it out and killed the man. He came from an island he called Ba-Rah or something, to the west of Skye. So peculiar was his speech, I could only understand some of what he said. His lady, he told me through one of the other wounded who understood him better, was the widow of Duncan of Mar, the brother of Robert's first wife Isabella. Her name was Christiana of the Isles.

There had been no sign of Lorne's Argyll men since Dalry, but even now we were wary, afraid to go out into the open for fear of discovery. I had no recollection of how many days we passed there in the glen, only that I was aware of the chill that crept over the land at nightfall and the frost that sparkled on the clumps of heather every morning when I rose and sat at the cave's edge, battling not warriors of Argyll or the Earl of Pembroke's knights, but my own persistent, nagging pain. When the swelling started to go down enough, Gil freed my arm of the crude splint he had fitted on it. He put it in a sling made from the lining of my colorful cloak—the one Robert's wife Elizabeth had given to me. I had never deemed myself worthy of it, but still I was grateful for it.

One morning, feeling stronger and itching with restlessness, I sat upon a rock as the sun rose pink in the east. Most of the men were still asleep, but a few had begun moving about quietly. Brisk air wrapped around me and I pulled my cloak close, hugging my knees to my chest. Robert walked along a meandering trail up to the cave. He held out a handful of berries.

"Take these," he offered.

I extended my left hand and he poured them, red and bright as precious gems, into my cupped palm.

"I've no penchant for them. I'd as soon live on beef and bread, as have my mouth puckered by something so tart." Wrinkling his nose, he wiped his hands on a tattered shirt and added, "You look like some skeleton the crows have picked clean. Eat."

I threw them in my mouth, let them swim there for a few seconds while their juice flooded my entire being like a surge of fresh blood, then swallowed them all in one gulp.

"Mmm, I don't think I've ever tasted anything so good," I said, my hand on my throat as if I could capture the sensation again. "Thank you, my lord king, with all my heart."

"Thank me all you want,"—he settled down on the rock beside me and glanced at his red-stained hands—"but call me Robert."

"Robert?"

"Aye. 'Tis my name." Shoulders hunched up toward his ears, he tucked his hands into his armpits. "Aside from Edward—and there's a voice I deign not to hear every day for the rest of my life—no one calls me that anymore. Not since Nigel and Elizabeth left. It's a lonely feeling, not hearing your own name. As a lad, sometimes there were three of us by the same name in the castle—myself, my father and grandfather. They had no trouble with it, but you can imagine the confusion it caused for a bold-spirited, sociable bairn like me. My grandfather . . . he is the one who taught me how to sit upon my horse so I would not fall, how to sail in strong winds and what words to whisper to make the maidens blush. He called me Robbie." He paused, smiling to himself.

They had called his grandfather Robert the Competitor, because he had contested the Balliol claim to Scotland's empty throne. Many agreed that it belonged to the Bruces. Even England's king, Longshanks, had promised it to Robert after his grandfather and father died. But when it became clear that Longshanks wanted Scotland for his own, Robert began to weary of empty promises. In time, John 'the Red' Comyn betrayed him to Longshanks, thinking it would earn him lands and titles. Greed has always been Scotland's downfall, whether Comyn or someone else.

When Robert called Comyn to meet him at Greyfriar's Kirk to confront him, Comyn attacked him. Though Robert only wounded Comyn, his companion Roger Kirkpatrick finished the scoundrel for him. I would have done the same.

Robert sighed, stood and cupped me lightly on my good arm. "Mend fast. We will head out in a couple of days."

"My lord . . . Robert? Marjorie . . . and the queen—where is Nigel taking them?" I had a fondness for both Robert's wife and his daughter. Elizabeth had given me a fine horse and a cloak when Bishop Lamberton sent me off to join Robert. And Marjorie, so spirited and curious... I don't know what I felt for her. The protectiveness of an older brother, perhaps?

The question forced his chin down. "To Kildrummy, if it's safe. If not, north to Orkney, then aboard ship to Ulster." The heel of his hand resting on the axe tucked into his belt, he shook his head in doubt. "Ah, James, how utterly selfish I am. Foolish, too. They would have been better off if I had sent them to Ireland in the first place."

"They'll be there, waiting for you," I assured him. "You'll see."

"*If* they'll have us in Ireland, otherwise we'll spend the winter adrift. Like rats on a piece of driftwood." An unconvincing smile flitted across his mouth. "Well then—eat. Get some rest."

"Thank you . . . for what you did." I meant to say his name again, but even the first time it had stumbled across my tongue.

"Pluck berries? Bit of a hike to gather them, but your gratitude is too much."

"Gil told me it was you who went back for me when I fell from my horse. I owe you my life for that."

"Ah, well, it would have been inconsiderate of me to leave you behind." He began to go, then stopped and added, "That was brave work at Dalry. Ten more like you, good James, and I should have the kingdom won back before next Michaelmas."

More like a thousand of me, maybe. But him . . . it would take only one of him.

3

James Douglas – Loch Lomond, 1306

WE LAID OUR DEAD out in rows in the cave, their arms crossed solemnly over their breasts, and piled the heaviest stones we could manage across the entrance. Nigh on starving, we left the secret cave of the glen near Balquhidder and crawled southward. We had only a few horses remaining that were not lame, and so our wounded rode those; the others we abandoned. Soon, Robert told me, we would have to cross a loch or a wide river and if we ever made it to the coast, we could not take them to Ireland anyway. While we trudged through dense forests and over burnished heather, I learned from Gil how to recognize wild thyme and mint to chew on, which flowers to pluck the petals from in the summer to eat, how to tell a nut tree from a distance and which plants to dig for their roots. I taught the rest where to look for the holes of mountain hares and how to snare a stoat or marten for its fur. Useless with my bow, I watched admiringly as Edward sent an arrow in a sure arc two hundred paces and brought down a young red stag in full stride. We ate only a small hunk of meat each. There was not nearly enough to go around.

It must have been late September when we saw Ben Lomond, its summit shoved up against a glowering sky that threatened to sink down on us as the rain began. There in its shadow, we found another cave that overlooked the loch, this one bigger and drier than the last we had inhabited. In the center, Boyd fed the fire with kindling that we had gathered along the way. Outside, the rumbling sky was dark as coal dust. A cold wind blustered in and the flames wavered before they burst defiantly back to life again.

Robert crouched on his muscular haunches before the sputtering fire. "If we stay here, we risk John of Lorne finding us. Or the English."

Should the Argyll warriors catch up with us again, they would kill us in a craze of bloodlust. The English, if they found us, would make prisoners of our leaders, as they had my father. There were many ways I wished to be like him, but living out my last days in the Tower of London was not one of them.

The broad, long loch below, called Loch Lomond after the mountain that guarded over it, was a daunting stretch of water and I, not being one with a love of water, would have preferred the longer journey around it. Once, when I was nine, my brother Hugh and I had stolen a little rowing boat. We only wished to row about on an adventure, but had sorely underestimated the strength of the waves created by a rough wind chopping at the surface. The little boat overturned before we were but a stone's throw from shore. Even though the water was only chest high, I was trapped beneath the weight of the boat. Hugh's frantic thrashing had only pushed the water higher inside my little dark, diminishing cavern of air. When he finally heaved the boat upright, it gave me a thump in the head hard enough to knock me out. Later, I found myself on the shore looking up at a blurry sky, coughing up water, with an awful ache in my skull and a lump that remained on my forehead for a week. Hugh, simple though he was, had saved me. Ever since then, the rocking of a boat upon the waves hurled me into a state of silent panic.

"If we can make it across the loch," Robert said, looking from face to sinking face, "we can go west, to the coast. I've sent Neil Campbell ahead. He'll be waiting for us with galleys. To take us to Ireland."

Edward had just come in from outside. Rivulets of rain trickled from his shoulders to pool at his feet. He sauntered closer and pushed his fingers back through slick hair. "Across?" he said with more than a trace of skepticism. "If you mean for us to swim, half of us will be drowned before we reach the other bank."

The sudden roar of rain filled the air. We all stared into the amber light of the fire, mulling over his words, wondering just how it could be done.

"A boat," Torquil proposed sleepily. He was sitting on the floor of the cave with his back against the wall, eyes half closed. Gil had given him some sort of infusion made from the crushed petals of a white flower and willow bark. Torquil let out a huge yawn. "Boats . . . I know. I sail."

Edward snorted. "Well, we don't have any, do we? And boat or no, it's a long way yet to Kintyre at this pace."

"We've made it this far," Robert reminded him tersely. "We'll make it even further."

THE NEXT DAY, AFTER the rain had stopped, Torquil and I slid down the hillside, over the next rise and along a muddy, winding trail among the trees. Torquil veered from the path and, with his small axe, he cut free two straight and lean saplings, hacked off their branches and tossed them over his shoulder. We wandered along the banks until we found a promising spot. With his knife, Torquil stripped the bark from the first one, then tossed it to me, pointing to the tapering end of the pole. I shaved the end to a sharp point, left-handed no less, until he ceased to grimace at my imperfect work. While he lay belly down on a rock and dangled there, I stripped and sharpened the next spear. Soon, he had skewered the first fish and tossed it onto shore. More followed. Torquil was patient enough to make his throws worthwhile, but swift enough to hit his mark with deadly accuracy. My mouth watered every time a tailfin swished at the surface. I was so famished I could have eaten them raw: heads, bones and all. I gathered the catch into my cloak. My hands smelled of fish. My cloak—the half of it that was left—was going to reek of it for a long time.

Wind rippled the water, pulsing waves over the lip of the bank. Water splashed at my leggings and my feet were soon soaked. My chest tightening with unease, I moved up away from the loch's edge to dry them as I waited to see Torquil take another jab into the water. He cursed in his own language at a pike too cunning for his methods.

My sights wandered in and out the length of the loch. Four days on horse to ride all the way around it, Gil had said. As battered as we were, it would take us eight. In a little cove to the south on the far bank, poked the roofs of a small fishing village. Four houses, maybe five. Hard to tell from this distance. On our side, directly opposite it, was a sandy beach broken by stands of reeds. A sandpiper wandered through the reeds, standing at times on one slender, blue-gray leg. Every so often, it dipped its long, pointed bill in the water, rooting about, then moved on, bobbing up and down. I lost sight of the bird as it moved behind something large and solid. After a time it appeared on the other side. Slowly, I realized that the 'something' was a fishing boat. Later, I thought, we could maybe take the boat out away from the shore and if I could somehow trail a hook there would be even more fish to eat. For now though, Torquil was doing well enough.

Far away to the north, the rock dropped abruptly into the water in places. There, the loch narrowed where it began as a river sprung from the mountains. Gil had told me that to the south the loch spread apart wide, pushing the earth miles and miles apart. A small army of islands floated there, he said, like a herd of whales skimming the surface. Behind us, the trees still wore their green summer cloaks, but some were now tinged with traces of gold or scarlet. Their leaves fluttered gently at the teasing of a steady breeze.

I wiggled my fingers and freed my arm of its sling. I turned it ever so slightly outward and tested my strength by plucking up small stones and squeezing them feebly in my palm. It would be some time before I could grip the hilt of my sword with ease. Longer yet, before I could pull a bowstring. Sinking back against a lush cushion of grass, the handle of my knife poked at my hip and I pulled it free. The sky was as blue as any summer day. In the branches above, a lark trilled incessantly.

Eyes drifting shut, I shifted the longknife to my weakened right hand and rubbed my thumb against the familiar worn cording of the handle. Water lapped rhythmically against the shore, lulling me to sleep.

I dreamt of home. Of riding along the Douglas Water and running over the hills with my simple-minded brother Hugh trailing behind. Of foxes loping through the meadows and a hare with its black-tipped ears peeking above a tussock of grass. I dreamt of my stepmother Eleanor rocking my wee brother Archibald in the ivory cradle of her arms as she sang to him and my father sitting on a bench before the hearth with a cup of ale in his hands, his thoughts consumed within the dancing flames. Of the Englishman, Neville, shoving Eleanor onto a table and yanking her skirts up, as she wept tears of shame. My knife, arcing through the air to cut him. Longshanks' boot slamming against my jaw to dislodge a tooth.

Then I dreamt long of two great armies staring at each other across an open plain, of a voyage in a leaky ship filled with rats the size of dogs and a journey into a strange land over a muddy field. Of Paris, cramped and reeking, and Master Andrae telling me to grab my ankles and bend forward as he tested his willow switch on the floorboards before laying it over my back. My father lying dead in a Tower dungeon. I dreamt of Bishop Lamberton reciting Mass from behind glittering relics and William Wallace walking away on a long, dusty road, never turning around, never showing his face, only the great sword strapped against his broad back.

And then, in the drifting mist of my dreams, Robert, tall astride his horse, twisted at the waist and beckoned to me. His embroidered cloak swung regally from his shoulders. Upon one of his fingers was a ring bearing a seal. Upon his brow sat a circlet of gold.

"James? Come along, James," he called, a soft, half-smile playing over his mouth.

As he began to go, I tried to follow, but something held me back. I willed my feet to move, but they could not. Further and further he went, saying my name, but never stopping to wait for me or looking back.

"Look 'ere," a gruff voice said. "A Scottish dog, good as dead."

The dull fog of sleep lifted suddenly like a blanket thrown off. It was not Wallace's voice, nor Robert's. Neither was it Torquil's.

Through barely parted lashes, I glimpsed a man with a bulging paunch standing over me. He grinned and flicked his tongue over lips pocked with sores. Drooping jowls rough with black stubble melted into a thick neck. The man had not suffered for lack of food, or from the guilt of gluttony. He reached beneath his oversized leather jerkin and scratched at this crotch. Then he lifted a nicked and rusty sword. Its point pricked the soft of my belly.

My heart thumped in a wild cadence. I curled my fingers around empty air. My blade lay tangled in the grass, only a few feet away. If I reached for it, I was dead. If I didn't—I was dead then, too.

His mouth spread into a macabre smile of jagged yellow teeth and irregular gaps. A guttural laugh shook his flabby gut and gurgled out of his throat, making him sound like a braying donkey. "Scared, are you? Don't worry, I'll keep you alive long enough to get some sport out of you."

I opened my eyes fully, gauging his quickness against mine. No contest. I would have skewered him in a heartbeat in an honest fight. Gutted him like the fat pig he was. That was when he pressed the point deeper into my belly, reminding me who had the advantage.

"Will, over 'ere!" he bellowed. "Look what I found me!"

With every shallow breath I drew, the sword point bit harder,

- 27 -

almost burning. I held my breath. Fear, or fate, whatever it was, held me entranced to observe the slow approach of my own death.

God's teeth, I had always thought I would die in a furious blaze of glory, not like this. Not in such a pathetic, helpless way.

Behind him, twigs cracked. Footsteps plodded, then stopped.

He chuckled, this time scratching at his buttocks. "What do you say we should do with him, Will? Strap him belly flat to a tree and fuck his Scottish arse till he screams with pleasure? Chop off his fingers, one knuckle bone at a time? Gouge out his eyeballs, maybe? I like that one, I do. Won't be pretty no more, then, will 'e?" He guffawed, amused by his own cleverness.

"Let him go."

The pig-bellied Englishman stopped laughing. He cocked his head sideways, not daring to take his eyes off me. "What did you—?"

A thwack cut off his words. He stumbled forward, as if someone had shoved him from behind. But there was no one there. A line—wet, burning—trickled warm across my abdomen to pool in my navel. The sword had pricked my flesh. It slipped from his grasp and thudded to the ground.

His tongue popped from his mouth, red foam bubbling around it. He lowered his eyes to gawp at his chest, where the tip of a wooden spear point protruded. Bright blood clotted in the Englishman's stubbly beard, spurted from the hole in his breast. Empty-eyed, he stared at me, making little croaking sounds—and fell.

I rolled away. My arm, not yet healed, flared with a bolt of pain. The spear point ripped my sleeve at the shoulder as he crashed against me, knocking the breath from me. Gulping in air, I shoved him aside with a strained heave. The man was dead, for certain, but smelling of his own shit.

"You could've killed me," I grumbled at Torquil as he stalked toward me.

With a yank, he pulled the spear out, stifling a curse when the haft split in two. He knelt down and whispered into my ear, "They come."

I started to sit up to look around, but he pushed me back down and pointed up the hillside to where a narrow bridle path led through the stand of trees from which he had been cutting spears. Rising on my good elbow, I peered at the rim of the small rise above us.

"English." I sank back down. "Ten, maybe twelve. They'll be looking for this one soon."

Torquil's fingers fluttered on his spear. I retrieved my knife from where it lay. It would be a quick fight if they found us—and not in our favor. I pointed to a thicket of bushes that crowded the nearby bank. Backs hunched to stay low, we dragged the dead man between us and rolled him under a young pine. We crawled deep inside the thicket, thorns lashing at our faces and snagging our shirts. Although their voices drifted clearly down to us, I could understand only snatches of their thick speech. They went by very slowly, pausing once directly above us a hundred feet up the mud-slickened slope.

As they at last passed to the south, Torquil turned to me. The wind tossed long strands of straw-pale hair from his ruddy face. "They find our horses. Follow us here."

WHILE THE SUN SLIPPED lazily into the west, they scoured the hillside, twice coming within a spear's throw. My fingers twitched on my knife, but Torquil kept his weapons idle beside him as they wandered off. Although I took joy in killing Englishmen—for I had never forgotten the terror of Berwick—neither of us was fool enough to deny the odds on this occasion.

When they had been gone for some time and daylight began to yield to dusk, Torquil and I crept down to the water. The boat that Torquil and I had found was big enough for only a few men. There was a leak somewhere in the stern, but Torquil deemed it slow enough that the boat could easily be bailed out before it took on too much water.

Darkness falling, we returned to the cave and told Robert of the scouting party.

That night, under a moonless sky, we rowed across to the opposite side of the loch in batches. The worst of the wounded—which was only a few by now, the rest having died—were set ashore first. After that went Robert, Gil and I, with Boyd returning the boat to the other side. I was eminently thankful there was no breeze that night and so, but for the sweep and surge of the oars, the boat glided across the surface, parting the mist that mantled the glassy loch. All the same, getting in and then out was motion enough to churn my stomach into a sour brew. While we waited for the others, Robert told the tale of Tristan and Isolde in French, the words drifting away into a twisting murmur as I slipped in and out of a fitful slumber. Every time I opened my eyes to look for the boat and who had made it, Robert was standing vigilant on the shore, his hands braced on his sword belt and his shortened cloak flared out over his elbows. A few at a time, our men were set safely upon the western shore of the loch.

Boyd had just left on the last trip, this one to fetch Edward and Torquil. Minds benumbed from sleeplessness and bodies drained by hunger, we peered into the mist as it broke, then rolled again over the silvery loch. In the east, above the blanket of fog, dawn crowned the mountaintops in a watery orange haze.

A scream shattered the silence. Metal clanged on metal, thudded on hide-covered shields to echo in the long, narrow basin of the loch against embracing mountains. Shouts. Another scream. The clink of blades striking metal bosses. A dying groan. The crash . . . of something hitting water. Then, quiet. Heavy, heart-stopping quiet.

I looked at those around me. Their faces were drawn. Some stood, swaying with closed eyes, their lips twitching in prayer. Others knelt, too weary, too hopeless. At last, the far-off murmur of rippling water filled our ears. Several men drew their weapons, but others edged forward to stand at the water's lip. Through the steamy fog, the little boat skimmed, its belly pushed deep by too much weight, with Boyd smiling devilishly at the prow and Torquil scooping out water with his hands. Grunting, Edward dipped hard into the oars, his cadence doubled. Some distance out yet, Torquil leapt into the water and waded ashore. He collapsed to his knees and touched his forehead to the sand.

"Thank the Almighty Above," Boyd said as he and Edward dragged the boat to ground, "he was carrying that bloody fishing spear and has a good aim. Killed one of the bastards before he could alert the others. We barely slipped out onto the water and they came tramping down the hill. Now, let's get the bloody hell out of here, shall we?"

4

Robert the Bruce – Loch Lomond/Dunaverty, 1306

HOPE AND FEAR FILLED my heart in those days. Hope that I would hold Elizabeth in my arms again. Fear that I might never. Both drove me. To wake each day, to take one more weary step, climb one more craggy mountain. To go both toward and away. Toward future's faint promise. Away from a past plagued with regrets.

Sleepless, we tarried only long enough west of Loch Lomond to beat up quarry and take enough venison to gain strength and set us on our way again. It was yet early morning when we crested the last hill and descended the rugged slopes of Loch Long. There, Neil Campbell was waiting for us, ten galleys arrayed along the shore, their sparse crews roasting white-fronted geese on spits.

I pulled Neil into my embrace and clapped him on the back. "More men—good, good. We'll take any we can find."

"The Campbells are fierce warriors, my lord. Worth three men a piece."

"What news do you have of Nigel?"

He stepped back and motioned me toward the nearest cooking fire. The wind had reddened his nose and cheeks, but he looked hale and certainly better fed than us. "None, I regret. Not a rumor, even."

I took the goose leg that he offered, plucked out the few stubbles of feather remaining. "If they'd been taken shortly after Dalry, we would have heard something of it. They've made it a ways, at least."

But even as I said it, a worm of doubt crawled inside my gut and burrowed there.

"Aye," Gil added as he joined us, "they could be to Orkney by now." He eyed the spit. Globules of fat oozed from beneath the charred skin and dripped, sizzling, into the fire. He reached out and stripped a long shred to stuff into his mouth, barely chewing before he swallowed.

"What of the Earl of Pembroke, or the Prince of Wales? Anything?" I squatted next to the fire and sank my teeth into the meat.

Neil shook his head. "None there, either. I suspect they've gone back south. I do know that John of Lorne's galleys are patrolling the waters."

Grease clinging to my beard, I dragged a dirty hand over my chin and gazed at Neil. "Aye? And which direction were they going?"

"South, headed for the mouth of the Clyde. *That*, I have on good word."

"We take the longer route then—and pray we don't meet them on the other side of Bute."

Afterward, we departed from the shore, watchful and hurried. I drew my cloak closed and huddled down in between the rowing benches. The first hour, James clung white-knuckled to the gunwale, puking his last meal—his only full meal in three days—into the water until there was nothing left to retch but spittle. The oars of our galleys dipped and pulled as our lean boats slipped into the broadening Firth of Clyde. As Bute rose up out of the water, I thought of James Stewart there at Rothesay where I had first laid eyes on Elizabeth de Burgh. The ice had been so thick that winter that leaving had been near to impossible. Marjorie was still a little girl then, enamored of Elizabeth, who had been caring for her since before Irvine. It was at Irvine that I had first offered my allegiance to Sir William Douglas, Stewart and William

Wallace, while the English advanced up the coastline. But my fellow Scots had not been easily convinced of my intentions, for I had been Longshanks' man for many years. They had argued over whether to fight or accept terms and in the end Wallace left. He had wanted to fight. Douglas convinced the rest of us to accept terms—that we would hand over hostages, my Marjorie being one. I had never fulfilled that worthless oath, knowing Marjorie was safely tucked away on Bute. When I finally went there to see my daughter, Elizabeth made me forget my sorrows over losing Isabella. I knew joy again. I was in love, utterly, helplessly. Her father, however, would not wed his daughter to a rebel.

What a challenge it had been to win Elizabeth's hand—courting Longshanks, fostering his faith in me with eager duty and all the while weaving the alliances that I was so blindly counting on now. If any of them failed me . . . if anyone betrayed me again, as Red Comyn had . . . What little I had so far won could be so easily lost.

"How fares the Stewart, Neil?" I asked my brother-in-law.

"He ails, sire." Neil grimaced as he picked at a festering scab between his thumb and forefinger.

"Greatly?"

"At times, aye."

"A pity. I pray his health returns. Will he send aid?"

Neil abandoned his sore to squint at me. "Will he? He has. Gave me these boats. Said he would send men and arms as he could. Longshanks granted his lands to the Earl of Lincoln, so the Stewart has his own battles for now. I would not count on him much . . . but if not for him, you'd still be standing on the shore waiting."

"Then I owe him." I recalled my oath to him that long ago winter night at Rothesay. The pact was that if he supported my claims to the crown, I would promise my daughter Marjorie to his son Walter.

Later, I took my own turn on the rowing thwarts so that others could sleep. But rest was not to be had for long for any of us.

"There." Torquil pointed to a pair of far-off coracles drifting off the western shore of a little island at the end of the Firth.

Macdougall spies? Or perhaps nothing more than fishermen as curious as they were timorous about the spectacle before them? Stealthily, they maneuvered into a small bay to watch us pass. We put our shoulders and backs into the oars and hooked a hard right past the tip of Bute into the sound that circled Arran. It was a longer route than going straight south, but the water was more placid and the change in direction gave us the favor of a slight wind. The sails went up and for a while we were able to rest our arms.

I went back to the stern and took the rudder to relieve Boyd. I knew these waters well and had learned how to sail from my grandfather. In between sucking the blood from my blistered hands I leaned into the rudder. James was by my knee rolled into a tight ball, his face blanched and his mouth slack. Not quite twenty and he'd already outdone his father Sir William's reputation on the battlefield, but the sea waves made him weak as a newborn kitten.

Our voyage continued around Arran, its sandy beaches dotted by seals sunning their great brown bellies. We skimmed past an otter as it floated on its back, chomping on the headless body of a fish. It seemed to watch us in droll amusement as its sleek body bobbed up and down on the waves. West of us ran Kintyre. The Viking ruler Magnus Barelegs had once had his men lug his boat across the narrow isthmus at the northern end of the peninsula while he sat in it. He claimed the land as his own. The deal he had struck with King Malcolm was that he, Magnus, could have any of the western islands that he could sail his boat around. The claim was a matter of contention and a sore point it was, but a grand prize garnered with a twist of words and ingenuity.

As Arran fell away behind us, the sea opened up to the south. We curved around, following the coastline of Kintyre. A barely fledged eagle, its feathers still spotted with white, soared above us a while, then peeled away as a brooding bank of clouds loomed gray and heavy ahead. A blustering wind picked up. I ordered the sails brought down and once more we took up the oars. Endlessly, it seemed, we were thrust away from our destination.

Stinging cold daggers of rain began to fall, cutting into our flesh. It came down so hard I could barely see the land. More than once I thought I had entirely lost sight of it. The whole world was so gray and smeared with rain that I could scarcely discern sky from land from sea. A tiny island rose suddenly to our left and I knew we were too far out. We veered north again, away from the little rock of land, as wind and sea opposed us. A shiver stabbed between my shoulder blades and soon gripped my whole body. My shoulders cramped until they were frozen in place. Water flooded the hulls of the boats faster than we could scoop it out. One of our galleys slipped further and further behind as the men, wrought with fatigue, battled to keep up. When I thought we could last no longer, a long, jagged shoreline broke the horizon before us. I laid into the rudder and shouted over to the next galley to head for the shore.

Torrents faded to a fine mist and by the time every one of us stood on solid ground, the clouds had rumbled angrily away to the east, leaving nothing behind but a damp wind and a tiny, battered, and soaked army of Scotsmen strewn over the beach like clumps of tempest-tossed seaweed. I sank to the sand. The earth continued to move beneath me, rolling and pitching. I pushed my hair away from my forehead. Sand fell into my eyes, stinging. Nearby, James and Gil were piling wrung-out cloaks on Torquil, who had succumbed to the chill worst of all.

Evening wore on and darkness fell. Seabirds jeered at our wretchedness. We had nothing to eat, no dry clothes, and no flint or firewood. I tucked my fist against my belly and bit at my lip as stony hunger ground at my insides.

"How far to Dunaverty?" I asked Neil.

He wiped his nose, stood and looked about. Waves surged against the gravelly shore, then retreated in a ripple of froth. As though rife with doubt, he shrugged. "Not so far. An hour by boat, but I would not wager my life on that."

"Then we should go there as soon as we can. This chill will take its toll on us all."

Neil glared at me—both of us miserable and defeated by the sea. "In the morning?"

"Aye," I conceded, not wanting to ask more of him or any man than they had to give. "In the morning."

For the mere promise of one small fire and a scrap of bread, I would have suffered the sea another whole day. I crawled onto a dune and rolled up inside my wet cloak amidst the rocks with the other men. Although I was certain I would never sleep, so utterly cold and hungry I was that somehow I did.

At daybreak, I pushed away my still sodden cloak and stood at water's edge, while the tide lapped at the toes of my boots and dawn's bold light shone upon my sea-weathered, sand-encrusted face.

DUNAVERTY. THERE IT WAS. A jumbled pile of stones tossed on top of a cliff. No beauty in its lines or welcome in its form, but oh, it was the eagle's eyrie on the crag. On a cloudless day you could see all the way to Ireland and beyond from its tower. While we should have been shouting joyfully at its appearance, instead we merely kept rowing toward it, pull after pull in a mindless rhythm, just as we had done all the way from Loch Long—an event that now seemed decades past. Dully, the men dropped over the sides of the boats and lugged them ashore.

"Ho there, fine fellows! Chins high!"

Perched jauntily atop a rock that butted out into the crescent bay stood a man in flamboyant checkered trousers. The top of his hair was lopped short while the back of it flared out full behind him like a stallion's mane. His twining golden-brown moustache cascaded from the corners of his mouth all the way down to his chest. Below him, a long line of MacDonalds were arrayed, swords sheathed and shields resting at their feet.

He opened his arms up in a broad flourish and announced in Gaelic, "I am Angus MacDonald, Lord of Islay! Welcome to humble Dunaverty, brave Robert, King of Scots!"

"Ah, but hardly humble yourself, Angus Og," I returned.

He leapt from the rock onto the beach before me, swept a sleeve-bare arm, clanking with bronze and silver bracelets, across his body and bowed to me.

I clasped his hand and said to him in English, "And not the babe I remember you as."

"Not so young yourself, if I may say respectfully," he returned in his whimsical accent.

"Your honesty is reflected in your wanton arrogance, MacDonald," Edward gibed, approaching us.

"Hah, Edward," Angus hailed. "You've finally outstripped your older brother in muscle. Thomas and Alexander are waiting in the castle."

Edward eyed him in annoyance. "Food and drink? It was a tedious long way from Perth. Or did your heathens lick the storerooms clean upon arrival?"

"Plenty to spare, my lords. Plenty to spare. This way."

We climbed beside Angus Og along the footpath up to the fortress. My men trudged behind, dragging their feet, all of us fighting the urge to let our knees buckle beneath us and fall to the earth.

THOMAS AND ALEXANDER GLOWED with health. Our own deplorable condition, however, was obvious in their reaction to our feeble embraces. Angus Og saw to it that we were all properly dried out, warmed and fed. Although my bones cried for a bed beneath them, I joined the revelry in the hall that afternoon. The ale had begun to flow early. Thomas was topped to his eyeballs by the time I took my seat.

My mouth watered as the smell of cooked pork, dripping with fat, curled inside my nostrils. The servants raced in and out of the kitchen door, dodging the wobbling, drunken soldiers that careened through the hall. A platter crashed to the floor. No one took any notice except me. It was the pork. A disappointment. I settled for some mutton that came my way.

"Thomas, you've let your beard grow long," I observed. "Hand me your knife and I'll take care of it."

At his seat, Thomas shrugged and mumbled, then hoisted his cup and called for another fill. When a pair of young maidens glanced at him from behind a column and giggled, he flocked to them, sloshing cup in hand.

Alexander, who had been sharing tales with Angus, came to sit beside me in the seat Edward was noticeably absent from. "Not to fear," Alexander said aside. "Thomas will never be mistaken for a monk. I have kept him from falling into the bed of every woman we came across—the married ones, at least—but the drink . . . it seems to find him. On any given night he would put dear Edward to shame. Edward is, at least, more discreet about his women and knows how to ration his ale. Thomas will destroy himself, if left on his own. He used to be lazy. Now he is reckless and lazy."

"Reckless, how so?"

"I would not give him command of any army, Robert. Not today, not ten years from now. He doesn't know whether to flail his sword at the first rustle he hears or run the other way. Thank the Almighty there are three of us between him and your throne. If he were next in line I'd say this kingdom was in dangerous straits." He tore a small chunk from the loaf of bread before him to nibble at it.

"Judgmental, Alexander. But if you are so sure to say it, I will take it to heart. Besides, this kingdom is already in danger . . . and it has been for twenty years."

"But not lost. Not yet lost."

"So I hope." I lifted my cup to Angus Og, who was leaning back in his chair as he laughed raucously at the jokes being shared. "Tell me, any word from Ulster?"

"Naught but silence," Alexander said. "But no protests of revulsion at your actions, either, if you want to look at it that way."

"Ah, our misfortune." I pointed to the end of the table. Boyd was standing on it. "He's about to sing. The kingdom may collapse after all."

"Can you be serious a moment?"

"Completely. You missed my performance at Perth. Very convincing."

"Pembroke was not convinced, I hear."

Even after swearing to meet us in battle the following morning, Pembroke had ridden out from Perth under cover of darkness with his army. We had nearly all been slaughtered while still in our blankets. What a fool I had been to trust him.

"It wasn't intended for Pembroke. His mind was already decided." I pulled my cup to me, swished the last of its contents around, and drained it. "But I don't want to talk about Perth. Not now."

My gaze drifted to Angus Og. A servant bent toward him and whispered in his ear. He left the room, purpose evident in his step.

Alexander's left brow arched. "You were the one who mentioned it."

"Forget I did. Shall we talk of something else then?"

"Very well." Alexander was now shredding the loaf. He tipped his head thoughtfully. "Christiana of the Isles has never hidden her attraction for you."

"Duncan of Mar's widow?" Christiana of the Isles had been the wife of my Isabella's brother Duncan. "What of her? She was far from faithful even when he was alive."

Alexander stroked his beard. "But very powerful. She has many islands in her possession: Uist, Eigg, Rum, Barra. Hundreds of galleys at her whim."

A silence gaped between us. Christiana was indeed the most powerful woman north of Carlisle and Berwick. And she had precisely what I was in need of. I found myself drumming my fingers on the table. If I fell in battle tomorrow, Alexander might have made an even finer king than me. A pity that Edward was born before him. "A foothold in the islands," I said.

"A stepping stone to the Highlands." He smiled pleasantly. "Lands where Longshanks' laws will never hold sway."

"And where loyalties change whenever the wind shifts."

Angus Og shoved his way behind the head table, his tankard of ale sloshing as he plunked it down. Golden ale splashed onto the shining rings on his wrist. He flicked the wetness from his arm. "Word from the mainland. English forces led by Sir John Menteith and the Prince of Wales will arrive here within the week. No rest for the weary and worn. Pack your gullets. Then up and away with you. You're crowding my hall." He dipped his head and added as an afterthought, "My lords."

"I expected a more lengthy welcome, Angus," I teased. "Always memorable when we meet, but far too brief."

Brief it was. Less than two full days in Dunaverty and my men and I were on our galleys again headed off into the channel. The weather held with us this time and we landed on Rathlin off the northeast coast of Ireland. A mile long and six times as wide—this, my kingdom. Ahead of us lay Ulster. Behind us Kintyre. Half a year since the crown had rested on my head at Scone and it had all but toppled from there.

Thrice I sent word to Elizabeth's kin in Ulster, asking, and then pleading for refuge. The first time I received no answer. The second time the reply was that they could not at that moment accommodate us. The last was a blunt suggestion that we go back to Scotland. That gave me small faith that Elizabeth and Nigel had arrived there and been able to argue my case. For now, I could but wonder and worry about the world beyond.

5

Robert the Bruce – Dunaverty/ Castle Tirrim, Garmoran, 1306

THERE ARE SOME WHO tire of fighting. Some who might plunge into a hole, who remember only the fall and the pain of landing hard. I could only look up to the light and ask myself how to reach it.

To do that, I needed two things: money and men. An abundance of one without the other was useless. But how to acquire them, and in large enough amounts, was a rather troublesome matter.

Boyd was sent to Carrick to collect rents due. Alexander was dispatched to the north of Ireland to muster recruits. Thomas and Edward wanted to go with him, but I ordered them to stay on Rathlin. Since the place was stone-dry of drink by then and had a thousandfold more birds than women on it, I reckoned there was not much harm they could do. All the same, if there was trouble to be found, they would find it, and so I encouraged Neil to watch over them.

With Torquil as my guide over the waters and twelve other men to man the galley, we sailed past Islay and Mull. The lordship of Garmoran clung like a forgotten growth to the western limits of the Highlands. Oars straining against the current, we traveled up the long arm of the sea loch. Deep green pines slashed by the silver-white of birches were reflected in the black water. As we went, the clouds sank down on us, as if they, too, were sluggish with grief, until at last they wept an icy rain. Sleet stung at our eyes, forcing our heads down.

Winter's misery bit deep into every sinew of my being. I tried to unclench my fists, but they were frozen, aching in every knuckle and joint. All sensation was lost in my toes. Lengths of land slid by in a gray, foggy blur. Moments stretched into hours, with nothing but the pulsating jerk and splash of the oars to break the drawn-out hiss of rain upon the water. The rowers sucked brittle air between chattering teeth, shoulders drawn deep into sodden cloaks. No one moaned of their misfortune, but it was plain to see they were all as wretched as I was. Time to put ashore. To rest, if that was even possible. Although if we slept, we might not awaken.

Merciful Lord, what I would not give to sit by a fire and thaw my bones.

I looked up to see a squat, gray castle hunched above a low cliff on an islet ahead: Castle Tirrim.

The tide being low, we beached the galley on the shingle-littered shore opposite the castle and trudged across a muddy bridge of land to the base of the cliff encircling the islet. Sleet had faded to a spitting mist. Arms wrapped about himself, Torquil led us to a breach in the cliff wall. Stiff with cold, we ascended after him, taking care not to slip on the moss-slickened stones. When Torquil scrambled over the top, he dropped to his knees, small stones crunching with the impact.

Before him stood a noblewoman in a hooded cloak, gloved palms open in welcome, and at her shoulder a glowering lord, his feet braced wide and one hand resting on the hilt of his sword.

Bending at the waist, the lady spread her arms wide, so that her cloak of crimson parted to reveal a green gown embroidered with golden knotwork. As she straightened, a rope of loosely plaited red hair swung from her shoulder, the end of it hanging to the inviting curve of her hip. Tall and imposing in presence, I was one of few men above whom she did not tower. She tilted her head and smiled pleasantly at me, ignoring Torquil and the dozen men huddled close and shivering at the lip of the cliff.

"A thousand welcomes to Tirrim, my lord king," Lady Christiana greeted. "I have watched for you from my window for weeks now."

"You couldn't have known I was coming, my lady." I took her hand, cold-wet with rain, and kissed her fingers just below the glittering facets of her emerald ring. "I sent no word. I dared not. Scotland is as thick with my enemies as there are pines in the forest. I must keep my comings and goings a secret, as much as I can."

She laid her other hand over mine. "There are some things a woman knows, even without being told." With a gentle tug she drew me close, her lips grazing my cheek with a kiss, her breath cupping my ear like a puff of steam as she whispered my name, "*Robert.*"

With every breath she drew, her bosom swelled against my chest. Fine droplets of rain on my face warmed, like a perspiration that has sprung to the brow with gentle exertion.

"Has it been ten years, truly? Not a day gone, judging by your beauty, I vow." I bestowed a brief kiss in return. "And you've still not found another husband? How can that be?"

When Christiana had barely been of marriageable age, her father, Alan Macruarie, had betrothed her to Duncan of Mar. Perpetually drunk and quarrelsome, she could hardly tolerate him and leapt at any distraction. I had been one of them. It did not matter to her that it was her wedding I had come to attend. But barely in my first full beard then, I was mad for Duncan's sister, Isabella.

"I'll not have just any." She poked a finger at my chest playfully. "You don't know how despondent I was when I heard *you* had married again. Did you not think of me? Cruel of you, it was. My heart has yet to mend."

The black-bearded lord cleared his throat. As I cast a glance at him, he raised his jaw. Finally, he dipped his head in acknowledgment.

"Reginald Crawford of Kyle . . . my lord." His hand drifted downward from his sword, indicating he would unsheathe it in a breath if given cause.

Christiana snaked a hand beneath my cloak and up my arm to cling seductively to me. "Come, my lord. Let me show you to a warm bed. But first, a fire, a full meal and a flagon of wine to bring you back to life, aye?"

As she led us over the rock-strewn path to the gate, her hip swayed against mine. I had come duly armed with my honor, but already it was proving a challenge. It would have been easier to leave altogether, than to stay and deny such an enchantress.

YEARS OF SOOT HAD blackened the knotty beams overhead. Along the walls, sconces blazed to throw a dancing yellow glow across Tirrim's broad hall. In the room's center, a great fire roared, heating the flesh, and the tempers, of the over-drunk. Platters of beef and mutton were emptied, bones flung to the floor where lank, grizzled hounds gnawed at them, growling. The skirl of pipes reeled through the boisterous throng to stomping feet and clapping hands. In the furthest corner, a girl of fifteen or sixteen with honey-colored hair danced atop a table, her slender body swaying rhythmically to the song, her hands caressing the air in wide sweeps and gentle dips, as if they were following the contours of her lover's body. At her feet, a young man reached out and ran his hand from her slim ankle to the curve of her calf. A dreamy smile spread across her lips and she sank to her knees to kneel above him. For a moment, her mouth hovered teasingly close to his. Impatient, he curved a hand around her waist and pulled her down into his lap. She swung a leg around to straddle him, his mouth devouring hers in a feast of passionate kisses. Cheers of encouragement and bawdy jests exploded around them.

Without warning, the crack of an axe splintered wood. The music tumbled into a maelstrom of discordant notes, until only a single, shrill keening stretched across the fractured air. Near them, a giant rose to his feet, shoulders hunched forward. His hair, with two long plaits framing his weathered face, was the same golden color as hers, but streaked with silver. He yanked the axe free, and with one sweep of it sent cups and bowls rolling to the floor in a great clatter. With his free hand, he hooked an arm around the girl and dragged her from the youth.

Except for an older man opposite them, cloaked in furs, the table emptied. The older man scraped the bench back over the planks and climbed on top of the table. "I'll not give on it, Macruarie. I told you what I want."

Macruarie shoved the girl behind him. Her bare feet tangled in her skirts and she crumpled to the floor, throwing an arm over her face. It was not until she peeked beneath her quivering forearm that Macruarie spoke to her over his shoulder, a scowl firmly pressed into the deeply creviced lines around his mouth.

"Remember, I have agreed to nothing yet," he said to her, "so save your wantonness for the man you'll wed, not some beggarly MacLeod who'll barely keep y'clothed." Then he climbed onto the table to face the older MacLeod. Timbers groaned with the strain of his massive weight. An arm's distance, they stared at each other: one clutching an axe, the other a short sword that gleamed in the wan light.

In moments, a riot-hungry crowd ringed them. A man in a tattered black tunic tossed down his coin and placed a wager on Macruarie.

I slid closer on the bench to Christiana until my thigh touched hers. "They look like a pair of cocks about to spar. Will it come to a fight, you think?"

Two places down, Crawford glanced at us as he called for a serving woman. She scurried forth, lifted a jug of ale from her hip and began to fill his cup. Her attention wandered to the two men eyeing each other. Ale spilled over the rim of the cup. Crawford cursed at her, even as she pulled a rag from the cord slung about her waist and mopped the table dry.

Bemused, Christiana smiled. "Those two? Sioltaich Macruarie is my cousin. He speaks affectionately of Tormod MacLeod. Always has. They've been dear friends for twenty years and have *yet* to kill each other. This morning Sioltaich betrothed his daughter to Tormod's son. This . . ."—she flapped her hand dismissively—"this posturing is nothing but a quibble over details, I assure you. Something about the number of cattle to be included in the girl's wedding price." With a wink, she slid her wine goblet to me in offer. "But I do think the entertainment will be, shall I say, 'lively' this evening. I suggest you slink shyly away if you don't like blood."

"I bathe in it regularly." I lifted the goblet, nodding my head in thanks, and drank from it. Clove-spiced sweetness tingled on my tongue. I swallowed and took another drink, deeper, letting its warmth slide down my throat, flood my innards and flow into my limbs. Sleeping as roughly as I had these last months—cloaked in salt-spray in a galley's belly, beneath the leaky roof a fisherman's hut and out in the brittle-cold open on rocky ground—had settled a rheum in my bones. The comfort of a proper bed beckoned, stuffed full with goose feathers and scattered with pillows atop smooth sheets. What heaven that would be!

Christiana's fingers stroked my arm. I slumped against her to keep from swaying, barely aware now of the brewing quarrel. Her head drifted to my shoulder, the scent of lavender oil wafting around her. I reached over and wound my finger in a rebellious curl at her temple.

"Shall I put a stop to it," I asked, even though I could barely have stood solidly, let alone stopped a fight, "before they actually do kill each other this time?"

"Who?" She lifted her head to look at me, blinking quizzically. Her gaze swept the hall until it found the brawling pair surrounded by whooping onlookers. "Oh, them? Don't bother with them. They've fought before."

"I thought you said they were old friends? That their son and daughter were betrothed?" My words were slurring, I could tell, but her nearness coaxed them freely from me. I traced my finger over her cheekbone, around the curve of her ear.

"Must friends always agree? Do allies not differ, lovers not quarrel?" She turned her gaze on me and I thought, for a moment, that in the depths of her pupils I could see the softness of the woman behind the strong façade.

I took her hand then, turned it over, and brought it to my lips to lay a kiss, light as a whisper, in her palm. "You'll show me your lands, tomorrow? Alone? I've a proposition for you."

On the other side of the hall, MacLeod jabbed his sword tauntingly at Macruarie. The mob pressed closer, hooting and stomping.

"You wish to go someplace quieter? More . . . private?" She brought her mouth close to mine, her breath tickling my chin. "*Now?*"

Crawford slammed his cup down.

Air hissed between Christiana's teeth. She drew herself up rod-straight, glaring sideways at him. "Lord Crawford, you will expel those two from the hall this moment—from the grounds entirely if they refuse to make peace. They still owe me for damages from the last time."

Fists clenched bloodless, jaw twitching, Crawford rose. Angrily, he whirled away and strode to the far end of the hall. He grabbed Macruarie by the forearm and yanked him to the floor. Macruarie landed with splayed legs, his sword skittering over the planks and clanging against the leg of a bench.

"Causing trouble again, Macruarie?" Crawford twisted a hand in the back of his shirt and dragged him kicking across the floor. "Best leave now or I'll cleave your bollocks from between your stumpy legs with your own axe."

When Crawford reached the outer door, two servants flung it open. With one brutal heave, he hurled Sioltaich Macruarie down the steps. The man's screams of fury were squelched by the slamming door.

I pushed my empty cup away. "I've no wish to intrude if Crawford and you are—"

"No," she said tersely, "we're nothing. We never were."

But her fingernails curled deeply into my arm told me that wasn't so. Jealousy between lovers is a vile thing and I had no wish to become the object of Crawford's spite. I realized, however, that she had thought that by 'proposition' I meant something more.

And I had not corrected her.

THE SUN CONCEALED BEHIND high clouds, we set out on horse late the next morning, just the two of us, although Crawford had led her palfrey from the stables for her and made sure the cinch was tight before he helped her up into the saddle, neither of them saying a word.

Over undulating moors, we rode side by side. The horses' hooves crunched softly over dry, yellowed grass and occasionally clacked on lichen-covered rock. Our breaths blew billows of steam into the crisp air. Snow, freshly fallen, rippled in low drifts between sparse clumps of winter-dead heather. Not wholly impervious to the December cold, Christiana wore a long, woolen cloak edged in fox fur, but with her hood swept back so that her flame-red hair fanned outward from her face.

She led us to a promontory, overlooking the endless water. Below, seabirds huddled against the cliff-face on tiny ledges. Only the tireless among them dared to battle the wind and glide above the white-capped waves. I slid from my saddle and locked my hands about her waist to help her down.

"Out there," I said, indicating a point of rock that thrust up from the water far out, "that is your island?"

"Hmm, yes, that one and the one beyond it. Those three specks to the left. The hills beyond Tirrim. Great swaths of forest and moor to the east and north. The dirt beneath your boots. Everything you see—and much that you don't." Chin lofted proudly, Christiana gathered her cloak across her to ward off the cold fingers of the wind. As she walked along the cliff edge, her mare followed her, its reins trailing in the snow. It nuzzled her.

She stopped to stroke its velvety nose and turned around to face me. "Am I different from her—your queen?"

In one heavy thump of my heart, the serenity of the past day was smashed by old, familiar sorrows. A pang of guilt followed quickly, as I realized I had not even thought of Elizabeth since arriving at Tirrim. Christiana's charms had ensnared me, allowed me to exist in the moment: carefree, comfortable, complacent even—until now. Now, I ached. Ached for some fleeting pleasure to displace my loss, make me forget . . .

Christiana moved within my reach, her cloak clutched tight to full breasts. I looked her over. There was nothing subtle about her. She flaunted her sensuality, invited playful courtship and teased unfortunate suitors to madness. If Elizabeth was the delicate flower sprung from melting snows, Christiana was the sprawling oak, deeply rooted and broadly crowned, unbroken by frost or flood. I opened my arms, inviting her into my embrace. "As the sun differs from the moon."

"And which am I?" she asked, fitting herself to me. As she lifted her face to mine, wind pulled at her hair, tossing it over her bewitching eyes. "Sun . . . or moon?"

"Sun."

She smiled. "Warm, bright?"

"Hot, blinding. Overpowering, perhaps."

"I could give you so much, Robert: a fleet of galleys, fighting men, arms, supplies." Her deerskin gloved fingers slid up my arms, went round my neck and locked together. "Give me what I crave—and I will give you anything you need. *Anything.*"

"And you crave . . . what?"

"You, Robert. As I always have. As Eve must have craved Adam's touch. Guinevere—Lancelot. And Delilah—Sampson. So I desire you.

Madly. From the first time I saw you. It was my wedding day and it was you I wanted to be with. I have never stopped wanting that." She laid her head on my shoulder, pouting lips brushing the crook of my neck. Her hands drifted downward, wandered beneath my cloak, fingertips making loose swirls over my shirt. "If you leave this time without coming to my bed, Robert, I vow I shall throw myself into the sea from this very place as you sail away."

Mother of God, she was tempting. What man, but one already cold in his grave, could have looked at her and not *wanted* her? I was no exception, but this threat—to kill herself—was preposterous.

"You will do no such thing." I caught her hand as it brushed across my chest. She gasped, stiffening in my arms. "Rather, you'll console your unrequited lust on some other man from your hall, like Crawford whose protection you seem to need . . . or some eager, trembling, fuzz-faced lad who creeps beneath your sheets by night, pleases you to perfection and is gone at first light. Aye, you are clever, Christiana. Clever and undeniably beautiful. You play all those men against each other, telling each one in turn that you love him and no other. Your gifts serve you now, but one day when what remains of your youth fades away, they will fail you."

Wrenching her hand away, she tried to pull free and flung her palm at my cheek, but I caught it before she marked my face with her temper and left it to sting.

"What I do," I said, wringing her wrist between thumb and forefinger, "is not to sate some fleeting desire. It is to secure a kingdom."

She snarled at me. "To secure your own crown."

"Ah, indeed. But better on my head that it should rest than on the puddle of character called John Balliol." I let go of her wrists, slid both hands down her waist and pulled her firmly against me. "If you would rather not have Norwegian longships invading your shores, then you—"

"Longships? From Norway?" Her large eyes suddenly became very, very small. For the first time, I noticed the crinkles at the corners of her eyes and the lines that finely etched her forehead, reminding me we had both grown shrewder with the years. Testing me, she provoked, "Are you king of that country now, too?"

"My sister is Queen Dowager of Norway, I remind you, and if you do not agree to my offer, then I will call upon her to send her ships to raid at will."

"If you have such powers, why not use them against England?" Arching an eyebrow, she lifted her chin triumphantly. "Hah, you don't and thus you cannot. Besides, if you dared to attack my lands, every clan from Kintyre to Orkney would come to my defense."

Laughter rumbled from my throat. "Oh, I doubt that, but if it comforts you to think it, then have your fantasies, dear Christiana. Truth is, you have as many enemies as I do in those lands. So hear my offer."

Waves crashed on the rocks below, filling the pause as she considered it. As if sensing an opportunity, she melted against me. "Then offer."

Cold wind nipped sharply at the rims of my ears. Even under the layers of clothing, I could feel the heat of her body and her hip bones digging against my thighs. Sweet Jesus, she was like a cat in constant season. Did she never tire of herself? "As long as I am king, no man shall take from you what is yours. Your men and galleys for my protection."

"And have I need of your protection? With what army shall you defend me, oh king? I think I liked my offer better."

I threw back my head and laughed again. "Yours would have left you breathless for a night. Mine will keep you well and safe all the days of your life, until you are old and gray."

"I shall never grow old and gray, my lord. When men will no longer have me I will hang myself in the stables. But, I *will* give consideration to your so-called 'offer'." She drew apart from me and called to her horse. It twitched its ears, tapped at the snow, then ambled slowly toward her, dragging its lips over the ground to nibble along the way.

I helped her mount, then took to my own saddle. We rode the distance back in silence. Every once in awhile she tossed me an appraising look. The wind gained force, making the day seem colder, despite that the clouds had raced off to the horizon. Finally, as we approached the castle gates, she said to me, "How many?"

"Of what?"

She reined her horse to a stop and looked at me with one eyebrow raised, as if I were ignorant of the obvious. "Galleys. How many do you need?"

"How many do you have?"

"That, my lord, would depend on whether or not you accept *my* offer. I can spare four, maybe five. More than that . . . You know where my chambers are?" With a cluck of her tongue, she signaled her mount forward.

I let her ride on ahead without answering. I knew.

THE NIGHT WAS HALF gone when I rose from my bed, crept up the tower stairs in darkness and raised a fist to rap on the door. My heart raced, sending blood rushing through every vein of my being, urging me on. Before my knuckles touched the aged wood, it opened partway.

Christiana peeked through the crack. An aurora of candlelight burnished her hair in bronze. From her shoulders, a sea-blue brocaded robe hung carelessly loose. She ran bare fingers through the swirling mass of ringlets that draped over her right breast. As if perplexed by my appearance, she tilted her head. "You are in need of something, my lord? Shall I send for my chamberlain—or will a servant do?"

I wedged a hand through the narrow opening and pushed against the door. "If I may . . ."

The moment I stepped within, she curved around me, rubbing against my leg like a cat seeking attention. The bar clicked into place and I turned to see her leaning against the door. "You may have what-

- 53 -

ever you—"

I wrapped an arm about her waist and pulled her to me, my mouth seeking hers. She whipped her head aside with a murmur of protest. Lightly, I kissed her neck, flicked my tongue over her earlobe.

"Whatever you . . . want, but . . . I—" Her words faded with a shudder.

With a mere finger, I turned her chin. Full lips parted at the pressure of mine. Hungrily, my tongue darted in and out, exploring. The robe slipped from her shoulders. She stepped from me, pulling me gently across the floor. White as virginal snow, her chemise clung to every full curve of her body as she moved, pert nipples jutting against the constraints of crisp cloth. My fingers tugged at the laces at the front as I followed her, loosening it.

Then, as she stood before the massive bed, she peeled the chemise away. With a whisper, it fell to reveal the rapture that awaited me.

6

Robert the Bruce – Rathlin, 1306

F OR A HANDFUL OF galleys, a score of fighting men, I willingly took what was given to me. Christiana of the Isles granted me the use of twenty-five sleek galleys. From Mackenzie of Kintail I received ten more. With those we already had from Kintyre, I now commanded a large fleet that could move armed men and supplies swiftly around the coastline. English ships could carry more men, but they were too bulky to maneuver far within the lochs like our galleys could.

Crawford requested to accompany me to Rathlin. My first thought was that he'd murder me in a fit of jealously one cold night and toss my body into the sea. But over a cask of wine, he confessed that it was Christiana he'd strangle if he spent another day in her presence. She released him without hesitation, no doubt ready to turn her attentions elsewhere the moment we were both gone from sight. In the few weeks I had been with her, she had gone from insatiable to insipid, her attentions wandering, her enthusiasm for mine dampened. Of late, she had been more irritable, prone to argue, and I sensed a pattern confirmed by Crawford's confession. For Christiana, the thrill was in the hunt, not the having.

The weather proved fairer on our return voyage, but shrieking gulls assaulted us all the way, no doubt expecting fish, which we did not have. The moment Rathlin's bleak, gray cliffs cut across the horizon, a knife of loathing sliced through my gut. Months ago, it had spared us from our enemies' pursuit and saved us from wandering upon the winter sea. Now, I saw it for what it was: an isolated, frozen slab of bird droppings. Oh why had I ever abandoned the intemperance of Christiana's hall and the transient pleasures of her bed—never mind her fickle mood—to come back to this purgatory of ice and stone? Surely a man who had known such hardships as I deserved some indulgences—and time enough to refresh both body and spirit?

My men were more pleased to see me back than I was to be among them, at least on this godforsaken island of forced asceticism, where a man could do nothing but pray and wait for winter's end. Depleted, I dragged my aching bones up an ancient sheep path that wound through a breach in the escarpment. There, an abandoned church served as my quarters. Wind howled through the ever-widening cracks between its stones and, glancing up at the roof to where the winter's gray light filtered down in patches, I could see no one had heeded my orders to repair the handful of buildings while I was away. I collapsed on a musty pallet next to the altar, sleep carrying me off to dreams of greater comforts before I had even pulled my cloak over me.

I awoke shivering. A puddle of rainwater had collected on the floor close to me. As it spread, my straw pallet had begun to wick the frozen water up. I rolled over, onto damp flagstones that left me colder still. Hinges creaked and I looked to the door, only to feel the frigid blast of a cold wind stinging at my eyes.

"M'lord?" Torquil stretched out his hand to rouse me. He gasped for air in between words. "On the water . . . coming . . ."

As I pushed myself into a sitting position, he pulled his hand back. Confusion fogged my mind. I rubbed at a neck so stiff I could barely look up. Torquil stooped over me, his pale lips buzzing with words that made no sense. Knees drawn up to my face, I cupped my head in my hands, grumbling at him in irritation.

"Wood and flint," I muttered into my forearms. "Any colder in here and I will damn well freeze to death."

"Later, you must . . . down to the shore . . . don't know who—"

"The shore?" I slid my arms down my shins to peer at him, letting his words slowly sort themselves in my muddled mind. "What's down there?"

"Who."

"Fine—who?"

He shrugged. "Two galleys in the bay. One taking on water."

Boyd had taken two galleys when he left for the mainland.

Into the darkening night I raced, down the treacherous cliff path and out to water's edge. Boyd's curses roared above the slap of rain turning to sleet. His boat crept into the little bay and lagged as they bailed the freezing water from it furiously. A vigorous wind pushed seawater over the gunwales and the boat pitched sideways, tossing two men over. Arms flailed above the surface. Someone grabbed a hand and pulled one of the men aboard. The other bobbed up and down, his body drifting further and further from the boat, even as he tried to swim back to it. A wave swelled up behind him, its crest rising in a ragged line of white like a lion's gaping jaws. Then, the wave surged and broke, the sea swallowing him whole.

Torquil and a few others were already pushing one of the landed galleys out into the water to go to Boyd's rescue. The two boats touched and Boyd and his men tumbled one by one into Torquil's vessel.

James stood at my side, the sleet cutting at our faces as we squinted into the dark, cold wetness.

Finally, swearing and stumbling, Boyd straggled ashore with a sack of money flung over his back. He slammed it at my feet and pitched forward. James caught him by the wrist and slipped beneath his arm to support him.

Boyd shivered violently. "Your rents," he muttered between chattering teeth.

"A bit bedraggled you are, but alive." I reached toward him. "Come. We'll sit you by the fire and dry you out. Alexander has just returned from Antrim with the Irishman Malcolm MacQuillan and a fierce host. He brought ale with him, half a galley-full I swear."

"No, no. You'll want to hear this first." Boyd took several ragged breaths, then raised his chin. He spoke from blue lips in an airy voice, like some ghost risen from the grave. "The English laid siege to Kildrummy. Nigel was there. He held it a long time . . . bravely. The English, near to giving up, promised gold to anyone inside who would give them access." He drooped. His knees almost gave way. James tightened an arm about his waist to hold him up. "Then, the blacksmith Osborne, who had tired of the hardship, set the stores of corn on fire. Everything burned. Even the castle gate. When they finally took the castle—"

He broke off as Alexander darted through the stabbing rain and skidded to a halt beside me, kicking flakes of shingle out into the water.

"They melted the gold and poured it down Osborne's throat." Boyd slumped against James, his eyelids flapping shut and then open, as though he struggled to remain conscience. "They took Nigel to Berwick, where he . . . was hanged and beheaded."

I dropped to my knees. My heart had turned to ice. "Elizabeth? Marjorie? What of them?"

Boyd leaned into James and shook his head. "I don't know. Only that the womenfolk left with the Earl of Atholl shortly before the English came. They never made it to Orkney."

"You don't know? How can you not know?" I leapt to my feet and grabbed the front of his shirt, yelling into his face, "My wife and my daughter were with him! How can you not *know* what happened to them?"

"Robert." Alexander hooked my arm to drag me toward the nearest house. He gestured for James to follow. "Boyd wasn't there. I'm sure he doesn't know any more than what he told you. Let him rest for now.

You need to get some sleep, too. We'll go to Carrick soon. Find out what we can."

But how does a man find sleep when his brother is dead? When he sends his wife away and has no idea where she has gone to? Whether she is dead or alive or suffering in terror as they rape and torture her?

Ah, merciful Lord . . . even as I try and try to weave this rag back together it frays between my fingers.

7

Edward, Prince of Wales – Tower of London, 1307

METAL CREAKED AGAINST METAL, rising steadily to a groan as
the wind nudged at the heavy cage, tipping it slightly. The con-
trivance hung from an iron hook, which extended from the wall of
Wakefield Tower in the outer bailey of the Tower of London. Bone-thin
fingers gripped the wooden bars. The girl peered down at me, her curling tresses twisted and snarled about a bloodless face. Even from the
ground, I could see her lashes, as black as a crow's feather, fluttering
over eyes of gold-green. Shoulders heaving, she sniffed and rubbed a
bare hand across her nose, then pulled the tattered hem of her gown
around slippered feet.

My sire's heels clacked unevenly over the cobbles, slowing as he
neared me. He tried to smooth the hitch in his stride, but his grimace
betrayed the pain. The long, muscular legs which had earned him the
name 'Longshanks' had withered to twigs of late. He had just returned
from Lanercrost Priory near Carlisle, where he sometimes went when
his health deteriorated. But instead of relief from his ailments, he had
returned with an unlikely prize: the Bruce women and the Earl of
Atholl's head, now adorning a pike above London Bridge.

"I sent you to Dunaverty," he said accusingly. "Was he not there?"

"Shortly after I left Berwick, I received word from Menteith that he had already fallen upon Dunaverty. Unfortunately, Bruce was not there, nor any of his brothers."

"So you accomplished nothing?"

Why did he always seek to find fault with me? Even though I expected such upbraidings, I could never shield my heart from them. Worst of all was how he had persecuted me for my friendship with Piers Gaveston. His banishment had nearly undone me. If I wished to hurry my sire's demise, it was not because I wanted his throne. Far from it. I only wished . . . no, *craved* to have Piers back at my side. Mother Mary, what torture it had been without him.

"The Bruce appears to have fled Scotland altogether," I said, hoping that would placate him, and added for further measure, "And you have, of course, heard of Pembroke's success in taking Kildrummy? I myself saw the crows picking at Nigel Bruce's head atop Berwick's wall."

"It would please me more if you brought me Robert's head." A cough tore at my sire's throat. He raised his fist to muffle it. The hacking startled a flock of ravens, sending them skyward in a whir of beating wings and petulant caws.

Like the arrogant, doddering fool he was, my sire denied that frequent illnesses had taken their toll on him. Too often, he was outside on days like this when frost rimed the rooftops, just as his once glorious golden hair had whitened. With every outing his joints stiffened so severely he could hardly walk for days afterwards sometimes. His French wife Queen Marguerite, who was my stepmother, trailed behind him with a gaggle of damsels. We exchanged perfunctory bows: a rehearsed ritual of mutual tolerance. I had it on the solemn word of her laundress that he still bedded her, hoping to get her with yet one more child, as if my two barely weaned half-brothers, Thomas and Edmund, were not testament enough of his enduring virulence. King now for more than half of his sixty-eight years, one would think my sire—whose portentous name I had been burdened with—would have given up youthful illusions years ago, but not so. Those who believe themselves born to fulfill greatness admit nothing of their own infirmities.

"Fitting, don't you think?" he said hoarsely. Glancing overhead, he pulled off his gloves and smacked them against his palm. "The Bruce's own daughter—Marjorie. My captive now. A tiny wren, her world no bigger than the stretch of her clipped wings. Poor, flightless creature."

The waif wormed her way closer to the edge of the cage, closer to me. Mouth downturned, she wedged her dirtied cheeks between the bars. One of her feet slipped beneath a crossbar, dislodging a shoe. It swung from her toes but a moment, before tumbling earthward. I snatched it up and tossed it at a raven strutting across the frost-crisped grass, missing by an arm's length. "Must we look upon her wretched face every day? The sight of her only reminds me that her perjuring father yet has his freedom."

His glove smarted against the side of my head. I sprang away, glaring at him.

"Why do you think I put her there, you daff?" A smile of wicked glee creased his mouth. "Bruce's sister Mary is dangling in an iron nest from the battlements at Roxburgh. Thrice a day she's allowed the use of the privy inside. This one's young; we'll grant her four such excursions. I've forbidden anyone but the constable to speak to her. Dare not take the chance that someone will take pity on her, bastard-spawn though she may be. The other sister—oh, what is she called? Damn, I cannot think in this cold . . . Ah, yes! Christina, the one whose husband, Christopher Seton, lost his head after that routing at Methven. Sick with grief. Shut her up in a nunnery. No comforts for her but her prayers."

My hand cupped a still-stinging ear. "What of his wife? Wasn't she taken, too?"

"Oh, she's here. But daylight will not shine on her pretty head until she's served my purpose to the fullest. I'd love nothing more than to see her suffer the same as this one, but she's too valuable. I cannot risk her taking ill and inconveniently dying on us—imagine the leverage that would rob us of. Besides," he said, steeling himself against a visible shiver, "her father's the Earl of Ulster. He may preside over savages, but he's loyal. I hear he turned down Bruce's request for refuge. Very wise of him." My sire stuck out an angular elbow for his wife. She slipped her hand in the crook of his arm, stroking his forearm with ringed fingers.

"Time for Mass soon, my son," the king proclaimed. "Shall we pay a cordial visit to our guest, first?"

"Guest?"

"Lady Elizabeth Bruce. Languishing in the Lanthorn Tower—at least until I can think of someplace more suitable. She hasn't had much to say yet, but I thought I might give her the chance."

He gimped away, leaning noticeably against his queen's arm.

I glanced once more at Marjorie Bruce, dangling exposed for all to see. She reached a hand downward, the palm reddened with rust where she had toyed with the lock, and pointed to her slipper.

My sire paused before the door through the inner wall nearest the Lanthorn Tower and said something to Marguerite. She swept her damsels on through the door first with a brush of her hand. Then, my sire bent his head and kissed her on the lips longer than I could bear. I looked away, although I could still hear the smack of their mouths. Dear God, had they no decency?

When I looked again, they were gone.

I glanced about the bailey and, finding it empty but for a couple of inattentive sentries—one propped against a merlon of the outer wall, the other making slow circles atop the Salt Tower—I sauntered over to where the shoe lay and picked it up. A ragged hole marked the place where her big toe would have stuck through. The shoe, I observed, was too large to have truly been hers and the leather soles so cracked and worn that I would not have allowed my own servants to go about clad thus.

"Pleeease," she begged, in a voice stripped raw by the wind.

Tapping the shoe against the buttoned front of my peliçon, I ambled closer as I cast one more glance about. Convinced no one was looking, I hurled the flimsy shoe at the cage. It smacked against the outside of a bar, but with cat-like reflexes she trapped it in her hands and pulled it inside.

"May God bless you, m'lord," she said.

I almost uttered an oath against her father, but the king's order that no one should speak to her reverberated in my mind. Better to simply carry out my revenge on the Bruce when the day arrived, than taunt a helpless girl for sport.

ELIZABETH BRUCE LAY CURLED in her bed like a fading infant, face to the far wall. My sire and stepmother stood at the foot of the bed. I walked around them to the other side, but Lady Elizabeth did not even blink when I entered her sight.

The chamber had more comforts than most of those in the Tower: a rag-stuffed mattress covered with clean bedding; a small table flanked by two stools; a hearth with a well-tended fire and a glass window, through which to view the outer world.

"Is she . . . unwell?" I asked. Aside from obvious signs of listlessness and her diminutive frame, nothing about her outward appearance suggested physical illness. She was dressed in a plain gray cyclas of linsey-woolsey, her russet hair pulled into a fraying plait at the back of her head. A coarse woolen blanket covered her lower legs, its tail trailing onto the floor. On the table, her supper from the previous night sat untouched: a congealed bowl of stewed beef and peas, a hardened loaf of rye bread and a cup of ale.

"They found her," my sire said, "lying in her own blood at St. Duthac's shrine in Tain."

I blinked at him, unwilling to ask more, lest he chide me for my supposed ignorance.

Marguerite spared me. "She lost a child."

"A blessing for her that she did,"—my sire went to window and gazed momentarily out at the late winter sky, choked with slow-moving clouds, then back toward Lady Elizabeth—"given the circumstances."

She stirred then, turned her head to meet his eyes. Although she said no words to him, her countenance conveyed everything: that she hated him and wished him dead. Just like her unborn child.

"It was the Earl of Ross, no less," he went on, unfazed by her look of damnation, "who uncovered their whereabouts and hunted them down. Old rivalries do run deep."

Bruce's spurious seizure of the crown earlier last year had done nothing but resurrect old blood feuds and Ross, a steadfast supporter of the Balliol claim, had been his most outspoken opponent. "Well, then, if you are not the Scots' undoing, my lord, they might well destroy themselves in time."

"One might hope," he said, appearing pleased with my observation.

Marguerite moved to the side of the bed, then eased herself onto its edge. Her mouth dipping in a frown of concern, she laid a hand gently on Lady Elizabeth's forearm. "I will send a physician for you."

Again, the Bruce's woman gave no answer. Moments dragged by. Wind wailed through the cracks around the window. The flames in the hearth wavered and dimmed. I shifted on my feet, feeling the tedium set in and wondering what the purpose of our being here was, other than to gloat.

There was a light knock at the door. Marguerite looked to my sire. "Enter," he bade.

Two servants—one bearing quill and parchment and the other a pouch of sawdust and an inkhorn—scurried in, bowing cursorily at the king. They arranged the implements on the table, resting the inkhorn in a slot in the table's center, and left.

My sire smoothed the parchment and pulled a stool back. Clasping his hands behind him, he strolled toward her. "Lady Elizabeth, you may send your husband a message. I suggest that you plead with him to give himself up. For if not, it will be a long time before you're together again. Say that and I will see to it that the earl receives it."

She closed her eyes for a moment. Slowly, she raised herself up and swung her feet to the floor. Slumping, she drew several breaths, then stood. What little color there was in her face drained abruptly. Somehow, she staggered the short distance to the table. But she did not sit. Nor finger the quill. Instead, she lifted the inkhorn from its slot and turned it sideways. Black ink streamed onto the parchment and splattered across the table. The inkhorn fell from her grasp, clattering as it bounced over the floor.

"My husband," she said, staring forlornly at the pool of ink as it spread across the table and dripped onto the floor, "is no mere 'earl', but the rightful King of Scots."

Hands pressed across the flat of her abdomen, she stumbled back to the bed and stretched herself upon its empty length.

Stubborn woman. At least the Bruce had picked a mate with an intractability to match his own—however shortsighted.

8

James Douglas – Rathlin/Arran, 1307

W HEN MANY OF US would just as well have walked into the cold, merciless sea and drown than go on, Robert refused to give up. He coordinated repairs of the church, saw that the galleys were properly caulked and formulated plans with Alexander and Gil for a return to the mainland. His vigor—however subdued his spirits may have been—spread like a contagion. Even Thomas, bored to excess, ceased to complain. Hands mended sails and stitched tattered clothing. Weapons were honed and polished. Men sparred with swords and shields upon the shore and practiced at makeshift butts with what few arrows we had.

English ships, we learned, were scouring the islands in search of us. As soon as could be managed, Thomas and Alexander left for Galloway in eighteen fully manned galleys. Over the winter, our supplies had run dismally low and if we did not replenish them soon, then there would be quarrels and thievery amongst our own. Even the fish, it seemed, had made themselves scarce. So while Robert waited on Rathlin for more galleys, I sailed off with a small raiding force. We hugged the coast of Kintyre, then pulled ashore across the sound from Brodrick Castle on the Isle of Arran. When night fell, we crossed the water and hid the galleys in an alcove beneath the cliffs to wait for our prey.

The silver outline of three English ships took form, sails at rest, provisions stacked and waiting upon the decks. Dawn's long fingers stretched across Brodrick Bay to flash argent upon scattered waves. As the sun broke boldly above the horizon, thirty Englishmen trickled out of the castle and rowed out to unload the ships: sacks of grain and casks of wine, clothing and arms.

My men waited for my signal.

Peering against the sun's light, I nocked my arrow and pulled the string taut, the feather tickling my cheek. At water's edge, a fat Englishman heaved a sack of corn from inside one of the rowboats and slung it over his shoulder. The bowstring flicked across my fingertips. An arrow sang through the silver dawn. It struck him in the back of the neck. The force jolted him forward to land, dead, in the water.

A circle of red seeped out around him as he floated face down, arms outspread like a fallen angel's. Those around him scrambled from the shallow water of the bay, grappling for weapons. Panic rippled through them, becoming chaos as we rushed at them in a frenzy of blades and shields. One after one, they fell dead upon the shore.

We took all three ships in the bloody mayhem and set them ablaze. Smoke drew the castle garrison down from their roosts. Halfway down the hill, the governor ordered his men back. We pursued them, catching some and taking down a few who stumbled or defied their commander out of obstinacy or pure arrogance. We did not cease in our slaughter until the gate banged shut and a few arrows warned us away.

With shouts of triumph we stormed back to the bay, where we crammed our galleys full. Later, as we rowed away, the castle above the bay blurred in a smoky haze.

Secure in their English arrogance, they had never expected us. A mistake they would surely repeat over and over.

Turnberry, 1307

"AND THEY FLED, JUST like that?" Robert sat close beside me on the thwart of our galley. He laced his fingers together and peered through the drifting February fog. After our raid, we had met Robert back on Rathlin. The awaited galleys had arrived and so we set off again. My stomach lurched. If I did not stand on dry land soon and stay there awhile, I would vomit up my bowels into a bloody puddle at my feet.

"At the mere mention of my name: The Black Douglas." In truth, no one had ever called me that before. I had chosen the name myself, though it sounded more sinister than I believed myself to be.

"I say you've earned a reputation. An infamous one." Robert's cheeks spread in a broad smile, crinkling the corners of his eyes. "Someday the nurses will tell little children tales of the Black Douglas and how the English dropped dead at the sight of him."

Beyond dark waters rippled with froth, stretched the ragged, purple outline of Arran's mountains, crowned by clouds of silver-white. An eagle soared above the shingled shore, its broad wings spread to catch the sea wind.

"A bit far-fetched yet, maybe," I said, pondering the thought, "but after I purge Douglas Castle of the English weasels who now sleep in my bed, harvest my fields and drink from my well, they may be saying that after all."

The oars plopped into the water once more, then pulled up. We had finally reached the southern head of Arran, where we would make camp. Torquil, the mooring rope slung over his shoulder, leapt from the prow to tow the boat ashore. Robert hopped over the side and splashed through the water. "Cuthbert! Cuthbert!" he called, searching each weary face as the other galleys came to shore.

A little man with a long torso and short, bowed legs flopped into the water and trotted up to the king. I had always rather imagined spies as being swarthy, lithe, cat-like men who hid in the shadows of obscure inns downing tankards of ale. This Cuthbert looked like nothing more than some simpleton with his hairy, tree-trunk arms and slick, bald head.

"Sire!" he jerked clumsily at the waist. Then he straightened and began to wring his clothes out.

"James, Cuthbert . . . Edward, over here." Robert sauntered eastward along the shore, tiny stones crunching beneath his feet. Early into evening now, the fog was just beginning to settle over the water in the windless air. "Thomas and Alexander should have landed at Loch Ryan by now. They'll be going into Galloway, then turning north toward Turnberry. Cuthbert, you understand your task?"

Cuthbert was now wringing his hands, rather than his clothes. His head bobbed at Robert's every word. "Sire, aye. What do y'wish to know about?"

"Who is with us. Who is against us. Go with caution, Cuthbert. I don't want anyone to know, just yet, that I am coming. They will figure that out when I get there. I also want you to send word to Alexander that we are waiting for his signal. A fire on the hill beyond the castle. He'll know."

Robert stopped and clapped him on the shoulder. "Godspeed."

Cuthbert nodded several times more, spun around and shuffled back toward the emptying galleys.

Arms folded, Edward's eyes narrowed to slits. "Your faith is blind, dear brother."

"For once I agree with you."

FOR ELEVEN NIGHTS NOTHINGNESS stared back at us from across the water. Turnberry was somewhere there on the shoreline, between a starlit sky and dark water, scattered with moonlight. Fat and content from the spoils of our recent raid, we watched and waited. A soldier's life is mostly one of boredom, broken only on occasion by fights to the death.

A wonder we tolerated either, but it was all for some end that we dreamed was a better life than this vagrant one we were leading.

On the twelfth night, I left my blankets and climbed with chilled, bare hands up onto a prominent rock pointing toward the coast of Carrick. Sharp edges scraped at my palms. At the top, I wiped bloody hands on my shirt. Watched. Nothing.

Hours later I groped my way back down and the next day at noon reclaimed my post. Snow began to fall. I stared long and hard up and down the mainland. Something glinted there and I looked away a moment to rest my eyes, then looked back. Through the wandering flakes of white, I saw a flicker, a tiny, amber flicker of light—a beacon growing stronger, pulsing, rising toward the cloud-glutted sky. I moved halfway down the rock and watched longer. It was still there.

Steadily, I worked my way down and picked through the milling bodies of our camp until I came upon Robert's small tent.

"Sire," I whispered, poking my head inside. "Come look."

A candle flickered weakly. Between his hands he held a single woman's hairpin, its looping end beaded with threads of gold and a lone pearl.

He stared at it forlornly. "Elizabeth's. I found it in the hem of my cloak after we crossed Loch Lomond. I don't even know how it got there."

"Maybe she put it there for you to find?"

He shrugged and put aside the hairpin, then threw on his cloak and came out after me. As we stood on the shore below the rock, he peered across the water to where I pointed.

"Alexander's signal." He nodded. "It's time. Get them ready to leave at once."

At first nightfall, we pushed away in our boats and slid over the open sea toward Turnberry. Fingers clenching the gunwale, Robert never took his eyes from the pinpoint of light atop the hill. He never blinked, never spoke.

Finally, as dawn's first light shone behind the low eastern hills, we neared land. Along the shore, a squat figure loped. It was Cuthbert. He waved his arms at us, signaling a place to beach the boats. Frantically, he ran toward King Robert, tripping over his own feet.

"Sire, sire, sire!" Cuthbert pulled at his stubby fingers and glanced at the spiral of smoke curling toward red-fringed clouds to the east. "No, no! It's not them—*not* my lords, Alexander and Thomas."

Among the first ashore, Robert halted abruptly. "What do you mean '*not them*'?" He jabbed a finger at the fire, still glowing on the hilltop. "That is the place. That is the signal."

"I saw it, too." Cuthbert glanced behind him, then shook his head. "Only a house gone up in flames from an ill-tended cooking fire."

The rest of the men were by then pooling behind us, awaiting orders and more than ready. Boyd and Gil stood shoulder to shoulder: the old, hulking warrior riddled with scars and the lean, tight-skinned one with his pinched nose and small, intent eyes like wet pebbles.

"Then where are Alexander and Thomas?" Robert questioned. "Isn't that why I sent you here—to find out?"

Cuthbert's head swung from side to side. He clamped his face between his hands to stop its motion. "Couldn't find them. Tried. I did. Honest. Asked everyone I could trust and some I didn't. Someone said there was a fight, with the . . . oooh, now, who was it? MacDonalds, Macdougalls . . ." He smacked himself on the forehead. "MacDowells, aye, that's it. A fight with the MacDowells at the loch."

"Bootlickers of Longshanks," Edward commented. "I've killed enough MacDowells over the years for raiding our lands that I'd have thought them extinct by now."

Robert pulled a hand down over his eyes as if to collect his thoughts. "Then if Thomas and Alexander are not here . . . Mercy, this does not bode well—for them or us. They had almost twenty galleys full of men. *Full* of men. It is peril and foolishness for us to throw ourselves upon Turnberry without them. We're going back to sea. Back to Rathlin."

As he turned back toward the boats, the men parted from him in a wave of disappointment.

Edward grabbed his brother's shoulder. "No, we won't. I won't. I'm not going back. No more waiting on that frozen, wind-battered rock in the middle of nowhere with nothing to do but grow old and mindless. We've had enough of being tossed about the sea in winter storms like a piece of driftwood. We're here, Robert. We need to take our chances, good or bad, but take them. We're back in Carrick now." He rattled his fist at Turnberry Castle, a gray lump against the broad night sky. "Take it."

Robert pulled from him and walked away three strides. He stared at Turnberry, a mile down the shoreline. His chin dropped. He kicked at the sand. "Who holds the castle, Cuthbert? How many are there?"

"Henry Percy, my lord. A hundred inside. Another two hundred without."

Edward swept up beside his brother. "Not impossible odds. We can take the castle if we attack now."

Robert, appearing less certain than his brother, looked at me. "James?"

"Impossible odds, no," I said. "But improbable? Most definitely."

Hands thrown wide, Edward scoffed. "What—so you, too, think we should creep away with our tails tucked up?"

"No, I don't. Far from it. But we must stop thinking in terms of all or nothing. Wound them. Steal their goods. Kill stragglers and brave fools, like we did on Arran. In short, harass them till they're driven to madness. Tonight, we leap upon those in the town while they sleep. Then fall back before they can rally and we suffer too many losses. Do damage, but preserve ourselves. And then we do it again—some other place, some other time."

"Edward?" Robert said.

Edward mulled it over. He wrapped his fingers one by one about the hilt of the sword at his hip and gripped it hard. "Done."

Robert split us into four groups: his, Edward's, Gil's and mine. Experienced hunters, the Highlanders crept without a sound behind me. We took the far path to the furthest side, that closest to the castle itself. The misplaced trill of a songbird cut the night air—Robert's signal. I put an arrow through the back of a sentry on the town walls as he turned to look toward the sound. Seconds later, the next signal came and my men and I were upon the stockade walls and scrambling over them.

Not a single English soldier from the town was left that night to tell how the Scots leapt upon them in the cold and dark as they sprang from their sleep. Percy never came out of the sanctuary of Turnberry Castle to rescue his forces as they were murdered in their masses. Too uncertain of his chances. Too unprepared. We took their horses and arms and fled before dawn. To find a lair in the hills.

9

James Douglas – Castle Douglas, 1307

MY FATHER, SIR WILLIAM Douglas, died in the Tower of London when I was still a boy. He had been sent there because he broke an oath of fealty to Longshanks—an oath made under duress to spare not only his own life, but his family's, as well. For my protection, I was sent to Paris to study. But I learned more of cutting purses from belts in a crowded market and pilfering warm loaves of bread than I did of Latin or liturgy. When finally I returned home as Bishop Lamberton's squire, I discovered I had no lands and no inheritance. The Englishman, Sir Robert Clifford, was now governor of Douglas Castle. It was a bone in my throat that I vowed to dislodge.

With Robert's blessing, I left for Douglas, taking only Cuthbert and Torquil so as not to arouse suspicion. Dressed in peasants' rags, we stacked crates full of squawking chickens onto the back of a cart and rumbled through the town. It had been ten years since I had walked that ground and no one from the town or castle recognized me. How odd that was, because I remembered so many of them.

Finally, I saw old Thomas Dickson haggling with the butcher's wife over a goose.

"Two pence—for *that?*" With a gnarled finger, he poked at it to send the gaunt carcass swinging. Flies stirred from the shop window to buzz about Dickson's face. He swatted them away, his tongue flicking over cracked lips. "A gosling, it is. I'll give you a halfpenny."

"Ha'penny would not buy you two eggs. Away with you."

"A penny then."

"Away!" The wart-faced hag grabbed a broom from behind the door, smacked him in the shins and slammed the door shut.

Cursing, he hobbled backward. I tossed a pebble at the door to get his attention. "Over here, old man. On my honor, I'll not rob you."

Defeated, Dickson ambled toward me cautiously, one hand rubbing at a concave belly. "That's what the last thief said."

I flipped open a crate, grabbed a plump white hen by the neck and thrust it at him.

He grabbed it by the wings to send feathers flying, then held it at arm's length. His lip curled, revealing two broken teeth. "You'll take a halfpenny? It's all I have."

"You're a poor liar," I told him, securing the latch on the crate. Torquil and Cuthbert sat crouched against a wall further down the street, where they watched beneath the drooping brims of their hats for soldiers. "Take it. Keep your penny."

Clutching the hen close, Dickson cocked his head at me. Stringy hanks of white hair fell across bloodshot gray eyes. "Who are you?"

"You lost those teeth at Sanqhuar fighting alongside William Wallace," I said lowly, winking. "You were my father's messenger."

He gawped at me, then took a step back. Suddenly, he dropped to his knees, mumbling. "M-m'lord."

A pair of older, barefooted lads clad in rags scurried from around the corner and began down the street.

I gave Dickson a swift kick in the shoulder. He let out a yelp. The hen squawked in his arms.

"A penny, you beggar!" I shouted at him. Touching a hand to the knife at my belt, I scowled at the boys coming toward us. They both stopped, shared a frightened glance and hastened away, arms flailing.

Dickson groped inside his shirt for a coin and dropped it at my feet. I bent to retrieve it, then gave him my hand and pulled him up, pressing the coin into his palm.

Lowly, I said, "I heard that Clifford tossed you from your home, as well, Thomas. The thieving magpie should learn not to take what isn't his. Do you live far from here?"

He shook his head, one hand rubbing his shoulder, the other crushing the wide-eyed fowl to his chest. "This edge of town, my lord. In clear sight of the castle."

"Good." I motioned Torquil and Cuthbert to their feet. "You'll take us there? We can roast a chicken or two while I share my plan with you, aye?"

Dickson nodded, a grin slowly splitting his mouth. He laughed then and inclined his head toward the end of the alley as he set off for his home.

FOR DAYS, MEN CAME and went from Dickson's cramped hovel, where we hid with his aged wife, daughter and her two young children. Dickson's daughter, Mariota, had no husband and by the fourth night Torquil was sharing a blanket with her. By the time the children were all soundly asleep, Torquil was grunting softly as he swived the lass. Between Mariota's drawn-out groans, Cuthbert's snores and the mice scampering across the floor, I do not think I slept at all. Just as well. I had important matters on my mind. Revenge being foremost.

The next morning, Palm Sunday, the castle garrison stumbled groggily through the town on their way to church. I sat hunched on the seat of my farmer's cart, counting them. By Dickson's count, there could not be many left, if any at all, at Douglas Castle. As the last of them passed by, a square-jawed soldier with hollow eyes spat in my face. I looked away, but not before I memorized his face.

When the soldiers were all inside, Cuthbert, Torquil and I shuffled into little St. Bride's Church after them and stood quietly to the rear. The handle of Cuthbert's knife peeked from the top of his boot. I nudged him, pointing to it, and he deftly stooped over to flick a dab of mud from his boot and slide his weapon further down. Dickson and the others filed in by ones and twos. Not even the priest seemed to notice that the women and children had been left at home that day.

I slipped my fingers beneath my cloak and wrapped them around the length of steel pressed against my ribs. Dickson glanced at me. As I brought my sword out, I gave the cry:

"Douglas! A Douglas!"

The soldier who had spat at me spun about, already reaching across his torso. He grasped the hilt of his weapon, drew it halfway and grunted as I plunged my blade deep in his belly. Blood gushed from the hole. His fingers fell away from his sword. He crumpled forward, clutching my blade.

"I gave you a sporting chance," I said with a grin. "I could have run you through from behind without ever having said a word."

I shoved my sword deeper and twisted, then spat in his face. His eyes rolled up into his head. With a jerk, I heaved my weapon free and he fell to the floor in a lifeless heap.

One less Englishman in the world.

Carrick, 1307

I RETURNED TO OUR camp with more than twenty men, our horses laden with the spoils from Douglas Castle.

From the back of the bone-thin nag I had used to pull the cart, I lifted a clanking sack and heaved it to the ground. I untied it, reached inside and drew out a short sword and a mail coif. Torquil and Cuthbert were handing out other treasures to the cheers and adulation of everyone.

"And what did you do then?" Boyd asked.

I flipped a coin in the air, then tossed it to Boyd. "Not only did we have ourselves a fine feast, but they left both their treasury *and* their armory unguarded."

"Perhaps they knew you were coming, good James," Robert said, "and wished to express their generosity."

"I should like to think. Unfortunately, though, Clifford was not there." My mouth twitched with a smile. "But at least he has no castle to govern now. And as long as they keep coming and trying to steal my home, I'll keep reminding them that Englishmen are not welcome there."

"A Douglas!" one of the men bellowed. Soon it was an uproarious chant. I grasped handful after handful of coins from the ground and flung them in sweeping arcs until the mound was gone.

"So tell," Edward said, as he weighed a sword in his hands, dug at the nicks in the blade with his fingernail, then dropped it at his feet, "what ruin did you inflict that left your men in such a giddy air?"

I fingered the last coin. "I will allow our faithful Cuthbert to relay the tale."

"Well, Cuthbert?" Edward slammed his foot down on the blade just as Cuthbert reached for it. "What wondrous feat did your good and noble knight perform?"

Cuthbert shrank away. He studied his feet. "Burnt it. Every last timber. Every sack of grain. Piled all the dead bodies on top of the corn in the cellar, hacked open the wine casks and set it all ablaze. Gone. Like that." He fluttered his hands above his head and blew a short burst of air between his lips. Slowly then, he bent to reach again for the sword. "And we poisoned the well with salt. Stuffed it with dead horses, too."

"One less fortress to be of any use to us. Not as if we needed it." Edward withdrew his foot. "We're doing quite splendidly in our cozy little cavern. A castle is always in need of such repair. So many tedious, daily tasks—tables to be set, beds to be made. The bother of it all."

Cuthbert nabbed the sword and ducked away from Edward. Then he hobbled off, flailing his prize in broad, swooshing arcs before him as he battled an imaginary foe.

"One less for the English, as well," Robert added as he stepped through the celebratory crowd.

"Oh, come, brother." Edward threw his hands wide. "Are we to go about destroying our own? I fail to see the wisdom in such vengeful folly."

"We all might learn a lesson from James." Robert tilted his head thoughtfully. "Unorthodox, that I'll grant you. But we cannot battle Longshanks on Longshanks' terms. We must make our own."

Had he been within arm's length, I wager he would have felt the impact of Edward's fist to his mouth. With a sneer, Edward turned on his heel and stalked off.

IN THE EARLY SPRING slop, the English were bogged down like over-loaded boats on a rapid river. From the forest's edge we watched them. They dared not venture inside the murky tangle with their unwieldy columns and rumbling wagons. We lurked and struck at night and were gone again. The great armies we let pass by, taking only stragglers or detachments sent off to steal provisions. Often we drove the cattle up into the hills, so by the time they arrived there was nothing for them to take.

Nearly every day, Robert ordered our camp moved. Being less than a hundred men, we could cover twice the distance in a day that the hulking English were capable of. We had no wagons, few horses, and only the armor we had taken on Arran and at Turnberry. Our greatest hardship was not being hunted or homeless, but that the people, even Robert's own Carrick tenants, were afraid to offer us succor. If it was discovered that they had given us aid, it could well cost them their homes, their crops, even their lives.

Springtime brought little more to fill our bellies than winter had. Occasionally, we stole a cow or two. Sometimes a herd, although that was not often. When we had a single cow, it was always a great debate whether to milk it or slaughter it. We were encamped in the wilds of Galloway, some of us sharing the comfort of a cave as our 'home' when such a debate raged. A ring of pines stood sentry and beyond them the green hills opened up, broad and surging. April's rains had abated and the breeze carried the first soothing warmth of summer as May passed. Gil had stolen a ruddy dun cow, far past her best calving days. A few of us were gathered in a clearing a hundred feet from the mouth of the cave, eyeing the moon-eyed, intractable cow that Gil led with obvious difficulty by a rope, tugging and cursing, into our starving midst.

Boyd poked at the cow's ribs. "You going to hoist her on your back or cradle her like a helpless bairn over the mountains while we run from the English?"

Gil settled on his haunches beside the cow, his fingers kneading the udders as he aimed and caught the milk in a bowl on the ground. The cow stamped a front hoof, then calmed as Gil began to hum to her. Boyd probed her bony hips with both hands.

"Keep your hands off her." Gil shoved his gaunt, pockmarked cheek up against her muddy, brown hide. "We'll get more from this one cow over the course this way."

"Ach, dry as a stone, I say. Douglas, meat or milk?" Boyd lifted up his shirt and scratched at his hairy paunch.

Just beyond our circle of trees, Robert shot arrows at a target marked in a stripped tree trunk with some of the other men. I was the only one among us who could better him—although sometimes I think he missed the bull's eye just to foster rivalry between us. He flicked the fingers on his bowstring and another arrow twanged dead center.

I pushed my tongue around a bone-dry mouth. My belly grumbled and flopped. "Meat."

Torquil dragged a forearm across his mouth and nodded. Boyd whipped out his knife. As he moved to the cow's throat, Gil shot to his feet so fast the bowl of milk overturned and splattered over Boyd's shins. Gil drew his fist back. I stepped between them and caught his forearm.

Boyd's mouth twisted within the dark red mat of his beard. He plowed his bulging chest against me. "What now? Soft over a cow, Douglas? Is that your pleasure, seeing as how I've never seen you with a lass beneath you? Let him go. We'll have this out and then we'll all eat well tonight."

"No." I nudged Gil aside and peered at the horizon. "Someone's coming."

Boyd drew his chest up and looked about. "There's no one."

"There," I said.

Riding double with Cuthbert, who had been on picket, was a lady I had never seen. Twenty mounted men accompanied her, some wearing mail and others only padded jackets. Both Robert and Edward were there to greet her, almost trying to crowd each other out. Robert yielded as Edward lifted her from the saddle.

"Aithne!" Edward cried, swinging her around in his arms. Her cloak sailed out behind her, circling them both. "Ah, my eyes are glad indeed."

When Edward finally put her down, he kissed her on the lips. She received him stiffly, then pulled back from his embrace. Edward let go of her, one hand lingering on the swell of her hips. Her hair was the color of a summer sunset after a storm, her eyes the azure of a cloudless sky.

"Sire. My lords." She beckoned a young boy to her side.

"Aithne of Carrick, welcome," Robert said kindly. "Who's this?"

"Niall. My son." She looked from Edward to Robert, and back again. Her cheeks creased with dimples as she smiled nervously. "He is seven now."

"A fine soldier he'll make someday." Edward tousled the boy's hair. "I'll show you about later, Niall. I have a fine horse. A stallion taken from an English knight at Turnberry. I'll let you sit on him. Would you like that?"

There was a glitter in Niall's eyes, though faint, like the first stars at night. His head bobbed.

"Likens to his father, does he?" Robert asked courteously. The boy had shining dark hair and eyes as rich as the tilled earth of a deep valley—both very unlike hers.

Her arms went around her son. "Some might say so."

"And how is Sir Gilbert? Any word of your husband since he gave up Loch Doon? I heard he fled to England."

Her eyes met Robert's once more. "He did . . . tried. He was killed before he ever got there."

"I'm sorry, I didn't mean to—"

"You assumed he was a coward or a traitor, did you—or both?" she said bluntly. "I reckon everyone did, and they always will. The truth of it is that when he heard of your loss at Methven and the English came, he was . . . unprepared. We abandoned the castle before they could lay siege to it. I went to Arran while he headed south, where he had kin. He meant to send for Niall and me when he knew that it was safe. He never made it. Anyway, it is done, in the past." She held her hand out to him, a sad smile barely lifting the corners of her mouth. "I have grave news."

A moment passed before Robert took her hand.

"My lord," she began huskily, "Kildrummy was taken and Nigel captured."

"We know that much," Robert said. "The manner of his death, as well."

Softly, Aithne brushed the back of her fingers across Robert's cheek as she gathered breath. "Then you know that before the English arrived to besiege Kildrummy, Nigel sent the Earl of Atholl north with your wife and daughter?"

"Aye . . . but no more than that."

"Then I shall tell you, though I wish to heaven I did not have to be the bearer of this news. They were seized near Tain at St. Duthac's shrine while seeking sanctuary and were immediately sent to the king in London. At Westminster, the Earl of Atholl was hung from a high gallows. His head rests on a pike on London Bridge. Your wife, Eliz—"

Robert held up his hand, shaking his head emphatically. His voice cracked. "No, no more news. Say nothing, Aithne, nothing. I cannot bear more."

"But they live, my lord. They live." She clasped his face in her hands. "In a sad, awful and lonely way, but they live."

"How so?" Edward interjected.

"King Edward ordered your sister Mary to be placed in a cage. It hangs from Roxburgh Castle."

In the murmuring press of the crowd, Neil Campbell groaned and hung his head. "The bastard," he muttered, and shoved his way free. "Bloody bastard!"

Neil's voice echoed across the valley and when it finally died away, everyone turned again to hear Aithne's news—for we all knew there was more.

"Marjorie was sentenced to the same fate—dangling from the Tower of London. Some say the king took pity on her because of her tender years, for she has since been removed. By rumor, she is at Walton, I hear. Christina . . . some other nunnery, but I do not know where. And Elizabeth, her father being an earl, was spared the humiliation. She was for a time in London, but is now under heavy guard at Burstwick-on-Holderness."

Like some ancient stone that would weather yet another storm, Robert stood unwavering. But only so for a moment. His brow furrowed, his chin drifted downward and his hands began to tremble slightly.

"There's more. Better you hear it all at once, so you know." Aithne lifted up his fingers in her own and squeezed them gently. She drew a deep breath, hesitating long before she began again, her voice quaking. "Thomas, Alexander and Sir Reginald Crawford were attacked as they landed in Galloway. Crawford was murdered on the shore. Thomas and Alexander met their fate, the same as Nigel's, in Carlisle."

Robert tore from her and shoved his way past the onlookers. In moments, he disappeared through the trees. Aithne collapsed, spent with the burden she had just unloaded. Edward knelt and put his arms around her. The two of them huddled there within the hovering circle of men—Aithne with her face hidden in her hands and Edward holding her against him. After a while, Edward lifted Aithne up and took little Niall by the hand and led them away.

The rest of us drifted apart and went back to our blankets, spread upon the ground beneath the trees or in the cave. Cooking fires were struck up as night came on. Robert was not to be seen. I left the fire I was sharing with Gil and Torquil and wandered through a nearby stand of woods toward a little stream cutting between two hills.

I found Robert sitting on the damp hillside, gazing up at the stars. His knees were pulled up to his chest, his arms locked tight around them. He glanced, red-eyed, at me, then laid his forehead on his knees.

"Her son is seven, she said."

I sank down a few feet away. "Her husband must have been proud."

He looked at me over the ridge of his forearm. "She never loved him."

"Ah." I wasn't sure that I wanted to know more, but he was going to tell me anyway.

"Aithne and I . . . we knew each other then. We have known each other for a long time. She was the first woman I was ever with. I wanted to marry her. My father always thought her beneath me. Her own father loathed my family. Called us 'pretenders', false princes . . . me, a worthless rebel. When I met Elizabeth I never thought about Aithne again.

Not until I saw her four years later—in Edward's bed. It was not their first time. That much I could tell. Nor was it to be their last. How very like him to take what he wants without thought or care."

My admiration of Edward Bruce did not extend beyond the battlefield. He thought himself the center of the world and the sole reason for God creating it. To him, women were merely another conquest. "The boy, do you know who . . . who . . ."

"Who his father is? I don't know if I should ask. I don't know if I want to know. Except that Elizabeth and I . . . we have not been able to have any children so far. If Niall . . . No, I don't want to know. It's better this way. It was better when I didn't know of him at all. He is indeed fine to look upon. Let Edward believe as he will. The boy is likely his, anyway." He raked his fingers through the sides of his hair. "In the morning, I'll send Aithne back to her home. Send her money, when I can. She doesn't need to be within Edward's reach."

An early summer wind caressed the tall grass of the Carrick hills. The hour was well past midnight, the whole world in slumber, but Robert was far from sleep. The matter of the boy's patronage was merely a diversion—something to be resolved some other day, if at all. All of heaven must have pressed down on him that night, the weight of it delivered in Aithne's sad words.

"What now?" I asked.

He sighed and raised his face to the endless night sky. "This morning, I thought I knew. Now?" His shoulders plunged lower yet and he thrashed his head around, digging fingernails deep into his scalp. "I'm a selfish bastard . . . and thrice the fool for what I have long dreamed of."

I let the wind answer him. The pines whispered and their branches rustled against one another. What could I have said or done to put such things right? We sat there, not speaking, for a very long time. I had come to know him not as a king, but as a man and a friend, and between friends the familiarity of silence is at times a comfort.

"It is not for men to know God's reason," I finally offered.

He scoffed lightly. "So they always tell us when things go terribly wrong."

"That is what my mother, my real mother, not the Lady Eleanor, used to say."

"Your mother—what do you remember of her?"

I thought for a moment and in my mind an image appeared: "The lilt of her voice as she sang me to sleep, the warmth of her touch, the color of her hair—dark like the night. Just like it is now." As I looked up at the stars and the darkness surrounding them, an old sadness overcame me. I was a small boy again, witnessing an event the portent of which I could not then comprehend. "On the day that Hugh was born, I crept into her chamber. For nearly two days she had labored. Then, all fell quiet. Knowing something was amiss, I had gone to see. There stood the midwife and a handmaiden, one on each side of the bed. The midwife took a knife and cut open my mother's belly. She was lying there, her guts open, the blood everywhere—on her, on the sheets, spilling onto the floor. A huge, dark puddle of blood. I screamed at them to stop. I thought they were killing her. I didn't know that women died sometimes, giving birth."

There I paused, recalling that Robert had lost his first wife, Isabella, in childbirth. I could see in the glow of starlight every painful memory clearly on his face. But I went on, even though I had never spoken of it before, because he understood. "The midwife shook me hard until I stopped screaming and told me I had a brother . . . told me to fetch my father. But I could only stare. The bairn . . . Hugh, he barely cried. He could not breathe well at first. He was blue. Deep, purple-blue. Ah, Hugh was never right. He is slow to understand, shy as a deer. My father . . . I think he blamed Hugh for her dying."

"Hardly Hugh's fault," Robert said.

"And it is hardly yours for what happened to your brothers. Or Lady Elizabeth or Marjorie. Longshanks is to blame. *Longshanks*, do y'hear? Do not, for a moment, blame yourself."

"Easily said," Robert muttered.

"Aye, but hard to remember sometimes."

"Leave me, James. I have had enough of words today."

"We all have pain, Robert. Any man without it hasn't really lived, has he?"

He gave me a damning look that cut deep into my soul. "Do you think that revelation lessens what I feel right now, James? In one day, I have lost three brothers and in the worst of ways. *Three.* In one day. Fair, errant Thomas, who could not find his way, even though the path was well laid out before him. Nigel, who could have shamed the saints. And Alexander . . . oh, beloved, luminous Alexander. I would have given my own life in return for his. And of the women I love, all are held captive by my greatest enemy. *Nothing* you say could make any difference at all right now. Now, I told you to leave. So go."

Having said all I could, I headed back toward the cave, the wind nudging me down the hill.

"Is this what it is to live?!" Robert shouted after me.

I turned and looked up at him, now standing with his arms spread outward. Ten thousand stars glittered behind him in a silver-black dome.

"Is this . . ." he raised his hands to the firmament, "*this* what it is to live?"

He slid down the hill and halted before me, the whites of his eyes shining bright with anger. "Cold and hunger. Fighting and death. When is the last time you fell asleep without your hands on the hilt of a weapon? Can you even remember what it is like to sleep deeply and not bolt at every little sound? I'll tell you what it is to live, James. To live is to hold your child, your own flesh, your very blood, in your arms. To see her smile and wrap five tiny fingers around just one of yours. To live is to hold your wife close to you as you lie in bed and listen to her breathe—to fall asleep, one against the other, fitted as if you were made for each other, and then awaken in the dawn when she turns to you and whispers your name. To live is to walk your land, knowing every tree and footpath and foxhole, and come home to the smell of a pot of stew, boiling over the fire. Home, wife, children. *That* is what it is to live."

He gripped my arms fiercely. "Have you ever ached for a woman? Loved her so much, that you thought that every time you lay with her, that if ever she was gone from you, you would die not to have her again? I have, more than once, and . . ." Suddenly, he let go. His hands slid over his face.

"Ah, James . . . how can I go on when I cannot live like this?"

I touched his forearm, but it did not seem like enough. So I put my arms around him. His head fell against my shoulder.

"You'll wake up tomorrow," I told him, "like the rest of us, and go on. Someday, the answer will come to you. But I cannot say when, Robert. Only . . . have faith in God's plan."

"Faith?" He took a deep breath, wiping away tears as he pulled back. "Aye, faith. I swear to you James, on my life, I'll bring them home."

"I know you will." I draped an arm about his shoulder, guiding him down the grassy slope, slick with the first drops of dew. "And we'll pummel those damned English so hard that they'll never come back to take our families and homes again."

10

Robert the Bruce – Ayrshire, 1307

THE ROAD TO CUMNOCK stretched empty. Sun and clouds flirted above. Below, the grass lay parched and sparse amid rock-strewn hills. Scattered behind the ridge that ran along the road, some of my men dozed in the warm, heady air.

Gil alerted us to the first sign of a light column of English, drawn out in a line just four across and straggling out lazily a quarter mile along the road. The Earl of Pembroke's pennons flopped in the breezeless air. Pembroke sat his horse at the fore with his nose held high. I crept along the ridge to gain a better view and crouched down beside Gil.

"How many on foot?" I asked, pushing away a bead of sweat from between my brows.

Gil squinted. He flexed his mailed glove. His lips moved as he counted the rows to himself. "Between a hundred seventy and a hundred eighty. Twenty . . . no, twenty-four horses."

I looked around. My men were drawn up tightly on the far side of the ridge where the English could not see them. We had left our horses behind, choosing the sloping, wooded ground as our advantage.

"Shall we attack when they draw abreast, just below?" Gil said.

"No. Wait until they swing around the bend to the west. That other hill there butts up against the road. The narrower the better. They'll knock each other flat trying to get to us."

He nodded and sank back down. "I'll tell the others."

Gil slunk off and spoke to Edward, then Boyd. The English slogged tediously along. Longshanks would have driven them along far more rapidly. Pembroke, however, was cautious and calculating. At length, the English began to round the bend below. I gestured to Boyd to wake two men near him who were sleeping. Gil gave the signal for our handful of archers to fit their arrows to the strings of their short bows. There was no sound but the tromping of English feet and the sharp breathing of my own men.

Out of the corner of my eye, I saw James sprinting as nimbly as a cat over the rocks and between the trees. He vaulted over a fallen log and dived to his knees beside me.

"It's a trap," he forced out, his chest heaving.

I yanked him in close and whispered, "What? How?"

"A lure. A diversion. The column on the road is a diversion. John of Lorne is to the north, just over the next line of hills, bearing hard and fast on our rear. Pembroke means to draw us down into the glen along the road while Lorne comes up from behind. We stand no chance. Our routes are constricted to the east and west by several bogs—we could cut through them, but just as well could Lorne and his men."

Damn. I had not wagered on Lorne teaming with Pembroke so soon. "How many?"

"More than at Dalry."

Think quickly, quickly. It is the measure of a shrewd commander and your men will judge you by such.

"Somehow," James began, his voice low so that no one else could hear, "they have received word of our position."

We were fewer in numbers. Fewer in arms. Trapped. Fight . . . or flee? Ah, how would we ever evict the English from Scotland if we were forever running from them?

"Robert? What do I tell them?"

The English cannot beat you if they do not meet you. Fight by your own rules, on your own ground.

My thumb stroked the binding on the hilt of my sword. "That we will not fight, James. The odds are poor—deplorable, actually. And I've no wish to serve as a martyr today."

We had only minutes to spare. I split the men into three groups. Edward took off with the largest number to the southeast, to draw Pembroke after him. James and the fastest on foot shot straight northward to taunt Lorne into pursuing them. I picked up my bow, took the ten nearest to me and we slipped away to the east, up into the hills, thickly nestled with trees and broken terrain littered with boulders and hard by the river, where we knew the places to cross, should the need arise.

We clung to the high ground, running a trail etched roughly over the jagged hills. But the further we went, the fewer the trees were, the harder the ground to navigate, the more and more tired we became. The rocky ground slowed us. Twice I stumbled, fell and cut my hands. As I reached the pinnacle of a bare crag, I paused to wait for my men. I looked to the ground behind us. There, a mob of English soldiers trickled over a far ridge. But worse than the sight of them was the sound that came before them—the baying of a hound, hard on a scent.

"Dogs," Neil said, as the rest caught up and reclaimed their breath.

I squinted into the sun and there at their front, maybe less than half a mile from us but following the very same steps as ours, I could see a single hound pulling on a lead, his nose to the ground. Every so often came the deep, joyous bellow from his throat signaling his quarry ahead.

"Not dogs," I said. "A dog. *My* dog."

Torquil twirled his spear in one hand. I grabbed his arm.

"Come with me, Torquil. The rest of you, split in two: one group to the south, one to the east. Torquil and I will follow the river. I dare not think it, but I fear it is I alone that the hound follows. The river is our only chance of throwing him."

Neil nodded and they went their different ways. Torquil and I ran as fast as our legs would allow. Stones flew from under our feet and skittered downhill. My lungs burned. My heart was near bursting. I picked the hardest ground I could find, plunging into a small ravine and then up a loosely soiled slope. As long as we were just beyond eyeshot they would have to follow the dog.

Torquil's legs were long and sinewy, making him a good match for my uncommon speed. I had picked him to accompany me, because I knew that he would lay down his life even as death itself bore screaming down on him. I had seen it in him on the sea as cold rain sliced at us and on land when our foes' arrows clouded the sky like a flock of jackdaws blotting out the sun as they swooped above fields of corn at harvest-time.

We ran . . . and ran. But still, we heard the dog—its long throaty bawl as it paused in confusion where we had turned or crossed over our own tracks or cut across rocky ground. The yip of exultation as it took up our scent again. The tenor of its cry sent a knife through my heart. I knew it as I knew my own voice in my ears. Coll, my own dog—taken from Kildrummy when Nigel was captured, no doubt. As the wind gathered strength, my hope waned. Coll would follow us more quickly now. He would leave the warm scent of our steps on the earth and cast his unfailing nose to the air. Somehow, we must get downwind of him or by God's eyes he would trail us to exhaustion and sure death. My loyal dog would find his way to me even if the very flames of hell rose up before him.

11

Robert the Bruce – Ayrshire, 1307

TO THE EAST, THE ground plunged away to a river, so shallow that a man or dog could walk across it, so narrow that our scent would have easily carried over. The forest, where we might have had some chance of throwing Coll off our trail, was far to the west of us now. Torquil searched my face as I stood there in mounting panic. Impatient, he pulled at my sleeve and together we slid down the hillside, our legs churning. Loose soil and rock clattered down into the ravine where the meandering river coursed through it. We leapt up to our calves into the cold water and with knees thrust high we ran upstream for what seemed like a long distance. Sharp rocks jabbed at the soles of my boots. My limbs twisted and tangled as I struggled to keep balance.

As Coll's warbling rang clearer, Torquil grabbed my arm again and pulled me up onto the grassy bank. There were a few trees here, although not enough to hide us. We were at a bend in the river. In the middle of the bend hunched a small mound. We ran a short way along the river's edge and dashed behind the earthen mound. On our bellies, we scrambled up the hillock and looked over.

Pitching hard on the lead, Coll sprang over the rise on the opposite side of the water. An English soldier strained to hold him back, the leash jerking and snapping. Two other men trotted behind, scanning everything in view to catch sight of us as they trailed down toward the river and into it. Torquil and I dipped back behind the hillock. I motioned for him to follow me.

Hearts hammering, we darted across a small, boggy meadow, the muck tugging at our wet feet, and into a narrow gully where a tiny brook trickled with the last rain. Barely waist-high at first, the gully soon deepened to just above our heads. The earth around us began to rise and fall in sweeping undulations. We squeezed around a huge slab of rock, which nearly blocked the gully, and stopped there. I unslung my bow, then plucked three arrows from the quiver on my back. I must have lost the rest during our frantic escape.

"I will handle the men, Torquil," I said. My hands trembled. "You . . . must kill the dog. Understand?"

He nodded and sank back behind the rock. My cut and bruised hands tenderly seeking handholds, I mounted the rock and stood, making myself as visible as possible. A gusting wind tossed my hair across my eyes. I swept it away and tucked two of the arrows into my belt. The third I fitted against the bow and pressed the familiar string between my calloused second and third fingers. The Englishmen debated tersely over whether to follow our trail into the narrow confines. The braver and more foolish of them won and Coll's warble fell to a low whimper. He knew I was near. He was glad. I glanced down at Torquil. His spear was gripped tightly in his right hand, drawn back from his shoulder.

The other Englishman popped over a low hill. He had taken the higher ground above the brook, meaning to serve as a pair of eyes. But I had him marked well before he saw me. He let out a yell, gripping his sword. I let the arrow fly. It pierced the base of his throat. His body sailed backward and impacted against a pile of stones. He drew his legs up in agony. His sword still in his right hand, he brought his other hand up to touch the bloody hole where the shaft stuck out. His feet kicked once more and he lay as dead as the stones beneath him.

"John? Ho!" came his comrade's voice. "What—"

I had another arrow snug against my bowstave when the second man poked his head above the tufted bank. I released the arrow. But the wind caught it and the shaft veered sharply to the right and fell aimlessly behind him. His head snapped around. In a second he was up and over the lip of the bank and screaming toward me. I reached for the third and last arrow at my belt. As I lifted it, it slipped from my dry fingers and bounced over the stone until it teetered halfway off the rock's edge. I lunged for it as his steps thundered closer. I grasped it by the feathers and slapped it against my bowstring.

I didn't even straighten to stand as I eyed the blur bearing down on me and stretched back the string simultaneously. He was less than ten feet from me, his axe arcing up above his head, when I put the arrow into his quaking belly. But he kept coming—the blood spurting from his open gut, the wind gone out of him. And still he kept on. I ducked as he heaved the shining axe head at me and felt the whoosh of air from its force. My balance off, I shoved him with bare hands. He tottered. His torso swayed and pitched. His foot slipped. Then he fell backward over the edge, his arms flailing wildly in the air.

I dropped my bow, leapt forward and peered down into the shadows. The wounded man lay in a twitching, gurgling heap exactly where Torquil had been waiting. But Torquil was not there. Coll yelped as Torquil's spear glanced off the dog's shoulder. Just on the other side of the rock Torquil grappled hand to hand with the last soldier. I leapt all the way down, my feet stinging as I landed. Clutching both my sword and axe I went forward. Coll's nose quivered. His head lifted. Ears perked. He bounded at me, his tail whipping with joy.

I hesitated, wanting to open my arms and let him bound to me. He barked in glee. And then I heard . . . other voices. English ones.

"My noble Coll . . . forgive," I said, as I pulled back my arm.

With all my strength I heaved the axe. It cleaved deep in Coll's ribs. Into his heart. He lurched forward one step and, his jaw smacking the ground first, collapsed onto his belly. Dead.

Torquil was on the ground, crawling backward, gravely wounded. I sprang at his aggressor, thrashing my sword. Again and again I struck, until the man fell lifeless into the shallow water and even then I stabbed my sword deep into his body, pulled it free and thrust it in again as the water ran over him. When my rage was spent, I stopped to survey the carnage. My knees wobbled. My shoulders and arms burned fiercely.

Torquil's fading voice came to me like a waking dream. "My . . . lord."

I went to him, dragging my feet through the bloody brook. His legs lay in the water, streams of red pouring from his wounds. I hooked my hands under his arms and pulled him onto dry earth. There was a curving cut that ran from the outside of his brow to just below his ear. It was deep—to the bone—and hard to look upon. I knelt and cradled him in my arms. His flesh was cold, deathly cold.

"We will get you up on your feet, Torquil, and back to the rest. And if you can not walk I shall carry you on my own back and Gil will sew up your cheek there and then you and I will—"

"No, I am done." He bit back the pain and shivered violently all at once. "Go on. I heard them. More coming. I heard . . . them. More."

"I do not leave behind those who have given me so much. I won't."

"A corpse is heavy." He no longer shivered. A stiff grin flitted over bruised lips. He looked at something up above him, happy. "There—a gull."

I looked there, too, in the big, open sky full of nothing, and when I looked back down at him his eyes were empty of life. Whispering rapid prayers over his soul, I pressed his face against my chest. Then I lowered his head to the ground, stood on weak legs and searched around for a place to lay his body and rocks to cover him. But through the valley came the sounds of Englishmen, still following me. I heard the distant voices, thick with their crude accents, and the clop of hooves. Numbly, I gathered up my weapons, sword and axe.

Once more, I glanced at Torquil . . . and at Coll. And I went—although I did not know to where.

I could not feel the ground beneath my feet, nor did I see the miles pass. The echo of voices haunted me, all mingling in a discordant keening: Torquil's, Alexander's, Nigel's . . . Elizabeth's. I stumbled, staggered, sometimes crawled. But I went on and on, until darkness fell and I could go no more.

My legs had stopped moving. My arms were cut and bruised. The earth chilly and damp against my face. I closed my eyes and breathed in. Somewhere a peat fire burned . . .

THE PUNGENT SMELL OF smoke grew stronger, nearer. Heat prickled my flesh. As I stretched, coarse wool brushed against my chest. Surely I was dead . . . or dreaming. Content, I lay like that a long time. My muscles were heavy. I slipped off to sleep again.

A wooden spoon thunked against the inside of a pot. I smelled a stew. I *was* dreaming. Of home.

"A long way in a short time," said a croaking voice.

I cracked my eyelids. It was dark, wherever I was. Shapes swam fuzzily around me. I could barely turn my head, my neck was so stiff. Smoke from of a cooking fire curled lazily toward a small hole in the roof. I focused on the wavering, yellow-orange flames and rubbed sore eyes. My bed was no more than a plank and some straw. I was in a cramped shepherd's hut—and it reeked of manure.

"English, you think?" came a deeper voice. "Fine mail. Too fancy for a Scot."

I blinked at the voice. "No, I'm . . ."

Too much effort to speak. I wanted to go back to sleep. I heard something slopping, something scraping. A hand, bony and calloused, propped up my head. A steaming bowl was waved under my nose.

"Eat," said the man. "You'll fetch more alive than dead."

Ill luck to have survived so much, only to be ransomed to the English. Death was now a certainty. What then would become of Elizabeth and Marjorie? And what of Scotland? There was so much that I had not yet done.

I turned my head away, even though it hurt to do so. There before me stood an old woman, her gray hairs hanging in sparse strings about a craggy, warty face and her spine crooked. Beside her was a man of middle years, his face dirty, but with shoulders hugely broad and splayed, rough hands that had seen hard work.

"Who are you?" I asked forthright.

"Nobody that matters," said a second man, standing by the door. Similar in looks to the other, he had a black-faced lamb slung over his shoulders. It bleated incessantly, but he took no mind of it.

A third stepped from the shadows, shorter, younger. "Aye, he's the one they're looking for. I wager they'll be back."

"Eat," urged the old woman once more.

But I was too tired to be hungry. I closed my eyes and slept.

LIGHT. IT WAS LIGHT now. I opened my eyes to the pale glow of morning. Quietly, slowly, I rolled over. The old lady and the younger man were asleep on the dirt floor. The lamb wandered about, nibbling at an empty sack of grain. It looked at me with its great black eyes, quivered its wet nose and went back to foraging through nothing.

"They'll be coming."

I gazed foggily across the empty table in the middle of the dank, smelly hut. The man who had been carrying the lamb yesterday sat cross-legged on the floor with his back against the door. He held a crook across his lap and was sopping up the last of the stew in his bowl with a hunk of bread. Calmly, I ignored him and looked about the room, searching for my weapons.

"Know what you're lookin' for," he said smugly. His mouth cracked in a slanted smile to reveal irregular gaps. He tipped his bowl up and drained the last of it. Belching, he dragged a hairy forearm across his chin.

"They here, Murdoch?" said the younger, lifting his head from where he lay on the floor.

"No' yet. Back to sleep, McKie. We've a long trek later to round up th'orphans. We'll leave soon as they get here and are gone again."

Did they know who I was? Should I claim to be someone else? Would they believe me if I did? No, I should keep silent. Slip away, if I could.

Uneasy, I burrowed back beneath my blankets. They had removed my shirt and washed it. It hung from a peg on the wall next to the door. Beneath it sat my boots. My mail was slung haphazardly over the back of the only chair in the place. My squire Gerald, who gave his life for mine at Methven, would have boiled to a fury to see it so carelessly arranged. My sword and axe were nowhere to be seen. They could well have sold them to buy that meat in the pot. The lamb hobbled over to a pile of straw, folded his knobby knees and plopped down.

Another hour went by. Murdoch did not budge from his vigil. Every time I glanced at him he was watching me intently, dark eyes tucked beneath a prominent brow, his broad face leathered by the sun. It was unnerving. Once I tried to sit up, but he swooped across the room and shoved me back down with one huge hand planted in the middle of my chest.

"Rest yourself," he ordered.

And so I did. I was too weak to fight him barehanded. He was fresh, fed and several stones heavier than me. He stared at me still and I closed my eyes and thought that for awhile I slept again, although fitfully.

Horses. I heard horses. I bolted upright and onto my feet. My knees folded. I barely caught myself by clinging to the edge of my bed.

The old lady and other man, McKie, were gone.

Murdoch leered at me, standing. "Going somewhere?"

He swung the door open. Light poured in. A shadow moved across the brightness. I sank back against the wattle and daub wall at my back. A cold sweat washed over me. I was nothing without my weapons. I would rather have died out there in the wild, fighting bravely, as I had lived—not here, not in a dungeon and certainly not as a spectacle of mockery on the gallows.

"Robert?"

James stooped beneath the sagging lintel and into the hut. My heart nearly burst at the sight of him. He threw his arms open and pulled me in.

"We eluded them easily," he said. "You had a harder time of it, I see."

"Hard enough." I clapped him on the shoulders, then stepped back. "But I'm alive, aye?"

"Barely."

Murdoch flushed the lamb from its cozy bed and clutched up my sword and axe from underneath the golden straw. He thrust them awkwardly at me.

"Yours, m'lord. Name's Murdoch—at your service. My brothers McKie and MacLurg, as well . . . if you've need of us."

"That I shall." I motioned for him to put them on the table as I sank to the chair, breathing in relief. "Torquil, did you—"

Edward brushed in through the tight doorway, gave a single nod and stepped back outside without saying a word, as if nothing had happened. Murdoch followed him.

"Aye." James hung his head low. "We buried him and the dog on a hill above the river."

Teeth clenched, I closed my eyes. So many dead. Because I would not bow to an English king. But in the years to come, how many *more* would die if I did?

James touched me on the shoulder. "Let's get you dressed and fed. The rest are outside."

He took my shirt from the peg and handed it to me. I bunched it in my hands, digging my fingers into it as if I could wring the answers from a piece of cloth. "Next time, James, we will be ready. We will fight. And we will win."

12

Edward, Prince of Wales – Lanercrost, 1307

GILBERT DE CLARE AND I sat on our horses just outside the priory at Lanercost, where my less than divine sire had collapsed and taken to his sickbed. Although Lanercost was very close to Carlisle, with all its comforts and security, my sire instead preferred to convalesce among monks. It seemed he felt his soul in need of more redemption than his honor.

The Bruce had again challenged that honor. Several weeks ago, reports had reached London of various skirmishes won by the Scots. The stripling scoundrel, James Douglas, had even sacked and burnt Douglas Castle, once his home, slaughtering the garrison and poisoning the well for added measure. More proof that they were naught but bloodthirsty heathens. And so the king, once more, had marched on his ruinous way to Scotland, intent on ending their rebellious ways for good. The levies were assembled and waiting in Carlisle. Today, he had ordered a litter to be prepared to carry him northward, since he had not the strength to ride. The king was going to lead us on. Or at least that was his delusion.

Let him have it. He will not have it long. He cannot even rise from his bed. If Fate calls his name, he might never.

"Pray tell, how did they manage it?" Gilbert, my nephew and dear friend, leaned forward in his saddle. A bothersome, hot July sun painted his sandy locks in hues of glittering gold. Reins draped across his lap, he uncorked his flask, washed the dust from his mouth with wine and spit it onto the ground. "How in God's kingdom do three hundred shabby Scots send five-fold that many English knights running? Court has been a dreadful yawn of late. Too little amusement in watching an old man wither and rot. I should have liked to have been there at Glen Trool to watch."

I scowled at the images he had conjured: a band of half-clothed Scots rattling their spears and routing the flower of English chivalry.

"A disgrace," I muttered in contempt. "Not two days after the Earl of Pembroke put Bruce's own hound on the trail after him, the Bruce decimated a detachment as they slept in a village by the River Dee. And at Glen Trool our haughty Pembroke sent a common woman as a spy into Bruce's camp. Ah, my dear Gilbert, never entrust a woman with a task better suited to a man. The weaker sex has no resolve, scarce courage, and less than little loyalty. Is it any shock that the self-anointed king had but to appear before her in all his wild glory and she swooned and told all—that Pembroke's forces were hidden in the woods beyond? The Jezebel would have bore his child, had he imposed himself on her. Hah. Women are worthless for anything but."

"And may your soon-to-be, comely French bride bear you ten hale sons, my lord."

"One would be sufficient. Ten would make me tens times as mad." It perturbed me that for one child, or however many times it took to produce a healthy son, I would have to stay hobbled to one woman until I died—or she died, whatever the case. I had heard from envoys to the French court so many times how beautiful this Isabella, the daughter of King Charles of France, was that I no longer believed them. It was as if they meant to convince me of it by repetition. The re-minders only served to turn my thoughts to my beloved Perrot—Piers Gaveston. Eternity had already passed since I had last laid eyes on him.

Sweet Mother Mary, how I wanted to be *with* him again. To gaze upon his Adonis face, to caress his sun-kissed cheek, feel the warmth of his skin next to mine . . .

Curse my sire for sending him away. The day would come when I would flout his condemnation of Piers and do as I damn well pleased. Soon.

I drummed my thumb against my thigh, impatient to get on with this blustering campaign. It was nearing noon. Half the day gone.

"Bruce himself, I heard," Gilbert began, "shot an arrow straight into one of Pembroke's best knights as he led the charge on the Scots' camp. Remember him at the tourneys? Best at lances, at swords . . . and an excellent marksman at the butts. Few could—"

"You forget"—I shot him a warning glare—"your company. You're a blathering sot, Gilbert. Quiet your tongue or I'll have a sausage made of it."

"Ah, I am humbled and submit, my lord." Gilbert threw a tight fist on his hip and thrust his jaw out. "But what of Loudon Hill? Was it as bad?"

"Worse," I grumbled. "Pembroke's knights tumbled headfirst into the Scots' trenches before they ever saw them. One on top the other, like a landslide, they said. Those that had a chance to rein to a halt and turn back collided with the second wave. Pembroke turned tail and cowered at Bothwell. Three days later, as your stepfather went to relieve the earl, Pembroke's forces were routed by that omnipresent devil and chased all the way to Ayr. A plague on both Pembroke and Ralph de Monthermer. Their flagrant incompetence has not only cursed our endeavors, it has leant impulse to the Bruce's."

"Lenience, I beg, my lord." Gilbert pouted like a chastised boy. "Ralph does as well as he is able. But I confess, I think his glory days of soldiering are long since past. His joints are stiff, his armor burdensome. I doubt he can see clearly beyond a spear's length."

"Save your worries, de Clare. The soothsayers will portend no block for your kinsman. And you shall earn your reward and station if you've any patience left to your name. First, let me test your ability to guard a secret."

He cocked one pale eyebrow at me.

"I shall recall Piers de Gaveston at the first opportunity."

"But not until—"

"Indeed. Not until. And when it is done, he shall be betrothed to your sister, Margaret—unless you can pose some reasonable objection . . ." I waited a moment, but his expression did not change. "Now say no more about it."

"But this will not happen too soon, I hope? Give matters time to settle. Appease those who—"

"Save it. If I want a sermon I shall open my ears at Mass."

Gilbert looked away, pretending to watch the door. "I meant about Margaret. She's not yet fourteen."

"Which is more than old enough. If I can wed Piers to my niece, it will make it that much harder for them to cast him off again. The sooner the better. They'll be less likely to quibble over such a seeming triviality when the kingship is in transition. If it ever will be—the Methuselah."

My patience had been tried to its tedious end on this journey. Every day I awoke and every day they told me my sire yet lived. It would have been more mercy than sin to add a drop of poison to his tisane.

A flurry of activity erupted near the priory gates and soon the King of England was borne pitifully out on a litter slung between two puissant steeds. How remote from regal he appeared, all wan and sunken back into his red and green silk cushions. He looked at me . . . or through me, and flipped his bony hand to signal the march onward.

Even greatness must yield to the fetters of age. Nothing lasts forever. Leather wears. Wood breaks. And iron eventually rusts.

13

<u>Edward, Prince of Wales – Burgh-on-Sands, 1307</u>

THE LEVIES HAD BEEN languishing at Carlisle for nearly a week by the time we arrived. Pembroke and Monthermer greeted us anxiously. I said not a word to them about the drubbings they had taken. The shame was sufficient. The king was transported to the cathedral, where the bishop said a hundred blessings over his litter and a hundred more over the army itself. The next morning, the king declared himself fit enough to sit astride his horse and so we departed—the glitter of polished armor flashing in the summer sun, wagons fat with provisions, Welsh bowmen by the thousands and a king who could not lift his head from his pillow without utterly exhausting himself.

We crawled, crawled, *crawled* from Carlisle. Our banners had not topped the first ridge before the king swayed limply and one of his royal guards caught him before he flopped over onto the ground. Three days and we had gone all of six miles. Six whole miles. *Six.*

He asked for a bed and his confessor.

Providence at last. Thank . . . *God.*

They carried him to the little village of Burgh-on-Sands and laid him up in the finest house there. He called for me. I came. More joyful than saddened. Sanguine, perhaps, but outwardly subdued. I knew how to play this part. I had waited for it a very, very long time. Dreamt of it nearly every night.

Candles flickered around the room. I stood at the doorway, watching. Queen Marguerite sat by my sire's sickbed, her rouged cheeks sucked in so that her lips puckered in a pout of concern. Another cough racked his chest and she unfolded a linen kerchief to wipe the spittle from the corner of his mouth. Then she took a goblet and brought it to his lips.

"Wine, my lord?" she said, the palm of one hand supporting the base of the goblet, the fingers of the other pinched around its stem.

He turned his head slowly toward me. Eyes as cold and hard as steel pierced my soul. "Help me to sit up," he uttered hoarsely, "so that I may drink."

Cringing, I shuffled forward and reached across the bed to grasp him beneath the arms to pull. My fingers curled into thin flesh, bones sharp beneath. He pushed with weakened legs, the muscles wasted from disuse, but I hesitated to grip harder.

He heaved a sigh of exasperation and flailed a blue-veined hand at me, knocking my arm away with surprising force. "Do you think you will break me? Use your head if you have not the strength. More pillows!"

I hastily collected the pillows that had slid to either side of him and propped him forward. His cracked lips parted and the queen, my stepmother, brought the cup to his mouth. He took one sip, gulped and gagged as though he had just swallowed glass.

Christendom's mightiest champion. Reduced to this. Brittle bones and sagging skin. His hair so thin I could see the blue of the veins on his scalp as they pulsed faintly. Sixty-nine years is enough for any man and thirty-two of those as king. He had yoked Wales to the plow, cowed Scotland, haggled with popes and eclipsed kings of France.

"Leave us," he croaked to Marguerite. She slipped away like the serpent she was.

I touched my forehead to his hand, lifted his cold, scaly, flaccid fingers and kissed the ring that bore his seal. Mine soon, although . . . I wanted him gone more than I wanted what was his. I would have been rapt at King's Langley hunting in the morning damp of autumn with Brother Perrot and Gilbert. I loathed sessions of parliament, detested these inconvenient campaigns, hated pointy-bearded ambassadors waving their documents about, prelates who nagged for funds and—

"Son?" His gray eyes glinted like winter sun off lake ice.

"Dear beloved father." I curved my lips in the semblance of a smile. How intriguing to observe him now. He had no eyelashes left. His hairs were as scant as those of a newborn babe. I had rather imagined him dying in a furious blaze of glory as he rammed Scotland clear into the Orkneys. Instead, he was like some tiny insect fading on the windowsill at the first frost—barely able to buzz, let alone fly. "You are chilled. Shall I have them bring more blankets?"

"You care . . ." He coughed feebly, swallowed back his phlegm and flicked a weak tongue over dry lips. "You care less about my comfort and more about how swiftly my end will come."

"I care that it shall come painlessly for you, my lord. Heaven hurries you, not I."

His pale lips parted to that cavernous orifice that had so relentlessly condemned me my whole life. I knew why he hated me: because he saw my love for Piers as a weakness—nay, a mortal sin. Piers was a part of me which I could not do without. But my sire would never, ever understand that. Even I could no more explain it than I could wish it away. The king drew air, rolled his eyes upward. I leaned close, watching.

"Last wishes?" I prompted. "Which saint do you wish to honor? A cathedral in your name perhaps?"

He clawed at my shirt collar with his twisted, yellow fingers and pulled my face to his. Death had a distinct odor. Not putrid so much as stale.

"I have honored saints enough," he said, raspy. "One last Crusade.

- 109 -

One final victory." His fingers began to lose their hold, but he gathered his will and held on, even as that one single act drained him completely.

"Whatever you desire."

"My heart to Jerusalem. But bear my bones before my army. Inter them not until Scotland has bowed to my name."

I loosened his fingers from my shirt and let his hand fall slack across his shallow, rattling chest.

Your name? Your name? Are you, my lord, in ranks with Charlemagne and Alexander the Great? Will you discourse with Saint George while peeling grapes and wash the feet of Christ himself as you take your ease in eternal blessedness?

I went to the window and surveyed the land. "As you so wish, sire."

Without looking back, I took my leave. As I closed the door behind me, my younger half-brother Thomas stepped from the shadows, blocking my retreat down the narrow steps to the lower floor of the cramped house. Hardly seven years of age, my doting father had insisted on bringing the seed of his fading years along for reasons only he knew why. Thomas' hair was a mess and his garnache had slipped to one side so that it looked as though he would lose the entire garment with a shrug of his shoulders. In the undersized hall below, there must have waited two dozen lords, barons, and holy men—none wanting to forego this momentous event. Already they had begun to bow more lowly to me, whereas weeks before they had afforded me only disapproving glances.

Beggars, I shall remember each and every one of you.

"Inform me when he is indeed expired," I said to my brother as I tugged at my collar and swept away the curse of my sire's touch. "He may linger for years simply to plague me."

Thomas looked at me in perplexity. He had his mother's vacant French eyes.

"Best to have the priest at hand, though," I added. "In case."

The king died within minutes. Little brother Thomas retrieved me from the garden. I stared at the king a long while as the priest chanted over him. I still expected him to gasp for breath, bolt up and curse at me with fire in his lungs. When they asked me what to do with him, I ordered his body to be laid at Waltham Abbey.

A pox on your brittle bones and shriveled heart. Let them lie within the hull of your rotting flesh while maggots feast.

You are dust. Your word, your will—nothing now.

I am king.

14

Edward II – London, 1307

A CANKER ON WAGGING tongues. I recalled Piers from Gascony. He bore more love and loyalty for me than anyone and for that I would always keep him by me. With my sire's damning voice forever silenced, it was I who would now judge my censors, not they me.

Diamonds of moonlight glinted off the Thames. As I paced along the quay, waiting for Piers' barge, I smoothed the creases from my tunic of scarlet velvet, its scalloped edge reaching only halfway down my thighs, fit snug with white hose. God's eyes, I should have chosen better. Red always made me look so sallow.

The rich smell of ale drifted from a nearby brewhouse and I inhaled deeply. I had come here, to the wharf at Queenhithe upstream of London Bridge, accompanied by only my manservant, Jankin. My secrecy was not so much about whom I could trust, but an overwhelming desire for privacy. Already as king I had so little of it. Once Piers Gaveston was known to be back in England, he would be watched, his every move scrutinized, my every interaction with him questioned.

A cool breeze carried the stench of a passing herring boat. The reflection of a half moon rippled in its wake across the Thames. I pressed a hand flat against my rumbling stomach. My nerves were so frayed that I had eaten no more than a white roll that day.

For a fortnight now, I had undulated somewhere between welling joy and an undercurrent of queasiness. At moments, I dreaded it might not happen at all. That for fear of his freedom he would choose not to return—or worse, that he would set out on the journey in good faith, as eager to embrace me as I was him, only to be intercepted and give up his life to envious scoundrels.

I cannot bear to think it. He will return. He must!

But hours wore on. The moon dipped lower—and with it my heart. The city slumbered. Only the occasional yap of a cur or the carnal squeal of a whore from a nearby alley rent the awful silence. Yellow eyes glowed like embers from the stairway. A small, black cat slinked down the steps to prowl along the dock. Her white-tipped tail flicking, she rubbed against Jankin's leg. Terrified, he froze, moving nothing but his eyes as he searched for an escape from the creature's unsolicited affections.

The rhythmic dip of oars reached my ears and I looked downriver. The pink crescent of a promised sunrise shone in the east. I squinted, peering toward the sound. But it was only a pair of small rowing boats, laden with fleeces, passing beneath the sprawling bridge that joined London to Southwark.

I walked to Jankin and picked up the cat to cradle her against my breast. "Come, my little grimalkin. You may rub yourself against me while I take rest." My fingers scratching at her ears and neck, she rolled in my arms and purred with contentment. "Stay, Jankin. If he comes after all, you know where I'll be."

Alone, I trudged up the stairs of the wharf and passed through the narrow lane squeezed between two leaning rows of buildings. Between a granary and the brewhouse, stood a gateway and from it ran a narrow alley leading to an inn. I slipped through the gate, along the alley and inside the inn's courtyard, where I went through a small, plain door. I fumbled my way up the unlit stairway to the backroom on the third floor. Once there, I went inside and set the cat down. In two bounds, she was up on the bed, piled high with the plushest of pillows and a down covering. A smoking oil lamp cast its amber light around the room. Mindlessly, I removed the red and gold striped surcote I had so carefully selected and kicked off the fashionable shoes that pinched my feet so horribly.

For awhile, I stood unmoving in the middle of the room where a square of moonlight lay. Nothing but my shirt and hose on. Here, alone, I was unburdened by the trappings of kingship. If only it could always be thus. If only I could live my life as I wished, simply, fully. A few merry friends. Drink. Music. And Piers . . .

I drifted toward the window overlooking the river and watched. Surely something not out of the ordinary had delayed him? An unfavorable wind, perhaps? A slight illness, come and gone within a day?

Staring at the river's mouth would not bring him any faster—*if* he was still on his way. My eyelids heavy, I settled down in the cushioned chair I had ordered delivered here earlier in the week. Next to it was a table stacked with gifts for my beloved Brother Perrot: a gilt-bronze clasp of a knight standing atop a lion and an adder; a jeweled chalice and matching bowl; and a small, oaken chest lined in velvet, within which lay a pearl-handled knife. I ran my hands over the relief of an ivory-backed mirror, depicting a mounted lord and lady, hawks perched on their wrists. I leaned back, my legs sprawled wide, and let my eyes drift shut.

A POUNDING AT THE door and Jankin's low voice startled me awake. Rubbing at bleary eyes, I stumbled to the door and slid the bar back.

"Bloody Christ, man," I complained, my forehead thudding against the doorframe as I blinked to clear my vision, "must you hammer at the thing?"

"He started softly," said a voice behind him, "but you were dead to the world, apparently."

Over Jankin's bony shoulder, I saw Piers' faintly discernible outline. Cracks of morning light edged the door below and the sounds of a stirring city—the rumble of cart wheels and the rap of a carpenter's hammer—drifted on the air. I shoved Jankin toward the wall of the landing and grabbed Piers' sleeve to pull him inside. The bar was barely secured when I noticed the bulge of his crotch against my buttocks. Slipping his hands beneath my shirt, his fingers roamed over my chest, fluttering about my waist, tracing each rib.

"Edward, sweet Edward," he breathed into my ear, "how I have yearned for you. Every night as I lay alone in my bed. Hungered for you until I thought I would go *mad*." His tongue flicked over my neck, its wet softness making my hairs prickle.

Heat singed my loins. Perspiration dampening my shirt, I stripped it off and, eager to mold his flesh to mine, turned and began to peel away his clothing. His cloak landed on the bed and the cat leapt up in surprise and scampered beneath.

"Then let madness have you." I undid the cord of his hose, sliding my hands over the prominence of his hipbones, moving them slowly downward as I sank to my knees before him. "And madness will give you all that you desire."

15

Robert the Bruce – Galloway, 1307

THE NEW KING, EDWARD of Caernarvon, had made it no further than Cumnock when his provisions trickled away and ran stone dry. He turned about on his heel and slunk home. We were that much in agreement—that he wished not to be in Scotland and that I wished him and his bevy of flaunting courtesans gone. Longshanks had been decisive to the point of defect. His issue was nothing of the sort. The new Edward was even so shortsighted as to remove Pembroke from his position in Scotland and replace him with the ineffectual John of Brittany, his cousin who was the Earl of Richmond.

With Longshanks gone, some sort of peace should have settled over Scotland. Ah, but not so. Not so. My countrymen are stubborn. Worse yet, they are flagrantly proud of that stubbornness.

For now, it served us well to fight only when we could do so on our own terms—when they were not expecting us. There were times when being fewer and more lightly armed was to our advantage. If only we could convince more Scotsmen to join us, we would have but one enemy, instead of scores of them.

We had blazed our way through untended Galloway, targeting the MacDowells, who had been responsible for the lost lives of my brothers, Thomas and Alexander—taking what cattle we could and burning what we could not carry with us.

The tall grass, tipped with yellow from the cool hand of encroaching autumn, waved and fluttered over the Gallovidian hills. I walked up a small hillock overlooking the road that followed the valley of the Nith, which stretched from north to south. The soldiers, weary lot that they were, crammed down the last of their bannocks and rolled up their blankets. The wind beat hard and steady at my face, making the climb, short though it was, ten times as arduous. I pulled cool air into my lungs. An odd weariness deadened my legs. The urge to sink down and rest tugged at me, but I knew it would be hard to get up again and so I resisted the dull, flaming ache in my body and concentrated on watching my motley army.

The clack of spear hafts reverberated through the glen as they fractured into sparring groups. Bawdy taunts and the occasional thud of a body meeting the ground or the thwack of a weapon against a padded jerkin mingled and ebbed. A few dozen others had drifted toward a line of bundled grain stalks, cut down before its harvest time for use as makeshift archery butts, and were fitting their strings to their bows. Soon the hiss and twang of arrows filled the air and all feeling of fatigue dissolved. My spirit, lofted by the smallest spark of pride, had renewed me. The drills were a morning ritual I insisted on and usually took part in. It kept us from turning idle, although it was the cause of as many arguments as it prevented. The evenings were set aside for the care of weapons and the gathering of supplies and food. The greatest benefit, I discovered, was not so much that they had sharply honed weapons, fuller bellies, better skills or bigger muscles. For their friends, for their brothers, they would rain one more blow, rise up after being knocked down, aim more truly and win.

Proudly, I watched them and thought of my grandfather, who had fought so hard to establish the Bruce claim to Scotland's throne. I reached out my hand and looked down my chainmailed arm, past my outstretched fingers, already riddled with a dozen scars. I touched the horizon where the gray above met the golden brown on which I stood. Then I grabbed at the vision that lay beyond, turned my hand over and pulled an empty fist to my chest.

Memories shattered as a cough crawled up my throat and ripped loose. I quickly unstopped the flask at my belt, tossed a swig of ale back and swallowed, but another cough forced itself out anyway. A full minute later I was still bent over, hacking uncontrollably, my eyes overflowing. When the mist finally cleared from my sight, there was James, the mountain goat, bounding effortlessly up the slope toward me.

"My lord?" James drew up beside me on the crest of the hill and leaned forward. Fat, dark clouds crawled sluggishly overhead. They had threatened rain for days now, but delivered none. The fields were as dry as kindling. He rubbed his unshaven chin. "Are you well?"

I cleared my throat and straightened, feigning a laugh. "What now? Are you my mother? Those whiskers say you're not. Damnable weather, that's all. Neither here nor there, but some irritating in between. Don't dare offer me some concoction reeking of turnips and leeks and tell me it will cure my ills. I was spoon-fed that rubbish from my nurse-maid since I was in the cradle and never once did it hold true. The only thing I ever got from it was a day spent in the garderobe expelling my innards."

Even in the prickling heat of impending battle James and I would jest with each other, but on this particular occasion he did not return the banter. On the road below, his men were pairing up for races. A favorite pastime of James' that he encouraged in his own faction. James was fleeter of foot than any and with the litheness of a cat. I had given him command of nearly a third of our forces to cover the southwest.

He shifted lightly on his feet and tipped his moppish head. His eyes narrowed to intense slits in the most severe countenance he could manage. "You're tired. It's plain in your face."

Ignoring his mothering, I started down the hillside. James came abreast of me in two strides.

"For your own sake, don't waste yourself, Robert. You can't win a kingdom in a day."

I stopped. "*Can't?* What kind of word is that? Poison to the mind. For certain I have never heard you breathe it. The day Pembroke was pummeled at Troon—we won. The day Longshanks died—we won. The day the Prince . . . *King* Edward dragged himself back over the border—we won. And when the day—"

"That's not what I'm saying."

"And when the day comes that he pricks his own finger and signs a document *in blood* that he will never step foot on Scottish soil again . . . the day my wife and daughter come home to me, *then* I will rest."

At the mention of them, James glanced away and nodded. He never spoke his heart, never coaxed me to reveal mine and on matters where we differed, he never confronted me outright. He would merely plant a seed and leave it to grow. He readjusted the manner in which his tattered cloak hung from his shoulders. Needle and thread were a rarity given our vagrant state. "What next? Where now?"

"I hear Clifford is still hovering over that pile of rocks you once called home."

He looked at me sideways. "Aye. Dangled it before a knight called Thirlwall. Clifford told him he could have it and the hand of some forbidden maiden if he guarded it from me for a year. As if it was ever his to give away." James spit with incredible accuracy at a beetle on a stone ten feet in front of him and planted his hands on his narrow waist. "I reckoned I would wait for them to graciously expend some effort repairing it. Then, I'll knock the notion out of Thirlwall's dense head and take it back."

"Good enough. I'll be moving on shortly. For now, you hold the southwest. Aye? Take back what you can. Give nothing away."

His thin lips curled upward as he looked slyly at me. "Oh, I shall do better than that. A little sliver of faith, my liege?"

"More than a little." I put out my right hand in a clasp of farewell and placed the other hand between his neck and shoulder. "A whole world of faith. I've given you the hardest task I could conjure up. Do you think I would risk leaving Edward with such a duty? I would be back in a fortnight to clean up his mess."

He gripped my hand with a tenacity that contradicted his unimpressive, sinewy frame.

"Godspeed, good James. May all the angels in heaven sit on your shoulder and the saints at your ear."

"If angels and saints can guide the aim of an arrow, I accept the company. England will think thrice before harassing a Douglas again."

"If they were wise that would hold, but count them for the damn fools they are. They'll be back."

He began to turn away and looked back. As he did so that same stray curl of hair fell over his right eye. Those blue eyes, apologetic and kind, stared at me through black, disobedient strands. How could any man be so contrary? Deceptively polite and soft-spoken and yet entirely formidable in battle. Fire beneath a sheet of ice.

"To my amusement," he purred. "And when do we bid farewell?"

"On the morrow. I wish to get where I'm going before the snow hinders."

Gil sprang from the fray, his sword wagging at his right side and his shield dangling from his other arm. "Hah! My lord! Come join. Boyd is pummeling the whole lot and deserves a lesson in humility."

"Some other time," I begged. "For now, find Neil Campbell and bring him to me. He knows the land west of here. I need his counsel."

Gil swept his torso in a bow and wove off through the melee.

"Going for Lorne?" James asked.

"Aye, but there are more flies to swat down than just him. Mark me, Scotland will stand as one or not at all."

The list would be long. My Scottish foes were more of an imminent danger than those beyond the border. With the new King Edward gone from Scotland and needing to keep his own affairs in order, time was for the moment on my side.

Slioch, 1307

WE LEFT GALLOWAY AND shortly encountered our new adversary, the Earl of Richmond. As a knife through parchment, we tore through his lines and never looked back. We assaulted the Macdougalls of Lorne by land while Angus Og harried them at sea. It was not until we encircled Dunstaffnage Castle, that John of Lorne capitulated. I was beyond gracious when I offered a truce. Lorne's oath, I knew, was a forced one, provisory upon his own strength and likely fortune. He would be watched. He would never be trusted.

Like a strike of lightning felt before it is seen, we took Inverlochy and Urquhart, where I joined with the Bishop of Moray, then stormed on to topple Inverness and level Nairn. Brother Edward, dare I say, was the bravest of all. He twitched and lurched at the lure of battle and while my men may have walked wide of him otherwise, on the field they willingly followed the swath of his blade.

As autumn gave way to winter, the sickness that had crept upon me months before settled in my lungs and bones. The fever came and went. The cough plagued me. I complained to no one and denied my ailing whenever they fussed, but in time I began to notice them whispering, telling me less and taking more upon themselves. They conferred with Edward. That vexed me sorely.

"Another log, Boyd . . . if you will." I wrapped myself tight inside my cloak and sank down in front of the first fire of another of our makeshift camps. I shivered, even though my muscles burned. Above, the stars shone like firelight reaching through tiny moth holes in a black sheet. "How dreadful cold and only a fortnight past All Hallow's Day. Has the world turned upside down?"

"All Hallow's?" Boyd shifted the log in his arms and set it at the fire's edge. He settled on his haunches and shook his grizzly head at me. "You've lost time somewhere along the road. That was a month ago, sire. It's three days to Christmas."

"Is it truly? Is that our Yule log, then?" My body quivered from my shoulders to my feet, even as the flames grew. A thick cloud of fog, or maybe it was smoke, billowed through my heavy head. My forehead drifted lower until it touched my drawn up knees. I yearned for sleep, but the cold and the pain in my joints screamed within me.

I heard Boyd's bearish grunt and the snapping of sparks as he added to the fire. Was vaguely aware of a woolen blanket alighting on my shoulders. Heard steps leading away. Voices—conspiring whispers, heckling laughter, weapons shifting in their scabbards, the hungry cracking of fire. Smoke scraping away at the inside of my nostrils. Saw Nairn burning. Ross upon bloodied knees, drawing back from me, clutching at his throat. Lorne smiling ghastly. Comyn lying dead as a stone at the altar. Darkness . . .

It was not sleep that came upon me, but the hell of all my transgressions.

I felt a chain go round my waist. Hard, cold links digging into my belly, tightening. My body lifted up. With all my strength, I forced my eyes open. Edward was beside me, holding me up. Snow fell lightly around him in the pale silver of morning. Had I slept indeed? He shifted the weight of my arm across his shoulders and was dragging me to my horse. As we stopped before it, Edward hoisted my dead weight into Boyd's care and mounted his own horse. Around us, my men moved through a haze with their nearly empty packs slung over their shoulders, standing there waiting with hollow cheeks and pale lips in their rent jackets and rusted mail.

"Where are . . ." I could not finish. The intense heat of my fever burned the breath from me.

"The Earl of Buchan is on our heels," Edward informed. His

squire, a scrawny lad of fifteen or so who I had never heard speak a word, handed him his gauntlets, then scrambled back to secure his other belongings on his pack horse.

I tried to free myself of Boyd's grasp, but the struggle was a useless one. I could not have beaten a six-year old lass at wrestling just then, much less unleashed myself of Boyd's bearish grip.

I said, "We face him. Fight."

Edward scoffed at me. He thrust out his hand for me to take. "You can't even sit your own horse, much less fight, brother. Look at yourself. I've seen specimens more fit for sparring in the loser's lot after dogfights. We're going to get you to the Bishop of Moray. He'll put you in better comfort and rally your health back into being."

"But Aberdeen?" I protested.

"Aberdeen? Forget Aberdeen," Edward commanded flippantly, wagging his fingers for me to come up with him. "We're all starving to death. We're all sick of fighting. You are evidence yourself to that fact. We're on to Strathbogie. Someplace away from Buchan and his men until we can muster more soldiers and find something to fill our hollow bellies to get us all up on our feet again. Bleeding Christ, what I wouldn't give for a dry shank of mutton, a swig of third ale and a lumpy mattress."

As Boyd began to hoist me up to share the saddle with Edward, I slammed my elbow backward into him with such surprising force that he stumbled backward. I staggered sideways and flagged my trembling fist at Edward. Faces swaddled in hoods of woolen rag strips ogled me. Only my own breathing cut through the bitter silence.

"We will not run!"

And with that obstinate effort, my knees buckled beneath me.

FOR THREE DAYS WE darted among the hills and hollows and staggered through the forests as Buchan's army trailed us to exhaustion. Every day, we sighted them in the distance and with each sighting they came closer and closer until we could see the color of their hair and trim of their beards. We were more accustomed of late to being the hunted and not the hunters. It was a prickly, sickening feeling.

Edward was right. I could not sit my horse. He held my limp, burning body to his chest as he sought to preserve me and gave me his cloak. I cannot say that I slept in such a precarious state, propped up in the saddle semi-conscious with naught but Edward's cramping arms to save me the fall, but I remembered very little of our flight. When we forded a river and the frozen waters cut across my lower legs I was shocked into temporary mental acuity. But just as fast, my mind, echoing the failing strength in my body, dimmed to darkness. Water brought to my lips invoked endless retching. Food had not passed my lips for a week. I recognized the haunting whisper of Death's specter as it breathed at my neck. I had seen the spirit's impending visit on my grandfather's ashen face in his fleeting days and I knew by others' reactions that that was how I must have looked.

By Christmas Day, I could not rise. My heart told me to listen to my dreams and live. My head told me to listen to my body and just let go.

As the snow tumbled down and deep upon the earth, my men straggled uphill, numb and weary. Boyd carried me in his arms and laid me on a thick piling of furs beneath an outcrop of rock, so that the snow would not bury me. I turned my stiff, aching neck to look. There, far beyond a boggy stretch of turf lay a village, wasted and emptied—though whether our work or Buchan's or perhaps even Pembroke's I could not tell. Edward began to array our men on the hillside, archers to the fore. And there in the distance . . . the men of Buchan marching forward, straining to churn their legs through the impeding drifts, their horses snorting clouds of ice.

Gil, who knew Latin better than any among us, sank to his knees at my side and began to utter, " . . . *terra sicut in coelo . . . dimitte nobis . . . nos inducas in tentationem . . ."*

He made the sign of the cross above me, glanced quickly over his shoulder, laid his hand on my chest and started again. *"Pater noster qui—"*

I laid my trembling blue fingers over his. "When did you take vows, Gil? Do I look so near to death?"

He feigned a smile, but it slipped away under the shadow of his beak-like nose. My brother-in-law Neil Campbell, his longsword dangling from one hairy-knuckled hand, hovered grimly over Gil's shoulder.

"Tomorrow will find you hale, my king," Neil insisted. "For now—Buchan, he is across the way. Rumors were amuck that you were already dead. That is why they've waited so long to come after us. They dared not while they believed you among us. But now, we've nowhere left to run. Our legs refuse to carry us any further."

"Time to use your arms, Neil," I told him hoarsely. "Time to fight."

"Aye." Neil tightened one of the carrying straps of his studded round shield and stood.

"Neil?"

"Aye?"

"For Mary."

The name touched on some strength deep and latent within him. He drew breath, raising his shoulders, and nodded. "And Elizabeth."

Before his sentimental side got the better of him, Neil took off scrambling sideways along the hill. I gestured to Gil to bend nearer to me.

Our archers ran their calloused fingers over their strings for one last test, then jabbed their missiles into the packed snow at their feet. They were well practiced and my faith in them was unfailing. But Buchan had archers, too, and no matter how stray or true the aim on either side, Scots would die this day.

"Edward—bring Edward," I whispered into Gil's scarlet-rimmed ear. I tried to raise my head, but the downward pull was too great, my power too little. "Tell him . . . I have a wish."

Gil left me. It was only a moment and yet more than an eternity when Edward's hulking shadow appeared above me. He studied me in his callous, cursory manner, half love, half hate, then knelt slowly beside me. There was not a thread of fear abiding in his conscience—only the cool glimmer of ambition at seeing his older sibling, that which stood between him and glory, heartbeats from death.

He bowed his head and placed his hand on my shoulder. "Your wish?" he prompted.

Of all of us this past year, he had fought the hardest and most dangerously, and yet he appeared unscathed, stronger, damn invincible.

I looked him straight in the eye and raised two fingers. Then I lowered one and said, "First, if you must go on without me, that you will finish what I started."

"That goes without saying, Robert. And?"

My hand began to shake and I let it fall to my chest. "Put me on my horse. Let me lead them one more time."

He scoffed at me. "And let you fall to an arrow? No."

"Edward, I am going to die here anyway. You know . . ."

He abandoned me with a surly glance. Ever defiant. Tenfold more so toward me than the rest of humanity. And yet . . .

I watched as Buchan's archers scurried forth. The call went up: "Take aim!"

For a moment, there was nothing but silence. Far, far silence resounding of mortality and snow all around, blinding to the sight.

"Pull!"

The twang and hiss. Bodies reeling backward. Buchan's lines faltered, then staggered on. Another command. Another cloud from our side, like diving swifts, cutting through the sky. More fell. Buchan's men began to weave and wade their way through the bog. My own men stood waiting with slack shoulders and pale, sepulchral faces.

I pushed away the furs covering me, turning over so that I could pull myself along the frozen ground, and searched for my sword and shield, for I had only my axe in my belt, nothing more. I trembled from the effort so much that I had to lay my head down to rest. Even though the surface of my flesh was drenched in fire, I felt the cold deep inside every muscle and my body yielding to it.

My dearest wish was to sleep until winter passed, then perhaps, in spring, awaken and move my resting place to some grassy knoll swept by a warm breeze. Come summer I might wander to the banks of a swift stream, there to dangle my hand in the cool water and watch the salmon flash like the last rays of sunset beneath the foaming swirls. But this existence . . . this marching on through winter's grip, swimming against the undercurrent of insurrection among my own countrymen, trailing them down, dangling retribution over them and at the last moment casting exoneration on them . . .

Heaven pity me, but that last was more draining than all my other efforts through the whole of my life. I only prayed that my generosity would not later prove me to be a naïve fool. Ah, but for certain it would. Let me rather pray that it would buy me more and stronger allies than enemies. I would need them. I had so few in the beginning and now—James, Boyd, Gil, Angus—blood brothers, all. But to die here to-day, while so much faith and loyalty yet lived . . .

Then . . . before me—the movement of hooves. My horse.

As Neil and Gil scurried to position me on my mount, Edward looked on, his sword lying ready across his lap as he sat astride his own horse. Neil and Gil held me fast while Boyd drew up on his bay next to me. Boyd brought our horses as close together as possible so that his knee touched mine. Carefully, he placed my sword in my limp hand.

"Hold onto this with all you have," he said. "I will hold the other end with my right hand to support you and hold you up with my left. We'll ride down the hill. When they see you, I'll let go. Raise it up. Let them know it is you."

I curled my fingers about the hilt. "I can't feel the damn thing. Not at all."

"Doesn't matter. We're taking wagers on the might of your reputation."

With Boyd beside me and Edward riding abreast, we went slowly down the hill. Edward had told our men to hold their position, a directive they accepted willingly, for none were in a state for an intense or drawn out fight. We picked a path through the fallen bodies. Arrows fell wildly about us and twice Edward blocked one with a swift move of his shield. Where the slope leveled out, we halted. Buchan's soldiers were now a hundred feet away.

Boyd let go of my blade. Even though it felt to me heavier than any boulder I had ever rested on, I raised my sword toward heaven.

Let God's will be done. Take me now or let me finish what I have begun.

Their lines began to falter.

"The Bruce!" someone shrieked.

The few still rushing forward drew up, then turned back. Buchan's lines broke. They ran.

I slumped against Boyd's burly arm and closed my eyes.

16

Edward II – Boulogne, 1308

ISABELLA. ISABELLA . . . *QUEEN* ISABELLA.

Daughter of a king, soon to be the wife of one and someday, should God decree, the mother of yet another. Born in a royal bed and taken to one. She need do nothing but receive me when I will have her, bear me a son, steward my servants and otherwise keep from me. A pampered life. One I would have relished, had I been so inclined to compliancy. Both misfortune and ease in being born woman.

I saw her for the first time in the cathedral at Boulogne. Between Bruce and his fractious rogues in Scotland and my English barons who nagged me to conclude my arranged union, this for now was the lesser of two evils. The documents had all been detailed, perused, re-penned, signed and sealed. Her dowry was already aboard ship. I was satisfied with her lineage as worthy of my own, pleased with the trinkets and property that came with her, but in the girl herself I was disappointed. Thirteen and by that age she should have had some budding to her bosom and broadening to her hips. She was a reed. Legs of a crane beneath that billowy skirt, doubtless. Layers of radiant silk and velvet did not distract enough from the thinness of her cheeks. And how was such a weanling to get herself bred? I might have suspected that in Louis' court they ate nothing but bean bread and turnips, judging by the sight of her, except that I had seen that the king himself was as corpulent as an overstuffed boar. We shall have to flush her after the tupping. She will have a fat baby, a healthy one, and after that I will be done with her.

Her eyes, though, they were ... pretty. But shy. Big and round, like a doe's. Her pupils swam in a pool of tears. Tears of joy at the promise of womanly fulfillment ... or tears of fear and repulsion? Probably some worldly, spiteful handmaiden had informed her of the horrid details of wedding nights and sent her into a dithering state of fright.

As she floated ghost-like up the steps to the altar, I experienced some relief at her displeasure. She gave a broken sigh, almost a whimper, her knees wobbling as she forced the last step toward me and placed her clammy hand in mine. I turned to the bishop and did not look upon her again until all was done.

Suffering the tedium of the ceremony, I yielded to distraction and glanced around at the spindly columns holding the ceiling aloft and up at the vaulted arches as they intersected in endless webs. A confusion of angels radiated from the narrow windows behind the altar and it was there, for a long while, that I fixed my eyes as the bishop canted on and on in mystic verse.

Only the peeling of bells roused me from my open-eyed slumber.

Although we walked side by side down the length of the nave and out into the shocking light of a winter noonday, we were yet separate entities, just as we had been hours before. Horses caparisoned in silks and bells awaited us. With a noisy string of mummers trailing behind the wedding party, we made way to the castle where a feast followed. Everything was, as is the usual French manner, in excess. I might have been reviled by it, but on this occasion it was a welcome array of distractions. My new wife waned. She slumped. She looked as though she might dissolve into a lake of tears from pure exhaustion at any moment.

"You should retire, my lady," I said.

She recoiled at my words. It was the first I had spoken to her, nay, even looked at her directly since leaving the cathedral. I leaned closer, intrigued by my effect on her. Her ivory hands lay tightly clasped in her lap.

"Wait for me," I teased wickedly.

Her eyes enlarged to the size of full moons. "Your forgiveness, but . . . I am exhausted," she said meekly.

"Ah." I gestured for more wine. When the servant finished filling my cup, I numbed myself with its contents. "I shall inform our guests that I, too, have wearied and need to retire."

She shuddered visibly and cast her eyes down. To her right, broad-bellied King Philip, resembling a lobster in his rose-colored clothes, was picking clean an entire stuffed capon. To my left, my stepmother Marguerite batted her eyelashes at the kings of Navarre and Sicily and thrust out her pouting, rouged lips. Was it the nobility of Europe I sat amongst, or the harlotry of a brothel?

I tugged at the ends of my sleeves, admiring the cut and hang of my peliçon. With a raging hearth at my back, the fur was stifling, but the fashion worth the price. "You wear your dread too plainly. Worry not, then. You are . . . how should I say this—not yet ready. I can see. There will be time, later, for the marriage bed."

To my immeasurable relief, she slid back her chair and rose, dipping at the knee to me for the benefit of our onlookers, but avoiding my gaze entirely.

"Isabella, my little butterfly?" King Philip slurred as he wiped the spittle from the corner of his drooping mouth. "Will you not dance with your new husband first? What shall I have them play for you?"

He jerked his other hand up in the air, sending droplets of grease from his roasted chicken leg splattering onto my new garments. I snatched his forearm and yanked it back down before the musicians were alerted to his wishes.

"She is weary, my lord," I begged, as I watched her turn and scurry off. "We will have years ahead of us to dance. Years ahead in which to get to know each other." But what was there to know of her? She was meek, uninteresting. A dainty violet whose petals would wilt with the first frost. What match was she for me? Certainly, Piers outshone her in every way. And it was Piers who had my love, not her.

Head down, Isabella tried to rush through the doorway at the far end of the great hall, but a young man with hair the same flaxen shade as hers caught her in his arms and held her protectively to his breast, smoothing a hand over her back in comfort. I recognized him as her brother, Charles, older than her by only a year.

King Philip fingered the golden lion pendant draped over his breast. Red light played across the rubies set within the lion's eyes like a fire within. Clutched in its paws, four pearls shimmered.

"Do you admire this, my son?" he asked.

Although I bristled at the endearment, I did covet the trinket. It would look even more dazzling on Piers. He loved such adornments. "I do. Where is it from? I might commission the same goldsmith, if you would deign to give his name."

"Why go to the trouble,"—he lifted it over his head and dangled it before me—"when you can have this very one?"

No sooner had I reached for it, than he snatched it away. "Ahhh, but you will promise, yes, to treat my daughter kindly and fairly?"

"With undying devotion, my lord." I afforded him a smile of reassurance, but all the while I was thinking of Piers.

The King of France dropped the pendant into my open palm, the serpentine links of its chain twisting over my fingers to fall upon the linen tablecloth. I closed my hand firmly around it. Air hissed between my teeth as the jewels' settings pricked my thumb. Opening my hand again, I brought it closer, inspecting the many facets of the gem and the impressive details of the lion's mane. I slipped it around my neck, feeling its weight settle over my heart.

As I gazed toward the door through which Isabella had vanished, Charles glowered at me, his feet braced wide in a taunting stance across the threshold. As if such a foppish stripling could pose any threat to me . . .

I raised my wine goblet to King Philip.

"May your offspring," he said, tapping his goblet against mine, "be the pride and glory of both France and England."

"Of course, my lord." I downed my drink in one long, greedy swallow.

17

Edward II – Dover, 1308

ON THE SEVENTH DAY of February, the towering white cliffs of Dover came into view. As our ship glided into the harbor, I espied my faithful Brother Perrot standing on the dock awaiting me. Cousin Lancaster had worked himself into a froth upon hearing that I had left Piers as regent during my absence. But I trusted the volatile Lancaster no further than I could pluck him up and toss him. An impossible feat, given his girth.

"Ah brother! Dear, dear brother!" I shouted to Piers as they cast the rope to the dock to haul us closer. He waved at me, a weary smile on his face. I raced over the plank to him and crushed him in my aching arms. Clasping his shoulders, I perused him head to toe.

"They've left you in one piece, have they?" I gibed.

"Unharmed."

"It went well, I trust?" Upon Piers' return from Gascony, I had made him Earl of Cornwall and to further entrench him I gave him the hand of my niece, Margaret of Gloucester, my sister Joan's daughter. Margaret was stout and long in waist, good for bearing children, and while she was agreeable company, she had the wits of an ox. He enjoyed her because she laughed at his quips, nothing more. A sound match. A peaceful existence for my faithful friend, my love of loves. I could only hope my own union would prove as pleasant.

"Beyond well," he said. "Governance is a mindless task. Promise everything. Delay, delay, delay. Give nothing in the end."

"Very politic of you. Any trouble from those cursed Scots while I was away? Still quarreling with their own?"

"Often enough."

"And Bruce?"

He sneered. "They say he had one leg in his grave not a few months past. Sadly, they also say he is improved now."

"Unfortunate."

Servants filed past us. Chest after chest was unloaded from the ship and piled onto carts for our procession to London. Furs, silks, jewels and all manner of riches—courtesy of my French father-in-law. I intercepted two servants lugging a large, ornately carved chest and had them open it. From its depths, I lifted several chains of gold, some strung with impressive, rare jewels, and draped them over my outstretched arm for Piers to admire.

He flicked a forefinger at the lion pendant. Pale winter light glinted off the facets of the ruby eyes.

"Do you desire it, Brother Perrot?"

He gazed into my eyes so long that I forgot what day and place it was until he spoke. "I admire perfection."

"Consider it yours. The rest I leave to your safekeeping. Wear whatever you choose, for as long and as often as you wish. There is far too much for me alone." I was rewarded with a broad smile, like that of a child presented with sweets. "No price is too great for the honor of your friendship." Lowering my voice, I added, "And your love."

"It need not be bought, dear Edward."

"A dung heap of an oath. You are more a popinjay than when I left." But for the one I had promised him, I dropped the other chains of gold and silver back into the chest. The two servants looming behind closed it up and I instructed them to place it with Piers' belongings when our caravan would later be assembled for the journey.

"I shall guard it with my life," Piers said.

I placed the lion pendant's chain over Piers' head, my hands brushing against his tawny hair. "Shine then, like the sun, brother. Shine with the riches of Midas. I shall wear you at my arm like a jewel unto myself. Had the rest of my barons half your devotion and less jealousy... what paradise my kingdom would be."

I was about to pull him into my embrace again, when skirts rustled behind me. Isabella stood at the dock's edge. She tugged the hood of her fur-lined mantle over her head. At her shoulder, her brother Charles narrowed his eyes at me in judgment.

Her voice was barely loud enough to be heard above the wind. "Those were for you."

"What did you say?" I asked, not certain that I had heard her correctly.

"The jewels—my father gave them to you, as gifts."

Unwilling to displace my merriment with argument, I resisted raising my voice and smiled tepidly. "He did. Which means I can do with them as I please. Piers deserves to be rewarded for his service. Certainly your father would not begrudge me to loan him a token or two?"

With that, I led Piers away. Arms linked, we strolled along the dock. "I trust you arranged her quarters far from mine?"

Piers laughed. "Of course." Abruptly, his smile slipped into a frown. "Unless you'd like her close, so that—"

"No, no. Not yet. Not for awhile—years from now, preferably." I draped my arm around his shoulder, pulled him close and said lowly, "I've missed you too much to keep from you for even one more night."

London, 1308

THE STREETS OF LONDON flowed with wine. The coronation would be such a glorious, heavenly affair that the Londoners would tell of it to their grandchildren. Flags of green, blue, yellow and red fluttered above the streets. Carpenters had erected miniature castles along the route and during the procession the members of every guild and organization beamed and waved at the onlookers as they paraded gaily by. Leashed bears and dogs danced to the delight of all and beasts of far away places paced in their cages upon slow-moving carts.

Where days before my queen had regarded me with disdain, she now glowed with proper regality. My subjects adored their new French doll and she in turn was pleased with their reception of her.

But good soon turned to worse. My contentious cousin, Thomas, Earl of Lancaster, saw Piers readying for the procession with the crown of St. Edward on a pillow.

"A royal coronation is no place for his kind!" Lancaster fumed. "For certain, he should not be leading the procession."

"Save your battles for bigger crimes, cousin." I plucked a piece of lint from Lancaster's shoulder. "Piers is like a brother to me and his place is at my side—as much on this day as on any other."

For another hour he ranted and raged like some beet-faced toad. I think it was Pembroke who finally convinced him to yield on the matter, lest the ceremony not go on at all.

If that was not enough, too many guests were packed into Westminster Abbey. Some lowly knight, whose name I cannot recall and did not know when I heard it, was suffocated beneath the crush of guests who shoved to get out the door. It was Piers who had been in charge of the guest list and Piers who took the blame for it, but such misfortunes happen every day.

Others complained of the ceremony's length. Tedious it may have been, but every passage, every ritual was imbued with profound, celestial meaning. Masses were said with routine monotony, but only once in their lifetimes were a king and his queen crowned.

But then, ah worse eroded to dismal. The dinner was not ready on time. The guests, tired from having to stand so long at the coronation, whined about the delay like unweaned pups deprived of their dam. Piers had simply ordered too much food to be prepared and, not being a cook himself, had no idea of the coordination that went into such an effort. How many of those malcontents would have volunteered to accept such a monumental task themselves?

It was evening before the food was brought to the tables and by then most of the guests were belly-full of wine. The pheasant was cold. The pork charred to cinders. Piers spent most of the afternoon shouting at the kitchen help, until he spun himself into a frenetic state.

My dainty French bride blubbered publicly. She declared the entire affair an outrage. I patted the back of her cold, delicate hand and called for the chief cook to be thrown into the stockades and for all his help to be immediately dismissed from service. It was not enough for her, but on what she truly wanted she bit her tongue.

I would not condemn Piers. Not at the behest of my new wife, nor at the abusive menacing of a jealous cousin or snubbed barons.

THEIR DISAFFECTION FOR PIERS brewed, until finally, in late April, the barons convened and expressed their strong dislike for Piers and my favoritism for him. Favoritism—was that how they saw it? If only they would all replace their own ambitions with loyalty. Only Hugh Despenser the Older spoke out in favor of leniency. I would remember, in years to come, who had crossed me and who had stood beside me.

In the end though, when I sat before the rumbling parliament at Northampton, I had no choice. I had to send Piers away.

Leaving the pouting Isabella behind, Piers and I rode casually to Bristol. Cherry trees and hawthorn bloomed in unabashed profusion alongside the roads. Fledgling robins tested their wings and nightingales, the surest sign of spring, trilled from the hazels.

"It will not be for long," I promised, as we watched them loading the ship with his belongings. To ease the distance between us, I had steeped upon him a large entourage, piles of clothes, stacks of plates and carts full of furnishings. "Tempers will cool, in time. All will be forgiven. You will see."

Looking askance at me, he narrowed his eyes. "Forgiven, perhaps—but never forgotten. Once I return, how long before they take offense at some insignificant gesture of your affection, Edward?"

"How can I know? Why even care? Lancaster thinks himself deserving of absolute privilege. He will forever test me, I fear." I lifted my chin, trying to look and sound hopeful when truly I was not. "But let's not taint this moment with such dismal talk. You're to be my Lieutenant in Ireland. Soon, I shall hear of your accomplishments there and all your naysayers will be shamed into praising you."

A sad smile flitted across his mouth. "Is that the plan? Make them regret their words?"

"Whatever it takes to silence them."

He scoffed. "I once said that your kingdom would command you, did I not?"

"Power has its price."

Looking away, he nodded. "And your love for me is that price."

I pulled him into my arms so hard I forced the air from his lungs. As I eased my embrace, my cheek brushed his and the warmth of his skin flowed into me. I kissed his temple, his jawline, his chin, my lips finally meeting his.

Piers shoved me back and stepped away, clenching his hands at his sides. "Edward, we *cannot* give them further cause to . . . to . . ."

"How can I hide my longing for you, Brother Perrot? How? This parting is purgatory."

With a single finger, he dashed away the tear that threatened to roll from his eye. "Then let our reunion be a paradise that, when it comes, will never end."

Heavy hearted, I waved farewell to him on the dock as seagulls cried with me. The journey had been too short, our parting long. My chest heaving with sorrow, I turned back on the road toward London. Back to my miserable consort, Isabella, and harping cousin, Lancaster. Back to Bruce's incessant havoc.

Curse kingship. And curse those subjects who pretend to serve while trying to command.

In my sire's overdue death, I have traded one devil for three others. In his grave, he laughs at me.

18

James Douglas – Peebles, 1308

MY MEN AND I lay low in the bracken and purple foxglove on the gentle slope above the bridle path. In the forest near Peebles in the long dusk of June, while on our way northward to rejoin Robert, we had happened upon a mounted detachment of English, not more than twenty in number.

Along the path that wound beside a crooked stream, the English rode. I thought to let them go by, for even though we had higher ground, they were far better armed than us. I might have let them pass, but . . .

"William?" I whispered to the older soldier beside me. William Bunnock had joined with Robert shortly after I did. A common crofter in times of peace, he had been fighting for the Bruces longer than I had been alive. "That man near the front . . . do you recognize him?"

He squinted until his eyes, permanently bloodshot, disappeared in the folds of his spotted, wrinkled skin. "Hard to say. Looks a bit like the king's nephew: Thomas Randolph of Moray."

"Is it him?"

"Could be, could be," William mused.

On the other side of me lay Sim of Leadhouse, who spoke little, if

N. GEMINI SASSON

ever. He ran a calloused finger along his knife blade. Then, testing its sharp edge on a piece of birch bark, he smiled toothlessly.

William scratched at his tangled, yellow-gray hair with dirty fingernails and kept his eyes on the straight-spined knight near the front of the line. Newly polished plate armor protected the knight's arms and legs, the latest and most fashionable of its kind—German or perhaps Italian, I had not seen enough of such to know the difference in the workmanship. His horse was a chestnut roan of pure blood. Spanish, judging by its proud head and sweeping mane. Although his face was partially hidden by the tangle of birches obscuring my view and I could not yet place it, the surcoat was oddly familiar—brightest blue with a white emblem. Not until he doffed his helmet to shove sweat-soaked fair hair from off his forehead did I recognize him.

"Aye, Thomas Randolph," I confirmed to William. "Riding with the God-damned English." Two years ago, Randolph had joined us at Kildrummy with word of Pembroke's approach. But at Methven, he had been captured by the English. All the while, it had been assumed be was rotting in a dark hole somewhere, tortured at Longshanks' wicked pleasure. A martyr, of sorts. Now, here he was riding with . . . no, at the *head* of an English force.

William's eyes bulged from their sockets. "Blessed Mary, 'tis. Alive and well. Fancy that. Don't look like no prisoner. Heard rumors he was in Carlisle with Clifford not long ago. Didn't believe it then."

"And you do now?"

"Aye," he growled. "The whoreson."

I pulled the cord of my short bow from beneath my helmet and, lying on my side in the grass, strung it to the proper tightness—not an easy feat. I told William, "I want Randolph as my prisoner. Kill the rest and strip them. Wait two arrows, then set upon them."

I crawled on my belly to the trunk of a twisted hornbeam tree. Slowly, I brought myself to my feet. William went on his hands and knees to the next man and passed the order. The sun was long over the hills and I could see only shapes of gray against a darkening background. But I had not lost sight of Randolph. There were two footsoldiers behind him wearing hauberks but no helmets. Evidently they believed themselves in little danger. I pulled until the feather tickled my cheek and looked down my shaft at one of their naked heads. The arrow sang as it sought its mark. Its steel tip plunged into the soldier's skull with a thump. As he clutched his head and tumbled, I brought up the second arrow from my belt and sent it into the neck of the other man beside him. He reeled backward and fell looking face up at the forest canopy.

Randolph spun his mount around and searched the thicket wildly. My men swooped down, saving their war cries for another time, so that all that could be heard was the frantic rustle of grass and snapping of twigs underfoot.

Half the English did not even have their weapons ready when my men dove upon them. I sent a third arrow to pierce an English chest, but I did not aim well and missed his heart. He staggered around, finally pulling out the shaft. Blood gushed from the hole between his ribs over his hands. He cried only once in agony before falling dead by another's weapon. With one more arrow I wounded a mounted man in his right arm, rendering him useless. In the chaos, three cowardly Englishmen had tried to run for their lives. The last to almost make it free fell to my blade as I descended the slope and blocked his escape.

By then, Randolph was surrounded. Though my men parried with him, they did not advance on him. At first there were only three on him, but as the other English fell, Randolph soon found himself set upon by nine, then ten. He flailed his sword with deft accuracy, wounding two in the first raucous flurry. Suddenly, he put spurs to his mount, attempting to crash through, but one of my Scots slashed at his horse, cutting it deeply in the foreleg. As the beast stumbled, Randolph's sword flew from his hand. He gripped the saddle to keep from being thrown. Someone grabbed the bridle and the horse—its foreleg nearly buckling whenever it tried to put pressure on it—backed and settled.

My blade outlined his heart. "I would say you are in a state of dire despair, my lord. Your horse deserves to be put out of its misery and you—you need to come with us."

"Douglas?" Randolph feigned a smile of familiarity, but in truth he had never spoken more than two arrogant, disdainful words to me between Kildrummy and Methven. His left hand drifted downward.

"Throw that knife at me," I warned, "and you'll have ten gaping holes in your chest before your next breath."

He shrugged and spread both hands outward while William plucked the knife from his belt. A moment later he was yanked from his failing horse and shoved to the trampled earth. The blood of his fallen soldiers stained his jaw.

"Douglas, when did you become a brigand?" Randolph taunted.

"I serve the King of Scots, my lord. I'm certain you will be delighted to hear we are taking you to him."

"Delighted . . ."—he scowled at me, as if I were to be chastised for my deed and not him—"more than you can imagine."

Sim shoved him to the ground and bound his hands with the twine that had tied up some of the grain sacks we carried. Someone brought him a horse taken from one of the dead English knights.

"No, no horse for him," I said. "Let him walk behind—and if he can't keep up, we'll drag him."

As Sim hoisted him to his feet, Randolph wiped his bloody chin on a soiled surcoat. "You should've shot me with an arrow, Douglas, and killed me when you had the chance."

"No sport in it, my lord." I gestured for the horse that had been offered to Randolph and climbed into the saddle. Feeling a strange rider, it danced nervously, but my gentle hand upon its withers calmed it. "Besides, I prefer the cat's manner: batting the mouse into a stupor before chewing its head off. Draws out the excitement."

I WOULD HAVE SWORN on St. Fillan's bones that every muscle in Randolph's body screamed for rest, but even days after stumbling along tied to the tail of a horse he had not uttered a word of complaint. His wrists were purple with bruises from the constant yanking upon the rope, his knees red where he had fallen and scraped them raw, and his feet so blistered his boots were stained with blood. It would take a great deal, I realized, to break this man's will.

We came at last to King Robert's camp northwest of Perth and were greeted with a host of curious stares. Men abandoned their tasks and trailed after us, eager to learn the identity of the prisoner on whose head William Bunnock had placed a sackcloth that morning. Thomas Randolph, long since stripped of his mail and clad only in shreds of his former dignity, was paraded into the midst of the encampment where Robert sat on a flat-topped rock, splashing his face and neck with water from a small bowl braced between his knees. He brought his knife up to shave. Just as he scraped the blade upward along his neck, he saw us. Setting the bowl aside, he waved his knife in the air to hail us, then bounded down and toward us.

"My good James! At last, at last!" A broad smile broke across his cheeks. Last winter, we had all feared for his life, so grave was the illness he had suffered; but his swift recovery after Slioch was nothing short of a miracle. He may have been weakened, his breathing strained, but as soon as he could rise and walk—feeble though he may have felt—he was back on his horse. If we admired him before for his courage and vision, we now thought him in league with saints. He glanced with only passing curiosity at my captive before crushing me in a welcoming embrace. "Ah, how many months now? A year come next, can it be? We have so much to talk of. I've a good cache of wine to share it over. Ale would not do it justice. You've had stunning success, I hear."

"Great success, my lord," I replied.

His words poured forth in a flood of ebullience. "As have we— Elgin, Aboyne, Fyvie . . . and so many of the old Comyn strongholds I

- 145 -

can't even recall all the names. The best blessing of all—Aberdeen's folk had finally sickened of their English chains. Rose up and slaughtered the soldiers in the streets. What a godsend after last winter' trials. Ah, but time for my tales later, James. Time later. And so, what of you? Have you brought me Edward of Caernarvon himself?"

"We destroyed a party of English knights several days ago. Fine armor—a pity we had to leave most of it behind. But their weapons and horses will be made good use of." I guided Randolph forward by the elbow. "I've brought you a prisoner."

I lifted the sack from Randolph's head.

The echo of his name rolled through the crowd. A sword scraped free of its scabbard. Boyd roared a warning and swept his way through the crowd, blade leveled before him. Robert lunged forward, his knife clanging against Boyd's weapon as he knocked it aside.

He threw Boyd a scowl of admonition before turning back to his nephew. "So the rumors hold true?" he said to Randolph, his brow creasing in perplexity. "When we rode into Aberdeen, a merchant who had recently sailed from Berwick told me you were there keeping English company. That you not only rode out with English knights to put down insurgence among the Scots—you led them. My God, I called the man a liar."

Robert's mouth was slack, the eyes kind to a fault, his voice low and controlled. One hand thoughtfully stroked his whiskers, the other was propped casually on his hip. "Thomas Randolph—you raised your sword against Englishmen at Methven. Yet now you, my own kinsman, fight beside them?"

Standing straight as a centurial oak lashed by tempestuous winds, Randolph ground his jaws together. His upper lip twitched. The words cut through his clamped teeth. "In return for my life, I gave my word to do so. I had no choice."

Incredulous, Robert turned his back on his nephew. "No offers of ransom were discussed?"

At that, Randolph smiled mockingly. "They were, but the price was absurd. Besides, a man swears things when his bones are stretched on the rack to the point of snapping. None of you know half my story, so don't dare to declare yourselves my judges. In my boots, you would have done likewise. Even if the ransom had been within reason, what kinsman of mine would have paid it? *You?*" He laughed, then gulped back the irony with bitter suddenness. "With what? Clods of dirt? Stones? What chance did I have, *Uncle* Robert? I sat in a lightless cell so cramped that I could not even lie down and stretch my legs to sleep. Lice and spiders crawled over my flesh every wretched minute of every wretched day. But what was a day, or a night, or a week or month? I had no way of knowing. They slid moldy bread to me through a sideways crack in the door and gave me a pot to shit in that was emptied not often enough. I thirsted so much that I even brought a cup of my own piss to my lips to drink to keep myself alive, but it was so thick and stinking I couldn't. I had neither blanket nor straw for a bed. I knew only darkness. Cold, damp darkness and no human voice. Even my guards were given orders not to speak to me. Isolated, weakened, wallowing in filth and fleas. Nothing but my thoughts to prey on my fears; my faith to feed me. Should I have cultivated my hopes of salvation in absurd dreams of a Scottish army marching on London to topple the Tower and set me free? *This* army? Where is the rest of it? Laying siege on York and Carlisle? I think not. I am just come from there and it is English lords and English armies who command."

Robert swept aside his nephew's bitterness and cynicism with a swift glare. Tucking the knife back into his belt, he walked to the rock on which he had been sitting before and leaned back against it. Only myself, Randolph and Boyd stood in the middle of the clearing now. Robert smirked. After a long pause, he tilted his head upward and spoke, each word measured. "And so feeling that you had no choice, you made an oath? That you would do as Longshanks bid you? That you would fight against me, your uncle . . . your own blood?"

"I did." Randolph looked about at all the faces gathered there, as if he thought he might find one among us to sympathize with him. "Besides, is this not Scotland where brother has fought brother since this land was first set foot upon? It goes on yet today—allegiance for a price, for land, for titles, for—"

"For life?" Robert strolled back toward Randolph, perusing him from head to toe. "And you're alive, aren't you? A fair exchange. It bought you enough time to bring you here and that, I hope, will serve some purpose in the end."

"Your amusement at seeing my head roll downhill?" Randolph suggested dryly. His eyes shifted to Boyd's sword, its steel flashing in the long light of a fading afternoon.

Edward pushed forward, his eyes ablaze with a rekindled grudge. "And do you still uphold that oath, Randolph . . . even now that Longshanks' puling son sits tottering on the throne?"

Unnerved by Edward's ire, he looked at him coolly. "I gave my vow long before I took up a sword beside you or Robert. When I was captured I was reminded of that oath and admitted my waywardness. I renewed it in the name of the crown of England, not Longshanks. I do not break my word."

"England?!" Boyd bellowed. He wrung the hilt of his sword in both hands, hoisted it high above his head and rammed its point into the stony earth with brutal force. The metal rang out cold and shrill. "Do we look like milky-arsed Englishmen? Did your mother whore herself out to an English bull to calve you? The cure for insane bastards the likes of you is to cut your heads off!"

Boyd tried to wrench his weapon loose, but the earth gripped back. Blood flushed his face as he grunted with the strain. A torrent of sweat gushed from his temples. Before he could whip it loose and send it screaming at Randolph's lean, bare neck, Neil Campbell rushed forward, hooked his arm and yanked him back.

"Let the king decide his fate," Neil said.

"Och! Let him swear himself to our good and honest King Robert," Boyd bellowed as he freed himself of Neil's grasp in one clean jerk and heaved his sword free, "or I'll plunge my blade through his navel and clear to his backside to let the truth of daylight through."

Before Neil could prevent him, he lurched forward. The tip of his sword pricked Randolph's belly, but Randolph did not flinch. He had been trained as a soldier from boyhood. Taught to stand his ground and rally, even when his opponent had beaten him to the ground. Blows and cuts were merely tests of one's inner mettle. And death . . . was a part of life.

Randolph cast his cold blue eyes upon his oldest uncle. "I do not fight in the name of cowards who flee from honest battle."

Boyd applied force until the tip indented Randolph's stomach. Then he pulled down, ever so slightly, so that the cloth of Randolph's tattered shirt rent and a fine line of blood trickled from the path of the metal's point. Randolph shuddered and blinked once, but his glare upon Robert remained as slick as ice.

Randolph had meant what he said. He believed it. Love him or not, there was something admirable about his obstinacy.

"Say the word, my lord." Boyd's sword arm shook with anticipation, waiting, seeking. "Just . . . Damn it, say it!"

Sifting for an answer, Robert glanced off into the tangled depths of the pines and spruces. "I think," he began, turning to look directly upon me, "that since James is his captor, I will let him decide what to do with Thomas Randolph. Tell us, James—do we let Boyd slice him open to see if there is a heart inside? Or spare him?"

I circled Randolph. The bindings had been wrapped so tightly about his wrists that the rope cut red into his skin. As I stepped behind him I clenched his shoulders with both hands and dropped him to his knees. Boyd's sword remained aimed at his entrails.

"If we spare him, there's not a penny's worth of ransom in it, him being a Scot." I entwined my fingers in his stiff hair, yellow as a field of corn in high summer, and pulled his head back so I could look into his pale-rimmed, penetrating eyes. "If we don't, what a fine example he would serve."

Boyd grinned like the devil invited to play, but I held up a hand to stop him.

"I say spare him," I said. "Let him prove himself the braver, better soldier than the rest of us, for I do not think he is. I think, indeed, that it is he who is the coward, who feared his own death too much to say, '*I am a Scot, born and bred, and King Robert is my liege*'. Let him swear that very thing this day and I say his life will be spared."

As I curled my fingers deeper into Randolph's hair, I nudged forward on his shoulder with my other hand just enough so that Boyd's blade bit into his flesh. A gasp escaped Randolph's throat. Every muscle in his body went taut.

"Swear," I commanded.

Instead of an oath of loyalty, he began to whisper the Lord's Prayer. *Pious son of a bitch.* As I brought my chin up to give affirmation to Boyd's dark urges, Robert spoke.

"No." Robert came forward and laid a pleading hand on Boyd's bulging upper arm, whose every muscle and tendon was poised for the kill like a tightly winched crossbow. "He brought men and arms to Kildrummy and news of Pembroke's approach. I myself witnessed him slaying ten Englishmen at Methven before I lost sight of him. Something not to be forgotten. I owe him . . . time, to think it over. Time to learn the value of forgiveness. Lay off, Boyd. James, untie his hands. And Gil, a salve for the ulcers on his wrists. Clean clothes and water for him. Some bread and salted pork, if we have any left."

As King Robert walked off, uphill along the path of the stream, toward the waterfall near where his blankets were spread—for he had no tent anymore, traveling as scant as the rest of us—half of those around wanted to pounce on Randolph and snap his neck or loop a rope around it and dangle him from the highest tree. The rest were in speechless astonishment at the king's magnanimous treatment of such traitorous scum. I, and perhaps only a few others, understood the motive behind the gesture.

If Thomas Randolph could be won over of his own volition, Robert would gain yet another strong ally and an indispensable soldier. If not, he had lost little. Randolph dead would soon be forgotten—carrion for the crows. Alive, and if loyal, he was priceless.

19

Robert the Bruce – Argyll, 1308

VICTORY CAME IN PIECES so small that I feared we might never see the whole of it. Following our victory at Slioch, Buchan fled to England. There he died, alone and disgraced. With the taking of Aberdeen, the northeast was now in our hands. But down in ever-wild Galloway, the MacDowells were again harrowing the folk with fierce persistence. While my brother Edward was more than gleeful to go after them, the rest of us went to Argyll in search of John of Lorne and his irksome Macdougall clan.

My nephew, Thomas Randolph, gradually abandoned his argumentative ways and instead kept his thoughts to himself. I insisted that my men treat him kindly, as a welcome guest and not a rank murderer destined for the gallows—although I said nothing when Sim of Leadhouse shoved him to the ground or William Bunnock cuffed his ear. The whelp deserved some abuse.

In his younger years, Randolph had been obsessed about practicing at swords and could barely contain his joy when he was given his first warhorse. As a close kinsman, he had been often in attendance at Lochmaben during Christmas and with us at Turnberry in the summers. He and Nigel would spend hours discussing scripture. Then he would wrestle my youngest brother Thomas to the ground and within the same hour outride Alexander or better him at chess. He had Edward's abrupt manners, then as now, but it wasn't the same sort of arrogance. It was justifiable pride.

Being ten years older, I had treated the fair-tressed Randolph like a rowdy pup, but I never overlooked that he was strong, able and intelligent. He was also a proper knight—true to God above all. And it was his faith in God that had helped him to endure his ordeal in the Tower and brought him here. Every night while my men were riled by their bawdy talk and every morning as they slept off their latest plunder of wine or ale, Randolph knelt in fervent prayer, forswearing all offers of drink.

One morning, as I lazed on a sunny hillside with James, Randolph was led to the stream below by his guards, Sim and William. He stripped to the waist and knelt. Eyes closed, he scooped up water to splash his face repeatedly, scrubbing vigorously with his fingers from his hairline to his neck. When he opened his eyes, Boyd was standing before him, his large hand stroking the round buttocks of a woman young enough to be his daughter.

She giggled as she kissed Boyd on the cheek. Tugging at one of her fire-red curls, she flicked a tongue over full lips and said to Randolph, "A beautiful morning, m'lord, is it not?"

He shrugged and dipped his hands in the water again.

Boyd patted her rump playfully. "I was about to find the fair Muirgheal here an escort back to her home, when she caught sight of you and asked for an introduction."

"I'm hardly free to escort her anywhere." Randolph smirked. "My apologies."

Letting out a guffaw, Boyd cuffed him on the shoulder. "Studying for the priesthood, are you?" He leaned over, his face intrusively close to Randolph's, although he still spoke loudly—the effect of a long guzzle of morning ale. "She thought you were quite comely. Says she's in love with you and wants to . . . get to know you."

"Priesthood?" James muttered, snapping a clutch of twigs between his hands. "Hardly. Sainthood is more likely."

I pressed a finger to my lips to shush him.

Randolph stood and turned to study Muirgheal. Her eyes dipped to his groin, then flicked to his chest, where droplets of water glistened from neck to sternum. Without looking away, she picked up his shirt from the ground and began to blot away the dampness. Starting at his shoulders, she rubbed the cloth downward until she was stroking in languorous circles from hipbone to hipbone. Just below his navel, she paused, glancing at him brazenly beneath fluttering lashes.

Stoic, Randolph wrapped his fingers gently about her hand and pushed it back to her own chest. "I'd sooner lie on hot coals," he said coolly, "than lie with a whore."

She blew a burst of air between her lips, her flagrant desire slowly turning to umbrage. "You mistake me, m'lord. No man has ever given me coin for . . . *favors*."

"Perhaps that is true." He inclined his head. "But you were willing to lie with me, were you not? Just as you did with Boyd last night. Aye, I heard the two of you, grunting like mating pigs."

William laughed, but Randolph sobered him with a glare.

"There was another man the night before," he continued, returning his gaze to Muirgheal, "was there not? Two, if I'm not mistaken."

He brushed a lock of hair from her cheek, his tone softening to compassion. "You're too precious, Muirgheal, to let yourself be passed around like a side of roasted mutton to be sampled by filthy hands."

She dashed his shirt to the ground, grinding it into the dirt with the ball of her bare foot. Spewing a Gaelic curse, she tried to bolt away, but Boyd grasped her waist and held her.

"Stay, Muirgheal," Boyd said. "He'll take back his words—or I'll cut his tongue out."

"His apology is worth nothing to me." Her fists hammered at Boyd's stout arm. "Let me go!"

When he finally released his grip, she stomped at Randolph, fists balled at her sides, and spit squarely in his face. "And you—who sold your loyalty, your heart—are better than me? How dare *you* condemn *me*! I harm no one. Can you say the same?"

The glob oozed down his cheek. He dragged a hand down over his face and flicked it to the ground. "How is it that you think no one is harmed by what you do? Half those men you've been with have wives. One day, it will be you with a husband, tending to the children and cooking his meals, waiting for him to come home while he's taking his pleasure beneath another woman's skirts. I would never dishonor my own wife so."

His words pierced my conscience. Tore a hole so huge I reeled from them. I leaned back in a sea of grass, dry stems scratching at my forearms where I had rolled my sleeves up. *I* had dishonored Elizabeth, saying it was for Scotland that I had lain with Christiana. In truth, I had traded power for pleasure as readily as one gives coin for goods at market. She had been there and willing; I had been weak and wanting, and in the bargain sacrificed fidelity for the sake of fleeting ecstasy—*not* for the preservation of a kingdom. If Elizabeth ever learned of it, would she find it in her heart to forgive? Would *I* forgive *her* for the same transgression?

A cold fist gripped my innards. No, I would not. The tally upon my soul was recorded and could not be erased. I was not worthy of her. I never had been. Yet once I had worshipped her, desired her enough to bow to Longshanks—until my dreams of a crown came to consume me even more than her.

Ah, how long had it been now since I had thought of Elizabeth, longed for her, lay down to sleep with my heart aching for her? Days, weeks? *Months?* I closed my eyes to shut out the sunlight, envisioning the flourish of her chestnut waves as she loosed her hair from its pins at night to join me in our bed. My fingertips recalled the silkiness of her skin; each curve, hollow and crease of her form; the inviting warmth between her legs . . . and the coldness of her tears as she wept for want of children, believing she had somehow failed me.

No, noooo . . . *I* had failed *her*!

Voices rose in anger. James was crouched in the grass, watching the scene below. I sat up.

Boyd slammed his fist into Randolph's jaw. Randolph staggered backward and, half-hunched, raised an arm in defense. Boyd stalked closer. Skirts bunched in her hands, Muirgheal turned and fled, splashing across the stream.

"Enough!" I shot to my feet and flew down the hill. Boyd halted, his chest heaving with rage.

"Enough, Boyd. Go," I told him. Jaw clenched, Boyd backed away, then scooped up Randolph's soiled shirt and flung it at him. I rounded on Sim and William. "I told you to keep him from harm. So do it!"

Sim and William looked at each other blankly, both nodding.

"Aye, m'lord. We will," William said, head hanging. Under his breath, he muttered, "Didn't actually think Boyd would kill him or anything."

Randolph snapped his shirt out and tugged it over his head. Muirgheal's footprint was imprinted on his chest. He glowered at me with those eyes so blue and clear I thought they might bore into my very soul. He had heard of Christiana, I was sure of it. But I was also sure that he would never breathe another word of it—to me or anyone. He did not need to.

My guilt was punishment enough.

Pass of Brander, 1308

AUGUST, AND ALREADY WE were deep within Lorne's territory. Too easily. Four days before, Angus Og and his Highlanders had joined us near St. Fillan's shrine, not far from the Pass of Dalry where we had suffered hard losses under John of Lorne once before.

Yawning, Angus stretched his arms above his head. "Is it over yet?"

"The truce?" I threw back the edge of my damp blanket and sat up. Droplets of morning dew glistened over the grassy hillside. Around us, men were already preparing to move on: putting on their padded jerkins, tucking arrows into belts and saddling horses. I rummaged in my sack, but found it empty of food. "Is it harvest season yet? I've lost count."

"More than a fortnight past Lammas."

I looked once more in my sack, as if expecting a full loaf of bread to appear there simply by wishing it. Turning the sack over, I shook it hard. Crumbs scattered upon the ground. One more shake and a frayed twig and a coil of bowstring too short to be of use fell out. My head light from lack of food, I stood slowly. "Already? Aye then, I reckon we'll come across Lorne soon enough. Has Cuthbert returned?"

"Just now. I'll fetch him." He gave a nod and darted off

"And fetch me a loaf of bread, as well," I called after him. "A bannock, a hunk of salted pork . . . peas, even. Something. Anything."

Without looking back, he raised his bare arm in acknowledgment. I had not even finished rolling up my blanket when Cuthbert stumbled through a group standing nearby.

He swept off his straw hat and jerked in a nervous bow. "M-m-my lord."

The poor rustic still lost his wits whenever he spoke to me. Nothing I said or did put him at ease. "Did you find Lorne?"

He smiled, showing off a mouth full of crooked teeth, but not a single one missing. "I d-d-did—and he was not hiding, either."

"Is he in the pass?"

His head bobbed. "In, above . . . around."

"Very good, Cuthbert. Today's to be the day, then." I tossed him a farthing, for whatever good it would do in these parts. He flipped it over in his palm several times, ogling at the way it reflected the light.

Under the watch of Sim and William, Randolph remained behind in a long-abandoned shepherd's hut, built of dry-stacked, crumbling stone and with half a molding roof full of roosting starlings. After Gil said a hasty prayer, we gathered our weapons and went, following the River Awe. The Awe's waters were deep and strong, for they rushed down from steep-sided mountains. One such giant was the great Ben Cruachan, overlooking the Pass of Brander. As we approached the mountain, Angus Og took his nimble men around its backside, where Cuthbert said that more of Lorne's forces were lying in wait.

Morning light spilled down into the chasm. Lorne's men gorged the Pass of Brander—thousands of them, although by numbers it was a fairly matched fight. Some stood atop stone heaps choking the road, baring their asses and whatever other puny parts they usually kept concealed under their breeches.

They rattled their spears and taunted us to come on, but we tarried at the mouth of the pass, biding our time as the sun crept higher. Down below, a long, shallow-bellied galley dropped its oars to slip from the place where the river widened out toward the loch, headed in our direction.

"We're being watched," I told James, who stood holding the reins of his horse—a fine roan taken from the English when he captured Randolph.

He raked his fingers through its mane to part a tangle. "John the Lame there. Staying out of the fray. Angus said he's been gravely ill of late."

"Not down enough, though, to miss seeing this fight. Shall we?"

"Aye. Looking a bit over-confident, they are. I say they're in need of being humbled today."

James handed his horse off to Gil, who in return gave him his bow. He caressed the length of yew, pulled the string from a pouch at his belt and strung it tight. With a glance toward Ben Cruachan, he strode away.

While James worked his way back through our column to join his burgeoning band of archers, I dismounted and called some of my knights to me. Doubtless, Lorne thought we were arguing last-moment strategy or debating over the sensibility of trying to plow our way through the rubble. Instead, we killed time with idle small talk as we waited for Angus to move into position.

"If the fool refuses to forfeit," Boyd said as he buffed his blade on the tail of his cloak, "I can give you fifteen ways to stretch out his death."

"Only fifteen?" Gil gibed. "Do any involve a near drowning?"

Boyd rolled his eyes and sighed heavily. "Of course."

"Death by eels?" I suggested.

Cupping his ear, Boyd leaned from his saddle toward me. "Ale, did you say?"

"Not ale," I said. "*Eels*. Forced feeding. Live eels, I mean."

Rumbling with laughter, Boyd hitched up his belt. "I thought you meant we could drown him with *ale*."

Gil crinkled his nose. "That would be a waste now, wouldn't it?"

"Hah! Right you are. Never mind, then."

The sun beat down, drenching us in our own sweat beneath our links of stifling mail and leather jerkins. Flasks of water were emptied into parched mouths. As the sun reached its pinnacle, I ordered the men back to their places.

A single arrow arced through the sky from the black slopes of Ben Cruachan.

Nudging my mount forward, I brought my sword up. I drew a circle above my head and jabbed the point of my blade heavenward. Spurs and bridles chinked discordantly behind me. Ten abreast, we pressed ahead onto the roadway that led into the pass.

Above the thunder of hooves came another sound. A bigger one. I looked up in time to see boulders crashing down the slope toward us. Lorne's men rushed from hidden crevices, hurling stones. A fist-sized rock clanged against Boyd's helmet, knocking him sideways. His horse veered into mine, before he shook off the blow and righted it.

The first swarm of arrows blotted the sky. Lorne's men faltered, then scrambled in disarray. James' archers were now rushing over the eastern rise of the slope. In moments, another cloud of arrows hissed toward their marks. Many clattered against the stones; others pierced bare flesh. Argyll warriors shrieked in agony as yet another volley followed.

A signal went up for the Argyll men who held the higher ground to fall back. James' band had no sooner slung their bows to pursue them on foot, when Angus Og and his men popped over a ridge far to the west, trapping the Argyll warriors between them.

While my right wing split off and guided their horses up the slope, the rest of us plunged toward the barrier. Abandoning our mounts, we scaled the loose wall of rock to meet our foes at last. The first horrible clang of weapons tore through the air. A hulking warrior in a rusted hauberk towered over me on his pile of rock. Clutching his long sword two-handed, he flailed it down at my head. I flinched backward, my feet slipping on the loose and uneven footing, and brought my shield up. The jolt of his weapon reverberated through my arm. I jerked at my shield, but his sword was embedded in it. With a guttural grunt, he tried to wrench it loose. The pull was enough so that my left arm slipped free of its straps and he reeled backward, his sword still attached to my shield. In the moment it took him to realize his blade was useless, I had snatched my axe from my belt. I swung it hard at his ankle. He toppled sideways with a curdling howl, his bloody foot flopping at the end of his leg. I plunged my sword into his chest to end his misery, then climbed over his corpse to meet the next man.

Confused by the assault from numerous sides, the Argyll men lost cohesion. They began to draw back and soon found themselves wedged in the very trap they had themselves set up. In the erupting chaos of retreat, they forced some of their own too close to the precipice. Bodies dropped like stones against the rocks below. Those who could retreated, clogging the only bridge over the River Awe. Even as some of their own were still struggling toward it, James' archers picked them off with precision. While bodies surfaced and were swept downstream, clouds of crimson spread across the dark waters of the Awe.

This time, it was the men of Argyll who had scattered and fallen.

Lorne's galley slipped quietly downriver, past the floating bodies, further and further away until it disappeared into a swirl of mist.

20

Robert the Bruce – Pass of Brander, 1308

TWO YEARS AGO, LORNE had broken us at the Pass of Dalry. That was the day I had last seen my beloved Elizabeth, watched her go from me, no time for farewells. I'd exacted my revenge on Lorne, defeated him—although he had slipped away—but little good that would do to bring my Elizabeth back to me.

Our casualties had been remarkably few, for the real fighting had happened only in the first clash. We stripped their dead for goods and cleared the pass. Parties of our mounted chased their stragglers and killed those who did not give up their weapons and swear allegiance. My men returned with cattle fat from Highland pastures. That night, after we slaughtered some, we ate till our bellies were near bursting. The flames of our fires licked the sky, heralding our victory.

Randolph sat cross-legged on a rock, his chin resting on his knuckles, elbows upon his knees. The firelight cast deep shadows over his features. His countenance was far too sober, the lines on his forehead too many for a man of his few years. By the time I was his age, I had bedded more women than I could recall, been married, widowed and raised a daughter. And after all the politics and fighting and rough living, I still managed a sense of humor, even in trying times.

He scowled at the hoots and whoops of my men as they heaped up the firewood and danced around in drunken jubilation. "Are they always so merry?"

"They're making up for the hard times, Thomas. We have a lot of those. Days without food. Nights without sleep or the comfort of a woman. Months without seeing or hearing of our loved ones. Nursing our wounds as we sit in the pouring rain and grieve at the unmarked graves of our friends and brothers." I paused there, knowing he must have known about my younger brothers and womenfolk. "You make merry when you can. Today is a good day for it. They'll be burying more of their own tomorrow, but I reckon there won't be any more on account of John of Lorne after this."

Boyd began to sing—always a sign that the drinking was at its height. Randolph rubbed at the stubble on his chin. "I need to shave. Your men won't let me do it for myself. I might turn the knife on one of them and run off."

"Would you," I said as I offered him a cup of ale, "still?"

He stared at the drink, then snubbed it. "I prefer my wits to that."

I downed half the drink, feeling its fire ease my aches. "But you didn't answer me. Would you?"

"Would I run? In a blink. But where would I go? West, deeper into Argyll? Never a friend for our family there, was there, Robert? South to Galloway? Uncle Edward would trounce on me and have a blade skewered through my gut before my head hit the ground. Back to Berwick? I'd earn myself direct passage back to London for playing the spy now, don't you think? Anything short of a proper escort to the border is as good as a hanging."

"Full of questions, Thomas, and too serious for your own good."

He rolled his eyes and sighed in exasperation. "What do you want from me, Robert?"

"Most men here call me 'my lord'. Although 'sire' is fitting, as well. I fancy the ring of that. I always shuddered to speak it to Longshanks,

- 163 -

though."

"Your name is 'Robert'. You're not my lord. And my sire is long since in heaven. I don't have anything to give you. Why can't you understand that?"

"I want your loyalty, desperately," I informed him, "but it has to be something freely given. I can't take it from you if it isn't there within you."

His pale blue eyes sparked like flint struck against steel. "You're one to speak of loyalty, *lord king*. You know best how to give it and take it back and then demand it from others. Teach me how to fashion 'loyalty'. Under what tree does it grow, is it made from clay, or do you keep it hidden in a hole somewhere?"

I took another draft from my cup. Feeling suddenly philosophical and caring little about the world except crawling under my blanket and sleeping off the day's efforts, I said, "You can't hold it. You live it."

A sneer contorted his face as he fixed his stare on the dwindling fire. Lord in heaven, but he was a stubborn one. Not altogether a bad quality, I mused.

"Oaths or not," I said, "think on what the English have done to you. They took pleasure in it, Thomas. Wicked pleasure. Reveled in watching a Scotsman squirm in agony and squeal like a babe, crying for their lord's mercy. They kept you barely breathing just to hold the power of life over you. You have noble blood. You're an able knight. Better than the brunt of all the knights on this entire damn island and half Christendom. But in King Edward's flock you're just another underling. Survive his battles and you'd have a square of land big enough to scratch a living off of and maybe, if you quibbled for better recompense, he'd toss you the youngest toothless, bow-legged daughter of some inglorious baron as a consolation prize. No one would remember who you were or what you did or where you were buried. Fight for Scotland and men will follow you. They'll remember you."

"Fight for Scotland," he muttered into his folded hands, "and perish like the rest of you under the might of England."

"Maybe. But I've killed enough Englishman the last two years to be able to tell you they're not invincible. They're men, not gods. And just like you and I, they have faults. Arrogance for one." I finished off the ale, stood and tipped my empty cup upside down to shake the last drops from it. "Sleep well. We've one less cocklebur in Scotland as of today."

Indeed, it was later learned that Lorne had fled to England to seek Edward II's protection. His father, the decrepit and half-witted Alexander of Lorne was uncovered at Dunstaffnage, which we besieged for only a short time before he capitulated. Powerless and devoid of the ambition that had fired his son, Alexander of Lorne was kept as hostage in his own abode.

Brother Edward swept headlong through Galloway. At a ford of the River Dee, he appeared from the fog with his army and shattered the forces of Sir Ingram de Umfraville. Later that year he took Rutherglen.

Galloway, Argyll, Angus, Moray . . . one by one they came into the fold. But my kingdom was not yet complete. Ross stood apart, still. So north we went, this time at an easy pace, better fed and rested, for nothing stood in our way any longer, the whole length of the land. Many castles in Lothian and the borders still remained in English hands, but the time for those would come.

Auldern, 1308

A STIFF OCTOBER WIND hammered its might across fields of stubbled corn. Upon a commanding hill crowned with red-barked pines just beyond Auldern in Moray, I sat upon my horse. Beside me on an aging gray was David, Bishop of Moray, wearing his silk belted robe and a red chasuble with the Savior embroidered on the back in gold thread. To his right stood a clutch of clerics—abbots, priests and monks—there to provide some solemnity to the occasion. If I had anyone to thank for having come this far, it was the clergy of Scotland that had served so absolutely: conveying messages, recruiting soldiers and most of all exhorting to the lay people the right and faculty of Scotland to stand by its own means. Behind us were my knights, those who had upheld me, fought beside me, saved my hope and starved, suffered and endured in the name of Scotland: James Douglas, Gil de la Haye and Neil Campbell among them. Brother Edward was still behind in Galloway, where disorder demanded his attention. My nephew Thomas Randolph sat upon a striking chestnut horse I had given to him. The binding on his hands had long since been cut loose and his guards dismissed.

"He said he would come?" I asked the bishop as we both squinted into the cold cut of the wind.

"Indeed, he did," Moray replied with a raised eyebrow, as if to question that I could even doubt his word.

"And he said that he would submit?"

"And beg for pardon."

Between two stands of trees to the southwest, a narrow road parted the way. A party of horsemen appeared there, their mounts pressed to a steady clip, their colorful cloaks snapping from their shoulders.

Malice throttled my soul. "Pardon has a heavy price."

"Vengeance—"

"Is mine, sayeth the Lord. Aye, I know." I glanced at the bishop, a thin fringe of dull brown hair peaking from beneath the miter that covered his balding head. "But if we all believed in that there would be no wars, would there? What men say and what they truly believe are two different things, your grace."

Clouds of turbid gray, pregnant with rain, marched across a foreboding sky. The man who had betrayed my beloved—pursued her and given her over to vile English hands—closed the distance between us.

The Bishop of Moray clasped his hands together, the reins lightly looped over his thumbs. "Could it be that men care more about this life than the next?"

"If you're trying to provoke an argument," I answered with a grin, "you've chosen the wrong man."

"I am trying to uncover your purpose in bringing the Earl of Ross here. I wonder, my lord, if it is as you said."

As his eyes met mine I nodded. "It is. Because I know this: that although vengeance is deeply rooted in my soul, as it is in most of mankind's, I know that I have much to be forgiven for myself."

He knew only a part of my meaning. Two and a half years had gone by since John Comyn died in Greyfriar's Kirk because of my anger and hatred for the man. And for two years now I had suffered in unspeakable anguish without Elizabeth and Marjorie. For two years, for every victory that belonged to me, I was reminded that I did not have them to share it with. And then I had bedded with Christiana of the Isles for mere ships. How did I ever think that infidelity would bring my loved ones back to me? This meeting with the Earl of Ross—this was God's test of me. I truly believed that.

If I have not been pure of heart, My Father, know that I am trying to put things aright.

William, Earl of Ross, pulled at his horse's reins and dropped to the ground. The rest of his party, the twenty he had sworn to limit himself to, dismounted also, but stayed where they were as he came forward. A roll of parchment was clenched tightly in his right hand. He kept his eyes downcast. When he reached me, he went to his knees and pressed his forehead to the ground.

"Rise, Lord William," I told him. I made eye contact with a distinguished-looking, silver-haired noble behind him. "Sir Robert Keith? I suspect the English king hovers over you like a hawk. Which side do you fall on this year?"

My question was a facetious one, as I suspected his heart had never wavered. Keith had served as Marischal of Scotland under Balliol and later, after his release, as a justice under Longshanks, doling out rulings that bordered on bias in favor of various Scots. He detected my sarcasm and answered with a comfortable grin, "Having spent quite some time in English prisons, sire, I can fairly say I have no desire to return there."

Slowly, Ross lifted his face. "Sire. Your grace. In utmost humility, may I speak?"

"That *is* why we called you here," I said. "I, for one, would like to hear what you have to say. I brought as many holy men as I could muster. They make more believable witnesses, I am told, than Scots nobles."

The jest fell short, as the blanched, wide-eyed look was still upon Ross's countenance.

"Please, William," I told him again, "rise. Such groveling does not become you. I remember, when my grandfather still had enough vigor in him to chase after the crown, you rallied to him. I don't forget those things."

"His was clearly the stronger claim. And he was the more fit man to wear the crown."

"Then did you think me not so?"

Lowering his eyes, he swallowed and squeezed the parchment tighter.

I leaned forward and put my weight upon my right elbow, which rested on my mount's withers. A fierce wind, cold and damp, beat at us without relent. It pulled at my cloak and tangled my hair. Wanting to appear neither mistrustful nor condescending, I had left both helmet and crown behind that day. Soon, it would rain and when it did it would likely go on for days.

"No, you needn't answer, William. I fought for England once, as well. At the time, I had my reasons. Even though a king, I do not claim myself to be without flaw. Now, up. And give me what you have there. We need to get on with this business before we're all soaked to the bone. I've been wet more times than I cared for these past years and am dreadfully sick of it. So go on. Straight to it."

Ross delivered an eloquent speech, wherein many times and in a very flattering manner he pointed out my grace in this matter. He went on to proclaim his oath of fealty, both for himself and his heirs toward me and mine. But also, he did not fail to mention the lands I had promised him. I forgave him that pettiness. It appeared his eyesight was not keen, as he read excruciatingly slowly. By the time he spoke the last words and placed his hand upon the Holy Gospel that the Bishop of Moray presented to him—

". . . I do swear upon the Gospel of God."

—it was misting. A cold, wetter than wet mist, familiar to Scotland. The Bishop hurriedly made the sign of the cross, blessed the occasion with a few words and tucked the letter beneath his robes to save its ink from the deluge. I thanked the earl and invited him to Nairn for a supper. As he climbed upon his horse and we readied to go, Thomas Randolph, who I had quite forgotten about even being there, stood before me holding the reins of his new horse.

"My lord . . . sire." He bowed his bare head and, with one hand swept across his abdomen, he knelt.

The formality of his address left me with no reaction but to look at him and wait for more.

"I ask for your pardon," he said.

I must have looked more than puzzled as he gazed up at me through the blur of rain, for he continued, trying to explain himself.

"I beg that you would grant me pardon for what I have done. For fighting against you. My faith, my loyalty—they are yours now, if you will have them."

I squeezed the water from my beard and blinked as the rain drove harder. I looked for James in the crowd of my most trusted fighting men and nobles. He was some thirty feet away and even so, he seemed to tell me in the careless tilt of his head that the choice was mine.

"Betting on my good humor today, are you?"

"The timing would seem to be good, aye," Randolph admitted.

"Honest and shrewd." I put forth my hand. "Lay yours in mine and we'll call it done."

He put his hand in mine.

"Up with you and let's away," I said. "I'm cold already. Can you hear my teeth clattering?"

That night we dried ourselves by a roaring fire while rain drummed upon the tiled roof. I had the Earl of Ross, Randolph and Keith at my side now. While all might have appeared well and good, my heart was ever empty.

Winter came on quick and fierce and when the New Year had just come, I received a letter from Rothesay telling of the passing of James Stewart. The signature at the bottom was that of Walter Stewart, the very lad who had once sat snotty-nosed and hollow-eyed at my knee while playing with my daughter Marjorie. Their childhood was long gone. James Stewart and I had made a pact. He had held up his end by sending me men and money, unable to join in the cause himself because of a long-debilitating illness that had left him weak of limb and barely able to speak. As for my end, how could I give Marjorie to Walter when she was being held against her will in England?

I could break the chains that bound Scotland to England and free an entire people, but I could not bring my daughter—or my wife—home.

21

Edward II – Wallingford, 1310

THE LITTLE VIRAGO HAD been scribbling a stream of letters to her doting father in France. I doubted that she was extolling the joys of wedded bliss to him. I suspected that she spoke against me. I knew it when I learned that King Philip himself had been corresponding with Robert the Bruce, petitioning the rebel to join him on Crusade to the Holy Land. Naturally, Bruce declined. Too fraught with English troubles, he said, to depart his country.

In the spring of 1309, the impudent Scots even gathered in St. Andrews to convene a parliament. They declared that Robert the Competitor had owned the rightful claim to the throne of Scotland and thus his grandson, that murdering Judas, was his due heir. Providence, they babbled, was the reason for Bruce's deliverance of their people. How conveniently oaths are tossed away like spent rushes when they no longer serve.

When my bickering barons arranged enough money for it, I sent troops into Scotland that autumn. It rained so incessantly that the supply wagons could not go one mile without getting stuck in the mud. When Edward Bruce gave one of my lieutenants a sound thrashing in Galloway, his brother made him Lord of Galloway. The arrogance! The lords of England begged for a reprieve. With my begrudging agreement, a truce was signed to last the winter.

We may have lost ground in Scotland, but at home I had won my battle. Perhaps my barons were pacified because they had been afforded some time to return to their lands to hunt in leisure or father children by the scores instead of freezing their cocks while standing up to their knees in Scottish muck; but whatever the reason for their goodwill, they eased from their haranguing and conceded to allow Brother Perrot to return to my side.

When Piers and I met in Chester that spring, it was a glorious reunion, made all the sweeter by our troubles. Oh, the Irish air had put a bloom to his cheeks. Hours upon hours riding over the verdant countryside had streaked his hair with bands of gold. If he had suffered from the same melancholy I had, he showed no trace of it. In his arms, I again found heaven. And I knew that every argument I had engaged in, every enemy I had made in the effort, every pain I had ever suffered to bring him back was worth it.

That summer at Wallingford, all the most skilled knights in the land gathered to tourney. Piers had already advanced far in the ranks when I entered his pavilion. He stood there rigidly, with his shirt pulled up to his midriff as he waited for his squire to tie his chausses. The boy, with the first fuzz of manhood on his chin but all the innocence of an angel in his countenance, crumbled to the ground at the sight of me. I gestured for him to continue his work. His fingers fumbled at the laces, but he somehow managed the task. Piers swept him outside with a wag of his hand.

"How is your fresh young bride Margaret?" I pried.

"Barren as a tilled field of stones," he stated. "The stable groom she so fancies poked her but could not get her stuffed. Neither could the butler, the lute player nor the local monk. My bet was on the cowl. Abstinence does miracles for fertility. There are more bastards of priests in Ireland than sheep, did you know?"

"I would beg you not to speak so ill of Margaret. She is, after all, my niece."

"I *jest*, Edward. Where is your humor today? Expelled in the garde-robe with yesterday's meal?" He sat down upon a stool to strap his poleyns over his knees, then put his spurs on. Arching an eyebrow at me, he shrugged limply. "And what of your brood bitch?"

"Cold as the driven snow and twice as pure."

"Still can't bear to bring yourself to bed her? Come now, you know how it's done. It's expected of you, begetting an heir and all that. Maybe we should pour some wine down your gullet and watch the dogs go at it to get you in the mood."

"I think that would nauseate me."

He stood and tapped me playfully on the cheekbone with the tips of his fingers. "You're looking quite useless. Help me on with my mail shirt, will you? I have a pain in my shoulder from unseating that goat Lancaster."

"I'll call your squire back in, instead. I'm due for an appearance. My pretty wife would rival Cleopatra and as a pair we are quite radiant."

"Twin suns? Blinding. Rather, a pair of peacocks, you are. Cheer for me."

"I shall."

"And the queen?"

"If any petals fall across your path, they will not be from her hand." I turned to go, then stopped as my hand parted the flap. "Make it look harder than it is. You enrage them by being so good."

"Perhaps they should put up more of a fight," he rejoined with a boyish wink.

Outside Piers' pavilion my page fell in behind me flapping a fan of palm leaves to keep the flies away. Jankin followed close behind, mute as always. I made my way through the row of pavilions, all decorated with pennons of azure, scarlet, emerald and gold. Even though his tent was the next row over, I could hear cousin Thomas of Lancaster lamenting over his misfortune at having too many lances splinter and his horse shying at an inconvenient moment.

"Hear that, Jankin?" I said to my manservant, who had startlingly red hair and ears so large they only accentuated his accursed looks. I kept him about because he seemed so utterly pleased to serve me, as if following in my steps somehow graced him. I stopped and glanced at him as his head, winged in appearance due to the ears, bobbed atop a neck as thin as a willow switch. The breeze from the flapping palm leaf cooled my face. "Our cousin the swine complains that it is only bad luck that caused him to lose the joust with Brother Perrot. A farthing says he could not knock an apple off your head if he were standing next to you."

As we began on our way back to the stands, a black horse led by a squire emerged from between two pavilions. The squire also carried one of his master's shields. He paused and bowed to let us pass, but then at his left stepped a stunted knight in dazzling armor.

"Greetings, Lord Pembroke," I said as he bent at the waist as much as his armor would allow.

His pinprick sloe eyes sparked with ambition. He shifted his black-plumed helmet to his other arm. "My lord."

I opened my mouth to wish him a soft fall, but thought better of it as I granted him a perfunctory smile and continued on my way. We strolled across the trodden meadow, which stank of horse manure. When I reached the stands, all those nearby but for the queen rose until I took to my velvet-cushioned seat beneath the bright silk awning. To Isabella's left sat my stepmother Marguerite and my half-brother Edmund, who was trying to pick his nose without his mother noticing. She slapped his hand away from his face and chided him in her nasal tongue. I lifted Isabella's hand and placed a kiss upon her ruby wedding ring. A year-and-a-half in England's amenable climate and lively court had put some fill to her face.

Above her knuckles, I said so only she could hear, "Your beauty and youth make jealous enemies of the sun and moon, my love."

"Who is next?" was all she said.

"Lord Pembroke and Piers Gaveston. The last joust. Pembroke is an excellent rider and although Piers matches him at the tilt, if it comes to swords . . . Pembroke is too short of limb to be of any threat. It shall be swiftly done then. Although Piers may draw it out, if only for our amusement." Her eyes had glazed over at the first word, but I kept her hand in mine and leaned close to push away a curl of hair that had fallen across her forehead. Just as I did so, Piers rode onto the field at a full gallop. The gentle murmur of the crowd died. He reined before the queen and me, spun his horse in a right circle and then just as swift one to the left. He swept off his helmet and bowed in his saddle.

"For my lady!" he declared. From his gauntleted hand he tossed a bouquet of roses.

Isabella closed her eyes as she turned her head away and they smacked her in the cheek to drop at her satin-slippered feet. With a smoldering glare at him, she whisked her hand across her cheek. "Did you not think to pick the thorns first?"

"An oversight, my queen," I said, picking up the blood-red flowers and placing them gently in her lap as shaken petals fell from the stems. "His enthusiasm overcomes his good sense at times. There now, there is no mark on your fair skin. You are preserved."

Standing, I paused as the roar of the crowd grew. "Our best wishes to you, Lord Piers. The Earl of Pembroke is a worthy opponent."

A bustle arose at the far end of the tilt field and Pembroke appeared on foot. Unhelmeted, he walked the length with his squire, who led his horse behind. Pembroke's black hair glistened with oil in the powerful noon sun, but he kept his chin low, glancing occasionally to either side, nodding here and there, flipping his hand in subtle greeting whenever a familiar voice called out his name.

"My lord and most fair lady." Pembroke bowed again and handed his helmet to his squire. Then he turned toward Piers. "May the better between us win."

"Veritably, I shall," Piers said.

With a smart kick of his spurs Piers was off to his appointed end of the field, where his squire hoisted a lance up to him. Piers flipped his visor down and shifted impatiently in his high-cantled saddle. Someone in the stands hissed at him and in moments it sounded like a pit over-flowing with snakes as others joined in.

Isabella tugged free the gossamer veil attached to the back of her coronet and rising from her chair she dangled it out before Pembroke. The inferno beneath my collar was not from the sun's heat. Pembroke tied the veil to the base of his lance and mounted, then sped off to his position. In anticipation, the crowd cheered and stomped their feet. I shivered at the noise, remembering another tournament during my youth where the stands had collapsed and ten people had been crushed to death. Trumpets blared. The two horses pawed at the sandy ground. Their tails swished as Pembroke and Piers both started forward. The rumble of hooves was swallowed up by the din of the crowd. Lances dipped. Piers hunkered forward. Pembroke leaned slightly to his left to steady his aim. Closer, closer . . . There!

The tips of their lances skipped off either shield and both knights continued on with barely a twitch. They wheeled around, checked their lances and began another pass. This time Pembroke veered away at the last second, so that neither lance made contact. The crowd booed.

Piers flipped open his visor. "Hah! Joseph the Jew—you are yellow-livered, indeed. Aim at my breast you dastardly Christ-killer. Or did you lose your courage when you took a shit in the garderobe this morning? That mad cur Warwick bared more fang than you."

"Mad dog, you say?" the Earl of Warwick bellowed from the end of the next box of stands. "Rather a dog than the bastard of a hung witch!"

Warwick had picked open a barely healed scab of Piers' in that comment. Piers was never proud of his mother's ignominious fate, but neither would he stand by and let such a jab go without parry. His visor clanged shut.

"Why does he call him a 'Jew', mama?" Edmund asked his mother, as the two flashing figures sized each other and dug spurs into horses' flanks.

She shrugged. Her thinly plucked eyebrows met above a sharp nose in perplexity. "I do not know. Because he is dark? I would say he looks more like a Moor."

"What's a Moor? Mama, what's a Moor? Is my hair dark enough to look like one?"

"Tell your brat to shut up and watch," I growled.

Marguerite's lips snapped together like a beak preparing to peck away at insects. I leaned forward, clenching the arms of my chair. The lances fell horizontal. Piers took aim, putting all his weight and might behind the point of his long-reaching weapon. This time Pembroke rode straight and unwavering at him. Which lance struck first was impossible to say. Perhaps it was Piers', perhaps Pembroke's. Pembroke's blunt-pronged coronel clicked at the joint of Piers' visor. The contact resulted in a barely noticeable jerk of Piers' head to the side—nothing more than a twitch. The slight sideways jerk, however, ripped the lance from Pembroke's grasp. It spun end over end through the dust cloud of Piers' thundering horse. But Piers' lance had struck true to center on Pembroke's black shield with a deafening crack. Pembroke was jolted into the cantle of his saddle. His torso swung to the right. His horse, feeling the lean of his master's weight, veered away from the chaos.

With deft ease, Piers wheeled his mount. In his grip, rested a splintered lance. He flung it to the ground with vehemence. Then in one great, scraping heave, he loosed his sword from its metal scabbard. He bore down on Pembroke, still tottering in his saddle. Piers brought his sword back. The move, however, was signaled too far in advance. Pembroke blocked his body with his shield, but the power of the blow lifted him from his saddle and hurled him to the ground. Pembroke lay motionless on his back, as Piers' horse danced in an angry storm around him.

"Get up, you bastard!" Piers roared. "Fight, God damn you, coward! I can kill you standing or lying down like a beaten dog, however you want it. But at least let them say you fought!"

Isabella gripped my forearm as Piers slid heavily from his saddle, encumbered by the weight of his mail, and moved in on Pembroke. Piers held his sword straight before him in challenge.

"Stop him," my queen begged, holding her breath. "Stop him before you lose one of your best knights to some meaningless quarrel of names. Do it now."

I laid my hand over hers, caressing it. "We should wait a moment," I said, "and give Piers the benefit of a fight fairly won. Allow him his victory and Pembroke his honor. Pembroke will yield . . . if he yet breathes."

All was silent but for the crunching of Piers' steps upon the packed, sandy ground. He unbuckled his helmet and dropped it to the ground, sure of his win and wanting everyone there to see his face and hear clearly what he had to say.

"Up!" Piers kicked Pembroke hard in the side. "Or yield to the greatest knight in all of England and Ireland: Piers de Gaveston, Earl of Cornwall!"

Pembroke jerked sideways and curled into a fetal position, gasping for air. Slowly, he dragged his gauntleted hand across the earth and fumbled with his visor, opening it only partway. His features were compressed in pain. His eyes rolled up toward his brow. His mouth gaped open, but no words escaped. The man had been dealt a blow hard enough to knock the air and wits from him.

His blade aimed at Pembroke's heart, Piers strode closer. Isabella dug her fingernails into my arm.

"Now," she whispered.

I grimaced at the pain and before I could respond, she had sprung to her feet.

"He yields!" she shouted. "In the name of his queen, he yields. Put aside your weapon."

Piers snarled at her, wanting to disobey, but knowing better. Grumbling, he sheathed his sword and began to walk toward the royal stands. I rubbed at the half-moons imprinted in my arm, then stood and gestured to Piers.

"Today, Lord Cornwall, you are our champion. Come and be showered with your prizes. A feast this night in your honor. Drink and dance. Hail the greatest knight in England!"

I clapped my hands together, but only silence answered. I clapped and clapped until my hands stung.

Pembroke's squire was at his side now, removing his lord's helmet. The rattling he received had proven to be only temporary, as minutes later his senses returned and he was carrying on some small conversation with a few friends who had rushed onto the field to aid him. Warwick and Lancaster were both there with him—Lancaster holding his shoulders so he could sit upright and Warwick offering him a drink of water from a cup. A suspicious circle already. And so stinking, bloody obvious.

Oh, they hate him more than ever for bettering them so easily. Is a man to hide his talents to allow others the false security of believing themselves his equal? Jealousy is an evil monster. I shall keep Brother Perrot close at my breast, safe, for they will not raise their hand against their king, else they desire their own deaths . . .

Not only in my homeland was I being assailed, but abroad as well. Whilst King Philip was consoling his shrew of a daughter, he was also corresponding with the Bruce. The greatest insult of all was that when he did so, he addressed the rebel as 'King of Scots'. I spilled out my anger in ink to my Janus-faced father-in-law. He told me, demanded of me, summoned me to come to France and pay him fealty for the lands I held there. I am a king, rightly born and acknowledged by nobility and holiness alike, unlike that mink Bruce, who flouted his own word. It does not behoove me to scrape my knees before another king. If I stepped one foot beyond this realm, the Lords Ordainers would be there like starving buzzards to swoop down on Piers and strip the flesh from his bones while he yet lived.

Westminster, 1311

MY BARONS WOULD NOT relinquish Scotland and yet they would not pay the price to keep it. The price of guarding the entry to all of Scotland—the castles of Stirling, Edinburgh, Berwick—were the leeches that drained the lifeblood from England. I told them so, over and over until my teeth nearly turned black from fury and they could not, *would* not listen. Neither would they vote me the taxes to raise a proper army. And while this quarrel raged on, they rallied against Piers, accusing him of insolence and undue influence over me. They said that he took from my money chests as he pleased and called my jewels his own. Did they believe me so mindless that I could not choose my own company or loan a true companion a few trinkets of finery?

In August of 1311, the Lords Ordainers demanded my presence at Westminster. Under immense duress, I signed the many papers they shuffled before me. I did it to protect Piers, as I had done before and would do again if forced.

But I stopped short when I read on the crowded pages an ordinance that thrust a cold knife into my heart. Silence gaped in the council chamber as the masters of my demise sat the length of the table, stoic in their countenances, but sure of the outcome.

"No." I thrust the parchment away. Ink dripped from the quill trembling in my hand onto the table. "Not that. All the rest, but not that."

Lancaster, who had been standing at my shoulder for the duration of this foul encounter, drew the paper back before me. "Sign here, my lord, and we have no more quarrels with you. You must agree to all."

"I will not banish him forever. I cannot."

Winchelsey, the Archbishop of Canterbury, circled the table in his gilded robes. He had come in full dress—his miter balanced on his pointed head and his crozier propping him up like a walking staff—to designate the significance of the event.

"The order must come from you, sire," the archbishop said, thrumming his fingers against his crozier impatiently, "to quell the masses."

"I suspect you will do it whether I agree or not."

Lancaster leaned close by my ear and with his stinking breath uttered lowly, "We could do far worse than just send him away. Now sign . . . or it's war you'll have and it won't be waged in Scotland, but at your very own threshold."

"Is this how you would have me reward loyalty?"

He took the quill from my fingers, dipped it and blotted the ink and put it back in my hand. A vain smile lifted the corners of his fat mouth.

Lancaster's rolling gut pressed against my shoulder. "We are merely trying to reconstruct what has been neglected, sire. Allow us this guidance and peace shall return in full."

Peace? I say you pick your wars poorly and Robert the Bruce should be the one who strikes terror in you, not Piers. As for me, you have emptied my pockets and now dangle me naked over a well. I have no dignity, no resources, and no friends I can call upon who do not fear for their lives, as well. Where is the choice in any of this for me?

They had diminished my power enormously—put it in a mortar and crushed it so fine there was nothing left but the dust of what used to be. The Archbishop of Canterbury had already excommunicated Piers.

Gladly would I give up heaven and earth to join him in the hell to which they had condemned him.

I signed my name and flung the quill across the table so that it left long streaks of ink in its path. Twenty-one triumphant faces stifled their grins and gloated silently.

22

Edward II – Eltham, 1311

THEY GAVE LESS THAN a month for Piers to quit the country. Hardly enough time to arrange passage. My older sister, Margaret, and her husband the duke had agreed to receive him in Brabant, but knowing Piers he would too soon grow restless there. Of the many stipulations the Lords Ordainers had imposed, one was that Piers was to be stripped of his earldom; another that he was not to be given the privileges of any office or permitted refuge on any lands owned by me. Why not just set him on a barren island without provisions, stripped naked, and let the wild beasts make a feast of him?

My every means of ensuring his safety had been suffocated. I was again the child who had no voice, no say, whose judgment was deemed inadequate, whose will was denied. Very little had changed in my twenty-eight miserable years. The only joy I had known had been realized in Piers' company. I wrote to him almost daily, but I doubt that more than a few letters ever reached him, if any at all.

Yet, if *I* could not offer him succor, perhaps Isabella could be of some good to me? Indeed, why not make her my instrument, rather than my undoing? Bound to me for life, would she not rather be my ally than my enemy? It would take wooing, compliments, gifts, but it could perhaps be done.

I arrived at Eltham Palace, documents in hand. Directed to the so-lar, I went unannounced. Even through the closed door, I could hear the high-pitched giggles of her damsels. The servant standing at the door put a hand to the latch, but I tapped him smartly on the shoulder with the parchment roll and stayed him with an upheld hand, listening. Court gossip, nothing more. I gestured for him to open it and stepped inside.

Laughter trickled away as one by one they turned their faces to the door. Patrice, who had been in the center of the room, whirling about in some sort of dance, staggered as she caught sight of me and backed away quickly. The others, Juliana and Marie, stood and bowed, then looked to the queen, awaiting an order.

"They may stay," I told her, tucking the parchment beneath my arm. Witnesses, especially those with rampant tongues, would serve well to spread news of the generosity I was about to impart.

"My lord?" Isabella laid her embroidery beside her stool and came toward me, but cautiously, as if she feared to ask what had brought me here.

I cast a smile at their curious faces, then at her. Behind her hung an unfamiliar tapestry, the work too intricate to have been spun by inexpe-rienced hands. "Your pilgrimage to Canterbury went well, I trust?"

She stopped an arm's length away and tilted her head. "It did, my lord. Very well."

I circled behind her to trace a hand over the tapestry, my fingertips sensing the blend of silk and woolen threads. Peering more closely, I realized it was a depiction of the archangel Gabriel, wings outspread and hands extended, as he appeared before the Virgin Mary.

Turning back to Isabella, I said, "I hear you left a sizable offering to Saint Thomas."

Her chin dipped to her chest, as though she were a child caught stealing warm bread from a kitchen window. A blush of pink colored her alabaster cheeks. The evening sun shone brightly upon her golden hair.

"All the more likely your prayers should be answered." I touched a hand to her elbow to get her attention and held out the roll of parchment I carried with me.

She blinked several times before reaching out to take it. Breaking the seal, she unrolled it and read. So long passed before she looked up that I wondered if there was some part of it she did not understand. I had thought it straightforward enough.

"This is too much," she said. "I cannot—"

"Eltham? Of course you can . . . and will. I know your fondness for it. Consider it a gift long overdue." I brushed the back of my fingers across her cheek, feeling the flush of blood there like a rising fever. "Sufficient moneys have been allotted for repairs, but if you need more, simply ask. Bourne and Deeping are in good enough condition, if I recall, but I leave the judgment up to you. Do as you wish with them all. You've a good head for such matters."

Again, the jaw hanging slack. The vapid gaze. Her eyes narrowed. I steeled myself against the inquiry of suspicion that was sure to follow.

Instead, she grasped my hand and, standing on tiptoe, kissed me full on the lips. Surprised, I stiffened, but before I could recover, she had spun about.

"Go on," she told her damsels with a wave of her delicate hand. "I shall call for you later."

The homely and timid Marie shuffled toward the door. Juliana, after a polite nod, followed. But Patrice's shoulders sagged in disappointment. She stood rooted to her spot, until Isabella took her by the hand and guided her insistently to the door.

"I promise, later I will read—"

"La Chanson de Roland? Oh, please?" A radiant smile flashed briefly across Patrice's face.

"Yes, yes. Although surely you must have it memorized by now?

After supper. Come to my chambers then."

Patrice shared a lingering glance with Isabella, implying unspoken secrets. But they were women. Always they made too much of too little.

The door closed after Patrice. Isabella turned to me. "I have written to my father."

"Ah, have you?" I had known. But I said nothing of it. I had long suspected that she harped to her father of even the smallest slight when I had not a chance to defend myself. Now, however, was not the time for confrontation.

"He has agreed," she said, "to allow Lord Gaveston safe passage through France."

"What do you mean?"

"If he should need to travel from Brabant to Flanders . . . or Ponthieu, even, no harm shall come to him there."

Stunned, I stumbled to the nearest stool. I pressed my palms flat against the tops of my thighs, waiting for the fog of confusion to clear.

She knelt on the floor beside me and laid one slender hand over mine.

I searched her eyes for some flicker of falsehood, but they were as innocent as a fawn's. "Why? Why have you done this for me?"

She curled her fingers beneath mine, squeezing lightly. "How long have we been husband and wife, Edward? Three years now? We are often in each others' company and yet it seems as though a distance as vast as from England to Egypt stretches between us. If we cannot work toward a common end, what hope is there for us?"

"But you have never spoken kindly of him." An understatement. She may never have said it in such words, but she loathed him.

"He was your friend, your confidante, long before I was thrust upon you. You love him. I only wanted it to be me."

She spoke of love like one would say they love the scent of roses or a favored pet. How could such a naïve thing know anything of a passion so consuming, so maddening, that reasoning flees because of it? No, she did not know. She could not. To her, love was a myth captured on the pages of a book or warbled by a bard: a man worships a goddess-like woman whom he cannot have, slays a dragon in her name and gives up his life for her.

So much is written and sung about the love of man for woman. But is that all there is, the only kind? If God can create such a boundless love as I have for Piers, how can it be 'unnatural'? Where is the harm in it? I can no more understand condemning what I share with him than I can fathom where the earth ends or what lies on the other side of it. And I . . . I have my own dragons to slay—but they lie not sleeping in caves or burrowed beneath the mountains—they surround me.

The warmth of Isabella's hand seeped into mine. Loyalty, if not love then, was what she bore for me. And if she wished to think I loved Piers as a friend only, then let her.

"Then you will stand by me in this?" I asked.

"It is a queen's duty," she replied, "to be her husband's greatest advocate. And I will be that, Edward. Never doubt it."

In time, I could grow fond of her. She was young, her skin so milky fresh it was a wonder kittens did not trail after her to lap at her fingers. Indeed, some would even call her 'beautiful'. Although she wore her youth like a mask of innocence, I sensed something of the diplomat in her and guile beyond her years. Traits which could prove far more useful than having a quivering lamb for a consort.

I slipped my hand from hers and cupped her chin in my fingers, tilting her head so the last of the day's light washed over her vernal features: the nose, so delicate it would not have looked out of place on a child; the chiseled planes of her cheekbones; almond-shaped eyes an ever-changing hue of green; and a smooth forehead framed between golden brows and the slightest widow's peak of a hairline.

In many ways and on many occasions, my father had cursed me, burdened me, and in the matter of betrothal to this French nursling deprived me of choice. But perhaps, this once, he had chosen rightly. If her whelps were half as fair, if she indeed remained as faithful as she now espoused herself to be . . .

"As a king's consort," I said, "your loyalty will be tested, often. More so as *my* queen, I fear. So many wish to bring me down, to take away as much of my power as they dare. I will resist them to the last, for to cede ground at any point is only to encourage them to push harder and take more. No, I will not yield, ever. The question, however, stands: How far, dear wife, will you bend against those forces before *you* break?"

Windsor, 1311

SPICED CIDER SLID DOWN my throat, numbing limbs weary from lack of sleep. In my upper story chambers at Windsor, rain drummed against the window pane so loudly that I did not hear the groan of the door on its hinges.

Gilbert de Clare, Earl of Gloucester, unclasped his sodden cloak and handed it to a servant, who scuttled from the room holding the garment at arm's length. Water dripped onto the flagstones, leaving a long, wet trail from the puddle collecting at my nephew's feet to the door.

I waved him to a chair on the opposite side of the hearth from me. Gilbert's shoes squelched as he dragged himself across the room. Blue-lipped, he slumped down in the chair with a drawn-out groan.

"God's eyes, Gilbert, you look pathetic. Did your horse drag you through the mud all the way from Gloucester?"

"Not quite so far." He sneezed violently and drew a sleeve across his chafed nose before continuing. "Only from Wallingford, Edward."

I leaned forward, my hands clenching the corners of my chair. "Did he send word through Margaret? And will she come with us?"

Sighing, he half-rolled his eyes at me. "Yes, and yes."

I bolted to my feet, although I resisted grabbing him by the shoulders to shake some urgency into him. "Tell me, then. What did he say?"

"He will join you, but he thinks it inconvenient for Margaret to journey so far in her present state."

"Convenience is not a luxury we have. But we cannot leave now. Not until the New Year. If I leave before Christmas court at Windsor, then Lancaster's hounds will be on our trail within the hour."

"The New Year? Dear Lord, Edward! Are you mad? She'll drop the child on the frozen road."

"There is time yet before the child is due. While I trust Lord Pembroke to keep her in his care, she'll be far safer in York than so close to Lancaster's reach."

Gilbert pressed his fingertips together and shook his head slowly. "Edward . . ."

"Do not say it, Gilbert." I turned from him and strode to the window to look out on a world as gray and bleak as my life had been. Beyond fields of mud and trampled grass, naked trees huddled bent along the banks of the Thames like old men with twisted bones.

"Only a month-and-a-half since—"

"No!" I whirled about to face him, stabbing a finger toward him. "You will not be among those who condemn me. You will not!"

He stood, his gaze hard and fixed. "I am not among them, Edward. I never have been. You know that. The Lords Ordainers have already heard rumor that Gaveston is back in England. They have been searching for him. What do you think they will do when he appears in plain sight?"

"His wife is with child. He should be with Margaret. Not in Brabant."

"Your reasoning is as thin as straw, Edward. If you go through with this, you gamble his life, his child's, your crown . . . And the queen? She will have you castrated and quartered alongside Gaveston."

"Ohhh, I think not, dear nephew." I leaned back against the wall, the rough stones digging into my scalp and snagging at my clothes. A smile crept across my mouth. "She has already agreed to it."

23

Edward II – York, 1312

IT'S A FOOL THAT falters for want of surety. Sometimes, one must act, even if out of desperation, or else leave one's fate to the whim of others.

But so little time to act and no room, not even an inch, for error.

In the biting dead of winter, in the darkest of hours before a dawn that was a distant blur to me, I collected my niece Margaret from Wallingford and fled north to York. Her belly near to bursting, she lay in a carriage bundled in ermine, whimpering her discomfort with each passing mile. I took with me only enough of my personal guard to fend off an attack and the minimum number of household servants I could manage with. It was imperative that we travel as swiftly and as unnoticed as possible.

We were somewhere past Bishopsthorpe by the River Ouse, when she let out a scream that ripped a knife of panic down my spine.

I reined my mount about and spurred its flanks, flying back along our small column to the carriage for fear that her shrieking would harken my enemies to descend like wolves on stumbling prey. With a flip of my palm, the driver drew the horses to a halt. Steam curled from their flaring nostrils. I yanked the rear curtain aside and peered in. Two handmaidens drew back, clutching their mantles to their breasts as January cold gusted into the confines. A third woman, her hands spotted with age, dabbed at my niece's forehead with a bunched cloth.

My personal physician, William de Bromtoft, pressed his hands to Margaret's taut belly. Her young face, too plain to be pretty, was distorted in anguish and the hue of her cheeks and forehead startlingly pallid.

"No trouble, I hope?" I said.

Bromtoft probed deeper, his knobby fingers kneading at her flesh, slowly moving outward and downward. Margaret opened her mouth as if to cry out, but she kept silent, her back arching with strain as she wrung the older woman's wrist.

"Not yet, my lord," Bromtoft said, "but the child has dropped. It could be hours . . . or days."

"God's soul, can't you tell?"

His single gray, feathered eyebrow fluttered. "If my lord would close the curtain, so that she may keep warm and have her privacy, I will . . . let you know."

"Hasten, then. Every moment we dally here is one nearer to death for us all." I dropped the flap. Impatient, I dismounted and paced along deeply worn ruts, centuries after the Romans had trod over these same tracks. The moors stretched to the horizon around us, nothing but a tiny church and a few cottages in view. Near the road, the river gurgled by sluggishly, its banks crusted with ice.

This time, I would not allow Lancaster or anyone to drive my Brother Perrot from England. Enough of their defiance and intimidation. If it took a battle to claim my rights back, then a battle it would be.

But I hadn't the men to defend myself just now if they came upon us. I had to get to York, had to know that Piers was there and safe. York's walls would keep Lancaster out.

If Piers' child insisted on coming into the world out here, now—in this barren, frozen and forgotten land—let it come. I marched back toward the carriage, lifted my hand to pull back the curtain when it parted and Bromtoft's face appeared.

"There is time yet," he announced. "But we have no more than a day, two at most."

"A day is all we need."

BY THE TIME WE arrived in York, Margaret's pains had pitched to an agony that signaled birth was imminent. I had not even made it to my chamber at the King's Tower, when the constable chased me down in the stairway and pressed a letter into my hands. I descended several steps to stand nearer to the rushlight there. Tentative, I opened it. Blotches of ink and smears marred the letters thereon. The words were crowded, chaotic strokes, written by a hurried hand, but I knew the hand that had formed them well. Piers was in Knaresborough, waiting for word that it was safe to enter York.

"Shall I send someone for him, my lord?" the constable asked, wringing his hands to warm them. "Or would you prefer to compose a letter? I can call for a clerk, if you wish."

"No, no need." I rolled the letter back up and returned it to him. "Saddle fresh horses and assemble my guard. There is yet daylight left. We ride for Knaresborough."

I left that very day to retrieve him myself. I could not wait one hour more for Margaret to expel the infant from her womb. Piers was waiting . . .

OH, THAT SEEING HIM again, pressing his cheek to mine, could make me feel such joy as it once had. Yet we greeted each other with a shared weariness of spirit—him looking as wide-eyed and frantic as a hare pursued by hounds and me wracked by the haunting fear that they would come, find him, and take him forever from me. I loved him beyond reason, but even that, I knew, might not be enough to save him. To preserve us, as it were.

There was a time when I believed that eternity existed. No longer. But there are moments when time ceases to move forward, when the world beyond our sight does not exist and when all that troubles us, for awhile, dissolves into nothing. So it was for Piers when we returned to York and they brought forth a fat-cheeked, bright-eyed babe. A log in the hearth hissed and crackled. Piers glanced toward the door to the adjacent chamber, where Margaret was. They would not yet let him enter, saying she was recovering from the birth, but well.

The midwife held out the bundled infant and smiled. "A girl. As healthy and content as any I have ever brought into the world."

Piers stood speechless, his arms dangling useless at his sides as he stared at the squirming lump.

"A daughter, Piers." I stepped up to his shoulder and nudged him forward. "She favors her mother. Are you quite sure—"

"She *is* mine." He snatched the babe from the midwife's arms a little too abruptly, but the child was undisturbed. With surprising care, he cradled her to his chest. Somehow, she had wriggled a hand free of the swaddling. Her tiny fingers flexed, reaching. Piers slid his forefinger into her grasp and her fingers curled tightly around it, her mouth curving into a gummy smile.

In that moment, I envied him his scrap of immortality, that little bundle gurgling in his arms.

They named her Joan, after Margaret's mother. Margaret recovered splendidly and the child thrived. Isabella arrived in time for Margaret's churching at the Franciscan friary. She was so busy coddling her new grand-niece that Piers and I were afforded some time alone to meander about the winter-bare gardens of the castle.

"I tell you, Flanders' people are as dull as its sky is gray," Piers reflected. "I could hardly remain there, dear Edward. The boredom alone would have killed me. Their court was so backwardly pious that they didn't even know the rules for dice, let alone have the interest in laying bets on races or cock fights. Their sense of fashion was abominable, their food bland and their language impossible to learn. After two months there, I had wasted away to a sack of bones. In an empty church in Utrecht—or was it Ghent—I found myself talking to the hideous carved figures hanging from the arches. A bloody sure sign it was time to leave. In Gascony the bastards would not allow me to disembark at any of the ports. Ireland lacks both comfort and civility, so that was out of the question. As for the alleged 'safe conduct' through France granted to me by King Philip—what good did that do me without a place to go to? So, I came back. To see my child born—and to be with you." He smoothed a wrinkle on the front of his blue brocaded garnache and hung his head. "I thought it would be as before—that they would have gone on and forgotten. But the queen says the Ordainers have already assembled in London. No doubt they will come for me soon. I should go then, back to Brabant. I'll take Margaret and the babe with—"

I grabbed his arm and swung him around to face me. "You will *not* leave England. Never again."

"But Edward, how can I stay? God knows it will ravage my heart to go from you again, but—"

"I said 'no'! Now cease with this gloom. They will cow neither you nor me again. The writs have already been written. Soon, it will be proclaimed: You are recalled, your lands returned. It is done."

He shrugged off my hand, shaking his head slowly. "You would willingly invite their wrath?"

"What I will not willingly do is give you up again. Nor will I allow them to take command of my kingdom while I yet live."

"Ah, the kingdom, the kingdom. Yes, yes." Piers stooped and plucked up a long-dead branch. He crumpled its brown leaves in the cup of his palm with his fingertips and scattered the flakes over the muddy ground around him as he began back toward the castle. "Well, how to win your kingdom back, then, eh? Piss on the Lords Ordainers. If you have the people behind you, Edward, you have all the army you need."

I far from had the people behind me now. As it was, I feared to so much as go out among them, let alone ask for their help. Why could they not love me as they loved Isabella, even with her French blood?

As I caught up with him, he halted momentarily and rubbed at his neck. "What an ache I have in my bones."

I pulled my hand from my glove and touched his cheek. "You're burning."

"Phhh . . . your fingers are frozen. Let us idle before the fire and have them bring wine by the tun. Call upon that lute player of yours. What is his name?"

"Robin Hobson . . . or Dobson, maybe. Does it matter? He comes when I call."

"I fancy his pluck. A far better musician than mine—although I haven't his service anymore. I haven't anything."

I slung an arm about his shoulder. "You have me, Brother Perrot. Is that not enough?" As I leaned upon him, we strolled through the door and into the great hall to escape a blasting wind that threatened a string of rainy days on its tail.

THE DOOR CREAKED ON its hinges and I rolled over, expecting to see my page scuttle in to tend to the fire one last time.

Instead, Isabella stood at my door, her pale hair coiled and set in a net woven with pearls. Even wearing her nightclothes, she looked as fresh and vibrant as a field rose in full bloom. She shut the door behind her and moved toward the bed, a nimbus of moonlight illuminating her nymph-like form.

I struggled to pull my head higher onto the pillows. "What brings you at this hour, my queen?"

Her hands adroitly freed her hair of nets and pins, so that a long braided rope of gold tumbled down her back. She pulled her fingers languidly through the plait to separate the strands. "You have heard that the Lords Ordainers met in London?"

"And did they call for my head?"

"Lord Pembroke dissuaded them from outright confrontation, but"—she glanced away, unwilling to meet my eyes—"there are rumors that Lancaster will come after Lord Gaveston."

"Which is why we are here and not there." Thunder pounded behind my eyeballs. I swung my feet over the edge of the canopied bed. Too little energy to do more, I propped my elbows upon my knees and cradled my head in my hands. The brush of her footsteps made me look up.

She knelt and laid her head in my lap. "You've been so distraught of late. I've worried for you."

"Yes, well, there is much to worry over. Piers has been excommunicated. And if it's not enough that they've condemned him to burn in purgatory eternally, they want to punish him in this life." Something compelled me to touch her hair. Seldom had I seen it hang loose to fan out over her back and shoulders in a veil of shimmering gold. It flowed like silk beneath my fingertips. As my fingers grazed her cheek, I felt her skin flush with fire. "But they'll do more than send him away or toss him into a dungeon to rot. No, those punishments would not be permanent enough."

One of her hands curled around my calf. She turned her head to look up at me, resting her small, oval chin upon my knee. "You forgive him so much, too much sometimes."

I stood, resting a hand upon the bed until the blood steadied in my head, and went to the table, where Jankin had left a pitcher of water. Ignoring the goblet beside it, I drank until I had emptied half of it, then leaned heavily with both hands upon the table.

"I would do anything for him. Even give my life for him." I said it not so much to her, but as a truth I could not hide. After the roiling haze had cleared from my thoughts, I looked at her, sitting upon the floor with her feet tucked beneath her.

She rose and took both my hands in hers. "Lancaster and his lords are wrong in what they do. Wrong by the laws of both man and God for rearing up against their liege."

Soon, if not already, Lancaster would be marching northward. And still I had no army. Only York's garrison. It would only take one traitor among them to throw open the gates and the enemy would be upon us. My spies had already uncovered some of Lancaster's sympathizers. Yesterday, three were hung in the market square. Today, two more.

"But without an army to oppose him," I said, "what could you or I ever do to exact a fitting revenge?"

Her mouth, plump and cherry red, twisted in thought. "Live in harmony. Bliss, even. I can bear you son after son—tall and strong, like you."

"Not like my father, I pray. I am not like him at all. I trust you've figured that out by now?" I drew my hands away. Sitting at the table, I leaned my head upon my fist. "I almost dread awakening every day, for it is one more day I must face the impossible. Tomorrow is just another bottomless pit in which to tumble."

She came to stand before me, arms crossed over her breasts. Moonlight etched a halo of silver above her. Her fingers slid between her garment and the skin at her shoulders. She peeled her dark blue robe down to her waist to reveal a thin chemise beneath. A firm bosom pressed against the sheer, white cloth. The frightened child that once resembled a reed was now a fully endowed woman. She lowered her linen chemise and stepped free, leaving her clothing in a rumpled heap on the floor to stand naked before me.

She extended her hand. "I will give you a son, Edward. A great son. A king among kings to conquer them all."

How do infants do battle, good wife? With wooden spoons? Cry until my enemies go mad with deafness? At least when I am old, I can send my sons to fight in Scotland in my stead.

She pulled me up. Her hands, though, they trembled.

"One condition," I told her, as she leaned back upon the downy bed that swallowed her smallness. "Tell your meddling father to leave Scotland to me and cease his courting of the Bruce. Tell him if he has any favor with the Pope to use it against the Bruce and relent of Piers.

"And tell him," I added, climbing upon the bed, "that you are content now and too enamored of your husband to write to him as often anymore."

I knelt between her legs and dropped my hose only as far as would be needed. Sensing a pressure in my loins, I cupped a hand beneath my stones and, to my surprise, discovered the first stirrings of arousal.

Like the effigy on a stone tomb, she stared unblinking up at the beams of the ceiling. I looked down on her ivory face, half shadowed, and lowered my body onto hers. Determined to have this over with, I drove between her legs several times, seeking entry, my organ swelling rapidly. Her breaths became quicker, shallower. But she was as tight as a goatskin drum. Her legs drew together in resistance and with each prod the blood rushed hotter to my loins. If she did not submit soon, I would waste my valuable seed all over the sheets. As I reached down to slip my fingers into her folds and guide myself into her, she dug her elbows into the mattress and scrambled backward. Her head thunked against the headboard, trapping her. *Damn her.*

I hauled her back down toward me. Clamping her jaw in one of my hands, I craned her face toward mine. "Do I so revile you that you will not have me—*me*, your husband?"

"No, no." She shook her head, the glint of a tear in her eye. "It's only that . . . I have heard that it hurts—the first time."

"That is what they tell young girls to keep them virgins," I said, half-laughing at her childish fears. So, she had thought herself prepared for this moment and when it was upon her, she became the diffident little girl again. Time to make a woman of her. Put a child in her and give her a purpose. Create my own perpetuity.

"Then . . ."—she dabbed at the corner of her eye with a fingertip, sniffling—"there is no pain?"

"If there is, it will pass quickly." I let go of her jaw, drew a finger down her neck, further down until I lightly circled the areola of her breast. The nipple tautened. I put my mouth to it, my tongue lapping at the firm nub, my teeth nipping soft flesh. She turned her head away and exhaled. Once more, she drew her legs apart, though not wide. My hand wandered to her hips, the joining of her thighs, the downy pile of hair modestly concealing her maidenhead. "Besides, if there was no pleasure in coupling, why would it be such a temptation to so many?"

She flinched as I penetrated her. Slowly, I moved deeper, then withdrew and waited before thrusting again. Her eyes closed, she bit at her lip so hard I expected blood to stream from her mouth. My thrusts quickened, her constriction hastening my rhythm. As I did my work, she lay beneath me like a rock at the bottom of the ocean.

The wave of my release was so swift and disappointing, that I rolled onto my back and tied the cord of my hose before the last of my fluids had been expelled. Some time passed before I noticed that Isabella was shivering.

"You're cold," I said.

"I'm unclothed," she mumbled, pulling the blanket over her body. Her arms and hands disappeared beneath the covers and, legs clamped tight, she turned over onto her side, away from me.

"Did it hurt?" I asked, trying to show some concern.

She responded with an unconvincing shake of her head.

"Did you hate it so much then—with me?"

Shoulders hunched forward, she sighed. Her words, although muffled in the pillow, cut to my soul. "Perhaps if you were not so ready to assume everyone hated you, Edward, it would not be so. Our child will love you, if you let him. *I* could."

Could you truly love me, Isabella my queen, even as I am? Could anyone?

I rolled over, far enough away that our backs did not touch. The moon had barely moved from its position as it stabbed its shaft through the glazed window to fall upon the same spot where she had stood in disinclined nakedness, offering her body as fulfillment of her duty. Our act had consumed little time. Pray she was fertile and we would not have to repeat it often.

THE NEXT EVENING, NOT having seen Piers about all day, I stopped at his bedchamber.

"Wait here, Jankin." I took the lantern from him, knocked once and hearing no answer nudged the door open. It was dark within. It stank so strongly that I drew back a moment before forging ahead.

"Brother Perrot?"

Hearing no reply at first, I entered the chamber and raised the lantern to throw light across the room. Normally, Piers was obsessively orderly, but there were clothes strewn about, plates of half-eaten food on the floor and an untouched goblet of wine on the bedside table.

"Here."

I turned toward the sound of a thin, leaking voice. Piers was slumped in a chair, his winter cloak still wrapped about him. He shivered. I stepped closer. His hair was soaked. I swept aside some articles of clothing and put the lantern on top of the Spanish chest I had given him as a gift many years ago. He had taken it everywhere with him. To Brabant, even.

"You are ill." I wiped his face with the nearest clean-looking garment I could find.

A long, thin sigh escaped from his barely moving lips. "Yes, I think I am. Maybe this will be the death of me and all your troubles will vanish the moment they turn up the first shovel-full of earth for my grave."

I did not leave his side for five days, until he was recovered. But even worse than watching Piers suffer was the news that Lancaster was at last heading north. Time was running out. What escape was there for us now? What hope?

Humbled by despair, I wrote to my enemy: Robert the Bruce.

24

Robert the Bruce – Forest of Selkirk, 1312

ENGLAND WAS IN UPHEAVAL. Whether fate or fortune, we took full advantage of it. The Northumbrians, who were short of defenses and shorter yet of funds, agreed to a truce to last the winter. No sooner had it expired, than we attacked Norham. They hastily and wisely paid another indemnity. Reparations for reprieve, perhaps, but little difference to what had been done to us in the past. Not only could I now feed my men, but I could pay them as well.

We were barely within Scotland's borders again when an urgent message arrived from my old friend, Bishop William Lamberton of St. Andrews: Edward of England wished to bargain.

A blanket of snow, so thin as to appear threadbare, stuck in clumps to the blue-green pine needles and mottled the ground where shadows lay. Puddles of slop in the road marked the tracks of the party that had come before ours, not long ago. We numbered twenty, the rest having been left behind in Lochmaben to guard the cattle while they grazed the scant winter grass along the River Annan.

Directly in front of me rode Gil de la Haye, his slight shoulders hunched against the cold. Randolph rode abreast of me. More than three years had passed since he had sworn himself to me. Not once since then had he given me cause to doubt his loyalty. Still, I often kept him close, not because I mistrusted him, but rather for his company and his counsel. A keen mind for politics, we passed the hours by speculating on the ever-perplexing stance of the Church. My nephew also had an intimate knowledge of the stratagem of many English commanders, which had quickly proven invaluable.

"You were right, Thomas," I said.

Straightening in his saddle, he narrowed his eyes attentively. "Right? Your pardon, Uncle?"

I flexed cold fingers on the reins of my horse as our line crested a ridge and began the descent into the glen. "About Northumbria. As unprotected as motherless lambs on an open hillside."

"Lancaster is gathering men in the south. That's no secret. Tournaments, he says, but the numbers grow with each one. I don't think it's us that he's after. Not yet, anyway." He gave me a wink. "Besides, he probably reckoned that even if you did venture across the border, you'd not risk staying long."

"Aye, a filching lot of rogues we are. There and gone before he even gets word of it. He'll either learn to regard us with more respect or reconcile with King Edward—an unlikely prospect. Two enemies is one too many, even for him. So right again you are. We are but flies about his ears—and Edward the rat gnawing at his ankles." Above the moaning of the wind, I heard only the squelching of hooves through mud. Even through the dampening cover of the forest, frigid air stung at my cheeks. Our line slowed as the path meandered ever downward. Off to the right and below, the trees parted, revealing a grassy clearing. "Over there, Thomas, do you see that circle of ground amid the fallen logs?"

Rising up in his stirrups, he peered past me. "Aye, Uncle, I do. But what of it?"

A pang struck my heart. I waited for it to pass before I spoke again. "That is where I knighted William Wallace and proclaimed him Scotland's Guardian. More than twelve years it's been. Struggling to sweep

England's footprints from our doorstep. So long a time and yet . . ."—pellets of sleet hissed through the brittle air and stung my eyes—"yet why are we not any closer? Despite so many small successes, it seems we are ever sliding down the mountain."

Gil, who had been silent until then, tossed a facetious grin over his shoulder. "Perhaps we need to look for a different foothold?"

"Devil take you, Gil. You think I have not thought of that? I say our 'foothold' is Edward of England himself. Soon enough, I wager, we'll purchase ground by his accidental grace."

The path leveled out, growing broader but muddier as we came onto low ground. Ahead, a black-caped figure, his hem trailing over dirty snow, emerged from the trees. Beside him stood a younger man—noble, judging by his ornately woven cloak. His hauberk was of an older style, yet gleaming from a fresh scouring of sand and vinegar. The undented helmet tucked beneath his armpit indicated his inexperience in combat. The older man snapped back his fur-lined hood to reveal a full crown of white hair. He bowed his head to me and sketched the sign of the cross in blessing.

I slipped from my saddle and bounded over the decaying logs, scattered now in the loose semblance of a circle.

"My lord," Bishop Lamberton hailed, "good day and welcome to Selkirk."

"Your grace, a good day it is." I clasped him in a brief embrace, then cast a glance at his companion. "And who is this?"

"David of Atholl, my lord."

The young nobleman knelt, his knee sinking into soft mud. He peeked up at me through thick brown locks, then looked quickly down, as a dog does when submitting to its master. I was never comfortable with such rote obedience, for it arose from fear, not respect. Fear was what I preferred to strike in my enemies, not my subjects.

"John's son? The last I saw you, you were no taller than my hound. You used to walk underneath him, as I recall." His father John of

Strathbogie, Earl of Atholl, had fought alongside me at Methven when the Earl of Pembroke surprised us that night and so brutally crushed our forces. It had rent my heart to hear of Atholl giving up his neck to the noose after being captured at Kildrummy with my brother Nigel. Brave and honest men should not die such ignoble deaths. I touched David's mail hood, wishing I could summon the soul of his father back to me somehow. "Rise, Lord David. Your father was ever faithful to me. I trust you will be, as well?"

David of Atholl sprang to his feet, tottering sideways as he scraped the mud from his leggings. Nervous fingers fluttered at his belt to read-just the weight of his sword. He drew breath, pulled his shoulders back and looked at me squarely. "I vow to try, my lord."

"'Try' will not suffice. You either will—or you won't."

His thin brow creased. "M-m-my loyalty lies with Scotland . . . and with you, my lord king."

The lad, who could not have been more than sixteen, was no James Douglas, but he would do. "Good enough, then. One more lamb unto the fold. One less on the side of the English. Now, what brings you here as an escort to our dear Bishop of St. Andrews? It's not a short while you've been in England—and you've not remained there against your will, as I understand."

He glanced at the bishop, then back at me, his mouth agape. "I, um . . . I—"

I held up my hand. "You needn't explain. I understand more than you know about the many pressures that bear upon us. And since you've come with the good bishop here, I trust you're not here to spy on us?"

The question, although meant in jest, struck an uneasiness in him. In response, Bishop Lamberton pulled a letter from his wide sleeve. Sleet pattered lightly against the parchment as he extended it.

I inspected the royal wax seal and pushed it back at him. "If you would, your grace. The honor belongs to the bearer on this occasion. I prefer to imagine that Edward of Caernarvon is standing here before me, speaking the words. Go on."

With slender fingers, more nimble than one would expect of a man of his years, he broke the seal and stretched open the roll to read aloud:

"Our Dear Lord Robert, King of Scots . . ."

His brows flitted upward. Above the top edge of the roll, I saw the crinkling of a smile at the corners of his eyes. He tilted his head quizzically and began again, the steam of his breath curling white around thin lips:

"Our Dear Lord Robert, King of Scots,

> *I call upon you as one who understands the implications of loyalty, or lack thereof. In my kingdom are those who challenge my authority to rule. The life of my dearest friend and truest advisor, Piers Gaveston, Earl of Cornwall, has been put in danger. It is these threats from which he must be protected, until a time that misunderstandings can be sufficiently and permanently resolved. In that, I beg your assistance.*
>
> *I offer you a lasting peace, as well as the acknowledgment of the title you have assumed as 'King of Scots'. My conditions are simple: that Lord Gaveston is given refuge in your kingdom, whensoever he shall have need of it. I ask no more in return.*
>
> *If agreed, then I give to you, Lord Robert, the kingdom of Scotland, to whit, freely and forever.*
> *Peace be with you.*
>
> *Edwardus Rex*
> *Given at York*
> *19ᵗʰ of February, 1312"*

"*Give* to me?" I echoed. "When was it ever his to give?"

Gil cracked a smile. "Generous of him."

Laughter bubbled from my throat. Although I tried to construct a serious reply, my amusement poured forth uncontrollably. Gil and Randolph laughed with me. A perplexed David looked from face to face. I clapped him on the shoulder and he responded with a sheepish grin, obviously unable to work out what the joke was. My sides aching, I clutched at my belly to quell my amusement.

"Lord Atholl and I,' Bishop Lamberton broke in, "are commissioned to return with your reply. How exactly are we to word it?"

Clasping the bishop by both arms, I laid my head on his shoulder for a moment. Finally sobering, I thrust him back to arm's length.

"He agreed to banish Lord Gaveston from his realm, did he not?"

Bishop Lamberton nodded.

"And already Gaveston is returned, aye?"

He hesitated. "Lord Gaveston arrived in York to attend the birth of his first child."

"And last I knew, York was still in England—unless they have uprooted every stone and dab of mortar and moved the whole city and its inhabitants to Flanders." I turned to the young Earl of Atholl and poked a finger at his chest. He shuffled back, stiffening against my jab. "Give King Edward this message: How am I to believe even the tiniest utterance of a fickle, *fickle* man who breaks the very oaths that he puts in writing to his own liege men, who themselves have given their homage in good faith? No, I do not trust him. Nor will I ever. Thus, I will never be deceived by him, as his own people have been deceived, time and time"—I thrust my finger so hard he stumbled backward—"and bloody *time* again."

"My lord," Bishop Lamberton said calmly, drawing a hand to the side, "a moment alone . . . please?"

He tucked the letter beneath his fur-lined cloak. Already great smears of ink were bleeding through the parchment and had stained his fingers.

His hand upon my arm, we walked toward the trees. "While I understand your reluctance in this, I think it prudent to consider it more carefully. He is offering a truce and to acknowledge you as King of Scots, surely that is worth—"

"He offers naught but lies!" I spun before him, halting him. "Your pardon, your grace, I do not mean to slough off your advice, but I know it in my heart that I am right in this. A man is to be measured by his actions alone. Words only convey intent if one's behaviors prove them so. To expect King Edward to act differently than he has in the past, to believe that he would uphold his word for any longer a time than what suits his own interests, is to play the fool. I believed his father when he said Scotland's throne would be mine and what did that get me? Nothing but the disdain of my own people. It took me years to prove I was no longer his servant. *Years* of acting as I believed, no matter the price. Not a mere few words spewed out in desperation."

"Then what would it take to make peace with England? Am I to tell him you are declining?" He let out a long sigh, as if to give me time to think on it. "Robert, I have been with you every step, through all your struggles. If not in body, in spirit. When I could not advise you directly, I prayed to God every day to grant you the patience and the wisdom to see your vision realized. Every time word came to me of your exploits—the battles at Brander, Glen Trool and Slioch—I knew that you were the one to question what has always been and bring about change. You inspire courage in others, you are a benevolent leader and a godly man. But your greatest gift is not your tenacity or your bravery, it is mercy. You forgave Thomas Randolph and the Earl of Ross and gave them another chance, when others would have taken their lives out of revenge."

"If you haven't noticed, I haven't the luxury of spare bodies. Every Scotsman dead is one less to fight alongside us. Forgive, rather than punish, and others will join of their own volition—like the wet-eared

Atholl there. But there is a difference between those men and Edward of England, your grace. And it is no small difference, but a very large, very egregious one. I trust I need not explain it to you?"

Looking down, he slid his hands beneath the wide sleeves of his vestments to clasp his forearms. "Remember when you called me to Turnberry? You gave me letters, two of them. You curried favor with both Philip of France and Longshanks . . ." As he raised his eyes to me, his voice took on a very solemn tone. "Because you wished to have Scotland's crown *and* marry Elizabeth. You have the crown now, but your wife, along with your daughter and sisters—they are still in England. The King of England controls their fate. If you forego this offer, however spurious it may seem to you, then you will be no closer to seeing them anytime soon again."

The sleet had turned to rain, slicing at my cheeks like daggers of ice. I felt the chill upon my flesh all the way down to the marrow of my bones. "Relinquish pride for love, you're saying?"

He shook his head at me. "I know it's not as simple as that, Robert."

"Indeed not. Because, you see, if I harbor Edward's beloved Gaveston, I'll have every discontented baron and grasping knight of England on my threshold, upturning every stone and torching every timber to flush him out. What would it matter, then, to have King Edward's word? It would matter not at all. Likely, it would make things even worse for us."

"Robert, I beg you to—"

"Beg, shout, throw yourself on the ground and wail if you want. If he cannot keep his word from one day to the following, why even begin to believe he has anything of lasting honor in him?"

Bishop Lamberton could not respond fast enough. Pulling a hand down over my face and beard, I flung frigid droplets at the ground. "Besides, he said nothing of releasing Elizabeth or Marjorie, did he? My answer stands. I will not parlay on a perjurer."

"What *will* it take then?"

"A document signed by every hand of parliament and"—I turned and began to walk away—"the blessing of the pope!"

"You will not get it, Robert!"

"I know, your grace! I know! But a man can dream."

25

Edward II – Tynemouth, 1312

WHEN LORD DAVID OF Atholl knelt before me in York's bailey and delivered the Bruce's reply, I threatened to remove his head if he ever showed his face before me again. More than a mere refusal, Bruce's words were provocative. Who was he, a murderer and a traitor, to say that *I* could not keep my word? Did he not understand the munificence of my offer and how greatly it stood to benefit us both? God's teeth, he was impossible! Pray I lived to see the day when I could make him pay for this arrogant mistake.

Lancaster, now on the move from London, was amassing considerable numbers. Thus, we went from York to Newcastle to Tynemouth, ever northward. But what good that would do us now I could no longer see. Piers' health went from bad to good to worse, sometimes all within a few days' time. Although my physician could not give a name to his malady, he declared it was not life threatening and said that my beloved Piers simply needed to rest. Small chance of that, wanderers that we were.

Gradually, my unions with Isabella became less gruff and more rehearsed. We were sequestered in the abbot's palace at Tynemouth when—exhausted from our forced travels—I had been with her one night and fallen asleep in her bed. Dawn pried its thin, pink fingers between the shutters. With a groan, Isabella threw back the covers, stumbled weakly across the floor and vomited before she could reach the washbasin on the other side of the room. Afraid that she had contracted Piers' illness, I bolted upright to stare at her, as she retched an ocher stream of bile onto the floor. The bits of rosemary and lavender strewn at her feet did nothing to cover the stink. Finally, she made it the last few steps, poured herself a cup of water to rinse her mouth, and spit into the basin.

"I am late," she uttered groggily, clutching her belly and crawling back into bed.

"Late?"

Amid a ghostly pale face, dark circles rimmed her eyes. She turned her head toward me, golden hair falling across her cheeks and lips. "Our child is the cause of it."

Relief washed over me. *Finally, an heir.* Naked, I rose and went to the window. Nudging open the shutters, I inhaled the faint scent of salt air coming in from the east on a light breeze. May was drawing near. Rain and warmer days had painted the land in lusher tones. Tynemouth was too small to contain all of us for any longer. "The day is perfect for hawking, don't you think?"

"I think I am not well enough to go with you."

I went to her and, gently, so as not to create a wake, I sat on the edge of the bed next to her. "Of course, you should rest. Eat well. Keep my son healthy."

Her eyes narrowed. "Perhaps it is a girl."

"The *next* one can be a girl." I brushed aside a stray tendril of hair from her cheek. Yes, one offspring would not be enough. Sons could fight for me. Daughters could be married off to build alliances at home and abroad. I would need those things in years to come. I more than needed them now. Perhaps this was the beginning of better times, but first—"As soon as Bromtoft says that Piers is well enough to travel again, I will be sending you—"

She clutched my arm fiercely. "No! You cannot send me away. Not now. Not as I am."

"What? You want to keep me near? Since when, good wife?" I gave her hand a squeeze. "Come now, we put up with each other for a purpose and it is, for now, done. You should not be near Piers in your condition. I will not endanger my heir . . . *our* child. And I want you safe, as well. You'll go to York and wait for me there."

"You'll be staying here at Tynemouth then?"

"Heaven knows I am weary of running, but I must take Piers elsewhere. Somewhere I pray they cannot get to him."

"Where?"

I pressed a finger to her lips. "You needn't know. That way, you have nothing to hide. If Lancaster finds you, tell him you are with child. He will not dare touch your pretty head then."

She grabbed my hand, kissed my palm, then slid further beneath the covers and closed her eyes, sighing. "How long before you return to York, Edward? A week? A month? More?"

"I will come as soon as I can." Her lashes fluttered as I kissed her on the forehead, but she did not glance up at me or say anything more. I know not if she believed me, but I truly meant it. She carried my child now and I would not let Lancaster or anyone bring harm upon her. Gathering up my clothes, I dressed and went to the door. I looked at her one last time before leaving. Her chest rose and fell in a peaceful rhythm. Her eyes remained closed.

I found Piers standing at the foot of the stairs, the door behind him gaping open. Although still pallid, he stood unwavering, appearing stronger than he had in many days. Dressed in fine clothes borrowed from me, his fingers worried at the lion pendant dangling from the chain of gold about his neck. There was something of surprise—or was it alarm—expressed in the wideness of his eyes, the slack mouth.

"Brother Perrot!" I held my arms out, ready to embrace him in reassurance as I hurried the last few steps.

He took a step back and braced his hands against the doorframe, shaking his head. "You must come to the priory chancel at once, Edward. There is a messenger."

No need to ask if the news was urgent or grave. I feared I knew it before I heard it. I laid a hand on his shoulder and inclined my head. "Come then. We'll bear this together."

We strode quickly across the open courtyard between the buildings, Piers' breathing labored by the exertion. A Benedictine monk, the front of his black cassock powdered with flour, emerged from the refectory and remarked on the beautiful morning God had blessed us with as we passed. Were he me, he might not say such a mindless thing an hour hence. The morning air was yet crisp, even though the sun was already burning brightly overhead. Gulls glided in slow circles out beyond the sea cliffs, dipping crescent wings to catch the wind. I slowed as we reached the steps to the chancel, wanting to delay the inevitable as long as possible. Then, I dragged my feet up the few steps as the guards flung open the doors and turned to wait for Piers.

His shoulders sagged. His eyes were sunken and his lips bloodless. The sickness had done this to him, I told myself. He would recover.

"Together," I said, extending my hand.

Head down, he trudged up after me. He kept his hands at his sides and, slowly raising his eyes to meet mine, said dolefully, "It will not always be so, Edward."

Bars of golden light pouring in from the tall, lancet windows dissected the expanse of the nave. From somewhere unseen, the sound of chanting drifted. Novices perhaps, learning. The nave was empty, but for a lone monk on his knees in a far corner, washing the tiles with a rag and bucket. I glanced behind me to make certain Piers had followed. He was there, but he had not followed closely, as though the distance would somehow shield him. When I turned back, the messenger had emerged from behind a column and was already on his knee.

"You bring word?" I asked.

His eyes flicked up, then back down. His appearance was that of road-weariness: the flesh beneath his eyes gray from lack of sleep, his hair knotted by the wind and his leggings and short cloak splattered with mud. "The Earl of Lancaster and his army approach on the road from Durham, my lord."

"How far?"

"Not more than four leagues hence by now."

Four leagues? Less than a full day's march. By nightfall, Tynemouth would be surrounded. I raised my face to the ceiling, as if I might find miraculously revealed there some answer amidst the vast expanses that stretched between the vaulted ribs. At the far end of the nave where the altar was, a cloud passed behind the great rosette window, throwing shadows across the openness and a seeping cold dread upon my soul.

"I'll see you are paid well for your service," I told the messenger.

"But there is more, my lord," he said. "The Earl of Lancaster has taken Newcastle."

No! Margaret and her child were still there. I clenched my fists at my sides. "Piers, we must—"

A draft blew in as the door opened and Piers disappeared outside. Abandoning the messenger, I followed Piers and found him on the steps, head in hands. I squatted beside him and pulled him to me, burying my face in his tawny hair.

He clasped my forearm and began to rock on his heels. "It begins."

"What begins?"

A roaring wind and the crash of waves below the cliffs nearly swallowed his words. "Our end."

26

Robert the Bruce – Carrick, 1312

S O MUCH. I ASKED so much of God. Too much for one lifetime.
Although by logic I knew I was justified to refuse King Edward's proviso, it did not lessen the nettle of Bishop Lamberton's reminder that my womenfolk were still being held captive. Not for a moment did I believe that taking Gaveston in would lead to their release. No, there was too much in the way, too far yet to go. It would take an event far greater than some rash bargain meted out in secret.

This year Marjorie would turn sixteen. Dear God, *sixteen*. No longer a child. A woman. Would I recognize her if she stood before me? Aye, I would. She would be her mother's very likeness. She always had been. Barely old enough to speak when I sent her to Rothesay for safety, Elizabeth had quickly become the mother she had never known or had.

Elizabeth, my wife, my beloved . . . Why did I find it so hard anymore to conjure her face in my mind? Remember the shade of her hair? The softness of her skin beneath my roving hands? Ever since Dalry, I had been plagued by guilt. Guilt that I had not protected her, better seen to her safety, sent her to Ireland when I should have. Regret now filled her absence, not fond memories. I had nearly lost those, too. It was all so long ago. And who knew how much longer lay ahead of me?

As we rode from Selkirk Forest, I led my men not north to the Highlands, but west. Toward Carrick.

Castle Loch Doon squatted on an islet above dark waters that mirrored a glowering sky. Eleven-sided, it was nearly round and there was barely room on the stony shores at the foot of its walls on which to land a boat. Shortly after our defeat at Methven and subsequent exodus, the castle had fallen into English hands. From between the crests of two hills, we studied the fortress, saw their sentries patrolling its walls and continued on our way. Through the burnished hills and dense forests. Spreading word as we went to gather in Ayr come July. The time to do more had come. England stood on the brink of civil war. King Edward could not defend two fronts at once. And we would need to be ready.

A fortnight after meeting Lamberton and young Atholl in Selkirk Forest, we were camped between the Rivers Ayr and Nith. The first greening of spring tinged the banks of the streams where violets shyly opened their petals. Some of the cattle had already been driven north and east to augment herds depleted by the plundering English army. Most, though, we kept to feed our burgeoning army for the coming months. Food, for awhile, was plentiful and we were grateful for it.

Evening shadows reached through the pines, thinning strands of amber sunlight broken by columns of darkness. Ten paces from my tent, a cow's carcass hung from a thick rope tied to a stout limb, the last of its blood dripping onto a mat of pine needles below. Beyond it in a small clearing, yesterday's slaughter was boiling in its own hide. The wood still damp from recent rains, white smoke billowed through the camp. Around smaller fires, bannocks cooked in iron plates while men mended clothes or scoured the rust from weapons.

The smell of stewed meat filled my nose. I drifted toward the cauldron of cowhide. Lumps of meat and organs bubbled to the surface. At the sight of me, the cook dunked a long ladle into the broth and spooned the contents into a wooden bowl. A jostling line quickly formed behind him. After barking at those up front to make way, Boyd snatched the bowl from the cook before anyone else could lay claim to it and approached me.

He made a flourish with his free hand and bowed low. "Fine Northumbrian beef, my lord."

I took it from him and sank to my haunches, cupping the warm bowl beneath my chin to inhale its aroma. With my knife, I speared a hunk of grizzled meat and popped it into my mouth. Its juices bathed my tongue, the fibers melting away as I ground my teeth together. The first morsel slid warm down my throat. Before I knew it, I had nothing left but broth, its surface pearled with shimmering droplets of fat.

I tipped my head back and drank until it was empty.

"More?" he asked.

"No, let the others eat first." I spat, my eyes watering as a cloud of smoke rolled across my vision, then dispersed. Beyond it was a small party on foot being escorted amongst the scattered bedrolls and tethered horses. One was a woman. Even from a distance in the waning light, shrouded in smoke, and clad in common rags, I knew her.

A small ray of joy burst free in my heart. The bowl still clutched in my hand, I stood and rushed toward her. I shoved the bowl at a nearby soldier, who clasped it greedily. Three men were with her: an elderly monk and two lightly armed men, protected only by leather jerkins checkered by age.

"Aithne of Carrick, welcome!" As I reached out to embrace her, she stumbled forward and drooped into my waiting arms. Beneath my calloused fingers, I felt the depressions between each rib, even the ridge of her spine against my forearm. "You've seen better days, my lady. Have you been ill?"

"No," she murmured. Brushing chilled lips against my cheek, she steadied herself on wobbly legs. The look in her eyes was so dull, her visage so pale that I was hardly convinced.

"Pray tell then, what brings you to seek out rabble such as this?"

She readjusted the hood of her patched cloak about her shoulders.

Her coppery hair—once a glorious mane—hung snarled and dull around her face.

"Food," she said hollowly.

"Come with me then." I thought she might protest when I swept her up in my arms, but instead she laid her head against me and closed her eyes. As I carried her to my tent, I ordered Boyd to make sure her companions were fed and to bring us two heaping bowls of stew and whatever else of sustenance he could find. Heads turned as I strode by, this worn but no less beautiful woman cradled against my chest.

I pushed through the tent flap and laid her down on a pile of furs. For a long time, I gazed down upon her, strange feelings of compassion and regret warring inside me. And stirrings of something pleasant, comforting, powerful. There was a time when I could have bedded her three times a day and never wearied of her. When I told my father I was in love with her, he hastily gave her away in marriage to Sir Gilbert de Carrick, to whom he had recently granted the stewardship of Castle Loch Doon. I had never quite forgiven him for that, but my love, or rather lust, for her died when my brother Edward took her as a lover. At least I thought it had. But where I had known a brief happiness before losing my first wife Isabella in childbed, Aithne's union had been an unsuitable one. Sir Gilbert was two decades older than her, taciturn, and a zealot who punished her if she did not pray often enough. Aithne was the wild rose in bloom, a bewitching nymph of hedonism, and he the splintered stump of an old crucifix.

Boyd arrived with two heaping bowls of stew and a half loaf of coarse bread. He set them down, scuttled out and quickly reappeared with two rare cups of ale. His eyes swept over her and he smiled broadly, his tongue working in and out between the gaps in his teeth. I waved him outside before he made some lecherous remark that she might overhear. Crouching down beside her, I ran the backs of my fingers over her cold cheek. She inhaled deeply. Her eyelids fluttered open.

Sighing, she pushed herself up, her back hunched forward, hair

hanging in long, wind-tangled strands over her breast. Her fingers fumbled at the clasp of her cloak and I almost reached out to help her, but
before I did she had slid the cloak, smelling of musty wool, off and
pushed it aside.

"You should have come to me sooner." I handed her a cup of ale.

"And where would I have found you, my lord? In Strathearn,
Badenoch, Galloway, across the border . . . or maybe in Garmoran?"
Aithne raised the cup to her mouth and tipped it up. A sip became a
guzzle as she drained the golden liquid. When she lowered the cup
again, a smile played across her glistening lips. "Besides, my husband
gave Loch Doon over to the English. I did not figure I was much welcome in your circle. I only came to you before, because—"

"You were always welcome. What Sir Gilbert did was not your
doing. Besides, he's long gone. I'd have thought you married again by
now." It was no more than a passing remark, but before she could make
anything of it, I added, "Where have you been?"

"Wherever my kinfolk would have me. But as you know, my family
has little money. None at all now, actually. Twice my parents' home has
been burned to the ground. After my father died, my brother began to
rebuild it, but he gave up the last time your men set fire to his crops. He
lost an entire harvest."

"If we had not, the English would have taken it to feed their army
and gone further north."

"Perhaps," she said with a shrug.

"And where is he now—your brother?"

She drank some more and drew a fur up around her. "Tending
sheep on Arran with my son."

"Then who is with you?"

"One is a cousin by marriage, the other his uncle."

"And the monk?"

"He joined us on the road. Gave us a loaf of bread for our company . . . and protection." Steam curled up from the bowl of stew. She

dipped her fingers carefully into it and plucked out a piece of meat.

"My brother Edward is on his way to Lothian and then north," I blurted out. "Trying to gather others to convene in Ayr."

Lowering her cup, she tilted her head at me. "I did not come here to see Edward."

An uneasy silence settled between us. I dared not breach it. The last time she sought me out, the news had been grave, unbearable. Outside, the rumble of conversation filled the air. The scent of smoke clung to every surface. I sat down next to her, although not too close. It seemed easier not to meet her eyes. At last, she picked up the meat and put it in her mouth, chewing slowly, as if to delay our conversation.

"Then why did you—aside from needing something to eat?"

Her teeth worked at the tough meat, until finally, she swallowed. "To see you," she said without looking up. Aithne dunked her fingers into the bowl again and stuffed her mouth greedily. Then she tore off a big hunk of bread and dipped it into the broth to suck up the meaty juices. "Times have been . . . hard, since my husband's death. For awhile, my family was able to survive off our lands. But too much rain one year, not enough the next, one too many raids and we have nothing left. No home, no byre. Nothing. So my brother left with Niall, while I traded work for food and shelter. Born low, I have returned there, it seems."

In all this time I had not given her welfare much thought. Not even after she delivered the news of my family's capture and my brothers' deaths. She had taken it upon herself to bring me word and I had not even thanked her. Worse, I had sent her away, because I did not want Edward fawning over her. I slid an arm beneath the fur. She shifted onto her left hip, her thigh pressed to mine.

Closing my eyes, I pulled her closer. "But you were warm and fed? And your son is safe?"

"Aye, I suppose. I was on my way to Arran when I heard you were nearby. So I came. It has been so long since I had seen you. It made me think of long ago. Of better, sweeter times." Setting the bowl aside, she nestled her head against my shoulder.

When I was sixteen, Aithne had been my first lover. For weeks she had tantalized me, teased me to madness. Returned my hungry kisses as her hand slipped beneath my shirt to stroke my then-bare chest. When once I led her to the cellar, desperate for privacy, she had explored beneath my breeches, touched me—there. Neither of us spoke as our bodies guided us in a primitive dance of desire. Her hands moved wider, rolling down my breeches to expose my swollen cock. I lifted her onto a stack of grain sacks and hitched her skirt up past her knees. And then . . . footsteps pounded on the stairs. Hastily, I yanked my breeches back up over my hips and pulled her forward so that her feet landed on the floor. The cloth of her skirt caught on the sacks. Just as she turned to grab the hem and pull it down, the cook's helper appeared at the bottom of the stairs in time to glimpse her bare buttocks. The spell of youthful lust had been shattered. But the desire had not been quenched. Each time we passed one another it burned brighter, our appetites whetted. Less than a week later, I met her in the stables at midnight and there, on a bed of fresh hay, we made love—wild, exhilarating love. I hardly cared about the prospect of burning in hell for fornication. The moment I discovered heaven within her, I had not cared what might happen to me after that.

As if she shared my memories, Aithne turned her face toward mine. Even in the growing darkness of night, I saw in her eyes the young woman, carefree and uninhibited. I wound a strand of her hair around my finger, grazed her neck with my fingertips as I did so. My hand trailed downward over her collarbone, to her breastbone. When I found the top button of her gown, a shiver rippled through her. She reached up and released the button, then the second and the third. I expected another garment beneath, but instead, her breasts were bare: two plump orbs, soft and inviting.

Slowly, I lowered her, turning so that I faced her. She gazed up at me and stretched her left arm above her head, inviting me to lie beside her. And I did.

Her fingers wandered over my face to brush the rough whiskers beneath my chin, my ear, my temple. My knee slid over her thigh and between her legs. I moved over her, admiring her. Fingers wound in my hair, she pulled my head to her breast. I bent toward her, explored her with kisses. The firm protrusion of a nipple met my lips and I closed my mouth around it, suckling gently as I cupped a hand around the fleshy cushion of her breast. Her legs strained outward, hands now grasping for her skirts. She nudged me to the side and, as I rolled reluctantly from her, she flipped her skirts up across her waist in one smooth motion.

"Aithne," I whispered, "you are so very beautiful."

"Still?" she murmured dreamily.

I pulled my shirt off to toss it aside and positioned myself over her again. As if time had never passed since we were flung apart, as if we had never stopped knowing one another, she tugged at the cord on my breeches and slipped her thumbs beneath the top, sliding them downward. Her hips bridged upward, ready.

"More than ever," I said, running a hand from her milky thigh to the full curve of her hips.

"Be my love, Robert. Let me give to you."

I eased into her, pleasure surging from my loins to envelope me.

Ahhh, Sweet Mother of God. How long has it been since—

She grasped my buttocks, pulling me deeper inside. A moan rose in her throat and I covered her mouth with mine to quiet her. *If anyone hears us . . .*

My rhythm quickened. Her folds, warm and slippery. My blood, rushing. Her body an eddy beneath mine. I probed my tongue deeper into her mouth, faster, in echo. Sweat poured down my chest, dripped from my lowest rib.

Outside, footsteps. The soft clop of hooves over drying mud.

My hips slammed her hard, yearning for ecstasy. I thrust in mounting excitement, searching for that plateau of rapture that was always in the next moment. Quicker. Deeper. Her legs went around me, her ankles twining together. Her fingernails dug into my back. Aye. Again and again. Almost there. I grunted as I drove toward release.

Voices. Closer . . . Randolph?

'I would never dishonor my own wife so.'

I stopped in mid-thrust, straining to listen above Aithne's rapid panting and my own. Her mouth wide in mounting rapture, she continued to rock beneath me. *Oh God, dear God, how I wanted to—*

The stomp of footsteps.

"Ah no, nothing serious," Boyd said. "A batch of bad ale."

My heart pounded in my ears. I ripped myself from Aithne.

She gasped, reached for me. "No, please nooo . . ."

I clamped a hand over her mouth to shush her.

Boyd cleared his throat. "Nasty stuff. I, uh, would not disturb him, unless you fancy a fist to your jaw. He puked his meal into his lap. Not a pretty sight. Rather embarrassing for a king. Best to let him sleep until morning."

"It can wait, I reckon," Randolph said. "But he'll be glad to hear the numbers. Seventy from Buchan alone."

"That's good, aye." Boyd lowered his voice to a soft rumble. "Come along. There's a bit of stew left, not the best of it, but . . ."

Their words drifted off as they walked away.

I flopped over on my back, my breeches yet halfway down my legs, the evidence of my desire now flagging.

"Robert?" Aithne whispered. Her hand groped for my organ, fingers gently kneading, coaxing, until the blood began to gather there again. "Do you remember, when we were young? How we—"

"No, Aithne." I gripped her wrist, moved her hand away. I had let it happen again. And I had not stopped myself. After pulling my breeches up, I rummaged for my shirt and put it back on. "That was long ago. We are not young anymore. I . . . I have a wife."

She pushed herself up. "But *I* gave you a son."

A son? I tugged the hem of my garment down, fingering a loose thread as I groped for a tactful response. In the end, nothing came to me. "What do you mean?"

Her skirts rustled in the darkness as she rearranged her clothes. "Why do you think your father married me off so quickly? Sir Gilbert was twice widowed, with no heir. Your father agreed to give Loch Doon to him if he claimed the child as his own. He kept his word until his death."

When I went to Perth that year with my grandfather and returned to find her gone, I had not asked the details. Some time passed before I learned of her marriage and Niall's birth. His age made it possible, except . . . "But Edward. You were together."

"Not then. You only assumed so. That happened much later. Gilbert—he couldn't . . . be aroused. He blamed me, called me 'impure', beat me for my sins. Edward gave me comfort. Made me feel desirable. It began innocently."

As Edward would have her think. And when he had won her trust, he bedded her and went away, returning from time to time to satisfy himself, while he mounted a dozen other willing women in between.

But I did not want to talk or think about Edward. At times, my resentment of him far outweighed any appreciation I held for him. I stepped into my leggings, pulled them up and belted them, then squatted down before her. "I would give you Loch Doon if I could, but I—"

"I didn't come here so that you could promise me a castle to keep me quiet. I came to tell you that you had a son. I thought you should know, Robert. That's all. And what happened, just now, that wasn't planned, either." Gathering her cloak, she stood and made for the tent flap. Without thinking, I grabbed her skirt and pulled her down. She tumbled backward, her rump hitting the furs with a soft thud.

"Stay," I told her. "As long as you like. When . . . if you decide to leave for Arran, I can arrange a small amount of money."

"I told you, I didn't come here—"

"Take the money, Aithne. The lad needs to eat, does he not?" Her jaw clamped tight, she swung her head away. I cupped her cheek and turned her face back to me. "Besides, my son's mother should not be starving or wanting for clothes or shelter. *Take* the money." I stroked her chin and neck, fighting hard not to lay a kiss upon those full lips and lose myself again. Aye, it felt like betrayal to admit it, but I still loved her—perhaps even more now, knowing her strength—but it could not be. Ever. "Sleep here. You'll be warm. I'll have more food brought to you in the morning."

I shared a tent that night with Boyd, although I slept not at all. In part because of his snores, but also because my conscience was again troubled. More than once, I had put Elizabeth from my mind in favor of another, simply because they were there and she was not. Miles and months, months that turn into years, have a way of making a man forget what it was about one woman that ever made him love her so much.

Morning found Aithne gone again. This time not by my command, but of her own accord.

And I was left alone with my shame.

27

Edward II – Scarborough, May, 1312

FOR TWO DAYS AFTER taking ship from Tynemouth, a southerly gale thrashed us about on spuming waves, nudging us so far northward we might as well have sailed for Scotland. On the third day, the wind relented and shifted to blow more gently from the west. Reinvigorated by the reprieve, the crew swiftly changed tack and we headed east, then gradually south, until we finally careened into the placid waters of Scarborough's harbor. A five day voyage that should have taken no more than two.

As it had been all my life, Fate was conspiring against me.

Scarborough Castle was situated on a finger of land that curled out into the bay. The only means of access was through the gates of a stout barbican on an adjoining promontory and across a drawbridge that spanned a deep ravine. The fortress was deemed impregnable. Which left only one means by which an enemy could take it: siege.

We had arrived without forewarning. Fed by a natural spring, the well was deep and untainted, but a cursory tally of victuals in the storerooms showed them to be inadequate to hold out for any length. And the garrison was woefully undermanned.

Trapped here now, we were merely buying time. Delaying death, as it were. In heaven—or hell, wherever he was—my sire was shaking his finger at me. He had never expected anything more of me than failure. Just as well. I had never inclined toward triumph and glory. My birthright had cursed me with the burden of power, made me an object of blame. My only wish for wanting to be king was so that I could fashion my own destiny, live my own peace. Not spend my life fighting battles I did not want or choose. Oh why could I not have been born a peasant?

I stumbled from the stairway out onto the fourth floor of Scarborough's square keep. The sights beyond the open, arched windows set my head to spinning. Perched on sheer, inexorable cliffs three hundred feet above the bay, for two centuries the fortress had absorbed the battering force of the sea's assault: the wind always there, always merciless. On that day—that fearsome, fateful day—a mocking gale slashed at my cheekbones, ripped at my cloak, and yanked the breath from my lungs.

Last night I had slept as if shrouded in the mantle of Death; but dawn had struck me with a fist of panic that hammered the breath from my lungs and left me gasping for air. Daylong, I had paced and fretted, doom gnawing at my innards like ship rats at a sack of grain. When the messenger arrived with the news, an odd, sickening calm overtook me. The inevitable was upon us.

With the faint brush of a feather, hope would perish over the precipice's edge.

A deep, gulping breath sounded behind me. I spun around, fingers flying to the hilt of my sword. In the darkest of the shadows, a form slumped shapelessly against the wall in the corner. Cloth rustled.

"He's coming, isn't he?" Piers croaked as he slid to the floor. The stones caught at his cloak, bunching it about his neck and shoulders.

I unclenched my fingers from around my hilt. "I received word this morning. Lancaster is no more than a few days away. His numbers are . . . considerable."

"Has no one tried to stop him?"

"No."

Piers slammed his head back against the crumpled pillow of his cloak. "The Bruce, then? You made an offer of peace?"

"I did."

"Did he reply? Surely, he did not refuse?"

A gull flapped at the window's ledge, squawking in complaint before it took to flight again. The Bruce's reply had reached me weeks ago, although I refrained from telling Piers of it then. "I went beyond extending peace terms. I acquiesced to call him 'King of Scots', if he would but keep you safe. He said he could not trust my word—as if *his* had any value. After six years of clamoring for his laurels, the ingrate has rebuffed me."

Piers' hands, coated in grime, crept up to cover his face, scraping over week-old stubble and rubbing at eyes red with wretchedness. He let out a strained whimper. On his neck, a line of nail marks raked downward to stand out against blanched skin.

This was not the Piers I knew, that brazen champion of tournaments, the reckless hunter, the merry reveler of song and drink, keen in wit, sharp of tongue, as lissome sober as he was drenched drunk . . . the one who held me close in familiar silence, long after we had exhausted ourselves in sensual delight. This, this was some apparition, some skeletal wraith plucked from the bowels of purgatory.

A gust of wind tousled my hair, obscuring my vision, but I had no will to tuck it back or even to turn my face. Even for so small a thing, the fight had left me. "I'm leaving for York. The queen is to meet me there. There are—"

"When?" He thrust himself away from the wall, eyes wild with terror. "I'm coming with you!"

"You can't, Piers. Shouldn't. If I leave here, there's every chance that Lancaster will follow. Even if he takes me—"

"No!" He swung about and slammed a palm against the wall with a thunderous crack. Fingers clawing at the stones, jaw quivering, he wailed, "No! Dear *God*, no. He'll kill us both and make himself king.

Don't you see?"

"He can be king, if it means he'll leave us in peace."

Piers turned slowly toward me, his head cocked in question. "How could you let it come to this, Edward? Why have you not done more for me? Kept this from happening?"

How? Clenching my fists at my sides, I reeled away. It was desperation that made him speak thus. What else could it have been? With heavy steps, I went to the far window and gazed out at the neck of the headland on which the barbican squatted. There may have been gates and drawbridges enough to repel an attack, but all Lancaster had to do was encamp his army along the road from the mainland and we were trapped like hares in the hole.

A wave of dizziness swept over me. I gripped the stones to steady myself. "I have done everything but pluck the moon from the sky and give it to you on a plate of gold—and gold aplenty I have given you. Three times I have called you back to me when they said you could not come, all at my own peril. What more *could* I have done?"

Footsteps rushed at me from behind. Far below, the bailey loomed. I braced my legs, and began to turn, one elbow flying back in defense. But instead of a shove, he hooked my arm and yanked me into the shadows with such suddenness that my breath caught. His hands flew up to lock around my face like a vise, squeezing my cheekbones, holding my jaw fixed. Cold. His hands were cold. His eyes, overflowing with sorrow.

"It *is* the end for us," he whispered. "I see it now more clearly than the sun above, feel it more firmly than the ground beneath my feet. But what a sweet life it has been, yes? Full of adventure. Laughter. Danger. Heartache . . . Paradise, rapturous, heavenly paradise." He stroked my cheek. Trailed shaking fingers around my ear, down my neck. "With every breath, every bone, every drop of blood, I have loved you, Edward. Damn them for ruining what we have shared, but more's the pity that they will never know such purity of love themselves."

I sucked in the cool, salty air, held it in my lungs, clasped my hand against his, still pressed to my cheek. "I'll give up my crown, if they—"

His lips silenced mine with a kiss, our breaths one. He leaned his forehead against mine. "What a stupid . . . *stupid* thing to say. If you give them that, how will you ever have the means to get back at them?"

Boots clacked on the curtain wall-walk somewhere. With a jerk, he drew back, stepped away. Soon, the sound of gathering hooves rang out on the cobbles of the bailey.

"To York, Edward. Fly fast."

"Swear that you will not yield to him."

"God's balls, do you think me so weak of will? Very well, I swear it. Now go. Godspeed and all that trifling midden. Just be certain that when you come back, you bring an army so big that Lancaster will piss himself and shed tears of fright on your feet as he kisses them."

My tongue was so thick and dry that I could not form the words I meant to say. He knew I loved him, more than my own worthless life, more than this prickly crown I had been born unto with all its accursed troubles. I had told him so a thousand times.

If I did not go from there, I was sure the earth would open up and swallow me. Forcing my feet to move, I walked away. I had to save him. Had to try.

28

Edward II – York, 1312

Reunited with Isabella in York, I quickly found myself severed from Scarborough by Lancaster's army. Pembroke and Warwick had descended on Scarborough and laid siege to it. I never thought to hear Pembroke's name among the wicked, but it was so. For ten days Piers held out, while I issued orders that they cease in their assault. I even offered to sit down with them, as brothers, and arrange a compromise. But all my pleas were ignored. Finally, Pembroke made a solemn promise that Piers would be permitted to see me before the convening of parliament and that he would be given a fair trial. Piers agreed.

What a *fool* he was! He may as well have delivered himself into the very Devil's hands. What good trying to save him, when he would not save himself?

When they sent their messengers to tell me of the deed, I was promptly reminded that any attempt to invoke war in my defense would open the door for the Scots to pour down upon us and inflict chaos and ruin. Yet if what Lancaster and his evil ilk had already done was not civil war, then what was it? Powerless, I could do nothing but plead for help. I prayed that Pembroke would honor his word and thus afford me time.

But in the end no one would come to my aid. Not a living soul. Not the pope. Not the King of France. And not my people. I was their king and yet . . . a pariah.

The scent of rain lingered in the air that June day. Clouds scraped the distant hills, the hollow roar of thunder echoing over the moors. From the highest window of the King's Tower, I gazed down upon York. People straggled over the mired streets like beetles amid the mud flats, hawked their wares from crowded stalls, and waited their turn at the city gates before passing through. A gust of wind carried the perpetual stench of sheep manure. My gaze passed over the verdant fields dotted with white beyond the city's walls and along the southern road.

There, a small group of riders, perhaps ten men, advanced swiftly. My heart hammered at the sight. The sun, which had not shone for three days, broke through a bank of clouds to the west and glinted off their plate armor. Cloaks heavy with rain hung from their shoulders, but before them a bright pennon occasionally lifted with the breeze. The colors were those of my nephew, Gilbert de Clare, Earl of Gloucester.

I withdrew from the window. My back against the wall, I pressed my palms flat against the stones.

Sitting on a padded stool at the other window, Isabella looked up from the book resting on the slight mound of her belly: a copy of a romance by Chrétien de Troyes, the leather straps of its spine loose from wear. She drew her finger from the page, marked it with a red silk ribbon and set the book on the floor. "Edward, what is it?"

"Gilbert is coming." Dare I to dream that some miracle had begun to play itself out whilst I rotted in this cloistered wasteland, robbed of hope? Surely, if they meant to force me to yet more impossible terms, it would have been Lancaster or one of his Hell Hounds bearing down upon me now, not my staunch companion and kinsman Gilbert?

For once, let the tidings be good. Merciful Lord, end this interminable agony. Let it be done.

Arms outstretched, Isabella started toward me, but I held a hand

up to stay her. The minutes dragged by like days spent imprisoned and
awaiting death. Eyes shut tight, breath held, I touched a shaking hand to
my abdomen, searching for some indication, some presentiment, of
what was to come. But I felt nothing. Nothing but an absence of what
once was.

A rap at the door stilled my heart momentarily. My hand flew to
the knife sheathed at my belt. Another knock and my heart began with a
thud, each pulse of blood slower and heavier than the one before. Jankin nudged open the door. Gilbert shoved his way past my manservant
and then came . . . the Earl of Pembroke, Aymer de Valance. In one
heartbeat, my dread turned to malice.

*How could you . . . you, of all those once faithful to me, join with them? For
your own sake, Aymer, I pray you did this to circumvent an even greater tragedy,
that somehow you will now redeem yourself.*

Pembroke doffed his mail hood, his black hair matted with sweat,
and tossed it to Jankin before bending a knee to me. Jankin scuttled out,
leaving the door open a crack.

"Why are *you* here?" I demanded of Pembroke, my voice clogged
with enmity. The urge to hurl myself at him to tear the flesh from his
bones with my bare hands was almost overwhelming. My fingernails
scraped at mortar, seeking anchor. "Tell me that you have set Piers free.
That he awaits me somewhere secreted. Or, at the very least, that he is
safe at Wallingford, as agreed."

Shifting on his feet, Gilbert glanced at Pembroke, who had not yet
raised his eyes. They were but shadows of omen beneath his Moorish-
dark brows. He stood, one hand flexing around empty air. His mouth
opened, but no answer came from it.

"Tell me what has happened to him, Aymer," I said. "Look at me,
damn you! Say what has become of him!"

He drew breath, pulled his shoulders back and slowly looked up.
"My king, I will not discuss matters of politics now, but it was better, I
reasoned, to join with them and temper Lancaster's fury, than allow it to

blaze untended. When I learned of Gaveston's whereabouts, I insisted on being the one to lead the siege. As you know, he gave himself freely unto my custody at Scarborough. I assure you, I am a man of my word and have never—"

"Already you feel the need to excuse yourself? This bodes ill of your involvement, Aymer, whatever it is. Get on with it. Tell me the truth, the pith of it."

He jerked his chin up. His cheeks and neck, usually neatly shaven, were shadowed by black stubble. "I had pressed the journey, wanting to place Lord Gaveston securely at Wallingford as soon as possible. We were near Deddington when he begged for rest. Early that evening, I complied and left him under guard at the church there, and went to nearby Bampton to see my wife. I swear—I did not know that Guy de Beauchamp, Earl of Warwick, had been following us closely." He glanced at Isabella, as if he had not noticed her before. Perhaps he hadn't. "At Warwick, Beauchamp was joined by Hereford and Lancaster. While they conspired, Gaveston was dragged from his bed at midnight and led to a place called Blacklow Hill, where he was . . . was executed."

"No, no . . . tell me that is a lie," I insisted. "They have sent him away again. That is all."

Haltingly, Pembroke approached me and extended a gilt chain. At its end dangled the lion pendant, eyes as red as blood. With a trembling hand, I took it from him. It was indeed the pendant I had given Piers at Dover. But it was heavier than I recalled, its surface scuffed from years of wear and the facets of the jewels dulled with a fine layer of dirt.

A chill gripped my spine and flushed the breath from my lungs with a forceful suddenness. "H-h-how?"

"Not by a traitor's rope, but by the sword. It is small consolation, I know, but the end came quickly for him."

Quickly? He would have been stricken with terror as his black-hooded executioner forced his head down upon some weathered tree stump, flinched as the mortal whisper of the sword descended. I wrapped my arms around myself and slid to the floor, the stones snagging at my clothes.

"Edward?" Gilbert's voice came to me as if muffled by a heavy rain. I glanced at the window, but the sun poured through harsh and hot. Feet shuffled. I looked up at Gilbert, who stood leaning forward before me, wringing his hands. He shook his head solemnly. "Edward, it is true. His body has been returned to Gloucester, though they could not give him a Christian burial. Lords Pembroke and Warenne came to me at once, irate at what Lancaster had done. They are guilty of nothing more than passing carelessness. They are not to—"

"Passing carelessness? Had they not been so careless, so . . . so bloody *incompetent*"—rising again to my feet, I swayed on watery knees—the pendant clenched so tightly in my left hand it pierced my palm—and threw a hand to the wall to steady myself—"then Piers would not be *dead*—if he indeed is. Oh, but you would want him dead, every one of you. You conjured falsities and embellished on every misstep he or I ever made, while you rallied against us to raise yourselves up. Upon God's soul, this is a grievous happening: for Piers, for me, for all of England. How can you, Gilbert, stand in league with these warring demons? Piers swore to me he would not surrender, that he would wait for me to return. He was unwitting, for he trusted Lord Pembroke to keep him safe. But Pembroke failed—or turned a blind eye while—"

"I swear to you," Pembroke interrupted, striding past Isabella and coming toward me, "I knew nothing of their plans!"

"Who *am* I to trust?! Should I trust you now, just as Piers did?" I shoved Pembroke away and rounded on Gilbert. "You all lie to me. You always have, like it is some perpetual joke you all take part in. You betray me and abandon me and leave me with nothing. Nothing! Now go from here—both of you!" I drew my knife and slashed at the air. Gilbert stumbled backward, bumping Pembroke's shoulder. The jeweled hilt lay rough in my uncalloused grip. "Go—or I will kill two more people I thought I once loved. Piers is already dead. The two of you are nothing to me anymore. Dead would make no difference, nor the fate of my condemned soul."

Pembroke grabbed Gilbert by the arm then and pulled him from the room. He knew when to claim his exit and save his own life.

Alone with Isabella, I lowered the knife, my hand trembling so violently I fought not to drop it. This time, she did not widen her arms to embrace me, but waited, her head down, fingers laced together beneath her rounded middle. Slipping the knife back into its sheath, I went to the window and lay my hands flat upon the ledge. The pendant fell to the floor, but I made no effort to retrieve it. "Go, Isabella. There is nothing you or anyone can do for me now."

Several moments passed and I heard neither movement nor response. Finally, her slippered feet brushed over the planks of the floor. The door latch clicked and without looking I knew I was alone now. I braced my hands on either side of the window and climbed up to stand on the ledge. My legs threatened to fold beneath me. The buildings of York, the scattered clouds, and the hills beyond tipped dizzily and blurred together. It would have been so easy to cast myself upon the courtyard stones, far below. I wanted to. For a long, long time, I contemplated it. What point in remaining here, to live as a lamb among hungering wolves? What point to live at all? One step forward, one slight lean, and I would suffer no more. Then, Piers and I could be together forever. Never again parted.

Lifting my head, I uncurled my fingers from the window's edge and drew one more breath. One final pull of this life's essence, this life's pain. I closed my eyes to the world, the fire of the sun burning my face, the wind beckoning.

No, my death would give them too much satisfaction. Pembroke would be free of his guilt. Lancaster would snatch the crown from my brothers and my unborn child. Bruce would run rampant in his heathen glee. And my sire . . . If I killed myself I would only prove the hateful bastard right.

Revenge must be my reason to go on living. Paradise must wait.

On my life and my crown, I will avenge thee, my beloved Brother Perrot. When the truth is out, the guilty will pay. And all their family and supporters will go down with them in pools of blood and burning flesh.

I opened my eyes to see a small crowd gathering in the courtyard below, faces upturned and mouths agape. Their voices buzzed faintly like hornets gathering at the nest. Sinners, all of them. "What sickness lives in the world, Piers. Our transgressions were trivial compared to what they have done to you and me. Oh, how they have judged and scorned us. They may condemn us for the physical act from now until eternity if they please, but you were right. It is the depth of our love they have failed to understand—for I will always, *always* love you, much to my own ruin. The pity of it, eh?"

I spit out over the ledge and stepped back inside. Then, I lay down, my cheek to the floor, my fingers stroking the pendant, and wept until my eyes were sore and dry of sorrow.

ON THE 12TH OF November, Queen Isabella delivered a healthy son. We named him Edward, so that long after I was gone my own flesh and my own name would remain to rule over those who had so viciously defied me.

Pembroke groveled as much as he could bring himself to do. Still swallowed by grief, I bided my time. If Lancaster and Warwick meant to bring me down, their act only served to soften public opinion toward my plight. With the arrival of my heir, their star was falling toward earth in ashes.

29

Robert the Bruce – Perth, 1313

SEVEN YEARS HAD LAPSED since I was crowned at Scone. Still the English held several key castles. With the money now to feed our troops and arm them, our tactics were soon to change. By siege or stealth, we would gain those fortresses back and make sure the English never took them again.

Leaving Randolph to surround Perth and starve them out, James and I rode on to Berwick. In the pale starlight of a December night, we stole upon its walls and with our spears raised two hemp ladders. Berwick had a special meaning to James, being the place where he first glimpsed Longshanks' savagery and saw his father fall a prisoner into the English king's hands. What a splendid prize that would have been, but a dog wandering loose beyond the castle barked as we hooked the top of our hemp ladder over the wall. In less than a minute, barely enough time for us to run beyond bowshot, the entire garrison was on the ramparts. Our plan was thwarted.

Since we could not snatch Berwick up, we wore away at Perth. James and I returned there to join Gil and Randolph. For six tedious weeks, we sat outside its walls, alternately freezing near to death under piles of snow or drowning in endless deluges of rain. Daylight was fleeting and so dicing by campfire was the most popular form of entertainment, seconded only by the scraping of mud from boots and the wringing out of cloaks. Little happened but that we traded volleys of arrows and insults with the English garrison. This time, at least, the Earl of Pembroke was not inside, but Sir William Oliphant who had once held out at Stirling while Longshanks mercilessly pummeled its walls with his great siege engines. Years in prison had convinced him be was better off fighting for England than dead.

I paced the stubbled cornfield between our encampment and Perth's towered walls. I had called together several of my men to consult—Alexander Lindsay, Gil, Boyd, James and Randolph. On three sides, Perth was protected by a deep moat and on the other by the River Tay. As I pounded a gauntleted fist in my palm, a crowd of starlings shot up and settled further away, protesting the disturbance. I turned to Randolph.

"Do they weaken?" I asked. "Any sign?"

"I don't think so." Randolph narrowed his blue eyes as he looked out over the sheen of drifted snow lying across the field. A weak afternoon sun struggled behind racing clouds that had begun to spit out more snow. "All is quiet inside. Normal, but for the seclusion. No word comes out. None has gone in."

"The church bells of St. John's toll the hours daily," Lindsay observed, "children play, people go about what business they can, and the roosters herald every blessed morn."

Boyd yawned enormously and swayed in his boots. He'd been in charge of the nightwatch, as I was taking no more chances like I had at Methven. Rousing him had earned me a stream of curses. Fortunately for us all, his drowsiness was returning and he was less bellicose than an hour ago. He thumped his chest and belched. "The roosters go first, you know. If they haven't slaughtered the chickens yet, they've stores enough to keep them awhile. I say in Perth they're still collecting eggs and drinking fine ale. With roofs over their heads, they'll last longer than we will. My feet are rotting in my boots, when they aren't frozen to them."

Gil blew a sore-crusted nose. His eyes were red from a cold he could not shake. "Aye, it's a miracle we don't have more down from sickness."

"When spring comes," James added, "the English will send more men into the Lowlands and elsewhere. We can't all be huddled here then. And our Highlanders won't sit about in this muck poking at their fires much longer. They want to fight."

"Aye, and they have been. I quashed two brawls this morning," Boyd grumbled, leaning against Lindsay's solid arm as he let go of a yawn. "They'll draw knives on each other shortly if you don't give them English throats to slice."

I pulled bits of ice from my beard. "Well, my good men, we can't outlast them and given that we've been camped here for six weeks we can't sneak up on them, can we? We lost our chance at Berwick. We can't keep letting the bastards slip away from us like this. We're making a dreadful habit of it. What now? Turn tail and leave?"

They all stood there dumb, their mouths twisting in empty thought, except for James, who stepped quietly toward me. Behind him, the city of tents and cooking fires hummed with monotony. Somewhere a smith was hammering. A drinking song filled the air. A dog barked.

"Aye, leave . . ." James looked at me between long, black lashes that glistened with snowflakes. A mischievous smile tugged at the corners of his mouth. "Draw all our men away. Let them relax their guard. Then when they least expect it . . ."

I glanced from James to Randolph, then to Lindsay and Boyd. Gil, staring at the frozen ground, rubbed his fingertips over a cleanly shaven chin.

"The ladders," James added. His eyes sparkled with excitement. "They would have worked at Berwick."

"Whatever would I do without you, my good James?" Cuffing him on the shoulder, I nodded. "Aye, they've wearied of watching us, I wager, and would celebrate to see us gone." I turned toward Perth's bulging ramparts, dotted with lazy archers and clasped my hands behind my back. "James, Thomas . . . give the word to decamp. We've just enough daylight left."

THE ENGLISH GARRISON CHEERED as we departed. A fortunate thing they could not see our slanted grins from their distant promontories.

Eight days later, leaving our horses and the better part of our army behind in our wooded retreat two miles to the west, we crept through the frosted dark toward Perth. Lightly armed in mail shirts and padded jackets, we took only a knife and an axe or sword each. The others, led by Randolph and Boyd, would follow in a short while and wait beyond a wooded hill until we had managed the walls and lifted the castle gate. The wind was rough and bitter and its roar covered the cracking of our footfalls on the crisp blanket of snow.

In the dark of night and cold of deepest winter, we waded through the frozen slime of the moat and raised our ladders.

The first English soldiers who caught sight of us had not enough time to call out or raise their weapons before James put an arrow through their throats. Within the hour, Gil's men had taken the gate. Randolph led his soldiers through and when a blood-red sun reared up in a cloud-scattered sky, Perth was ours.

We let the townspeople, mostly Scots, go free and questioned none of their actions or allegiances. The English garrison was put to the knife. Sir William Oliphant had taken an axe to the jaw and, unable to eat, died ten days later. As Perth was being razed to the ground, I left to join Edward at Dumfries, which was being slowly starved. Since Edward could barely tolerate the boredom, I relieved him from his task so he could go and thwart the train of English supplies being carried over roads to the south. By early February Dumfries was given up by Dugald

MacDowell who was one of the leaders of that same clan that had beaten my brothers Thomas and Alexander in Galloway and handed them over to the English to die.

Angus Og and I sailed from the Ayrshire coast that spring and landed on the Isle of Man where we took Rushen for our own. I had hardly stepped foot back on the mainland at Ayr, when James caught up with me and urged me frantically on to Stirling. In my absence, Edward had been given the duty of laying siege to Stirling, for we had no hope of throwing the English forever from our country if we could not shake them loose in the midlands. They were like a hand clenched on the very heart of the kingdom.

"You'll not like it," James warned me.

When he told me the whole story of the many things that Edward had done . . . the same rage I had felt toward John Comyn consumed me. My brother had proven impetuous once more. Beyond exposing his own fatal flaws, he had put at risk my kingdom, dividing it from within and had gone so far as to invite the enemy to opportunity.

My Lord, your tests of me are infinite. I wonder how many trials I can endure before I fail?

Dumbarton, 1313

AS I SAT IN one of Angus' galleys, watching the shoreline glide by, listening to the rhythmic stroke of oars upon the sea, I turned a thousand thoughts over in my mind. I prayed for tolerance and understanding, searched for some truth or reasoning I may have overlooked, but everything escaped me. The water flashed silver under the searing light of midsummer sun. Fifteen other galleys fanned out behind like a flock of geese. Angus stood at the prow of his ship, as we turned hard into the river from the Firth of Clyde. The sea-wind blew his long, flaming hair across his reddened face, but his eyes stayed intent, reading each landmark. Suddenly, he hooked his arm overhead and the vessel veered sharply to the left. A low rocky strip of shore drew closer. The oars sank and grabbed at the moving water as the wind pushed back. Finally, Angus closed his fingers in a fist. The oars drew up and hung suspended out over the water.

"Dumbarton, sire!" he shouted, even though I was not ten feet away. Then more quietly, but with a facetious tone, "And your loving brother is already there and waiting eagerly for you."

"Damn," I muttered, realizing that what James had relayed to me was bitterly true. Edward was further up the strand riding toward us with a sizeable force of knights and foot soldiers. The horses' hooves clacked sharply against the flakes of stone littering the shore.

He should not be here. He should still be at Stirling.

Angus hopped over the rowing thwarts to stand before me. "Happy to see your brother, as always, m'lord?" He propped his fists on his hips.

"Do not nettle me, Angus." I buried my face in my hands for a moment, then looked up at him between splayed fingers. "I should give you my weapons. Remove temptation."

Angus put out a hand to help me up. He pounded me on the upper arm. "Och, I knew enough of your brother's company at Dunaverty. I would not pick a quarrel with him. He'll finish whatever is started."

I hopped over the gunwale and immersed myself up to my ribs. The smell of saltwater mingled with that of muddied river water. Side by side, Angus and I waded toward land.

"I differ there, Angus. He'll not leave a fight unfinished, but as for a simple task, suffice it to say that persistence is not among his virtues. If only he had finished what he started at Stirling . . ."

"Ho! Robert!" Edward sprang from his horse and waved his arms in the air. "Come, let me tell you the news."

As we sloshed through the water, waves lapping at the backs of our knees, Angus gave me a sideways glance. "He's not wearing mail. I can throw a knife at this distance, if you'd like to make short of it."

"You're a poor influence, Angus. I can see why your people have such a sordid reputation."

"And proud of it, sire." He chuckled into his beard.

Angus and I emerged in our dripping clothes and water logged boots. Edward jogged toward us. He had shed his armor in favor of velvet and fine hose, looking more the king than me in my ragged battle garb, my face and hair beaten by the force of the sea and sun. With a wan smile above his trimmed beard, Edward bowed slightly. He threw his arms open to embrace me.

"Robert, well met. Did it go well on Man?" he asked.

"Not so well met, brother. In fact, our situation is horrid. I don't think it's ever been worse. I should think you'd be aware of that. What is this I hear about you getting the Earl of Atholl's sister Isabel with child and denying it? My sources tell me you are now wooing the sister of the Earl of Ross, worshipping her like the Virgin Mary, and making Atholl's sister out as a Jezebel. It's dangerous play to pit Atholl against Ross. I gave too many years trying to bring them together to have you rent them apart because of your inability to keep your breeches on."

"Atholl would leak that lie to you because he wants his fallen sister wed to a Bruce. It's a common ploy among women, an age-old conspiracy, to immediately bed with the most desirable nobleman they can find after they've already gotten themselves plowed and sown."

"And you consider yourself desirable?"

"As do you. But you hush your women properly. If I could shower their brats with slabs of rock and empty titles, I'd do the same. You bed women for passing pleasure, Robert, as you know—not to test their fertility for marriage. Isabel of Atholl is a harpy and a leech and she can keep whatever bastards she bears well fed with those ample breasts of hers . . . and her brother David has more than the means to look after her brood. The worst thing I could do to encourage her is admit that her bulging belly has anything to do with me. Atholl concocted this whole, fabulous, overgrown lie. Believe him, or believe me."

I covered my eyes with my hands for a moment, trying to wring the thoughts from my brain and shape them in a way that would go over as well as possible. But this situation with Atholl and Stirling—it was impossible. I was angry with him, for a hundred reasons. I would not let him ply at my infidelity in order for him to shirk off his own guilt like a mantle he had tired of wearing.

"My God, my God." When I uncovered my eyes, I found that I could not look at him and accuse him at the same time. "David of Atholl's father died trying to help Elizabeth, Marjorie and your own sisters escape. He has been back in Scotland himself not a year, trying in vain to prove his loyalty and forget whatever divided us all in the past—and this is what you do, call him a liar and opportunist? You fathered a child on an earl's sister, Edward, not a peasant girl who can be brushed away. If I could give away lands or titles to fix everything that you have broken, I would. But this is beyond that. And there is one thing you have done that I won't be able to fix. My kingdom is in a shambles . . . because of you. Everything I have gained thus far stands to be lost."

His mouth sank in confusion. "But with Og's galleys and men, surely you—"

"Not that. Rushen fell. Quick work. But I hear . . . understand that you and Mowbray, Stirling's commander, came to an agreement. Is that so, Edward?"

Behind him, Gil, who had been left on assignment with him, shrunk at the mention of Stirling. I could see that he, at least, had some inkling that this reunion would not go smoothly.

Edward forced an unconvincing smile. The gravity of my disappointment in his deeds was starting to seep in. He took a step back. "Aye. I thought you would be glad to hear of it. I agreed to lift the siege. He agreed to hand us Stirling if the English did not relieve it by midsummer next. The castle will be ours without so much as bending a finger."

The tenor of my voice deepened. "What in Christ's sacred name were you thinking?"

His dark eyebrows lifted. "Thinking?"

"Not at all, I reckon. What will happen if they come?" The men trailing behind him kept their distance as my patronizing queries rose to a bellow of inquisition.

He shook his head. "But they won't. I assure you. Edward of Caernarvon is too troubled in his own court to care. He hasn't stepped north of Berwick since—"

"Damn it! And damn you to bloody hell and back!" I stomped at him and jabbed a finger at his chest. "Fool, idiot and imbecile! You've given them reason and invitation now to come with a full invasion force. You could have gotten away with such stupidity elsewhere, but they'll not hand you Stirling. I can barely believe you would act with such blind carelessness. Had you no time to think this through? You had them, my God, had them right there in your palm—supplies to last you weeks yet and if those had run short we'd have sent you more. More men, if you needed, too."

His pride challenged, Edward moved closer to me until our chests nearly touched. "More men to sit idly about and count the clouds in the sky? No, Robert, I caution you not to hurl such rubbish at me. And listen well first. It was Mowbray who made the offer. I indeed gave it thought. Stirling sits on a rock so high it parts the clouds. It was untouchable. I freed our men to fight elsewhere for you. How many times have you bemoaned the fact that the English outnumber us? I have saved you a world of trouble. Stirling will fall like a ripe apple into our open hands. For that you should thank me, not berate me like a spoiled infant."

I raised a fist to hammer him in the breastbone, but drew it back, beating at my own chest instead. I raised my chin and shouted in vexation. "Agh!" Yanking at the roots of my hair I turned back to him and shook my head. "You gave King Edward an entire year to gather an army. A whole year. Did you stop to consider that if Mowbray were willing to throw out such a lure, that maybe his victuals were beginning to run low? Or that sickness had set in? That if you had only waited another week, another month, that Stirling might now be yours? He held out before at Stirling against Longshanks himself as long as he could. Have you no memory of these things? Heaven tests my patience in your very form. I told you when I left you were not to break the siege for any cause or reason. Yet you neglected my wishes and thought better of your own. What arrogance you possess."

"You would wish me different, would you? *You* have always been this way, Robert. You smack of the very arrogance you accuse me of. If you loathe it in me, first change yourself. I am but a mirror of my older brother."

"In more lawless times I would have throttled you by now for your impertinence."

"When were you ever one to heed the convention of laws?" He smirked. "You murdered John Comyn in God's house and then crawled on your raw belly to Bishop Wishart and groveled for forgiveness. Tell me, who between us is arrogant, given that?"

"I defended my own life."

"Call it what you will. You drew your sword. You put a hole in his gut. He would have drowned in his own puddle of blood if Christopher had not acted on mercy and set him free. The man died, Robert."

"You should not speak of that day. You were not there to witness it. Say no more on it and leave my sight, Edward. If you don't, then I'll—"

"You'll what? Will you kill me, too, brother?"

I tightened my fists into bloodless stumps. Aye, there were moments I had considered it. God alone knew that I had often wished myself free of the curse of having Edward as a brother.

I held my breath before I answered. "For now I have to deal with your mess. You've brought upon us what I've long tried to avoid and succeeded without having to do—meeting the English in full battle. But it's a year I've got as well to prepare. And a year from now you *will* be there at my side."

"Sweet Jesus, Robert. You were ever the fatalist. They won't come. You'll see."

"Oh, they will. They'll come like a market parade stretching from London to Carlisle. You will be there with the rest of us—a stand of reeds against a tempest. And you will watch your kin and faithful fall. Do you wish me to be among the heaps of the dead, so that this hollow crown will then be yours? What will it be worth when the war is lost? Edward, I would rather have toiled another ten years, gaining a foot at a time, than risk all in one day. Why have you forced us to the edge? Why?"

Edward whipped away. He clenched and unclenched his fists. "I have stood behind you from the first, brother. Ask yourself: would you be where you are without me?"

The men who had gathered about us exchanged glances. None of them loved Edward. I questioned if I even did. I had heard enough of the derogatory remarks under the breath of each one of them pertaining to his selfishness.

Gentle waves lapped against the shore. The late June sun had begun to dry my clothes out. But there was a chill that went deep beyond my flesh and down into my very soul. I let my chin sink. "No, Edward. I would not."

Slowly, with tilted head, he turned to face me. His eyes were drawn tight, his jaw clenched, his voice barely controlled. A sliver of the devil danced upon his tongue as he spoke. "Then you'll live with things as they are. Maybe this isn't the curse you've made it to be, but the way things ought to be. If you think King Edward will be here come next year, then you've that long to think on how to beat him."

Because of you, Edward, I have no choice.

30

James Douglas – Roxburgh, 1314

A S A LAD, I seldom slept peacefully, rising often before first light
from the lumpy bed I shared with snoring Hugh and creeping up
the tower stairs on bare, silent feet. With my knees tucked up to my
chest, I would sit on the parapets and peer out over Douglas Water,
which often lay hidden beneath a cloak of shifting fog. There, I envi-
sioned kelpies dancing mischievously at water's edge and waiting for
some wayward beggar to tumble into the water and drown so they
might claim his soul. I feared the trickery of kelpies more than I feared
damnation by God, the possibility of which the priests were forever
warning us.

This night was ideal for ambush, but instead of kelpies, there were
my men and I, tasked to take Roxburgh Castle and release it from English hands—for good. As well, I did not sleep that night either. A winter
mist had lingered all the day before and by the time darkness came on in
full, a thick, tangible fog had rolled down from the Lammermuir Hills
and sprawled across the valley where the Rivers Teviot and Tweed met.
The whiteness swallowed Roxburgh Castle whole and threatened never
to spit it out again.

At the brink of the apple orchard near where my men and I huddled, a small herd of penned cattle lowed. On one of our forays previously from the Forest of Selkirk, we had stripped the bark from the apple trees, leaving their leaves to yellow and float to earth and their branches go barren. Their fruit would never again fill English bellies. Now they stood like harpies with their hair blown wild by the wind and gnarled, outstretched hands, waiting to snatch wandering bairns. Limbs felled by winter storms littered the weedy ground beneath them. Between the castle and us lay an open stretch of field, soaked by winter rains. I pulled at the corner of the black cowhide spread over my shoulders and wiped the snot from my nose.

The years had been both good and hard. The forest from the top of Clydesdale all the way to Jedburgh was mine. I had lost men—good men, honest, hard fighters—but the English had lost more. All that was left in English hands was a thin strip of land running from Berwick to Stirling, but even those possessions grew more and more precarious with each passing day. In September, Linlithgow had fallen to the rustic wiles of good William Bunnock, delivering a cart of hay in which was concealed eight Scotsmen. Robert rewarded William heartily for that prize. Randolph had been tasked to take Edinburgh, but I could hardly see how that was possible.

I peered through the fog as it parted momentarily to reveal the faint outline of Roxburgh. One more day from now and there would be one less jewel in King Edward's rusting crown. A sentry passed over the battlements and the fog billowed upward to once more envelope the slumbering fortress.

No more the lank lad, I had strung my bow a hundred times a hundred since the day I had joined up with Robert nearly eight years past. My chest had broadened and my hands grown strong and coarse, but I was far from the giant in strength that Robert was. It was an advantage, I discovered, to be underestimated. When an enemy came at me and saw a lean man, few in years, he would either laugh at his good fortune or half try to kill me, sure that I would falter or flee. I did neither.

I would fight until my very end, just like my father had.

I knew the places where mail gapped. How to deflect every angle of my foe's every blow and how to vary the strength in my parry to upset their leverage. How to shoot an arrow every third heartbeat with unfailing accuracy. How to wait through torrents of rain, crouched among the nettles, nursing an empty belly until the sentries fell asleep on the towers, or the archers dropped their breeches to piss from the crenels of the battlements, or the guards arrived at the barbican swaggering with too much drink. I knew the crumbling, low places in the walls that had gone unmended from English assaults. The depth of moats and the places where the latrines drained into them. And the doors in the walls through which crucial supplies came and furtive letters went.

When it came to my foes, I knew what tempted them, what bored them, what frightened them, what rankled them and what aroused their suspicion. I knew all that and I used their soft, unguarded spots to defeat them, preying first upon their fears, nibbling at their sanity, just as a kelpie would.

I knew, as well, the pain that their evil left in its wake. The English had ravaged the women in these surrounding villages, then tossed them inside their cottages, barred the doors and set the thatch afire. Too many wretched times we came upon those scenes when all that was left was the rotten stench of charred corpses and swirls of smoke rising from the ashes. More than once I found a child, now an orphan, crying inconsolably beside the blackened bones of his parents, the burnt down house and the carcasses of dead animals—cows, pigs and old plow horses with their bellies split open and their blood roiling in the muddy, trampled grass. Most of the wee ones had witnessed the whole sordid thing. The lucky ones were those too young to be able to remember, too young to understand. When we found weeping bairns, we tried to feed them and clean them up, then carried them to the nearest abbey to be cared for. The monks were never happy to see us, whether they were

Scotsmen or no, but they had come to an understanding that when we arrived with children we would take nothing from them. I would thank them in Latin, which would always set them back in astonishment, and we would go on our way.

Rain began to fall again. I burrowed deeper inside the fresh cattle hide, still stinking of blood. Drops pattered against the hide, fine and soft at first, but soon they were bigger and harder. Silver fog drifted down toward the river, revealing again the stark outline of Roxburgh. My men hunkered still as stones—two dozen donned in cattle capes, as many more spread about in the broken orchard around us, and ten deeper back in the woods holding the reins of their horses. None complained—they knew I would not allow the smallest grumbling. Any complaint was followed by a sound thump to the head. Bairns cried, I told them, not grown men. My boots were soaked, my feet frozen to the leather. It had not seemed cold when we first took up our position on a slope at the wood's edge about half a mile from the castle, but a few hours in a miserable rain, unable to move, and eventually it was damnable cold. I wiggled my fingers and blew warm air into my cupped palms. I had to piss, but didn't dare.

It was hard to tell when the first light of day actually came. In time we could see the castle more clearly. We waited. The rain softened. When we could make out the sentries on the walls, the ruse began. I gave the wren's whistle and the herd of underfed, black cattle were unpenned and prodded toward the open meadow. In the dawn gray we crept forward upon hands and knees, mingling with the cattle. My fingers squelched in the cold mud and steaming cow dung. I wiped my hands on the grass, moved forward as a startled heifer danced over one of my legs with her enormous weight and found myself sunken again in more shit. I clenched my teeth to keep from crying out. Sim was behind me and gave her a shove in the flanks with his round shield, barely dodging a flash of angry hooves as she braced on her front legs and swung her rear to the side. Fearing a stampede, I struggled to regain my feet. Sim yanked me to my knees, then disappeared with a grunt into the herd. Tomorrow there would be a bruise the entire length of my right calf. The big, wet hide weighed me down like a sack of rocks. The muck sucked strongly at my hands and knees. My lower right leg throbbed. I checked my belt for my arrows, to be certain they were still there. My sword was slung over my back beneath the hide, so as not to drag on the ground, and just beneath it closest to my flesh, was a small round shield. Their constant weight was a comfort.

Shouts went down from the walls to the yard within. Chains rattled and the edges of the portcullis groaned against its stone grooves as it was raised up. Most of the garrison streamed out through the gate to come claim its feast. They charged across the open land, whooping with excitement, the few horsemen reaching us first. But before the first spear was hurled from English hands, Scottish arrows flew from the trees and pierced their breasts. The men on foot did not know yet what was happening when the first horseman slammed onto the ground, crying in mortal agony. They kept coming and did not falter until we threw off our hides, raised our weapons and rushed at the horsed soldiers. By then my own horsemen had already set off from the woods to cut off the footsoldiers. Every step on my right leg was a bolt of pain, but it was pain quickly forgotten in the rush of battle.

While we rained our blows and poured out our strength—cutting, thrusting, jabbing, slashing—Sim parted from the fray and scaled the ladders put up over the walls. A dozen followed him. There were not enough men left inside the walls to sufficiently defend the castle. By the time I made it through the gates of Roxburgh and led my men into the bailey, a pale sun was overcoming the fog and a dry, even colder wind blew down from the hills.

What remained of the garrison had withdrawn to the central keep. I tried to keep up with my men and they maneuvered across the bailey, but every step I took shot me with pain from ankle to hip. An arrow smacked on the cobbles beside me. I snatched it up and ducked behind a cart loaded with broken barrels. A scrape and scuffling beside me drew my attention. Sim wheeled before me, his huge hairy forearm flailing through the pale dawn light. An English archer, barely weaned from his mother's breast and now in his horror of horrors reduced to fighting on foot, wielded a clumsy sword. The Englishman's sword jerked swiftly toward Sim's head. Sim ducked to avoid the blow. His axe blade glinted high as he whipped it back and upward, then arced it down. It cleaved the archer's face from hairline to nose. I closed my eyes as blood sprayed over me. Instinctively, I wiped away the wetness from my lips and cheeks. The English archer lay on the slick cobbles, his eyes wide and lifeless. Sim wiped his axe blade on the Englishman's jacket and went to find more prey. Carefully, I took the bow that was slung over the archer's back before its string could soak up any blood. He had three arrows stuck in his belt. Two had been broken in his fall. So I took the one left and gathered more, scurrying in between bursts of fighting, before I returned to the cover of the cart and its jumbled barrels. In my own belt, I had but one arrow—the last one fletched with swan's feathers. The rest I must have lost in the first wave of fighting.

An occasional arrow still pelted us from the keep and it was there I set my sights. A figure appeared in one of the crenel gaps. He was an older man, his forehead fringed with silver. His red and blue surcoat marked him as someone of importance. The visor of his helmet was flipped open, so that he could better see the state of fighting below. Daring fool, he was, to stand there so long and vulnerable. I fitted an arrow to my newly found bow, marked him for his boldness and let fly. The white swan feathers sailed upward and struck him in the face. He toppled backward, out of sight, and someone else upon the battlements there dashed from behind the merlon to his aid. I waited for more men to appear, but by now they were wise to me. I chanced a few more gray-feathered arrows wherever I noted movement, but whether more found a mark I did not know. Likely by now they were barricading the doors, bent on holding out for the long term.

When I had spent my cache of arrows, I abandoned the bow, left my post at the barrel cart, slipped through a tower door and made my way up a flight of winding stairs, climbing over the bodies of two fallen Englishmen. The next that I came upon was not quite dead and I paused a moment, considering whether it was worth my time to finish him. The side of his head was smashed in. Brain matter was spattered onto the steps above him. His pupils were well back into his head. His face was contorted unnaturally and his body gripped with small spasms. I left him, figuring he was past pain and cognizance.

My leg throbbed as if it were being struck every pulse with a lead hammer. I swallowed back the cries that I longed to release and went on. The first two doors I came to had already been thrust open, the contents looted and the confines cleared of habitation. Before I reached the third I could already hear the hammering of an axe on the door latch, then the abrupt splintering of wood as the planks yielded.

"Sim?" I called up, as I spied his broad back and two other Scots, McKie and Murdoch, at his shoulder. He turned to look at me, his great, grizzly head speckled with dark brown mud and drying blood. I scrambled up the steps, each stride sending bolts of pain up my leg, squeezed past the others and reached his side. "Does anyone call out from inside?"

He shook his head at me. I brought my shield up before me and tucked my sword between it and the wall. "Let me go first," I said, nodding at him to take the door from its hinges.

The whites of his eyes glowed in the half dark as he flung his axe again and again at the parting planks. No sounds emanated from within. He managed a gap, hooked his axe and yanked more of the wood away and when it was wide enough he shoved his arm through to fumble for the latch. He flipped it up, but the door was plainly barred and so he squeezed his arm through further and braced his shoulder against the door as he pulled up with all the might in his one arm. Grunting and sweating, his arm shook with the weight and tightness of the bar. Then it slid upward with a groan. He heaved it up over its hooks and away. As he began to pull his arm clear, his eyes shot wide and wild. He winced and pulled a blood streaked arm back through. Metal clattered sharply onto the floor on the other side. Sim's wound was but a superficial cut, but the stinging of his flesh angered him.

"Armed," I warned, glancing at the two men with us. "Caution."

Sim rammed his shoulder into the door and threw it wide. Light poured in from tall windows to show a solar, packed with weaving looms and stools and baskets overflowing with thread and needles for embroidery work. Our enemies amounted to six women and an infant. Tapestries covered the walls and at once McKie and Murdoch went at them, slashing the threads and pulling them down to make certain that no armed men were hidden behind them. Two of the women were aged, one of those visibly feeble. The others were young and all ladies of high breeding. The fairest of them, hair of midnight and skin like January snow, clutched a writhing bundle to her breast.

Sim gave his big, gaping grin as he stepped toward them. The women retreated toward the windows in a huddle, aghast at the intent in their intruder's eyes. Only the black-haired lady stood her ground with stubborn denial. A cry, high and thin, escaped from the swaddling in her arms. Eyes shut, she pressed her face to the child she held and began to sing as she swayed side to side:

"Hush, hush, do not fret ye."

Her voice leaked frailly from a trembling mouth. The babe cried louder and I thought of Archibald in my stepmother Eleanor's arms when Neville exploded into our room after the massacre at Berwick. My God, what had ever happened to Hugh and Archibald? I had been too enthralled in my fighting all these years to seek them out. At one time they had been safe at Rothesay and Eleanor was cloistered somewhere with nuns. But that was all I ever knew.

Sim dropped his axe into his drooping belt and wiped at his face, looming closer to the flock of women. He reached out his blood-streaked arm toward the infant.

"The Black Douglas will not get ye," she half-cried, half-sang.

"No, stop!" I ordered. I sheathed my sword and rushed between Sim and the young woman, kicking a stool over on the way. A white bolt of pain ripped up the right half of my body. I stumbled and caught myself. Even as the stool toppled and fell loudly, still the lady kept her eyes shut and sang the song over and over and over. Sim yielded his ground with a low grumble.

"Stop!" I shouted at her with all the wind in my lungs. My vehemence was aimed as much at her as it was at the shattering pain in my calf. I tried to stand without revealing my injury, but managed only a lopsided stance and sharp breaths.

She flinched at my bellowing. I shifted my weight slowly onto the bad leg, went a stride closer, studied her. She was still in her nightclothes. Her fluttering fingers ran over a blanket draped about the bairn's small back. She touched her forehead to its downy crown and the top of its swaddling fell away. The babe twisted in her grip to look at me. It fell quiet in curiosity. I guessed it was not more than a few months old . . . and a girl, judging by the delicate nose and small forehead.

". . . do not fret—"

I spoke over her plaintive song. "We mean no harm, my lady." I willed her to look at me, but she kept her eyes closed, droning on and on in that false lullaby.

"The Black Douglas will not—"

"Please, enough," I demanded. "Douglas . . . he is not like that. He would never do you harm. Never."

I reached out to touch her on the shoulder and break her trance, but as I did so one of her hands whipped toward me with a flash of metal. I caught her by the wrist. The same knife she had cut Sim with hurtled from her grasp and spun across the floor.

At last she looked at me. But the hatred in her dark, smoldering eyes struck me harder than the blow of any blade.

"Your people have raped and murdered mine," she accused, her red lips curved into a bitter snarl that turned her beauty into outright ugliness. "Have us all if you will. But I beg you—make it quickly done. What is one more mark on your conscience among thousands?"

"I have violated no one, my lady," I replied. Still clenching her wrist, I lowered her arm and pulled her in even closer to me so that she would not miss a word of what I had to say. "Not today, nor yesterday, nor in all my life. And any who have lost their lives to me made the choice to place themselves in danger. I am waging a war against the King of England. It requires that I fight . . . and win."

Proudly, she drew her chin up. "Then kill me. Now. But however, honor mercy and do not leave us to your pack of dogs. It doesn't matter if it's you or those who serve you who commit the deed. The stain is on you."

Aye, my men had taken women along the way. In the border towns we sacked it was an inevitable part of the aftermath. I discouraged it, punished them for brutality when I discovered it, hung them even, but alas, I could not be everywhere.

I let go of her. "Tell me your name first, so that I may know the degree of the *crime* I am about to commit."

Just then the bairn thumbed her mother's nose and cooed. The lady's features softened with the boundless depth of her love for her child. The first tear spilled from the corner of her eye. "My name is of no matter."

"It matters if you are the governess of this castle and your husband is William de Fiennes."

At that a cloud passed over her brow. The governess of Roxburgh sank to her knees in defeat. The bairn cradled in her lap tugged at a loose strand of her hair, but she paid it no heed. The very moment Sim had ripped open the door, she had decided her fate was sealed and this was to be the day of her death.

We Scots are not all savages, my lady. Perhaps this is the day you should instead learn a lesson of our humanity.

"Sim." I turned to him. He brooded yet over the prize that had been denied to him and thus this was no place for him. "Go. Find out if William de Fiennes has been captured, or," I added lowly, "if he has fallen during the fight. I reckon most likely he is shut up in the keep. Murdoch, McKie . . . search for more weapons here, but harm none of these women or the bairn . . . or else it's you I'll kill. The lady is worth a fair ransom. A shame the governor abandoned his womenfolk and saved himself."

"It happened too quickly," Lady De Fiennes protested. "He did not mean to part from us. My ladies were asleep in the adjoining chambers. My child was crying from colic. I came here to soothe her and by then we were under attack."

I retrieved the knife from beside a loom and twirled its jeweled hilt between my palms.

"Forgive me for leaving your company so suddenly, Lady De Fiennes." As I went toward the battered door, I motioned for Sim to accompany me, and gave McKie and Murdoch a warning glance to keep them in check. Without looking back, I said to the lady, "Things are not always what we imagine them to be."

Kelpies in the mist came to mind. And the Black Douglas . . . he was no child-killer or violator of women, either.

WILLIAM DE FIENNES, AS it turned out, was indeed confined within the castle keep as no accounts of him were found among the dead or captured. I had lost yet more men in taking the castle, among them the shepherd MacLurg, brother to McKie and Murdoch, and so I chose not to risk any more if I could avoid it. The defenders of the keep had a store of arrows, but their best archers had been posted on the outer walls and fallen in the outset. Whatever arrows were loosed from the keep did not fly true. They fell short or curved wildly—sure signs that the men behind them were not well practiced in the art. And whenever they shot their arrows, my men replied with more.

For two days we held them there. Their numbers were unknown, but clearly they had suffered from the suddenness of our attack. My men laid out their dead beyond the outer wall for the local womenfolk to search over and bury. I had expected De Fiennes to surrender immediately, surrounded and disadvantaged as he was, and so it was not until the second day with no word from inside the keep that I ordered Sim to lead a company of men in battering at the keep's door with a ramming rod. For nearly an hour, he and twenty other men heaved the monstrous pole at the timber door which was reinforced with iron straps. A dozen archers and I were positioned around the keep, arrows nocked to pierce the first Englishman who tried to pour boiling oil on Sim and his crew. But no one ever tried. When the door began to cave, a flag of truce appeared on the highest point of the keep, waved by the captain of the garrison. I motioned for my men to lower their bows and perched myself on the parapet of the tower nearest the keep. The day was bitterly cold, although bright, and a light, brisk wind nudged at my chest.

Upon seeing me, the captain called out, "My master, the governor of this castle, requests his freedom in return for the castle keep and wishes to know your demands."

Standing with the toes of my boots over the edge of the wall on which I stood, high above the inner bailey, I cupped my hands around my mouth and responded, "Tell him, that I will permit the governor his freedom, but that I shall keep his wife and daughter until he pays me the sum of fifty marks. Less than two year's wages for a knight. A small sacrifice, given the value of the goods."

"My master wants to know who it is that makes such a demand."

"I am known as the Black Douglas by the English around here. Surely you have heard of me?"

"We have, m'lord."

"Ah, then you know that I get what I ask for?"

"We do."

"Then who are you to bargain on his behalf?"

"John of Wigton, captain of this garrison. A moment, m'lord, while I consult."

"Take an hour, John of Wigton. It will all come to the same no matter how you delay."

He left his post and reappeared only a few minutes later. I found the action merely ritualistic, as I doubted he had indeed consulted over much of anything. Why that was so intrigued me.

"My master requests that if you would but hand over his wife and daughter so that they may accompany him back to England, he will pay you an annual indemnity of your choosing—within his means, of course."

"Tell your generous master that I will take the fifty marks from him and an immediate indemnity from the peoples of this county as well as other payments due through the course of the year. I will compromise by giving up the daughter, but keep the wife in my care until such payment is met."

John of Wigton's gruff laughter echoed over the empty courtyard as he held his belly. "Leave the lady in *your* care? M'lord, I would not entrust you with the village laundress for a day and a night, let alone the Lady Rosalind for a matter of weeks or perhaps months until such monies could be raised."

"Tell your master that is my offer . . . or can he speak for himself at all?"

Wigton threw his arms open. "Indeed he cannot. He was gravely wounded by an arrow morning before yester and is in terrible pain. But on the matter of his wife, m'lord, he asks that you take into consideration his condition and release her, for he fears he may not live to see her again should he depart here without her."

Wounded by an arrow. My arrow. I stepped down from the parapets and paced, my arms folded, one set of fingers drumming against my mailed arm. My archers stared at me as I swung back and forth. A minute later, I bounded back to my roost. Pain shot through my lower leg, reminding me of the deep bruise there.

"Half an hour," I said. "I shall meet him in the courtyard at the foot of the keep. He is promised safe passage from here to Berwick, but is to take nothing with him."

"And on the matter of the Lady Rosalind."

"I have given my terms, John of Wigton. Half an hour."

Before the captain could interrogate or plead further, I had left and was headed for the ladies' solar. I knocked twice upon the poorly re-paired door and gave the order to open. Murdoch complied.

I had not seen Lady Rosalind since the day of the attack. I had, however, given firm orders that she and her women were to be afforded comforts. They had been brought appropriate clothing for a journey, fed well and passed the time reading to each other, so Murdoch had re-layed to me. Rosalind herself was modestly and warmly dressed in her fur-lined winter cloak. She was a woman in her prime, yet young, and with the dark, mystical looks of a Spanish princess.

"When will you permit a fire, m'lord?" Rosalind addressed, placing her sleeping daughter in a rocking cradle and approaching me quite boldly. One of the two older women, the one with silver-black hair and a shape of brow like Rosalind's, went to the bairn and began to rock the cradle gently. Rosalind had shed her resolution of impending death in favor of confident demands. "The few candles we have been given will not warm a drafty chamber like this in the middle of winter."

"I am not your host, my lady." Dragging my leg noticeably, I moved away from Lady Rosalind and further into the chamber to inspect it and make certain that they had been kept in comfort.

"Yes, I know," she said cynically behind me. "We are your prison-ers. We have looked from the window and seen our dead tossed in piles on carts like carcasses of beef."

I picked up a book and opened it long enough to see it was written in French. Then I returned it to the small folding table on which it had rested on top of a stack of other books. "How long have you been in residence at Roxburgh, my lady?"

"A year."

"Then that is long enough to have seen your husband's soldiers leave from here for days and return. What do you think they were doing in that time?" I turned to her.

She gave no answer and so I continued. "I can tell you. They went out into the villages and to the farms and demanded taxes in the name of King Edward. Sometimes they took the money and left. Sometimes they stayed and took what they wanted from the people. My people. Scots. Sometimes they burned their homes to the ground when the people had no money or goods to pay them with. They raped. They killed. And it was not only soldiers they killed, but also common folk: old men, women and sometimes the bairns who stood in their way. So aye, you are my prisoner, but to prove to you I am not as much a savage as your own kind, I am giving you this chance to go from here—with all your women and your child—and go back to England with your husband and live out what's left of your lives."

Puzzled, the faint lines on her forehead doubled up. "Then . . . we are no longer your prisoners?"

"Not unless you want to be." I stood away from the door and raised a hand to it. "Go."

She hesitated in disbelief, then turned to the nursemaid, who was already lifting the infant from the cradle as it stirred from sleep. She took the baby girl from the lady's outstretched arms and held her to her bosom. As the rest of her women scurried past, as though still suspicious that some threat awaited them, Rosalind paused before me.

Her arched lips partly slightly, but when the nursemaid placed a hand upon the small of her back, she turned and went on her way down the tower stairs and out into the courtyard to wait on her husband.

Hobbling, I followed at a distance and as she stood there in the courtyard hovering at the door of the keep I sensed her eyes upon me. For a very long time I did not look at her, remembering the vile hatred she had served me with when we first discovered her. As the inner bar of the keep's main door groaned, I glanced her way—only a glance. Curiosity. But all her focus was now on the door and what was behind it. The babe was quiet in her nursemaid's arms as John of Wigton appeared first from the keep. Over his shoulder was slung the arm of an old man: William de Fiennes, well into his fifties and his head heavily bandaged from his right jaw, across the bridge of his nose and toward his left temple. A huge, red blood stain marked the linen over his right eye and several likewise stains, old and brown, spotted the bandage at various points, indicating that they had used it for some time and turned the bandaging as it soaked through in one spot. I wondered if he had lost the eye, but judging by his dazed and feeble reactions, that was not the worst of his wounds.

At once Rosalind, herself only half his age, flew to her husband, pressed herself against his trembling chest and whispered soothing words against his cheek. Weakened, he slumped against her.

Under poised arrows, the remainder of the keep's garrison trickled out, throwing down their weapons in a haphazard pile. Like sheep sent out to pasture in spring, they were herded out the gate and escorted a good ways down the road by Scots soldiers who prodded them with spears and taunted them all the way.

I motioned to Sim to have the horses brought forward for the governor and the women. "I would have had a cart ready, but I am afraid even had I done so you would have found the roads impassable this time of year."

As a few of my men helped De Fiennes onto his horse and steadied him, Lady Rosalind took to her own mount, accepted the bundled bairn from her nursemaid and looked once more at me.

"You never said your name," she said.

"No, I didn't."

"Well, what is it?"

I bowed to her. "James Douglas, my lady—your liberator."

She half-smiled at the irony. "On behalf of my husband, I thank you, Master Douglas."

AFTERWARD, I SENT A letter to Walter Stewart, the son of James Stewart, at Rothesay asking the whereabouts of my brothers. Hugh was still there, he wrote, hurling spears at haystacks and caring for the horses, as his lacking wit made him good for little else. Archibald had gone only recently to the abbey in Inchafray to study scripture. I then wrote to Archibald, told him to collect Hugh from Rothesay and join King Robert and me at Bannockburn before the middle of June.

Gil de la Haye arrived at Roxburgh shortly after we had taken it. He had been with Edward Bruce during his harrowing of Cumberland—a ploy to distract the English levies as they trickled northward along the eastern coast. Upon inspecting my injured leg, he pronounced that it was deeply bruised, perhaps, he surmised, it might even have had a fine crack in the bone. I feared that he might bind me up in an awkward splint, but he said it would do little good and insisted that I refrain from walking as much as possible and instead ride my horse everywhere. He did apply leeches to suck away the blood spreading beneath my skin from the bruise and in between bleedings packed my leg with a poultice of moss and the powder of ground willow bark. Naturally, in my stubbornness and intoxication to fight and travel swiftly, I ignored his advice to rest. Scars and lingering injuries were but evidence of a soldier's courage. They told that I had cheated death. The more scars I bore, the more invincible I deemed myself.

When we heard that the English were beginning to assemble in Berwick in greater and greater numbers, we abandoned Roxburgh, its walls demolished to useless rubble. As Gil and I journeyed by

Selkirk, we met a merchant, Flemish by birth, but raised in Scotland and traveling to Ayr in order to join his daughter's family and leave Berwick before the English overran it. He told us that the De Fiennes' company had made it safely back across the border; however, William de Fiennes made it little further than that. His wound was severe. The arrow had punctured his eye and buried itself in his brain. He died in a fit of convulsions in his young wife's arms.

31

Edward II – Berwick, 1314

THE EARL OF HEREFORD'S lips moved on in an endless drone, the sounds coming from his mouth no more to me than an insect's annoying buzz.

My fingers rubbed at the pearls set within the clutching paws of the lion pendant as it lay upon my chest.

For nigh on two years, my tolerance had been tested. And in all that time I had neither forgotten anything, nor forgiven any of them. After Piers' murder, there had been threats of war, riots, envoys dispatched to Paris and Avignon. Lancaster, Hereford and Warwick had even dared to come to London when called. God's breath, I did not actually believe that they would. Of course, they denied any offense. Eventually, it was Gilbert's influence that calmed me. Pardons were granted to them in return for promises of support against the Scots. My perpetual curse, it seemed, was that I could not bring the Bruce down without them. When that was done, I intended to seek my revenge, but only when the moment presented itself. For now, Stirling awaited. A victory on Scottish soil would serve me well in more ways than one.

And after all that bartering on Lancaster's part, the beggar was late to the campaign. I would deal with him later.

Beneath the tip of my finger, I balanced a skipping stone on its edge. I let go and, for the hundredth time, it fell flat upon its water-smoothed side. This had been my obsession for the past two hours as my councilors bickered over minutia in Berwick's great hall: which order to arrange the marching columns in, what to do with the problem of roads pocked with holes so hardened by the sun that they broke the wagon wheels, how to get water to parched horses and men, where to encamp . . . and the ridiculous guessing game of how Bruce would face us, or if he would dare at all once he saw the perennial menace of his people bearing down on him and his ragged band of thieves and murderers. I sighed out of tedium. How many war councils had I attended in the past year? The count exceeded memory. How many more would I have to endure before I could embrace peace and prosperity? If such things existed, would I know them when I had them?

Footsteps shattered my trance and I glanced up to see Pembroke in full battle gear enter the far end of the council chamber of Berwick Castle. Pembroke's mouth was scored in a firm sneer, as if someone had etched a straight pair of lips upon a rock and painted eyes and a nose above it.

"Is it warm outside, Lord Pembroke? There was a chill this morning, although yesterday was like breathing in a pot of hot stew. Surely we are past sext now, although I swear I did not hear the bells." I pinched my middle finger against my thumb, then flicked the stone down the length of the table. It glided across a scattering of maps and narrowly missed the jutting elbow of Humphrey de Bohun, the Earl of Hereford. Still droning on, he did not so much as blink. I spoke over him. "I do love May. Trees in blossom. Bees abuzz. My favorite month, I think, of all. Gilbert, don't you agree with me?"

At the furthest end of the table, Gilbert balanced his chin on top of folded hands, yawned in reply and rubbed at his bloodshot eyeballs. "Sext, did you say? Already? I'm hungry."

Pembroke strode up to him and popped him in the side of the head with a roll of parchment. Gilbert lurched sideways and toppled clumsily from his chair with his legs in the air. Hereford, at last, ceased his rambling to gawk.

"You were due to inspect the new archers from Chester with me just past dawn," Pembroke admonished. "Where were you? Sharing your bed with a flea-infested tavern girl?"

Gilbert sprawled upon the floor, then got to his knees and cupped his hands on either side of his head. Snarling, Gilbert bit back. "I am as faithful to my lovely wife as you, my good lord. And with better reason, as mine does not resemble a horse."

"Ah, a sharp wit you have. Too drunk to make it to bed, then? By the looks of you, you slept draped across a table." Pembroke continued on down the length of the table and slapped the parchment in front of me. "My lord, you will find this of remarkable interest."

"Just tell us what it says," I told him. I leaned back in my chair, wishing the cushions were thicker. My pelvis and back ached sharply already from the morning's stagnation. "Judging by your entrance, you already know its contents, do you not?"

His dark-lined eyes swept around the table—at Hereford, old Ralph de Monthermer who had been sleeping upright until his stepson Gilbert fell from his chair beside him, Sir Robert Clifford, Sir Henry Beaumont, Hugh Despenser the Younger and Sir Ingram d'Umfraville. Working his jaw back and forth, Pembroke took the empty seat next to Hereford. "They admit guilt, beg forgiveness, claim loyalty and then . . . foul, damnable liars. Lancaster and Warwick refuse to reply to your summons, sire."

"Ah, I see. Refuses, does he? At my consort's urging, I threw a banquet of peace for cousin Lancaster. 'What good,' I asked her. 'So they will aid you when it comes time to march on Scotland,' she said. Stinking pile of shit that was. Should I be surprised that this is his repayment? The arrogant pig." I exchanged a glance with young Hugh, who besides Gilbert had been the only one to remain true to me at every convolution. "A dog is a dog, even if you pin an ass's tail to it."

Clifford shook his head in disgust. "Lord Pembroke, did they send any footmen? Cavalry?"

"They did," Pembroke replied. "As if such a hollow gesture could buy their innocence. They should all be dealt with after this, sire, completely and properly."

Hereford rattled his fat fist on the table. "Power-mongers and troublemakers. Better off without them, we are. What base reason did they give for their truancy?"

"That the consent of parliament was not given first," Pembroke said.

"By God's soul!" I shoved back my chair and threw my arms to the ceiling. "They would have worked every hole they could find to turn parliament upside down on this matter. We have been challenged openly by the Scots. Are we to dawdle while fusty old men squabble over taxes and question every farthing that was ever put into or taken from the treasury?" I took my knife from my belt and gripped its hilt with all the strength in my fingers. Then I turned its blade downward and slammed it into the point on the map in front of me where Stirling was marked.

"Never was a war more just than this one," I stated. Bracing one hand flat against the map I yanked the knife violently across it. "Let the false bastards rot. More riches for us then. We shall carve Scotland into a hundred jagged pieces. An earldom for each of you. Hugh, to you I will begin by granting the lands of that two-faced Janus, Thomas Randolph. And to the rest of you, like will you be allotted the estates of the fallen—of Ross, Keith, Douglas, every one of them. Let the rivers flow with the blood of Bruce and his screaming, naked heathens. We will flatten those Scottish shit-flies and afterwards attend to the festering pox within our own land. We march at once on Stirling!"

The thundering of my own voice echoed off the rafters and returned emptily to me.

"Sire?" Young Hugh's velvety voice slipped through the heavy air to redirect matters. Even in times of heated argument, he remained outwardly dispassionate—sitting back observantly, waiting for the pot to boil over so he could quench the flame beneath it. "We yet await various knights, of Brittany, Germany and elsewhere, who have pledged their service. D'Argentan is en route from Byzantium."

"And many supplies have yet to reach us," Pembroke added. "Without them we will have neither the means to feed our host nor the arms to equip them entirely."

Temporarily defeated, I dropped back into my chair. "How much longer then? A day? A week?"

Pembroke shrugged. "Two weeks. Maybe three. There are ships due at Leith which will fill much of the void."

"We cannot tarry here," Clifford grumbled as he cracked his knuckles, "while time erodes. The date has been set in stone. Fail to meet it and Mowbray tosses his meat scrap to the Scottish wolves."

"This is an enormous undertaking, my lord," Pembroke said. "We have over two-hundred horse and oxen carts to move. Fifteen thousand foot soldiers."

Clifford interrupted, "Which do nothing but stumble and crawl and pule like slobbering infants who have shit themselves. I told all of you that it was more infantry than we needed. I have gone up against the Scots more than any of you and you're fools, all, if you don't think they're any match for us man for man. They were bloody born to fight. Beat them with what they don't have. Archers and cavalry will get the job done and right."

"And if during all these skirmishes," Pembroke said, "you had figured the Scots out so well, you'd have beaten them back to the Shetlands by now. Of heavy cavalry there are nearly—"

I rolled my head. "I thank you, earl, for reminding us of those counts yet one more time. I doubt you are one to advise any of us, since he thrashed you soundly at both Glen Trool and Loudon Hill." Weary of doing battle with nagging and unwavering barons, I slumped back in my chair, dangled my arms over its sides and swung my feet up onto the table. I laid my hand across my eyes to shut out the light. "We shall march when supplies are in order. As for the knights seeking easy glory, for them we will not wait. Impatience overrules me. Ah, damn it! Someone call on Jankin to bring me a drink of poppy and peony root. This ceaseless prattle will cause my head to explode. If anyone breathes the names of Thomas of Lancaster or Robert the Bruce again this day I will have his tongue hacked out and tossed in the pig slop. Damn it. Jankin!"

Leith, 1314

AN EASTERLY WIND RATTLED the riggings of the fleet of supply ships at Leith's port on the outskirts of Edinburgh. Goods were being ferried to shore from some of the larger ships by brown, bare-chested men stroking the oars of their sluggish little boats through the rippling water of the firth. Gulls floated and jeered above in a terrible clamor, trained to follow sea vessels in hopes of freshly caught fish, and occasionally landed on the decks to harass the sailors. The smell of brine scoured my throat and scraped at the pit of my stomach. North, the Firth of Forth divided the land, gaping broader and broader as it ran eastward until it mingled indistinguishably with the sea. Four days ago we had left Berwick—an entire week later than planned. Today was the 21st of June. Our pace would have to be doubled to reach Stirling in time. It could be done. Calculations had proven it. But with each hour, my barons became more irascible, the troops more troublesome and I more impatient.

Mounted on my bay and followed by a legion of nobles on horses with gay trappings, I passed through a swarm of grumbling footsoldiers. They parted with downcast heads as they saw me. In their midst, a captain lashed at the bleeding back of a soldier whose hands were roped to the back side of a supply wagon. The soldier wailed in agony as the whip seared across his flesh. The captain, taking perverse delight in his work, cast back his arm again.

"Hold there." I leaned forward upon my saddle. "What offense has this man committed?"

Lowering the whip, the captain dragged a scarred arm across his half-toothless mouth. His chest heaved with exertion. He let himself down on one knee, bowed his head of sweat-matted hair and said in a voice choked with dust, "Said his feet were too sore to go on, m'lord."

I studied the soldier's feet. His leggings hung in shreds about his knees. The sole of one shoe was entirely gone from one and half from the other, so that the bottoms of his feet oozed with blood and pus. Where his toes were not likewise raw, they were completely bruised green and purple.

"His duty is to serve his king," I said, "and his king commands him to march to Stirling." I straightened in my saddle and signaled my horse onward. "Carry on, captain."

As we proceeded to the port, the sharp crack of the whip rang out again and again. Usually, other soldiers mocked and shouted derisions at offenders. This time, they did not. Perhaps they had all wanted to voice the same complaint, but the rest had been wise enough to hold their tongues. The footsoldiers would have to tolerate their blistered feet and wearied legs. Surely they knew there was no element of comfort in their calling? In their ignorance, they probably expected riches from this expedition.

We came to the rocky strip of shoreline which began the eastern border of the harbor. I looked behind me and squinted against a blaze of June sun. Edinburgh Castle rose up ominously at our backs—a great, black rock dominating the horizon and shadowing a long reach of land at its base wherein huddled a town no longer protected by its power. Months ago Thomas Randolph had taken the castle. I both marveled and fumed at the feat. "Without sorcery I would say it was impossible.

How did they manage?"

"The Scots are like goats, sire." Hugh Despenser swished the flies from his horse's ears with the ends of his reins. "Done at night. Randolph and his men climbed the rock face. The devil must have had some hand in it."

"You can see to the other side of the Forth from there," Clifford observed.

"They are not watching us from there now, Sir Robert," Pembroke said. "A skeleton garrison. Victualed to the highest stone. With orders, no doubt, to starve themselves, rather than surrender."

I wadded the cloth of my surcoat at the shoulder and wiped the sweat from my brow. "So Bruce would rather rule over a country of byres and burnt fields. What of Linlithgow? Roxburgh?" Lightheaded, I gripped the edge of my saddle. I had not stopped thirsting since the day we rode out from Berwick. The constant weight of my armor had wearied me. The fiery knot between my shoulder blades burned like the first singe of a branding iron.

Pembroke freed his hands of his leather gauntlets and wiped the sweat from his tanned brow. "Linlithgow fell by deceit. A farmer named William Bunnock brought a cart full of hay to the gate as he had done for months before that. But on one particular day the hay had hidden within it a handful of Scotsmen. They forced open the gate and more poured in. Roxburgh, on the other hand, indeed had the devil playing for it. The Black Douglas employed an old ruse—dressed his men up as wandering cows. When the garrison came out to raid, they were set upon and slaughtered."

Deceitful bastards. Have they no chivalry?

The ships, two days overdue, were finally being emptied and provisions and arms loaded onto their bursting carts. I coughed dryly as another cart, this one heaped with sheaves of arrows, rumbled by in a cloud of dust to take its place in line. It had not rained a drop since we stepped foot in Scotland. The low hills around Edinburgh were as brown as cow dun. The ground had begun to crack. Soon the cracks would grow into a chasm wide enough to swallow a column of footsoldiers.

"If we push out tomorrow, Lord Pembroke, can we make it there in time?"

"If nothing stood in our way, sire, yes. The men are weary, but if we drive hard tomorrow, it will be less far to go the next day to Stirling. My estimation, however, is that Bruce will have blocked the most direct path."

Clifford's eyes narrowed in thought. But he kept what was on his mind to himself for the moment. There was a constant tacit struggle between the two men. I should have liked to fling Pembroke and Clifford into a pit and watch them fight to the death like dogs with spiked collars and be done with it. Their quarrels were the cause for many a headache of mine.

"Good then," I said, casting a terse warning glance at Clifford to hold his tongue. Not quite noon and already a sharp pain was splitting my skull into two halves. "It will finally come to outright battle. That is why we came—to get this over with. Dear God, I am sick unto death of this place. A stinking, burnt out, God-forsaken hellhole. If I never come back again it will not be soon enough." I plucked up my reins and turned my mount toward the southwest where my quarters were. As I rode out between the writhing, grunting lines of soldiers, rolled in dust, unloading the supplies, I said to Hugh beside me, "How many times have I said that before? This country is my curse, I think."

"Perhaps, sire," Hugh said, "it is your opportunity at greatness."

Clever fellow. I enjoyed his flattery.

Come, come, Bruce. The final day of reckoning is well past due. I have an army that Alexander the Great would have envied. And you? What have you? A herd of brutish hill men waving their pitchforks and fishing knives as they charge suicidal at the greatest army in Christendom. Come. Fight. I will finish the work my sire began. What an even greater revenge that will be for all the times he mocked me for being weak.

Make room in your grave, great sire. Robert the Bruce is soon to join you.

As Pembroke drifted off to inspect and direct supplies, Clifford rode toward Hugh and me.

Clifford glanced furtively about us, not wanting to be overheard, and said lowly, "If Bruce guards the entry to Stirling along the Roman road, as we all know he shall, our army cannot pass through without first fighting them. We have lost precious time. Let me bypass them and relieve the castle. Is that not our first objective?"

Hugh and I exchanged glances. His eyebrows lifted and drew down as if in a nod of agreement.

"Indeed, it is," I acknowledged to Clifford. "You know the land. Go by the shortest route. Just get it done. Smashing Bruce into historical oblivion is secondary. But I should like that pleasure to myself."

Clifford's whiskered cheeks bunched into a smile. "Gladly, sire."

32

James Douglas – Leith, 1314

A SEA OF POLISHED SILVER glimmered in the first hazy beams of morning sun. Spearheads glinted like the fins of fishes breaking the surface. Surely, my eyes deceived me. Yet time and again, I counted and calculated the mass of English cavalry and footmen. The number was staggering. Their encampment clogged the area along the Forth between the castle and port, where two dozen ships bobbed empty-bellied at anchor. A train of wagons stretched out to the east, each one heaped with boxes, barrels, or bundles. Some of those bundles, I knew, contained arrows by the thousands: broad-heads with their flared barbs for shredding flesh and sharply pointed piles for driving through mail. I remembered the pale-haired boy at Berwick during Longshanks' assault when I was ten, caught in the shower of arrows, his brain torn open by a single shaft.

Out of habit, I ran my fingers over the string of my own bow, slung over my back. Its length was much shorter than that of the English bows, but the strength required to pull it was much less and because of that I could turn out more archers quicker. For our closer work, lurking in the woods then springing to attack, it suited our purpose. But the army before us would not be an object of unsuspecting ambush. They would line up before us in the open and from a distance would send those arrows and blacken the very sky with them. The bow that had so faithfully served me on Arran, at Perth and Roxburgh seemed an insignificant tool in light of what lay before me.

"How many, would you say?" Sir Robert Keith, whom the king had appointed as Marischal of Scotland, crouched beside me. His question brought my heart to a halt. Keith was more than twice my age. He had known my father and known him well. The years had not soured him as happens to some older men, who become cynical, languid or stubborn. On the contrary, he was open-minded, pensive at times and, although less fleet, as strong as many of my archers not past their twenties. Being of noble lineage, he was to command the cavalry. As a horseman, he was the most excellent I had ever known. His horses were not only his servants, but also his guarded treasures. He looked to the nails in their shoes himself, kept his farrier always at his side and his horse groom just a step more behind. Our horses were tethered fifty feet away on the southern side of a long, wooded ridgeline where we had huddled the night, waiting for the sun to chase away the half-darkness of mid-summer so that we could take inventory of our opposition and their strength in numbers.

On my other side, Gil de la Haye sniffed. "Two thousand mounted knights. Maybe more. Ten times that in archers and footsoldiers."

I nodded in affirmation. Keith scooted along the ground and sank down behind a tree. He drew a hand over his face and pulled down on his beard so that his mouth hung open.

"What a slaughter of man and beast we will see," he prophesied. Finally, his hand slipped down to his throat and he looked up at the canopy of leaves overhead, undisturbed by wind. "Heaven help us all."

"I would not leave it to heaven," I said, "but to King Robert. And he would say that we shall have to help ourselves." I continued to watch the English army as they stirred from their places to gather into lumpy columns. Their commanders shouted tersely, angrily. It took a long time for them to seek out their marching positions and assemble into columns, something which, by now, should have come as naturally to them as a blind man moving about his own home.

Edward of England believed in the power of numbers. But when it came to fighting, numbers were also a burden. The giant Goliath had been no match for David with his little stones. The English army was so cumbersome that they had lost the ability to move with speed. They were late getting here. Weary to the bone. Short on time. Their bellies were empty, their throats were dry and they hated the land they walked upon. I wagered they would not have dallied there at the port if they had not been in dire need of those supplies. They could not go on without them. Edward of Caernarvon had bitten off more than he could swallow in bringing such a vast horde so impossibly far. His ambition had exacted its toll. We had suffered for wanting our land back and Edward of Caernarvon should suffer for trying to wrangle it once again from us.

We could only hope our disadvantage in numbers had spawned enough ingenuity in us to make the difference. Robert had more than a few stones in his pocket and a good aim to tip the scales.

"Can you tell by their standards who is with them?" Keith asked, rejoining us. "Lancaster? Pembroke? It's all a blur of color to me from this distance. They say the eyes are the first to go from age."

"Truly? I heard that was the second," Gil jested.

"Oh, a lie," Keith said, "I assure you. But who do you see?"

"Aside from the king's standard on the oxcart to the front, I can't tell from here either. Not worth the risk of finding out. This time let curiosity yield to caution."

"I should rather like to know," Keith mused, grinning, "whose head I have the chance to cut off, that's all. Some English I hate more than others."

"Time to go back now, then?" Gil prodded, already sliding down the short hillside toward the horses.

"Don't like being here?" I teased.

He stopped and pounded the dust from his surcoat. "The three best Scottish soldiers against thirty thousand English?" His thin lips twisted into and out of a smile. "Wouldn't be fair to them, I say. So let's go back to Stirling and at least play by the rules, aye?"

"Aye. Back to Stirling. 'Though I don't know how fair a fight it will be."

Bannockburn – 22nd of June, 1314

IT WAS A HARD day's ride under a hot sun that threw our mounts into a thick lather, but there was no threat of the English army being on our tails by the time we arrived. As we neared the vacant hamlet of Bannock, lying on the south side of the meandering stream which began up in the hills and wound its way sluggishly downward and across the peat bogs and marshes before spitting out into the Forth, the men of the Scottish pickets hailed us. At the burn, we turned our horses upstream and made way toward the place where the Roman road dipped into and crossed the murky water. There I found King Robert, leading the reins of his low-slung pony, as he walked through a milling of soldiers, who were hefting piles of sod and long sticks in their arms.

He raised his hand as he saw me, Gil and Keith and beckoned us to him. We dismounted and bowed our heads once as we moved toward him. Robert took no heed of our gesture, instead dropping the reins of his pony and darting toward a trio of soldiers.

"Iver, Gram . . . not so heavy they cave in. You understand?" Robert had spent the months since spring not only scheming and plotting, but learning the names of the soldiers as they slogged in from various parts of Scotland. He drank with them and shared stories with them as they sat around their cookfires at night. The familiarity not only allowed him to win their allegiance, but it also gave him license to

criticize when the moment called for it. He strode up to one of the soldiers, who was barely able to peek over the thin mats of layered sod
cradled in his bare, grubby arms. Then he plucked a stout branch from
one of the other men's loads. "This one—it's too big. And this, John, it
is too green and will bend before it breaks. The green will work if it is
small enough, but any larger pieces must be well dried out, brittle, understand? I want the English to fall like boulders. See their horses' legs
snap like kindling. I want to watch those bleeding armored knights
flounder like pregnant cows tipped over, while the lines behind them
rush forward and fall on top of them."

"My lord?" John's face, deeply scarred from a pox, became ten
shades of red all at once. He blinked repeatedly as rivulets of perspiration streamed down his temples and into his eyes. "We're working as
fast as we can. And we hadn't enough of these things for all the pots."

John indicated an object on the ground nearby, cast from iron and
with four pointed spikes of equal length.

"That 'thing' is a caltrop, lad. Its sole purpose is to maim horses,
which will then be of no use and worse than dead. The screaming
wounded animals will serve as barriers to those behind them. Hardly a
means of fighting fairly, but the purpose of war is to win, isn't it? Now
do you want the whole English cavalry to come bounding over your
traps without missing a stride? If you've not enough caltrops, then litter
them with jagged stones or line them with pointed sticks. Whatever
does the trick. You will wish you hadn't compromised when the first
lance pricks a hole in your brain or arrows pierce your chest so that you
leak blood like seawater through a fishing net. Don't bumble now.
Figure it out. And if you have any doubts test the cover yourselves.
I'd sooner sacrifice one of you to a broken leg than to lose an entire
schiltron to a wall of English cavalry."

The three soldiers exchanged blank glances, none of them willing
to vault up and down on a flimsy pile of grass and twigs laid over a
hole in the ground to see if it would hold them up. Then in shrugging

acceptance they shuffled on toward the pots, now completely dug and being covered over artfully to conceal their exact whereabouts. From a distance, it was near to impossible to tell the ground had been disturbed at all on either side of the Roman road nearer to Stirling.

"Sire?" I swallowed, not wanting to share the news.

Absorbed in overseeing his vast project, it took a moment for Robert to shake his thoughts and give me his full attention.

"The barricades?" Robert inquired, panicked.

"Done days ago," I assured him.

Before he asked for my report, he thumped a fist on my shoulder. "James, someone came asking to join you, but damn if I can remember who or from where. It will come. Give a moment."

He screwed his eyes shut in thought. I glanced at Gil and Keith, who both nodded for me to go on.

"It will wait, m'lord. Our report first. You'll want to hear it."

His eyes flew open. "Ah! Aye, do. You all look a wee bit grim, though. Should I hear?"

Although Robert could bound lighthearted into even the darkest of moments, I could not for once reflect his outlook. "I wish I did not have to tell. They are over thirty thousand. A tenth of that is cavalry, heavy cavalry. More banners than I have ever seen in all my life. Some, I would guess, from far away places. They have plucked up half of Wales to wield their bows. The wagon train stretched out beyond the horizon. Miles."

"Many," he said to himself. A grin of amusement played over his lips. "I should have sent my brother Edward along with you to see for himself. Ah, but what use now to rub his nose in his own shit pile? He'll smell the English soon enough."

For a good while he said nothing, just turned to watch the soldiers as they bent over their holes in the earth, laying the long branches across them that had been taken from deep in Torwood many weeks ago for this very purpose. The work, although tedious at times, had kept the soldiers from falling idle and turning against each other, as might have happened in the face of bringing together so many traditional enemies in one place under one premise. When they had not been fel- ling trees, gathering branches, shoveling up sod or clawing at the earth, they had been drilled rigorously in arms and archery, often by me. The movements of each schiltron had been practiced to unthinking exact- ness, planned out like a party dance. Robert had kept their faith by encouraging them all on while I, Gil, Edward, Randolph and Keith demanded effort and precision of them, shouting till our throats were raw and our chests aching. He shook his head helplessly as one of the soldiers who had been carrying the wood collapsed. Someone hurried to him with a bucket of water and doused the man while he lay on the ground, twitching.

"The heat," he said. "Getting to them. Long days. Hard work. But it must be done. Should have been done by now. A blessing, I suppose, that the English have been in no hurry. But whether they get here by the set date or not . . . it will not matter." Suddenly he turned to me, his face clear of worry and the dark circles that had haunted beneath his eyes all the last year gone for a change. "This is fate, good James. God cursed me with that bastard Edward for a brother so it would all come to this. Battle. Scot against Sassenach—face to face. If He had wanted it to be easy for us, He'd have kept King Edward at Windsor. We're as ready as we are ever damn well going to be. I say let them come. Let them test the faith of Scotland and the love of her people for their land and their freedom. I have no fear of whatever may befall us. I am ready, James. Are you?"

He said the words as easily as any saint preparing for the Second Coming. Said it as one who understands God's wishes and never doubts the impossibility of his task. But in that certainty, he seemed somehow removed from the present, like he was already looking back on what had not yet happened. It unsettled me, not because I thought him deranged, but because I could not muster the faith in myself, given what

I had witnessed. "We have had . . . time to prepare. I agree. But what do I tell men like John, Iver and Gram there when they ask how many bloody English are going to be marching toward them along this road we're now standing on as we have this very profound conversation about God and fate?"

He winked at me. "Tell them there are a lot of them. Most of them can't count past ten, so showering them with vast numbers won't mean a thing, except there are more of them than us, and I reckon they all expect that. Tell them that the English argue, straggle, and suffer from the heat and terrain. That sickness plagues them and they've run low on food. Don't mention any cavalry and if they ask, plead ignorance." Robert drew me in close, his hands pinching either side of my face. "They are ready for this, James. Ready. Don't do or say anything to dissuade them from believing that victory is possible. Because, dear God in heaven, it is. *It is.*"

His eyes were mere inches from mine. Even through the hot air, I could feel his breath on my face, feel the sweat thick upon his calloused palms, feel his blood pounding through the veins in his fingers . . . and I believed him.

I touched him on both shoulders to draw strength from him, then pulled away to go back to my men and ready for the day to come.

As Keith handed me the reins of my horse, Robert, who was heading back toward the pots, called out.

"Ah, I do remember now. Too many things crowding my head these days. Some young man and his brother from Ross . . . no, Rothesay." He clucked at his pony. It lifted its shaggy head to follow him at a leisurely pace, stopping on occasion to pull at a clump of grass. "They went on over to Walter Stewart's tent to wait for you. I wouldn't mark either as archers, though. The mute one had broad shoulders and was already fondling a spear. Put him in one of the schiltrons. The other is barely weaned, but Walter will find a place for him. He seemed to know them already."

"Rothesay?" Keith said to me as Robert wandered away. "Stewart's men?"

"My brothers," I told him. "Hugh and Archibald."

"Brothers?" He slipped his foot into his stirrup and swung himself up. "Didn't know you had any."

"I wasn't sure if I still did, until now."

"Is Walter Stewart within?" I asked the soldier loitering at the entry to Stewart's tent. His face was unfamiliar to me, but he looked the part in his leather-trussed hose and over-sized hauberk. After leaving Robert down by the pots along the Roman road, I had gone with Keith back to the encampment at the edge of the Torwood. There we had given our horses over to squires for tending, then parted ways to manage the hundred details apiece that had to be looked over in too little a time before the inevitable finally came to pass.

The soldier blinked at me and narrowed his eyes. "Who calls?"

For months now we had made our camp in the Torwood, two miles south and uphill of the tiny village of Bannock, the inhabitants of which had departed soon after our arrival dragging their life's belongings in rickety carts or in empty grain sacks tossed over hunched backs. In that time we had hewn tall spears from the saplings and practiced with them in the clearings. We had fashioned thick barricades across every path that led through the Torwood for miles, to destroy any plans the English might have of avoiding us by that route and relieving Stirling. I had wielded my axe alongside my men, not burrowed inside my tent and emerged merely to spew orders. I had suffered from the raw pain of oozing blisters and my fingers were lumpy with calluses. I had bedded down each night weary to the bone and arisen stiff and barely able to walk or raise my arms above my head.

By now, any man who had been at camp for more than a few days would have known me. This one had no idea of my identity and I wondered if he might truly be my brother or was just another upstart, lately come. I studied the young man. In years, he was probably not yet twenty and because of his sinewy limbs and clear skin could have passed for less. The sword hanging from his belt appeared so awkwardly heavy in comparison to his frame that it threatened to topple him over. He had let the downy fuzz on his chin and upper lip go unshaven, but it did little to age him. The eyes, surrounded by thick, dark lashes, were honest and innocent and their constant shifting to take in every face and going-on revealed he had not seen much of the world before coming here. His hair was golden-brown, but loosely curled like mine.

"I am the Stewart's cousin—James Douglas," I said.

He took his time answering, scrutinizing me every inch as if he were yet doubtful of my identity. "They said you had the king's confidence—that you were important." Tentatively, he put out his hand. His palms were smooth and pink. The only callous he had was on the inside of his middle finger, where a quill had rested. Crescents of ink stain showed beneath the ends of his nails. "Archibald."

"Archibald!" I crushed him in my arms and as I thrust him back to look at him again he stiffened, uncomfortable with such an endearing gesture. "I would never have known you. A bairn when I left. Ah, but look at you now. Look. You have Eleanor's eyes and chin, true. Father's mess of hair, though. Where is Hugh?"

He pointed down the length of the corridor between the two rows of commanders' pavilions. There crouched Hugh, dipping his dented bascinet into a bucket of water intended for horses and pouring it over his head to cool off. When I called out his name, he turned his wet head and seeing Archibald curve an arm in beckon he dutifully rose and loped toward us with his bascinet tucked under his arm. He paused only long enough to scoop up a long spear, dragging its end along the ground, stirring up a trail of dust on the way.

He stopped and stood looking blankly at Archibald, ignoring me until I said his name again.

"Hugh? It's me, James. Your brother. Do you remember?"

Staring at me beneath that large forehead and bulging brow, a smile as wide as the Forth parted his lips. His shoulders were indeed broad and his bulk accentuated by the lack of neck and shorter limbs for his mass. But for the tangled loops in his hair, he looked nothing like Archibald or me.

"You remember who I am?" I asked of him. "I don't look the same, I know. Neither do you."

"H-U-G-H," he replied. He squeezed the too-small bascinet onto the top of his head, so that it more or less just sat there, and planted his spear proudly in front of him. "I fight. Good?"

"Aye, good. We'll make a fine soldier of you, Hugh." Unlike Archibald, whose hauberk sleeves dangled down below his elbows, Hugh wore no mail—only a padded jacket, covered in studded leather and with bared arms that showed his enormous, tree-trunk muscles. Hugh, I realized, had been preparing for this since we were lads out slinging stones across Douglas Water in the summer twilight when we should have been in bed. But when I glanced at my youngest brother, I saw that he cringed at the thought of going into battle, of metal tearing flesh and men killing men. Having inherited Eleanor's love for letters, he was not cut for the soldier's mold. "Archibald, you didn't have to come. You're too young yet for—"

"No, you were my age when you joined King Robert. Is that not so?"

I nodded, wishing now after having seen him that I had not sent for him at all. I could have waited until this was all over to find him, but in truth when I wrote to him I did not know if any of us would live past the day. Despite his words, I was not convinced he wanted to be here. I had known too many like him who had said the words because they thought that alone would make them brave and when they were up against the first hail of arrows, that false courage stared them hard in the face and made liars of them. I would speak to my cousin Walter later and find a place for Archibald, far from the first wave of battle. "Aye, well, you could not let Hugh come alone, could you? He would have lost his way before he ever got off Bute."

Offended somehow, Archibald looked away. He watched half a dozen men, who were carrying the tall spears that would stand against the English cavalry, make their way down the corridor among the tents in silence. Entranced, Hugh strolled after them a ways.

"Hugh's done well enough on his own while I've been gone—" Archibald said, "not that you would know. As long as there is someone to tell him what to do, he manages. I reckon he'll fit in well enough here. As for me, I'm not so certain now. I was content where I was . . . but you wrote, so I came."

The truth after all. "Aside from me asking you to, why?"

He shifted on his feet, clutched the pommel of his sword and raised his eyes to gaze at me through those long, boyish eyelashes. "Because I'd heard about you, James, the Black Douglas, for years now. Sometimes you were so close to Rothesay I could have ridden less than a day to seek you out. But I no longer knew you. Didn't even remember you. Eventually, I went to Glasgow, then on to Inchafray—more to escape boredom than to study. I heard more talk of you. About the Bruce and Randolph. Unbelievable tales. So I came, James. To see if it was true. I came because you asked and I was curious. And now you say I'm too young and maybe I should have stayed away? I thought it was more than an escort for Hugh that you wanted. It was quite a bit out of my way to go back to Rothesay and retrieve him before coming here, you realize? But I did it, because you bloody asked me to and I'm here now. Wouldn't you have done the same at my age, come here, if you could have? You contradict yourself a bit, I think."

The small, ragged group of spearmen descended the gentle slope in the slanted light of evening, then turned up the Roman road toward St. Ninian's Kirk where Randolph's men would be stationed later. More men were going that way. Walter Stewart hurried toward us, leading a clutch of nobles, among them Angus Og, Thomas Randolph and the obdurate Edward Bruce.

"There's a place for you, Archibald, if you'll not think it too trivial a duty for one of your birth." At his age I was squire to a bishop, which meant I fiddled my time away running mundane errands on church business I neither knew nor cared about. He would get little better until he had proven himself. "There are a mess of folk up on Gillies Hill." I pointed to the place up above the humble church of St. Ninian's, just west of the road there, where the camp followers milled about— late-comers and tradesmen, as well as the womenfolk, some of them wives and others belonging to no one, or to anyone for a penny or a loaf of bread. "Some untrained, most without proper weapons, but all willing to fight, if needed. Go there. Ask for Sim Leadhouse. He'll put you where needed. As for Hugh, I'll entrust him to Thomas of Moray. A few days from now, God willing, we'll talk again when you have your own tales to tell."

Archibald took a knife from his belt and held it out to me. The leather binding on the handle was cracked and the blade itself, although recently whetted, was pocked and nicked in several places. It was no more than a huntsman's knife, and a poor one at that which would have served better melted down than as it was. Failing to understand, I returned it into Archibald's palm.

"Keep it. You may have need of it."

"You don't understand," he said with a frown. "It was Father's. You left it behind when you went away to Paris."

Obligingly, I took it from him and fingered the worn binding of the handle. I remembered the day Father gave it to me. I was only ten. The day Longshanks stormed Berwick. The screams. The smoke. The smell of blood . . . I shook away the memories and tucked the knife beneath my belt.

"Archibald!" Walter Stewart called out as he passed by Hugh, who was still watching after the spearmen fading far off into the distance.

Walter drew up to us and clapped Archibald sharply on the upper arm. "You've found your brother, I see. I feared there wouldn't be time before the battle. I have lacked for a good conversation ever since you went off. Have those monks converted you yet? My friend Annice nearly wasted away from starvation when you abandoned her."

"Not completely," Archibald replied.

Angus og and Randolph hung back, discussing plans, while Edward Bruce stood with arms crossed.

"Ah, but forget about her," Walter said. "Better to let her rot. She started rumors that you were . . . how does one say it kindly? *Unnatural.*" He put his lips closer to Archibald's ear, although he barely lowered his voice. "I did not tell her that the miller's daughter knows different. She named the bairn after you. Sadly, the wee one took a fever his first winter. He did not make it."

So, Archibald's youthful embrace of the restrained life inside an abbey had less to do with devotion and more to do with seeking penance.

"James, how long has it been?" Walter turned to me and nodded in acknowledgment. Near to the same age as Archibald, duty had been thrust upon him very early on as his father had waned after suffering from apoplexy. Being the hereditary steward, he had harkened to the calling naturally and although sometimes plagued by a weakness of the lungs, he had a bright and eager mind that had earned the attention of Robert. Since he was not yet of age though, Robert had seen fit to nestle him under my wing for this undertaking, although I full well knew that part of that doing was because many of the men of nobler birth did not readily accept me as their commander, being the son of a mere knight and not an earl. Walter was my cousin as well. My mother and his father had been brother and sister, but since my mother Elizabeth had died when I was young, I had not ever seen much of my uncle James, for whom I was named.

"The king has called for us all to take up our positions," Walter said. "Can it be, so soon? I had hoped they would not come after all. I wished in vain."

Edward Bruce said nothing. He had sworn, believed, they would not come, but now they were almost here. But like the rest of us, he had accepted the inevitable and despise him though we all did, he would hold his ground when the time arrived . . . or die doing it.

Randolph said, "The English will be in Falkirk, or close there, by nightfall."

"Bannockburn tomorrow," Angus Og said. "We'll get to see the bastards eye to eye, then."

Enough of this waiting and making ready. Enough of sleeping on rocks in the stabbing rain and the bone-cracking cold, of sucking the juice from blackberries for sustenance and drinking brackish water, of creeping upon packs of strayed Englishmen and putting arrows through their ribs and knives in their overfed bellies. One more battle and let it be done. Once more. Once and for all.

As they began to disperse, I turned to Archibald. "The Abbot of Inchafray will perform Mass at daybreak, Archibald. We've all a need to purge ourselves before tomorrow's done. In the morning. A good night's rest to you."

I hadn't intended it as judgmental, having a number of sins to perfunctorily clear my own soul of, but he lowered his chin in disgrace and refused to meet my eyes. I had failed his expectations in my welcome somehow, but mending that rift would need to wait. Archibald's fleeting romp with a willing lass was an insignificant matter. In the face of Scotland's survival, it meant nothing to me or anyone else except Archibald. I doubted the abbot would even pause over such a confession, having heard our own noble king's share of improprieties. If the sins of all humanity were piled up to make a mountain, Archibald's would not have amounted to a grain of sand. But being milk-faced like that, proud and meek at the same time, the whole world was what lay within his sight and all of history was the length of his own life.

By sunset, I had my men stationed midway between the divisions of Randolph and Edward Bruce in a triangle of land that stretched from the point of St. Ninian's to the Bannock Burn. Thin clouds of red cut across the sky in omen, likes streaks of blood trailing from wounded flesh. The day's final light bathed the wooded slopes of Gillie's Hill in deep purple. There Archibald would be, waiting nervously with his pocked knife and cumbersome sword, morbidly contemplating the vast weight of his sins while the English horde poured onto the carse with their shining spears and silver-white armor. I looked toward the feeble peaked roof of St. Ninian's, by where Hugh was—Hugh, who I doubted either feared or hoped or felt any guilt. Hugh who would fight, because I asked him to, because he had always wanted to.

How strange that our lives had wandered in this way. I might curse Longshanks for casting my brothers and me apart, but I had his incompetent son to thank for bringing us together again.

33

James Douglas – Bannockburn, 23rd of June, 1314

MAURICE, THE ABBOT OF Inchafray, progressed along a meandering line of Scotsmen who bowed their heads to him as they knelt on soiled knees. His fringed head glistened with fine beads of perspiration and his plump cheeks were as red as ripened apples from weeks in the sun. In one hand, he clutched a gospel, its binding frayed and its pages slightly splayed from having absorbed too much dampness over the years. A tattered ribbon marked a passage that he read aloud from time to time. Translated, it said:

"Greater love hath no man than he would lay down his life for his friends."

A crucifix dangled from a fine silver chain wound about his knuckles. In the other hand he held a small, plain wooden casket, purported to contain the knuckle bones of St. Fillan. At intervals he broke from his Latin droning, as someone stretched out their hands to touch the box and utter a prayer. Occasionally, a soldier poured out a brief confession and the abbot placed the palm of his hand upon the man's forehead and absolved him of sins past.

I looked to the sky where the sun labored to climb. A lion-sized hunger growled inside my empty belly. Priests floated by, tearing off crumbs from loaves of coarse bread and offering sips of water from a community bowl. My greaves pressed painfully into my shinbones as I knelt. Down the lines, snatches of prayer drifted heavenward. Men took a pinch of earth and placed it beneath their tongues. Here and there a cough broke the silence, a horse snorted, a weapon scraped against a shield. My horse's sour breath warmed my neck, then his lips brushed against my coif and shoulder plates. He nudged me forward. I caught myself with my left hand, still grasping the hilt of my sword in my right as the tip of its blade dug into the earth.

"Damn you," I muttered, as I twisted around to scold an absent squire for not minding my mischievous horse better.

"If it's the English you're referring to," Abbot Maurice said, "Our Lord will do the damning, not you."

"I was not." I scraped my dirty palm on a tuft of grass, then wrapped it around the hilt of my sword, interlocking my fingers and touching my forehead to the crossguard. "Your blessing, Father."

"First, a confession, Master James?"

"God knows my sins and to Him I will answer. Must I need repeat them aloud before everyone here?"

Indignant, the abbot snapped his Holy Gospel shut and snorted at me with the peculiar familiarity of a barnyard pig. "Given the circumstances, I would say a private confession is out of the question. Now, I haven't time to barter with you over conveniences and matters of trivial privacy. Have you anything to confess to?"

"Nothing I care to admit."

"May God have abundant mercy on your soul, James Douglas. Given all your deeds thus far, you need it as much as any man here."

I peered at him over the iron wings of the crossguard of my sword. "Is that an admonishment . . . or a compliment, dear Father?"

Shocked at my glibness, he tucked his chin into the loose folds of his neck and rattled his egg-shaped head at me. I dropped my eyes as his fat fingers pressed into my scalp. He rumbled in Latin, parts of it yet familiar to my faded memory, and quickly moved on to the next man beside me—Boyd, who had tenfold the number of sins to his score, but had figured long ago that you could commit as many as you pleased so long as some holy man purged you of them, as if none then ever counted against him. Boyd had also learned that you did not argue with Abbot Maurice unless you wanted your own private sermon and a staff cracked across your knees.

When the Abbott had moved further down the line, Boyd cleared his throat, spat at the ground and elbowed me in the side. "Tell them what they want to hear. They'll leave you the bloody hell alone then."

I cracked a smile, but it turned to a grimace as I stood. Pain sliced through my calf where the cow had stomped on my leg at Roxburgh—a pain I would never be rid of. Beneath my left mail sleeve was a deep indentation where the arrow had pierced my arm when we had scaled the walls at Perth on a frigid winter night. I glanced down at my knuckles, riddled with lines of pink, the outer two fingers on my left hand gnarled when they had broken a fall from my horse more than once. I had not so much the want to look after my soul this day, as I did to preserve my body through to tomorrow. If I made it that far . . . I would re-examine the matter of salvation then. "Priests are mere men, Boyd. They stumble like everyone else, then throw on their robes and tell us all to repent. Pious, filthy liars, most of them."

Boyd gathered his shield from the ground and stood. "You're in a righteous and uplifting mood today, *Master* Douglas."

"I'm in a mood for killing Englishman, Boyd. That's what I am. Join me?"

"Well, I didn't come here to be blessed over some dead monk's bones or doused with holy water from Ireland."

"Her name was Saint Skeoch and the water comes from a well in St. Ninian's. She was Irish, though what brought her here or the cause for her sainthood I don't know. As for St. Fillan's bones, Robert would not begin this battle without them. They give the men faith that God is with them in this. If that's what they need, I say give it to them." I gathered the reins of my horse. "Will you go back to your wife when it's all over? How long since you've seen her?"

"Five years. But she died two years ago . . . tertian fever, or some such thing, so one of my sons told me."

"You never said."

"Thought I did. I had a lot to drink that night, so maybe it just didn't make sense when I said it."

"You're drunk every other time I see you, Boyd."

"Ah? Well, it was one of those times that I learned about it. She was a strong woman. A good mother. And a fist like a smith's hammer. Fought me every time I took her, but we both liked it that way. I won't marry again, though. Got myself a woman, down in Lanark, when I can get there."

"I'm happy for you, Boyd."

"And you? Do you have a woman?"

"*Had* women, aye. But not 'a' woman. No, I don't have one all to myself now." The implication was that I had been with many. The true count, in all my life, totaled two. One had been a prostitute in Paris, when I was a student there, that I nearly knocked over while running from a merchant whose bag of coin I'd stolen. She offered me a hiding place and her sexual favors in return for a few of those coins. Half curious, half afraid to go out in the street again for fear of being discovered, I took her up on her offer. The whole affair lasted not five minutes and in the diversion, an accomplice of hers in turn stole the money from me. The second time had been with a camp follower while encamped in Selkirk Forest two years past, who, it turned out, already had a husband. For that I suffered guilt, because the man was one of my own soldiers, who I suspect, never knew of his wife's infidelity. Since then, I'd been too preoccupied to make any effort to impress a woman.

"I seem to have a reputation that precedes me," I said. "Scares them." That was a scalding lie and Boyd knew it. Exceedingly shy with women, I compensated for my lack of courage there in battle. Put pretty before me and I was tongue-tied and a bumbling fool.

"Pity, James. You've a fine face and an honest manner. Perhaps a wee bit less manners would serve you better?" He tugged at his beard, extracting a thought from beneath that big, red mat of hair. "I've a daughter, seventeen—ripe for marriage."

"Who said I was looking for a wife? If I had a wife, just where would I keep her?" I pulled myself up into the comfort of my saddle. The smells of leather, horse hide and newly oiled metal revived fresh memories of hard-won fights and times spent haunting English armies from the shadows of the woods and hills. I could hardly recall my life before such times.

"What about Lady de Fiennes? She's a widow now, aye?"

"I have no home, Boyd, and that would be a sore point for any respectable woman. Besides, she's English."

"I hear your father took your mother captive and held her until she agreed to marry him. She was English, wasn't she?"

"They were in love, Boyd. Her father wouldn't allow the marriage—at least not until she became pregnant with me."

"You could always—"

"What? Take off for England? I haven't time right now and I doubt she'd be willing. That's not my way, Boyd." It was true I'd never be as bold as my father—stealing a women with the intent to put a child in her—but I had thought often of Lady de Fiennes. Never before had a woman's beauty so haunted me.

I searched passing faces for Archibald, Thomas Randolph, and Gil de la Haye . . . but saw no sign of them. Old Alexander Lindsay strode by, his sword at his hip and his eyes as keen as ever. Close behind him, Neil Campbell moved wordlessly among a grumbling clutch of spearmen. I looked toward the carse, broken by coarse tufts of marsh grass and bordered by the deeply cut, looping burn. Across it wound the bridle path, now empty. Between our scattered lines on the slopes of New Park and the mixed expanse of the carse, the Scottish divisions were gathering up in expectation. A year's worth of anticipation . . . and dread. Centuries' worth of struggle. All of us waiting to offer blood in exchange for hope.

Boyd squeezed his rebellious head of hair beneath his helmet. Idly, he swung his axe upside down at his side. "Fine day for a battle, aye?"

"If there is such a thing, aye." I tugged the reins of my horse to turn, then pulled back on them. "Boyd? If you see Gil or Randolph before . . . before it begins, tell them something for me, will you?"

He shrugged at me, curious.

"Greater love hath no man than he would lay down his life for his friends."

"Och!" He spit at the ground and scowled. "Priest's dribble. Speak for yourself, James Douglas. If it should come to preserving you or me, then I can't say I love you that bloody much."

"You're a goddamn liar, Boyd. Tell them, will you?"

I clucked at my mount and went to my place beside my cousin, Walter Stewart. Admirably, the manhood of Scotland bore out the tedium of the day, maintaining their lines, weapons at hand, as they passed flasks of water. King Robert, who had shaped this quarreling mob into a cohesive and skilled machine of war in an impossibly short span, was perhaps the most anxious of all. If any of us pondered upon the possibility of losing our lives this day or the next, it was all menial when compared to what he gambled.

The reflection of a late afternoon sun sparked off the plain, golden circlet adorning his helmet as he sat on his pony between his own division, guarding the north side of the Roman road, and mine. He had wiled away the day riding along the road so that all his soldiers could see him, lending courage in the bare essence of his presence—his own eye watchful of the carse beyond the ghostly village and the road from Edinburgh to Stirling that shot through a densely wooded archway before leading out to the more sparsely wooded slopes of New Park.

"How many were there?" Walter asked me. "More than at Falkirk or Stirling, would you say?"

"I was not at either place, Walter. I would not dare to guess."

"But can we beat them, James? Beat the English here, on our own ground?" His words were more trepidation than anticipation. He would wear himself out with worry before the English came into sight.

"Robert believes we can," I told him . . . and said nothing more, for as I looked toward the road by where Robert stood vigil on his sturdy gray pony, there . . . a knight rode at a full gallop from the place where the road just north of the burn yielded itself to New Park.

An English knight, his lance held high, riding toward our king. And Robert, who had all the time in the world to retreat to his own lines, waited there to meet him.

34

Edward II – Bannockburn, 23rd of June, 1314

SIR PHILIP MOWBRAY KNELT on the road before me wearing a coat of dust. He cradled his helmet on his knee between gloved hands.

"I trust you came bearing good news, Mowbray," I said, "or else it would have been better of you not to come at all. You appear much wearier than the last time I laid eyes on you."

"I do not think I have been in your presence for many years, sire. This past year has been worrisome. It has taken its toll on everyone."

"The Bruce as well, I trust?"

He raised his eyes, bloodshot from the fine grit kicked up by pounding hooves on the road. "I would not know."

Above the trees, a lacework of clouds in a pale, blue sky was broken by the rugged, dark rock of Stirling's base. At its peak, the fortress stood guard over the broad valley of the Forth, beckoning me like a purpose unto which I was born. To either side of me, Gilbert de Clare and Pembroke were mounted. Directly behind me, young Hugh Despenser. We were but miles from our destination and as we had approached a small stream that fed into the Forth, the whole English army was grinding to a halt while we gathered to receive our messenger and determine a precise course of action.

"So, Mowbray," I said, "where is Scotland's honor? Crouched in the wood with slings and rocks in their usual cowardly manner?"

His eyebrows lifted well onto his deeply lined forehead. "I came here by a very wide route west of New Park, sire. The roads through there are impassable for an army of this magnitude. The Scots have done good work of damming even the slightest deer-path."

Pembroke spoke. "So if not huddled there, where do we find them?"

"Not celebrating at Stirling?" I added with a flare of shock, imagining the worst.

"No, sire," Mowbray said. "Bruce is utterly a man of his word. You have met the terms that Edward Bruce and I agreed to by arriving this day within the assigned limits for relieving the castle. One day more and—"

"One more day and your head would be somewhere else than upon your shoulders." I glared at my counselors in consternation. "But you failed to answer the question. Where precisely do we find the Scots?"

"Arrayed on the slope falling between the woods of New Park and the Bannock Burn, sire. They will not let you pass without a fight, I regret to say."

"Regret why?"

"You do not owe them a battle, sire. I urge you to send forth an envoy, reminding them of the terms, but not until after you have taken your army far west and to Stirling."

"But you yourself have said we would have to go a long way about. This army is a large one, Mowbray. We would lose days by that fashion. Furthermore, we have not dragged ourselves from the virtual paradise of England into the steaming bowels of hell known as Scotland only to skulk behind the arses of our enemies as if we lived in fear of them. This is the army of England. *My* army. Even the might of the continent cannot stand against it. We have no hesitation of sweeping aside

Highland rabble to claim what now belongs to us. Why is it that you think they will not flee when they lay eyes on this?" I swept a hand behind me at the lumbering column, stretching miles yet down the road along which we had come by way of Edinburgh, Berwick, London . . .

"They very well might, sire," Hugh contemplated. "And yet, they might not."

Everyone turned to look at him, wearing a bemused grin. As if his remark were an insignificant thought, considered and passed over, Hugh swung his leg down and slipped the other foot from his stirrup, landing nimbly in his armor upon the baked dirt of the road.

Behind him, Hereford jammed his helmet onto his head and clenched his reins in both hands. "Send me with the cavalry along the road. Let us give Bruce a test of his mettle."

"You're too eager, Hereford," Gilbert berated. "Stirling is relieved. Our footsoldiers are weary and our horses parched. We require a day of rest."

"To what end, Gilbert?" I pressed. "We're all ready to fight and yet you would prefer to *rest*?"

"What end?" Gilbert echoed. "To renew ourselves. You can't possibly ask them to face the Scots now. Twenty-two miles yesterday, you whipped them along. Another ten today and now you want to throw them at the feet of several thousand fresh and exhilarated foes, hungering for their blood? Edward, pause a moment and consider it, damn it. Hold back one day. Sweet Jesus in heaven—*one* day! You have naught to lose, Edward."

"My pride, Gilbert. I would lose my pride if we dallied here one more day. Already it has been chafed raw. It is not enough that we are within sight of Stirling. By tomorrow we shall ride through its gatehouse. And if Robert of Scotland cares to throw himself across our path, then he will be trampled for his folly. So take the cavalry, on that road and across that stream, and beat the bloody bastards back into the woods."

"And if I refuse?"

"Surely, Gilbert, my eyes will never see the likes of that. Not from you." That my constant companion since boyhood would turn against me sat with impossible unease upon my conscience. He was weary, irritable. We all were. Yet it remained that I was his king, the overlord of every man on the isle of Britain, and I had long ago wearied of being defied. I held his gaze and laid down the gauntlet. "But if you do, then take your disloyal, insubordinate face, alone, back down that road on which we just came—all the way back to blessed England."

Hereford spurred his horse so that it lurched forward, nearly trampling the still-kneeling Mowbray who scurried aside, and pranced before Gilbert. "It is my right to lead the vanguard! Mine, I say!" He flailed his boulder-like fist at Gilbert. "I am High Constable of England and by tradition I should lead this army onto the battlefield. It's bloodless men that balk at a fight. Let me ride out and I vow I will shatter them in the first blow!"

Gilbert's face reddened in resentment. "Oh, great, bloody Christ! What will you do if they don't run at the sight of your ugly face or fall like flies in the wake of your rotten odor? What if they fight and fight well?"

Hereford held his breath. His eyes bulged. His hand plunged across the lower part of his torso and yanked his restless sword from its scabbard.

Anticipating Hereford's actions, Pembroke maneuvered his mount between them. He thrust open palms at both men. "A brief moment, lords." He held his arms aloft until both men showed signs of settling. "We cannot take the Scots from behind in New Park, as Mowbray has advised, nor bypass them by that route as our king has so sagely pointed out. The Scots will either flee or hold their ground. What we need to do is test them. If they flee, the road to Stirling is clear. If they stand, we will have time to array ourselves before the morrow's dawn."

"So you," Gilbert delved, his countenance set as hard as granite, "would send our cavalry forward today? Without reconnaissance? Make good your reasoning, Lord Pembroke, because I am hard pressed to see the hurry in all this."

"We have all the reconnaissance we require from Sir Philip Mowbray." Pembroke eased back against the cantle of his saddle. "Besides, we have come this far without them taking so much as a swat at us . . . and when has Robert the Bruce ever not run from a fair fight, earl?"

I raised a hand to interrupt them. "We will dispatch Beaumont and Clifford along the track toward the river where they can cover the Scots' rear flank if they take flight, should the vanguard be engaged. If not, they can proceed on to Stirling with all haste."

Pembroke narrowed his dark eyes at me, noting the omission of his own name in these rapidly dispersed plans.

"You, Lord Pembroke," I said to him, "will keep by us. I require the benefit of your counsel ere tomorrow breaks."

Satisfied with that, he gave a subtle nod and fell quiet.

"What of my right to lead this army?" Hereford bellowed.

"On that I defer to the king," Pembroke prudently said.

"Well?" Hereford's breath came in broken gasps. His fingers opened and clasped the hilt of his weapon repeatedly.

The Earl of Hereford was a veteran of many tournaments, but in an intimate knowledge of military matters he was limited. On that account, I laid my trust in my nephew, Gilbert, despite his present unwillingness. "Hugh? Call Clifford and Beaumont forward and inform them of our instructions, per the Earl of Pembroke's plan. Hereford, ride forward . . . but with Gilbert de Clare as your joint commander. Understood?"

Hereford did not need to be told twice. He pricked his horse so hard in the flanks with his spurs that it bucked. Then he flew off toward the cavalrymen to prepare them.

Gilbert tarried behind. He eased his horse toward mine, the bright colors of its trappings dulled by dirt. There was a coolness in his tone as he spoke to me. "I'll do as you command, my lord, but damn you if you think that blundering swine was ever more loyal to you than I."

"Then do more than talk of it," I said.

He snapped his reins smartly and wheeled away to join Hereford.

When the larger part of the army had drawn up along the old Roman road—the men, the horses, the carts and arms—all choked in a swirling, hot cloud of dust, details of the plan were worked over and set in action. Beaumont and Clifford assembled their men toward the river and the cavalry set off toward the stand of woods embracing the steeply sided stream known as the Bannock Burn. I sent Mowbray back to Stirling with a curt reminder to hold the castle in waiting for us until the Scots were dealt with.

Much to the disdain of both, Gilbert and Hereford rode side by side in the fore. But as their front line dipped down toward the stream, one of them took the lead, galloping hard through the leafy archway, his lance balanced skyward. I could barely make out a flash of yellow and red—the colors of Gilbert's surcoat—as he disappeared from view.

You were never like that in the hunt—never out ahead. Usually, you were asleep beneath an oak tree while Piers took down a stag with his bow or speared a boar. But it was always you who spun the tale of the hunt later on as we nursed our cups of wine and filled them again.

Have a care and hasten back. I might find it in me to mete out a soothing word or two for you, whom I love as a brother.

35

James Douglas – Bannockburn, 23rd of June, 1314

THE POWERFUL STEED OF the red and yellow clad knight galloped out into the open. With every strike of its hooves, its muscles rippled. Dark patches of sweat stained its brown hide. Its deep muzzle was tucked to a bulging chest. Black eyes, surveying the ground before it, begged no forgiveness from a hard-driving master. Some distance behind the knight, there followed the splash of hooves crossing the burn and the clatter of other mounted knights in the wake of his thunder. The road itself had been left free of the waist-deep pots, so as to give the appearance that nothing had been tampered with. Just beyond where the road crossed the burn was a small stretch of woodland and it was there the traps had been laid on either side. The lone knight was a hundred feet or more free of the line of trees and still the rest had not appeared. He was far out ahead, but to what purpose other than sheer insanity . . .

Robert had not moved from his post, nor had he looked to his lines or called out for assistance. He lowered his visor. Gripped his shield. Coaxed his pony into a canter.

Walter gasped beside me. "My God. What is he doing?"

Baffled, frozen in disbelief, I watched as witness and could not move or speak or breathe.

The English knight braced all his strength against his lance and lowered it as Robert came at him. The Englishman's horse dwarfed the king's and was pressed to a full gallop. Robert by now had slowed his mount to a gentle clip over the parched grass of the meadow. The lance tip bore down—aiming for Robert's heart.

The hooves of Robert's pony plodded. The heavy feathering on its forelegs danced with each restrained stride as it kept its course. The knight leaned into his long-reaching weapon, yearning toward a victory beyond expectation. The distance closed. Robert's pony dipped its head and veered suddenly to the left, crossing in front of the knight. The move was too swiftly done for the knight to shift his lance or alter the direction of his own mount. As his lance bolted harmlessly past the king, the knight jerked his head to the right, only long enough to see Robert shoot up straight-legged in his stirrups to gain height and swipe his axe downward.

The axe blade struck squarely on the front of the knight's helmet. And the blow had been delivered with such power and accuracy, that it cleaved the metal and embedded itself in the knight's skull.

Robert's arm whipped back with the force. The knight reeled in his saddle, swayed left, then right and finally back as the panic-stricken steed reared. When its hooves struck the ground, it spun tightly, tossing the knight from its back. The knight's head struck the ground in a spray of scarlet—the axe blade still buried in his riven skull as blood bubbled from the cleft. One foot, twisted in the stirrup, entangled his lifeless body, which bounced and kicked up dust as the horse continued on.

Gripping nothing but the splintered handle of a broken axe, Robert watched the knight's body being dragged across the baked earth. For a stunned moment, there was absolute silence. Then, as the English cavalry broke through the trees, a war cry rose in challenge from the throats of a thousand Highlanders who spilled down the hill where Robert's division had lain in wait.

But the host of English horsemen, who had followed behind the now fallen knight, were emerging in disorder. The pots had claimed their victims—swallowing heavy horses burdened with their armored masters and sending other animals in such a tumble that they screamed with the terrible agony of shattered bones. The riders that broke over the northern bank of the burn and out into the open were cautious, glancing back, holding their mounts in check until others could come abreast of them. Those to the fore had gained daylight by luck alone. But those behind, if not horseless because of the spiked caltrops driving into their horses' legs or crushed by the weight of others falling on top of them, were either hindered by the erupting chaos or crying out from the rear. In utter futility, the English were attempting to draw up into a line to meet the onslaught of frenzied Highlanders tearing down the hillside, their bare legs churning, swearing oaths of annihilation in the Gaelic tongue, drumming their round shields, their faces streaked in blue, their limed hair flying out behind.

Robert turned his pony back, at last. He waved madly, trying to signal Angus Og to recall his men. Angus gave the word and a horn sounded over the valley and the wild men slowed, still screaming, still beating their weapons against their shields in a terrible, deafening clamor.

And the English, turned . . . and went, back to where they had come from.

As if in a fog, Robert stood and stared at the splintered axe handle in his palm. After scouts had been sent and returned with new information of the progress of King Edward's army, Randolph, Edward and I had parted from our divisions and joined Robert's temporarily.

"And what the bloody hell was that about?" Edward scolded, dropping from his saddle as he rode in. Arms swinging, he strode angrily toward his older brother.

But Robert said nothing. Just stared at the jagged wood of the axe handle, then glanced vaguely off toward where the body of the fallen knight was being laid out behind the front line of his division. A few Highlanders had managed to calm the terrified knight's horse and cut through the stirrup strap to free the dead man. It was with a watchful eye and numerous curses that Angus Og restrained his men from stripping the body of its valuables.

Edward slammed his palm into Robert's shoulder to get his attention. "What in the—"

"Gilbert," Robert said with a twinge of melancholy, blinking. "Gilbert de Clare . . . of Gloucester. His stepfather once saved my life."

"An Englishman, Robert. I prefer them all dead, myself." Edward pulled off his gauntlets and smacked the dust from them. "Speaking of 'dead'—you could have been killed. That would have left me in charge and I hasten to say I doubt that was your wish as you sat there like a blatant fool begging to have your heart rammed through the back of your spine, was it?"

Robert ignored him, gazing off into the distance, his eyebrows twitching with concentration.

Boiling under his mail, Edward stepped in front of him. "For a year you never once failed to remind me of the risk I had put upon you. This is no bloody time for heroics. Dead men don't lead armies."

I could never be certain if Edward Bruce had his own abrasive way of displaying a protective side for his brother, or if he merely grabbed at every barb he could because in patronizing Robert it elevated him. One thing was without question: Edward believed he had been cheated in the birth order.

Chewing on his patience, Robert lowered his head a moment. Gil spared him a reply by speaking.

"I would say," Gil calmly observed as he tightened a bothersome strap of his right arm plate, "that I have never seen so many Scots up on their feet and cheering at one time. Sinclairs, Macdougalls, Frasers and

Campbells, shoulder to shoulder with Highlanders and . . . my God . . . do you ever recall seeing them all on the same side of a fight at once? Incredible."

The others nodded in agreement. Edward gave him a killing glare that went unanswered. Most men knew that the best way to keep from getting trampled on by Edward was to ignore him—a tactic which only infuriated Edward further at being so offhandedly dismissed.

The mood turned quickly somber again, as Robert glanced at the bloodied corpse of the Earl of Gloucester being laid out and wrapped in a sheet. Randolph spoke, "If you wish, I'll tell them to have the earl's body taken to the kirk in St. Ninian's."

"Should I fetch Abbot Maurice?" I asked, not knowing what was proper or timely, given the circumstances.

"Of course," Robert answered tersely, as he brushed past me. He rushed forward several quick strides, out away from the front line clinging to the edge of the wood. He glanced at Randolph, then back toward the land beyond the village of Bannockburn and raised a finger to point. "Thomas? Do you see? They couldn't penetrate by the road, so now they're evading us by the bridle path. As we guessed. Vain, rock-headed bastards. Best go from here, Thomas, or else you'll miss your opportunity altogether."

In a moment, Randolph was remounted and flying down the road toward St. Ninian's. Another English division of cavalry was moving along the narrow bridle path on the carse. Unlike the vanguard that had been scattered by the pots on either side of the old Roman road, this division was a cohesive one—riding at a steady, yet unhurried pace, their lines tight and straight.

Randolph's men were on their feet and armed by the time he arrived and called them into formation. Moving as one, the circle of spears went forward. The English had their opportunity to go on and avoid battle, but it appeared that today they would not have it so. Pride had a way of compromising sensibility. Drawing out in a line, the first wave of cavalry rushed at the prickling mound of spears.

There are never times as helpless as watching a friend toil for his very existence and sitting there, doing nothing about it. Bridling, I rode my horse from where Robert was, stoically watching the fight go on, and to the vacant ground between the king's division and my own. Randolph's schiltron held, but there were casualties—as many Scots as English. More times than I could count I rode that distance back and forth, finally plunging to my knees before Robert and begging for him to allow me to take my men and aid the Earl of Moray.

"Not yet, James. Not yet." Compulsively, his right thumb stroked his left forearm. He leaned forward, squinting. "There. Another English knight down. And another. But it is hard to tell with our own. They just . . . disappear."

"Then let me go, I beg." I lifted my shield from its holding place on my saddle and strapped it to my forearm, as if I knew he would yield at that. "If you let Walter and me go to him—"

"No, no. Not yet, I told you. Don't take what belongs to Thomas. Faith, faith. He will persist."

Exasperated, I took to my saddle, slapped my horse on the rump and sped back to my division, where at least I could watch more closely and go to him if his men fell into worse trouble—with or without Robert's blessing.

The sun began to slide behind the looming silhouette of Stirling Castle. The fighting had slowed, for their strength was waning. A wounded Scottish soldier, one arm hacked off just above the elbow, crawled from beneath the crowding legs of his comrades. He pulled himself along with that bony stump of a limb and one good hand, biting his lip in silence, trying to escape without notice. But an English knight, or perhaps a squire judging by his piecemeal, rusted armor, who had been pushed from the fray and could not find a hole to go at the schiltron, saw him and ran him down, clubbing him in the back of the head with a mace. Leaning from his saddle, the knight struck again and again as the Scotsman lay there helpless, his legs twitching and his face drowning in his own pool of blood.

Now. I motioned to Walter and told him to make ready to go to Randolph's aid. He called the men up into their circular formation and as our lines shifted forward and took their first steps, several English knights fell back, shouting to the others to retreat. They had suffered too many losses and could neither rip nor hammer their way through. Randolph's schiltron had held together, warding off last moment blows of desperation. The English trickled away, beaten and bedraggled on wounded horses, back along the path and over the burn. With a collective moan, Randolph's men sank to their knees. They leaned against their spears and looked around them.

A cheer broke—first from my own men and then from each of the other divisions. Randolph managed to rally his men back up the slope a ways, collecting the wounded and clearing away the fallen as they went.

That night, there was a great celebration among the soldiers of Scotland. King Robert called together his commanders and we met in the woods of New Park at the southern foot of Gillies Hill as dusk yielded to darkness. But while we floated giddily about, voices raised in song and men already re-telling the tale with the usual Scottish embellishments, the English were beginning to move onto the carse. Not a detachment of vanity-laden cavalry, but the whole of the English army. They took their axes to the houses of Bannockburn and ripped loose the doors, the rafters and the thatch of those empty shells and began laying them down across the boggy places so their men, horses and wagons could pass over. I watched for a long time at the edge of the wood. Their progress was so slow and the number of men yet needing to cross so huge, that I surmised it would take them most of the night. They had come a long ways in a short time and would get no rest this night.

Sunrise would come early. The day had been brutally long. I had divested myself of my mail and all but my sword, intending to gain a few precious and direly needed hours of sleep before the morrow arrived. First, I would attend to Robert's call and so I went from the edge of the wood to the place where Robert's tent stood. Joyful voices came from within and the light of a lamp threw shifting shadows on the canvas walls. Just outside, Randolph parted from some of his men. The infusive exhilaration of their victory had washed away all traces of fatigue.

"Hugh? How is he?" I asked uneasily.

"Never better, James. Brave and strong as any Douglas. I will tell him that you asked after him when I see him again. Come on."

I followed Randolph inside.

Boyd crushed Randolph in his brutish arms. "Ah ha!" he laughed. "By God, you sent the bastards off with a sound thrashing!"

Robert stood in the middle of the gathering. His hands were clasped behind his lower back. "You have done well today, Thomas. Edinburgh and now this. You and your men are to be congratulated."

A sheepish grin flicked over Thomas Randolph's mouth. The lamp-light revealed a bruise, slowly purpling, on his right cheek. He nodded in thanks. "I fought as a Scotsman, that is all."

"And tomorrow, my lord," I addressed the king, "tomorrow, what would you have of us? The day is here. We are armed. They have come and shown they'll fight. Tell us . . . what to do."

All went silent inside. The evening's jubilation continued on outside the crowded tent. Robert came to me and laid a hand firm upon my shoulder. "The English came thinking we would do nothing but watch as they passed by. Twice today we stood them down and sent them running. So what do you suppose they think now, James?" He gripped both of my shoulders, then let go and turned to the others in the circle. "Thomas, Edward, Gil, Keith?"

Sir Robert Keith, one of only three yet in full mail, said, "I would think we had come up against a mob of stubborn fools begging for a lesson in humility."

"Ah." Robert raised a single finger and tapped at his temple. "You're thinking as knights, though. Boyd, what would a footsoldier, an English footsoldier, think of his predicament? Of facing us, after his own leaders have been turned back by mere Scotsmen?"

Rubbing at his belly, Boyd chuckled. "I'd think I might as well be a lamb on a spit." He sniffed. "And I could damn well smell my own flesh roasting right now."

"So?" Edward jumped to the heart of the reason for our gathering. "You're saying we're going to fight?"

"I won't tell any of you that," Robert said. "But I'll ask you what you want to do. Stirling is only one castle among dozens. Between Roxburgh and Inverness, how many fortresses are yet in English hands and how many lie either in ours or obliterated? For eight years, we have slowly whittled away at their possessions without ever meeting them in full battle. Clan by clan, stone by stone, Scotland is becoming one. One country, as it has never been before. The process has been long and tedious to many of you, but has it not served? Without shame, we could go from here tomorrow and live to fight another day in the same way we always have. And we could win everything back that way . . . in time. But the question remains—how will you fight them? When? And where?"

Randolph shifted in the weighty silence that ensued. His shoulders humbly stooped, he raised his chin from his chest and said, "Order us to the field at first light. We will not fail you. Some will die, but better that they should do so fighting for their freedom, than having given it up."

"Very well. As you would have it. In the morning—make ready, my friends."

36

Robert the Bruce – Bannockburn, 24th of June, 1314

A S I LOOKED OUT on a sea of faces—their eyes set on the thin strand of tomorrow, their heartbeats echoing with the rhythm of all their yesterdays—I thought surely I looked upon all the sons of Scotland of all the ages there in one place at one time, ready to fight for the very fistful of dirt they were each standing on. And in that I never saw more truth . . . than to truly live, was to have something worth dying for.

I held my fingers out to the new day. In that virgin light—bold strands of pink and orange breaking over the rim of the horizon—I saw hope, and I wrapped my fingers around that light and brought it to my heart. Dawn's long shadows stretched across the land and the golden light of summer filtered down through the green-cloaked trees where my men stirred and woke. Prayers were whispered. Soldiers made the sign of the cross over and over. They kissed the ground. Counted arrows. Tightened straps. Memorized the faces around them . . . Small things that had already been done a hundred times. Then we began to assemble beyond the wood, out on the high ground where we could see what awaited us . . . and be clearly seen by those who had come to meet our challenge.

That same light pouring over the army of Scotland, that was that day spread out on the gentle slopes of New Park, also shone down upon the army of England, gathered now upon the carse in the openness between the loop of the Bannock Burn and the Pelstream. The tide was up. The water would be deep behind them. They filled the whole place, with as many men as I had ever seen in all my life put together. James and Keith had not exaggerated. Pennons and banners fluttered in a rising breeze, heralding the nobility of England and abroad.

The noble Gilbert de Clare, Earl of Gloucester, was already among their fallen. His stepfather Ralph de Monthermer had spared me from Longshanks' gallows when he warned me of Comyn's plot to betray me at Windsor. Because of Ralph's debt to my grandfather, he had shown me a grace, allowing my escape, so I could live to see this day. Now that I was here, I prayed God would have the grace to bring me through to tomorrow. But of late, I could not discern one day from the previous or the next. The sign of a soul living in a dream. Of a body that has known too little sleep.

Last night I had knelt in prayer through most of the dark hours next to Gilbert de Clare's body. He had been laid before the altar in St. Ninian's Kirk, wrapped up in a shroud stained brown with the seeping blood from his deep, singular wound, his sword and shield set honorably upon his lifeless chest. Behind his corpse glowed a hundred tallow candles, flickering like points of starlight, as if this one knight had already been taken into heaven.

Up above him on the yellowed wall behind the altar dangled a cross wrought of bronze. In its center was set a small dark, blood-red jewel, surrounded by the writhing knotwork of the people who once roamed this land freely—a people who had left as their legacy not the written word or great, soaring castles, but jewels and weapons and mysterious relics such as this one. A nearly forgotten people, overrun throughout the centuries by greedy neighbors and far-traveled foreigners whose own riches were not enough for them. And now come the English, once more.

I called to me James and Walter, among others, and laid the flat of my blade upon their shoulders as they knelt in newly granted knighthood.

I mounted and put spurs to my pony. My helmet tucked under my arm so that all could see my face, I rode past the tiny cluster of houses of St. Ninian's, between the watchful divisions of Keith and Douglas and on past Randolph's until I reached the edge of Edward's men. Their voices rose in a rolling wave, until I raised my hand in the air. The rumble broke in places and fell away like the surf meeting its end against a ragged shore.

"This is the day . . . when you ask yourselves, how great is your faith in God and your love of freedom? For eight years, I have toiled to make this kingdom one. And in that time, I have lost three brothers and more. Who among you has not lost a kinsman or friend in this struggle? You have paid the price in blood. Scotland has paid the price. You see there those who have exacted that price and say that you have no right to freedom. They come, on their warhorses and in their mail, to destroy you and take what little you have. They want what is yours. Will you let them have it? Your wives, your children, your freedom?"

They rattled their weapons and cried out. Again, I lifted my hand to heaven and spoke:

"Nay. You are here with me, of your own will, so for that, I say you will not bend in slavery one more day. I have fought with you, known your courage and your honor. Within your hands, lies victory. So with those hands and with all your strength, pray to God, that His right will prevail—for this is the day that they will one day say honorable men came and fought for what was theirs. But to win this day you must be valiant. Do not let your hearts fail you. Be steadfast and brave. Go forth, my men. God is with you!"

Abbot Maurice blessed the army of Scotland.

The English had barely moved. Their archers had not yet been rallied to the fore, as was the English custom.

Ah, a blessing, Edward of Caernarvon, that you are so dull in your arrogance. You bide your time, expecting to make the first move at your leisure. One day you leap before looking at the size of the chasm before you and the next you are yet in your nightclothes while your enemy is pounding on your door. Wake now, Edward, before we set fire to your thatch and smoke you out. You came for a fight. You have one.

As the brave of Scotland roared on, I resumed my position behind the first three columns with my own men. To my far right, my brother Edward's standard fluttered—the blue lion on a field of white. Directly to his left, Randolph waited. My division was stationed in reserve just behind Randolph's and James Douglas'. To the far left and further behind, Sir Robert Keith sat with his light cavalry to take the English flank.

I gave the signal to my standard bearer. The red lion dipped, rose, then swept to the left before returning upright. Edward's division started forward. They continued on over the open ground, unchallenged until they came within a hundred yards of the English. There, Edward halted them. They knelt one last time in rapid prayer, for never were enough prayers said when battle impended. Then quickly, as had been practiced a thousand times, my brother's men formed their schiltron.

The call to arms sounded from the English camp. In a sleepy and yet frantic fashion, one of their cavalry divisions began to mobilize. I squinted hard. *No bloody archers.* Perhaps King Edward thought our schiltrons would scatter at the first charge. Clearly, he had never listened to the events of Stirling or Falkirk. His father had learned from Wallace's use of the spearmen at Stirling. At Falkirk, archers had been employed to tear holes in them. *Still, no archers . . .*

Prematurely, a ragged stream of mounted English knights flew forward. Scottish spears were anchored into the earth, their points arrayed at varying heights and reaching a full twelve feet from their ends. Hooves drummed wildly across the ground. Brave, blindly loyal warhorses forged on. English lances slammed into braced shields. A few ripped open the chests of valiant Scotsmen. But a lance once used in the charge is a worthless instrument. And so the English knights, who had snatched at what they believed would be easy prey, were now reduced to flailing swords a fraction of the length of the spears that jabbed at them and rammed into the flesh of their horses, so that the beasts reared and screamed and tossed them. Once on the ground, the knights were set upon by nimble Scottish footmen, armorless, but lightning-quick, who hacked at them with stunted swords and heavy axes.

Edward's schiltron held.

"Signal Randolph forward," I said to Angus Og.

With a fiery smile, Angus gave the word. Randolph's division drew up on Edward's left, pressuring the exposed flank of the English cavalry, some of whom broke off to ward off the new threat. More of the same. English knights jabbing at Scots through a forest of pricking spears. Riders thrown, trampled, their throats cut, blades thrust into the small places where their mail gapped. And riderless horses, seeking escape, crashing into other mounted knights trying to press forward and attack. Many of those horses, wounded and fraught with hysteria, raced directly at the lines of Englishmen waiting further back on the carse.

"Now Douglas," I said to Angus.

When James' division went forward, the army of Scotland covered a straight line from the Bannock Burn to the Pelstream, so that the English for now had no way to attack but to their restricted front. King Edward's archers were penned behind. There was only forward for them and in front of them a wall of Scottish spears so thick that it looked like a forest of blood-soaked trees. On the hot breeze, the stench of death—blood and excrement—fouled the air.

They held. For hours they held. And I could do nothing yet but watch and wait for them to do their work as the dead and dismembered piled up in that long, writhing line. Far, far into the distance, Englishmen dropped from the banks and crossed the Pelstream, but whether they were in retreat or making way to Stirling to claim it or . . .

They were drawing up on James' left flank and still on the opposite bank they staggered out in a measured line. I saw the bows, faint slashes of brown against a field of dull yellow shot with tufts of green where the ground was marshy. Then the streaks cutting through the blue of the sky. And Scotsmen dropping. Pools of red flowing from their pierced bodies.

"Keith. Now!" I shouted at Angus.

While more of James' soldiers were cut down, Keith took to the expanse with his horsemen. The battle cries of Keith's men broke the rhythm of the English archers and was followed by a moment of indecision. Some of the archers turned to face Keith's cavalry, while the rest continued to rain their shafts at James' division. But fast, Keith was upon them and they scattered like field mice back downstream, clambering to wade the Pelstream and find refuge amongst the helpless ranks of English infantry that had yet to be engaged.

The stink of blood floated on the hot air. The cries of the dying drifted heavenward. Sword struck spear haft. Axe clanged on shield. And Scotland held. And pushed forward, compressing England's force back, until it began to cave in on itself. Englishmen toppled from the steep lip of the Bannock Burn into its waters and as they struggled to gain their feet, more fell. Horses plunged from the banks in a flurry of legs and ear-renting screams, crushing the bodies that broke their fall.

Angus sat on his horse before me. He crammed his helmet down over his head. It had no visor, only a slit in the shape of a cross, so that I could see nothing of his face, but for his bloodshot eyes staring hotly at me, the reddened tip of his nose and that ragged moustache flapping as he spoke.

"Now, my lord?"

"Aye," I answered. "Go now, Angus. They're failing and the weight of the scale rests in your hands. Faith." I nudged my pony forward and extended a loose fist toward him. He reached out and clasped it. I shook my fist once, then pulled it back. "Our Lord be with you."

Angus paused and beamed with the exultation of joining in the battle. "It would seem, my lord king, that He is on Scotland's side after all."

I nodded. "So it would seem. So it would seem. But take nothing for granted, least of all God's favor. He can take it from you in a heartbeat. The day is not yet done."

"Done for King Edward," Angus yelled over his shoulder as he raced away, filled with joy and battle-lust. "Someone should let him know, don't you think?"

A body of heavy English cavalry nudged and shoved its way toward the Pelstream, where they began to cross on a bridge of drowned and broken bodies. For a moment I thought I saw among them the flash of King Edward's colors. But my eyes must have been tricked, for when I looked again the standard was gone and the horsemen were over the stream and headed for Stirling.

Among all the miracles of that one day, the greatest was when the small folk gushed over the crown of Gillies Hill, waving their hand-painted banners and flourishing crude spears and shouting loud enough to lift the roof off the sky. Seeing hundreds more coming to kill them, the infantry of England began to flee in every direction they could. They piled over the mangled and the drowning and the dead in the Bannock Burn and Pelstream. Some fell in the marshy places, where they were run down by Scots or run over by their own. The vestiges of a once large and mighty army lay in scattered ruins. Its leaders had abandoned it—fled, to save their own lives so they might go back to England and live off the fat of their lands.

The brave sons of Scotland had won their battle. Not because they were more—no, they were outnumbered four-fold. Not because they were better armed or paid. They won because, in order to live, they had to.

In exchange for the English nobles that had been taken captive today, I would not ask for ransom. Instead, I would bring my wife and daughter home.

Eight years, it has been. Soon, I will hold Elizabeth in my arms again, gaze upon my daughter's face. And I pray they can find it in their hearts to forgive me for the suffering I have caused them.

As I ride to join in the fight, I cannot see, for I weep. I weep for the dead and dying. Weep for God's grace that I have lived to see this day. Weep for freedom—which I have never truly known until now.

Epilogue

Edward II – Stirling, 1314

D' ARGENTAN RIDES KNEE TO knee beside me, so close that our mounts bump frequently. But as we fly over a waist-high ridge, the last of the hobelars bearing down on us, he glances behind us and grins morbidly at me.

"I take my stand here, sire."

With those words, he peels away, cutting behind me. Immediately, I hear the crash of metal and a heavy thud. Grunts and more clanging. I dare not look back. All I can do is ride on. On toward Stirling. Away from Bannockburn and the army of Scotland. Nothing left around me but the remnants of what, only a day before, was the greatest force ever to set foot on Britain's soil.

God spare me. I am not ready to meet my sire, not yet. I would rather plummet to hell and take my eternity there with my flesh forever burning. Could he have foreseen this? Known it would come to this end? Is that why he spurned me so?

At last we reach the cobbled road that leads up the rock upon which Stirling sits. Already, my English soldiers are collecting at the foot of the crag in refuge. Most look as though they had fled without ever striking a blow. Deplorable cowards. Houses crowd the view, so that I can see nothing of the way from which we have come. We halt our lathered horses at the gatehouse. Swinging down from his saddle, Pembroke elbows his way through the front group of my guard and bangs on the gate with the butt end of his sword.

"Open!" he cries. "Open, Mowbray. In the name of your king, Edward of England!"

No answer comes. Soldiers peek at us from the ramparts and disappear. Pembroke pounds again and again. His face, already red from the heat and extreme effort, begins to purple in vexation.

"Damnable hell, man. Let us in!"

Mowbray's head pops through one of the crenels of the southeast gate tower.

"I regret to inform you, my lords," Mowbray says with a nervous grin, "that it would be most unwise, for all considered, to permit you entrance."

I tremble violently. Pembroke steps away from the gate until he comes to stand beside me, so that he can see Mowbray directly.

"If I could kill him from here," I utter, "I would. Have we an archer?"

"Allow me." Hugh Despenser removes his helmet, wipes the sweat from his brow and cocks his head back. In a loud, strained voice, he calls, "Sir Mowbray, by your own words, the castle is relieved. The king is here. He commands you to give him entrance to Stirling Castle. Open the gate—or cast your name among the king's enemies."

Mowbray snorts in ridicule. "Ah, no. I would dare not say you have relieved it after that routing. I saw everything from up here. Quite a plain view, I have. An ugly one, if you're an Englishman. I would say the King of England has many enemies this day that will outlive him. You've nothing left to defend this place. If I let you in here I promise you Robert the Bruce, having already torn your army to shreds, will surround the place and starve us all to sickness and make a fine prisoner of your lord. Take it as a sign of concern for your welfare that I've turned you away. You would not be safe here, unfortunately."

With that, he withdraws.

I leap from my horse and claw at the gate until my nails are bloody and I am white with rage. I yell curses, accuse Mowbray's mother of lying with the devil, vow to put his head on a pike on London Bridge after gouging out his eyes . . .

Somehow, during my madness, Hugh wrenches me from there, puts me on my horse and leads me away as I scream on. Pembroke takes his leave at the edge of town, saying he intends to gather his men and lead them away. I think it a vain act and am certain I will never set eyes on him again.

I take no food. Have no thought of hunger. Drink only when they push a flask of water to my lips. Sleep not at all. I only ride. On and on. South through the tangled depths of New Park. East by Torwood. Past Falkirk. Linlithgow. Edinburgh. Names of places I would rather never have known. All the while Scots trail behind in our clouds of dust. Pushing us further, faster. They dare not engage us, because we are yet five times their number. Bruce has failed in his ultimate genius, sending only so few. A foible worth a king's true ransom.

Day becomes night becomes day again. East. Ever east. Haunted. Hunted. Chased down like hares by a pack of hounds. I cannot look back. They are always there.

A horse begins to pull up lame among my personal guard. All the other men look at the unfortunate knight with only fleeting pity. His horse falters. Refuses to go on. No one cares to save him. His ill luck, not ours. The knight is left there, alone. His one sword against three score Scots as they run him down.

I hear the cry I fear most: "A Douglas!"

I do not look back.

At Dunbar, I fall from my horse, leave it lame and dying, and run on foot . . . stumbling through the castle gate. Around me, familiar faces begin to gather. But many are missing.

When the gate draws shut behind us, my knights packed in the bailey like livestock in the market pens, Dunbar's handful of archers pelt the Scots with arrows. The thieves take our horses. Most will be of no use to them, ruined as they are. In a distant fog, I watch from the parapets as the Scots ride into a setting sun, leading four horses apiece. Someone speaks to me. Asks me something. I do not answer.

Still, I can hear the echo in my head of the banging tenor of the Highlanders' drums. The primeval battle cries. The crash of weapons. The grunt as a sword is plunged into a belly. The sucking sound as it is pulled out. The slurping of boots through rising pools of blood. The wails as horses trod over the wounded and crush their bones. The guttural pleas for mercy.

Slipping a hand beneath my mail coif, I feel the links of the gilt chain around my neck. The lion pendant is still there, guarding my heart.

Author's Note

There is a great deal of folklore surrounding Robert the Bruce and the exploits of his steadfast followers. It is impossible to determine how much is truth and how much is myth. I have employed both in the telling of this tale in hopes of embodying the spirit of his quest for the autonomy of Scotland. Some of the errors on these pages are wholly intentional; some are not. Only the people who lived during the time this story was set know the actual events. And even then, reality is colored by perspective.

To learn more about the history of the Scottish War for Independence, Robert the Bruce, James Douglas and King Edward II of England, I suggest the following works of non-fiction:

Brown, Chris. *Robert the Bruce, A Life Chronicled.* Stroud, Gloucestershire, U.K.: Tempus Publishing Limited, 2004.

Haines, Roy Martin. *King Edward II: His Life, His Reign and Its Aftermath, 1284-1330.* Montreal: McGill-Queen's University Press, 2003.

Reese, Peter. *Bannockburn.* Edinburgh: Canongate Books Ltd., 2000.

Ross, David R. *James the Good: The Black Douglas.* Edinburgh: Luath Press Ltd., 2008.

Scott, Ronald McNair. *Robert the Bruce: King of Scots.* Edinburgh: Canongate Books Ltd., 1996.

Acknowledgments

Without the help of a few generous souls, this story would never have been sculpted into its final form. I'd like to thank Anna Rossi for her unwavering ability to remain encouraging while letting me know what worked and what didn't; Jack Ramsay for his honesty and thorough attention to detail while he kept his editor's hat on; and, as always, Greta van der Rol, who not only keeps me focused on the big picture, but keeps me grounded on a daily basis, too.

About the Author

N. Gemini Sasson holds a M.S. in Biology from Wright State University where she ran cross country on athletic scholarship. She has worked as an aquatic toxicologist, an environmental engineer, a teacher and a cross country coach. A longtime breeder of Australian Shepherds, her articles on bobtail genetics have been translated into seven languages. She lives in rural Ohio with her husband, two nearly grown children and an ever-changing number of sheep and dogs.

Worth Dying For, The Bruce Trilogy: Book II, is her third book. She is also the author of *The Crown in the Heather, The Bruce Trilogy: Book I,* and *Isabeau, A Novel of Queen Isabella and Sir Roger Mortimer.*

www.ngeminisasson.com

CPSIA information can be obtained at www.ICGtesting.com
Printed in the USA
BVOW040150291112

306705BV00002B/456/P